Revenge after twenty years

by

Hugh Chare

Publication Data

Book, and cover design by Hugh B. Chare
ISBN: 978-1-940012-14-8

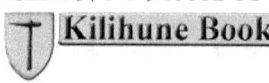

Other Books by Hugh Chare
African Encounter
Just off the Great North Road
The journal of Jan Englebrecht
The Sagitta Mishap
Flight 5 to Johannesburg
British Spy in the Bushveld
Federica
Across the Zambezi
Death in the Mopane

Preface

This is a work of fiction. Any resemblance in the featured characters to actual persons, living or dead, is purely coincidental.

Contents

Release

On the 18th of October 1991, the gates of the Francistown prison opened long enough to allow three men to depart and get into a waiting Land Rover. Two were officers of the Botswana Police, and the third was an ageing, thin, bearded white man, in handcuffs and shackles. He was placed in the back, behind the grillwork that separated the rear of the interior from the rest of the cab. There was no escape possible from the Land Rover; his shackles had been attached to eye bolts set in the sides of the bodywork, and the rear door had been shut and locked with a bolt that ran all the way across the back with a padlock at the end. Still, it was not a bad experience for the prisoner, after twenty years in the prison, the open grill of the back of the Land Rover allowed views of the world as they travelled, once dawn broke, and the fresh air came in from all sides, except the floor. The party had left Francistown a little after five in the morning, and they made their first stop at the police station at Palapye, just after seven in the morning. There, the prisoner was taken from the Land Rover and escorted to the cells, where he was temporarily incarcerated. He was given breakfast, and coffee, under the watchful eye of the Palapye staff, while the others from Francistown had breakfast; after he had finished the staff made sure that they collected the tray, paper plate, the plastic fork, and paper cup, leaving nothing for the prisoner to take with him, no paper clips, no tines or tools of any description, they had had escapes before. There was little conversation between the officers and the man, and in his hearing, they said nothing to one another. They had been briefed that he spoke Setswana and had no intention of having their conversations overheard. At eight, they were on the road again, stopping only when they reached Gaborone just after eleven.

Watching him arrive at the Central Police Station from an upper office window was Assistant Superintendent Marieke Englebrecht of the Botswana Police, who wondered who he was and why he

1

was being transported. She was joined at the window by Assistant Commissioner Mochage.

"Who is he, Sir?" she asked.

"Hansie Pretorius, released today after serving twenty years in the prison at Francistown," the commissioner replied.

"Why was he there?" she asked.

"Twenty years ago, he was stupid enough to try and shoot his way out of an arrest for ivory poaching," Mochage replied. "I was the arresting officer. Your cousin, Katrina Martin, was involved; she and her husband, James, were there at the camp of Piet and Anna Englebrecht, and she helped us corner Pretorius, something we never made public. If he hadn't shot at us, we probably would have just kicked him out of the country, because although we could link his rifle to some of the elephants shot, there was no other physical evidence in his vehicle. The ivory was transported some other way, we believe by a lorry driven by someone else."

"So, there were others involved in the poaching?" she asked.

"We believe so," Mochage replied. "Our information was that there was also a cousin of Pretorius, Danie Pretorius, a Koos van de Merwe, and we believe our now solid upstanding citizen, Jan Lamprecht. They also had help from a number of trackers and skinners from Zim. We apprehended the other Pretorius, and van de Merwe near Kasane, they were completely empty handed but, we booted them out of the country because we had your cousin's eyewitness testimony of seeing them in Namibia, across the river, then again in Botswana, so they had been crossing, and re-crossing the border illegally. We never saw Jan Lamprecht in the country, so we only have hearsay evidence that he was ever here, even our border crossing records were incomplete at that time, so no passport number, no record of entry, nothing."

"I had heard something about Jan Lamprecht having a shady past," Marieke said. "Has he given us any trouble at all since he moved to Botswana?"

"Not a bit," Mochage said. "He apparently decided, or perhaps his wife, Mbali, decided that he should give up those ways. He came into the country with no record of arrests or anything in South Africa, so he has no official history of any wrongdoing, either criminal or civil. We kept a file on him for the first five years he was living here in Gaborone, but he never put a foot wrong, no speeding fines, no drunk and disorderly, nothing. He certainly seems to have put whatever past he may have had firmly behind him. He became a citizen, as did his wife, Mbali, and the two girls were both born here, so were naturally citizens. Now he employs quite a number of people in his diesel repair shop, and the reports I get are that he treats his people really well, and the business is thriving."

"So, what happens to Pretorius now?" she asked.

"He'll be taken to the border post at Kopfontein and sent on his way. We've already alerted the South Africans that he's coming," Mochage explained.

"Will he be back?" Marieke asked.

"Who knows," Mochage said, shrugging his shoulders. "He's been denied entry permanently, but our border is still very porous, and he could slip over in any number of places. I understand from the people at Francistown that he learned Setswana while he was imprisoned, so he could make his way through the rural areas quite easily. We'll take new pictures of him, with the beard, and without, and we'll take a new set of fingerprints, handprints, and toe and footprints. All that is useful for is identifying him if he breaks the law here, but it does not stop him from entering the country illegally. What is there to stop him crossing the Limpopo or the Molopo?"

"Nothing," she agreed. "If he walks, he could arrive in any number of places; if he drives, his options are more limited, but the border is still fairly porous. He could probably ford the Limpopo in a number of places, and the Molopo is generally a dry riverbed for much of the year, so if he knows how to drive in sand, that would present no barrier. I think one day he will be back."

"Sadly, I agree with you," Mochage said. "We will just have to stay vigilant."

Pretorius was taken to the cells and then to a room where he was provided with a new suit of clothes, a new shirt, and shoes. His fingerprints and the other prints were taken, and he was photographed, then he had his hair cut, and was shaved by a barber brought in specially, and then photographed again. The Botswana Police wanted the best description of him they could get, so he was also weighed and measured. The new details were added to his file, already a thick one, from various infractions committed in the past, apart from the poaching episode. Pretorius was then given lunch and then taken to the border with South Africa, and shown the door. He walked over to the South African side, where he was now their problem.

Marieke went to the old records department, pulled the case file about Pretorius, and read through it. It had all started when Piet Englebrecht and a group of tourists had come across a small herd of elephants that had been slaughtered, and the ivory taken. From then there had been other small incidents and sightings, including one where her cousin, Katrina, and husband, James, had been shot at from across the Namibian border, allegedly by Pretorius. When the police and game guards moved in, the operation was already over, and they never found any of the ivory, but they were definitely able to match the bullets from Pretorius's rifle to those dug out of some of the dead elephants. Pretorius claimed that he had lent his rifle to a Mr Strydom, who was never found, and who, in the opinion of the Botswana game guards and police, never existed. Although there was a statement in the records from her cousin about them coming across the dead elephants, there was no mention anywhere of her assisting in the detention of Pretorius; Marieke thought that they probably decided that it was easier that way as at that time Katrina, and James were living in Zambia, and coming back, and forth to testify might not have been that easy. She closed the file and sent it back to the records department.

She then turned her attention back to current cases. There were a few things happening: a car theft ring that had sprung up in Gaborone, some diamond thefts that had been occurring at the big Orapa mine, and the hint of some ivory poaching in and around the Chobe National Park. In the cases of the diamonds and ivory, her department was acting in more of an advisory role, but the car theft ring was all theirs to pursue. She called in Sergeant Maphosa, and they went through progress, or lack of it, and discussed how to change their approach to get better results. That done, she locked away all the files and then left for the day to have dinner with the once-wayward Jan Lamprecht and his wife, Mbali.

Marieke drove to the house of Jan and Mbali. She enjoyed their company and did business with Mbali, who was the manager of one of the larger banks in town.

"*Dumela Mma*," she said when Mbali opened the door to her.

"*Dumela Mma*," Mbali replied. "Please come in, the girls were asking when you would be here."

"*Dumela Rra*," Marieke said to Jan when he also came to the door.

"*Dumela Mma*, great to see you again," he said. "Nandi, Khanyo, your Auntie Marieke is here."

"*Dumela Mma*," the girls said, almost in unison.

"*Dumela*," Marieke replied. "What's new and exciting today?"

"I'm going to apply to the University of Kent next year to study wildlife conservation," Khanyo replied. "Then I'd like to look into a Master's program that focuses on the economics of wildlife conservation. If we want to keep the Botswana parks, they have to be worth as much as an alternate use. I suspect that in the future, someone will find big ore deposits in national parks, and then it will be money that talks."

"The studies sound like fun, but you are probably right about the competing interests, and then it will be who pays the most, and sadly we in Africa have a history of corrupt politicians who will give approval to the project that pays the most, both above, and below the table," Marieke said. "And you, Nandi?"

"I can't decide," she replied. "I'm still interested in being a mining engineer, but also in being a pilot for Air Botswana.

"Quite a dilemma," Marieke agreed.

"I know, Khanyo wants to preserve everything we have, but there are always more people, and the government is expected to provide for them, and the only way to do that is taxes and royalties, so diamonds pay for a lot," Nandi said.

"What cases are you working on?" Khanyo asked, changing the subject so that she and her sister did not get into another of their endless arguments about the merits of mining.

"Nothing really exciting at the moment," Marieke said. "We are helping with a diamond smuggling case and an ivory poaching case, so something for each of you. I did see a man today, who was just released from prison, and deported, a man by the name of Hansie Pretorius. I looked into his case, and he had been involved in ivory poaching some years ago."

"Has it been twenty years already?" Mbali said. "I remember reading in the paper years ago that he had been sentenced to twenty years in prison. So, he's gone?"

"Gone, across the border at Kopfontein," Marieke confirmed.

"Well, twenty years is not long enough for ivory poaching," Khanyo said.

"It wasn't the ivory poaching that got him the twenty years," Marieke said. "It was shooting at the police. We never really had firm evidence that he had actually been poaching."

"When's your French friend coming back, Auntie Marieke?" Nandi asked.

"Melisende said that she'd like to come back sometime next year, perhaps in May or June," Marieke replied. They were talking about her friend Melisende Garnier, with whom Marieke had gone to university in Lyon, and who was now with the National Police, previously known to most as the Sûreté, in Paris. She and Melisende had shared a flat and had developed a deep relationship that went far beyond being merely fellow students. "She told me that she had had such a good time last December that she wants to come back."

"Maybe we should book something at your friends' camp in the Linyanti?" Mbali suggested.

"Come, and eat," Jan suggested. "I've got the *braai* all done, we can talk while we eat."

"Just not at the same time," Mbali cautioned the girls. "No talking with your mouths full!"

When the meal was over and things were being cleared up, Marieke went out to the *stoep* and talked to Jan about Hansie Pretorius.

"He's gone then," Jan said.

"He's gone, Marieke confirmed. "What was he like?"

"He was a butcher from Zeerust who had a side business that dealt with poached meat and trophies. He was a typical Afrikaner. He said he hated the blacks, but he would go to Swazi for his entertainment, and he had a collection of Playboy centrefolds up on his office wall, some of which were of black girls. He could be fun to be with, but he could just as easily be an idiot. He set up an expedition to meet an order he got from this *ou* calling himself Smith. We sent a lorry across the Limpopo with the guns and ammunition, and the rest of us came in quite legally as tourists, but back then record record-keeping at the border was quite spotty, so I doubt that there was ever any official record that we had crossed. We went to the Linyanti area, crossed the river there into the Caprivi, and set up camp. We hunted for ivory and other trophies that Hansie had orders for, some in the Caprivi, and some in Botswana. I thought Hansie was a genuine *ou* but when we had filled the order, and were preparing to leave, something changed, he refused to pay the *ouks* that came from Rhodesia to help him, he left his cousin Danie, and Koos to do that," Jan said. "It was every man for himself. I was to drive the lorry loaded with the ivory, and the rest, and Koos, and Danie were going to drive back together, through Zim. Hansie was going to be sure that he was long gone before anyone else left, so he left before me, taking his gun, but with none of the ivory or other trophies. I'm still not sure how he got caught back up in the Linyanti."

"As far as I can tell from the file, he went the wrong way onto a side road that was going to take him towards Chobe, a game guard saw him, and asked where he was going. I suppose he panicked and went back the way he had come," Marieke explained. "But, by then, the game guards and police were after him, and it was only a matter of time before they caught up with him."

"*Ja*, I saw them going north, I was *kakking* my *brooke* that they would stop me, and search the *bakkie*, we had Botswana number plates on it, so they probably just passed by without thinking," Jan said. "It was really loaded, and we had all the guns, except Hansie's, hidden away in a compartment under the *bakkie*, but which probably would have been found with a decent search."

"Will Hansie stay in Zeerust?" Marieke asked.

"Don't know," Jan admitted. "Danie was the hell in because Hansie had left him to pay off the *ouks* from Rhodesia, so was Koos, they were his friends, they'd been in the army together. What happened after we all left Botswana, I don't really know. We all went our own ways. I went to Phalaborwa, and Koos went to the Caprivi, and I suppose Danie went back to Zeerust; the three of us only met once after that, and that was in Cape Town to deliver the order. What happened to the butcher's shop that Hansie had in Zeerust, I don't know. The *ou* who ordered the stuff, Koos identified as a colonel in the South African army intelligence branch, by the name of de Villiers, so corruption in high places, Koos called me once two years after we'd been to tell me that, I suppose to warn me in case I ran into him, but by then I'd left the army, and was here in Gabs. I've tried to put all that behind me; since I've been in Botswana, I've been absolutely straight. Mbali would divorce me if I put a foot wrong, and that would be the end for me, no Mbali, and no girls, I couldn't take that."

"I know," Marieke said. "The Assistant Commissioner told me that you'd never given us any reason to look at you, and it was all twenty years ago, so well past any statute of limitations. He said that they had hearsay evidence that you might have been involved, but no actual evidence that you were ever in the country."

"Well, I'm glad Hansie's out of the country. I saw a different Hansie towards the end of the trip to the Linyanti. He was devious and was ever looking to make a plan about something," Jan said, then looked up and saw Mbali come out onto the *stoep*. "I'll just go, and help with the washing up, and leave you to talk to Mbali."

"So, Matshwana," Mbali said, using the nickname that Marieke had earned while she was stationed at Tsabong. *Matshwana* is the Setswana word for the ratel or honey badger, an animal known for its tenacity. "Your Melisende wants to come for another visit."

"She does," Marieke confirmed. "She still talks about her trip last Christmas."

"Will you call your friends, Will, and Bridget, and book us some time at the Pitse Safari Camp?" Mbali asked.

"I think I will," Marieke said. "When are the girls off school?"

"They have a mid-term break in May, with the last day of school on the 8th, and they go back on the 1st of June," Mbali replied.

"So, we could take two weeks at the end of May," Marieke thought. "That would be right at the beginning of the season, I'll have to find out if they're even open then. I think they are; they typically run from May until November, obviously depending on the rains. It would be a difficult place to get to in the rains, so if the rains are late, and they can't get in there in April, it may delay the season opening."

"How do they deal with that if people have already booked?" Mbali asked.

"You know, I really don't know," Marieke said. "We should ask them that when we see them."

"Another glass of wine?" Mbali asked.

"Thank you," Marieke replied. While Mbali was gone, Marieke fell to musing about things in general, about Mbali, a Zulu being married to Jan, a white Afrikaner, something that was not unheard of in Botswana, but which was still technically illegal in South Africa, but which might change in the near future, now that the political winds had changed, and it seemed fairly certain that Nelson Mandela would be elected to high office. Marieke herself had been in the same situation as Nandi and Khanyo, a child of mixed parents, except that in her case, her mother had been Motswana, and her father a white Afrikaner, which is why she was able to claim Botswana heritage. They had lived in the wilds of then South West Africa, now Namibia, and she had gone to university in Lyon in France. The South African authorities just ignored them, living out in the wilds of South West. If they had lived in Oudtshoorn, where her father's family lived, or somewhere else more populated, they would have been at least harassed by the government, at worst arrested. She had discovered parts of her white family the previous year on her first big case as an Assistant Superintendent when two headless bodies had been discovered on the Pitse Safari location in the Linyanti area. Will and Bridget, who ran the camp where the bodies were found, were not direct relatives, but Will's brother, James, was married to Katrina, who was her cousin. The Piet and Anna Englebrecht that the Assistant Commissioner had referred to were also cousins, albeit distant. While interviewing Piet, and Anna about earlier visitors to the camp, she had been introduced to Katrina's father, her uncle, who told her a little about the family rift after her father married her mother, something that was a little hard to fathom as her great-great-grandmother had been San, the native people of Botswana, so many of the Englebrechts had a mixed heritage.

"Penny for your thought?" Mbali asked when she came back with the wine.

"I was just thinking about things, and how you and Jan may be able to go back to South Africa if you want in the next year or so," Marieke replied.

"It does look as if things are changing," Mbali agreed. "But, a simple change in the law won't change people's views of things, so in many places, it would still be difficult for Jan and me. My folks are finally coming around, they're getting used to Jan, my Dad even asks him for help with his car, they love the girls, and are planning another visit later this year, Jan's folks are still distant, they love the girls too, on their visits here have been polite enough to me, but it obviously still bothers them, I suppose they're products of their generation, and upbringing, so may never fully accept us. Jan doesn't care if they do or don't, he says that that's their problem, and if they want to miss out on things, then that's their *indaba*."

"Has Jan ever said anything about this Pretorius?" Marieke asked.

"He told me the whole story once," Mbali said. "It was before we got married, and he promised me that he would never again go poaching, either for the pot or for money. He told me that Hansie seemed to change while they were on their trip; he became bitter and fought with almost everyone else there. Jan thinks that there will be trouble in Zeerust when Hansie goes back, because he and Danie fell out, and when they delivered the ivory to the buyer, they split the money three ways, and left Hansie out. Apparently, Danie thought that Hansie had taken more than enough upfront, so didn't deserve anything else."

"Well, at least Zeerust is over the border," Marieke said. "Any issues might well stay there."

"True, but how difficult is it to cross the border?" Mbali asked. "You'll let me know if you hear of any goings on in Zeerust?"

"I will," Marieke promised.

"So, what are you *tannies* gossiping about?" Jan joked as he and the girls joined them on the *stoep*.

"We were just talking about families," Mbali said. "And not so much of the *tannie, pas op neefie*!"

"When are you going to get married, Auntie Marieke?" Nandi asked, to the horror of her mother, who looked at Marieke in alarm.

"Not just yet," Marieke replied. "I haven't found the right person yet."

"But you will one day?" Nandi pressed.

"Perhaps," Marieke said. "But, tell me, pilot or mining engineer?"

"I was thinking," Nandi said. "You are a pilot, but you are also a police officer, so I could be a pilot and a mining engineer. I wouldn't fly for Air Botswana, but perhaps being a mining engineer is more secure than being with an airline. Could you take me flying again soon?"

"I will," Marieke promised. "And while I think of it, Khanyo, if you have some time in December, I can arrange a trip for you to spend some time with one of our San trackers. How does that sound?"

"Really?" Khanyo asked. "That would be wonderful, can I, Mom, Dad?"

"Of course," Mbali said. "We've already talked about it, and your Auntie Marieke has made arrangements for you to stay with a policewoman in Maun, then the tracker, Tushay, could take you out from there. Would you be prepared to let Nandi go as well?"

"Of course, Mom," Khanyo said. "If Nandi wants to come, it would be fun."

"Will you fly us up there?" Nandi asked of Marieke.

"I will," Marieke promised.

"Then I'd love to go with Khanyo, and your Mr Tushay, who is the policewoman?" Nandi asked.

"Sergeant Constance Sephoto, she's stationed in Maun, but is from Ghanzi," Marieke explained. "Well, if you will excuse me, I should go, I have an early start in the morning, I have a court appearance to get ready for."

"Let me see you out," Mbali said. "I'm sorry about Nandi, one day I'll explain to her about you, and Melisende, but only when I think she won't go blabbing to anyone, most of all your own department or any other part of the government. With the changes in South Africa, I wonder if Botswana will ever change the laws on same-sex relationships. I suppose, given the huge AIDS problem we have, and the perceived connection, that that may not happen soon."

"I'm afraid you may be right," Marieke agreed. "Still, for now, I can just immerse myself in work and stay busy."

"Still, I would like to see you happy," Mbali said.

"I'm happy enough," Marieke assured her. "It was lovely to spend time with you again, thank you for the dinner; stay well."

"Go well," Mbali said.

Marieke went home and looked with dismay at the pile of mail yet to be sorted out. She quickly put it into piles: bills, rubbish, and personal. She would pay the bills on the morrow and answer the personals, which were both from Melisende, later in the week. She thought about Melisende, regretting as she always did that they lived so far apart. She had tried a heterosexual relationship once, even, to the delight of her parents, announcing an engagement, but then Danie had been killed in a traffic accident, and her parents had both died when their car struck a land mine, so there being no parental expectations, she had given up on men, and reserved her affections for Melisende. Theirs was truly a long-distance relationship, but each time they were able to meet, the affection was still there, as deep and as strong as ever. Perhaps in the future, she would move to France to be with Melisende; that would be something to discuss if Melisende were able to come for a visit. She would get some details from Will and Bridget and send them on to Melisende. A trip to the bush camp sounded wonderful and was something she would really look forward to.

Marieke sat up in bed, reading the letters from Melisende. They were full of news, and what she had been doing since her parents had both been killed in a traffic accident. Apparently, a drunk driver had hit them and had managed to walk away himself, but kill them. Melisende had been winding up the estate of her parents, long distance from Paris. She also reminisced about their times together and talked about longing and loneliness. Marieke understood, she had the same feelings and usually tried to bury them in work, so that she was always busy with no time to dwell upon the past or what the present could be. In many ways, it was most unsatisfactory, but to change things would mean a big decision on the part of one of them.

Murder in Gaborone

Marieke was on her way to work in late April of 1992 when she heard on her radio a call about an incident on Independence Avenue. She quickly made an about-turn and went to the address given. There was a police Land Rover already there with a sergeant and a constable. Marieke knew them both, and after she had greeted them, asked what was the issue.

"Murder, *Mma*," Sergeant Phiri said.

"What do we have?" she asked.

"A man in a car in the garage, apparently shot in the head," Phiri explained.

"Who called you?" she asked.

"The gardener," Phiri replied. "He saw us driving in the street and called us over. He's over there."

"Is there anyone else at the house?" she asked.

"No, *Mma*, the gardener says that there is no one else here," Phiri replied.

"Let me take a quick look at the scene, then I'll talk to him," she said. She walked to the garage and looked around. There was a fairly new BMW parked in the garage with a man slumped over the steering wheel, and blood spattered on the windscreen, and bullet holes in the glass. Clearly, the man was very dead, judging by the wounds in his head. She looked over the car quickly and noted that all the doors were closed, but when she tried one, it proved to be not locked. The keys were in the ignition, but the ignition was not on.

"Did you turn the ignition off?" she asked Phiri.

"No, *Mma*," he said. "This is exactly as we found things."

"Very good," she said. "Call in, and get someone from forensics here. Let me talk to the gardener."

Marieke talked to the gardener and learned that he normally started work at seven in the morning, and had been on time that day. When he had opened the garage to get tools, he had seen the car, which was not typical as the owner was usually gone before six-thirty in the morning. He had seen the blood on the windscreen and the person behind the wheel, and had run out to look for help.

"Who is the person in the car?" she asked.

"Kagiso Katse, *Mma*," the gardener said.

"Did you see anyone around?' she asked.

"No, *Mma*," he replied.

"Fine, please give your statement to Sergeant Phiri," she said, then she turned and went back to the garage for another look. She put on some gloves, opened the driver's side door, and looked more closely at the victim. It was Kagiso Katse; she knew him from all manner of criminal cases that she had been involved with. He was well known in police circles as a solicitor who would take clients with really shady pasts, and was reputed to be mixed up with all manner of enterprise, legitimate and otherwise. Marieke had not known where he actually lived; all her dealings with him had been either at the police headquarters or at his office. She felt in the pockets of his suit and determined that his wallet was still there. She carefully removed it, without disturbing the body, and quickly looked through it. There was a driving licence in the name of Kagiso Katse, 560 Pula in cash, four credit cards, and some business cards. So, robbery seemed an unlikely motive. She walked around the car but could see nothing on the concrete floor that offered any clues, no footprints, no trails of dust, no extraneous leaves or twigs, nothing that might tell something about who had done this. She crouched down and looked under the car, but that told her nothing. She peered along the floor at ground level and did see where the floor had been swept, perhaps recently, judging by the sharpness of the ridges left by the brush bristles in the dust. She stood up, looked at the bullet holes in the glass, and then at the garage wall, and spotted where the bullets had entered the wall. She would wait for the forensics people and then have them dig them out. She went back to the gardener and asked him if the garage door had been closed when he arrived.

"Yes, *Mma*," he confirmed.

"Was it locked?' she asked.

"No, *Mma*, the lock has been broken for two weeks, Mr Katse kept saying that he would have it mended, but he never did," the gardener replied.

"How did the lock get broken?" she asked.

"Mr Katse did not say," the gardener said. "He just told me that one day he came home, and it was broken. He said he looked inside the garage, and nothing at all was missing or had been moved, so he thought that I must have broken it. He charged my wages for a new lock."

"Did you break the lock?" she asked.

"No, *Mma*," he said. "I have a key, see here, I did not need to break it."

"Have you worked for Mr Katse long?" she asked.

"Twenty years, *Mma*," he replied. "He paid me well, the same each day, he would leave early, before I arrived, except on Friday, when he would wait to pay me, always in cash. His day was the same, each day, he would go from here to a yoga studio, because he liked to watch the girls there, then he would go to his office. Once a month, on the last Friday, I went with him to work on the small plot that is by the office, but that never took long. This garden here takes many hours."

"Tell me, is Mr Katse married?" she asked.

"Oh no, *Mma*," the gardener said. "Mr Katse never marry, but he has a girlfriend who visits quite often."

Marieke was thinking of what else she might draw from the gardener when another police vehicle arrived, and Thabo Mosiwa, one of the police pathologists, got out with his assistant, Neo Mogotsi.

"*Dumela Mma*," Thabo said.

"*Dumela Rra*," she replied.

"So, what do we have?" Thabo asked.

"Kagiso Katse, it looks as if he was shot from behind while he was sitting at the wheel of his car. The gardener found him this morning at seven when he came to work. There is what looks like a bullet hole in the wall at the back of the garage," she explained.

"Katse?" Thabo said. "Did someone finally decide that he had cheated them enough?"

"Good question," Marieke agreed. "I'm afraid that the suspect list could be a rather long one. I'll leave you and Neo to get busy.

Would you see if there are house keys on the ring with the car keys?"

"This looks promising," Thabo suggested, pointing to a key on the ring. Marieke tried it, and it fit the door between the house and the garage. Inside the house, there was an entryway with a tiled floor. The tile was clean, no mud, no dust. Katse either did a good job of cleaning himself, or he had someone come in regularly. Marieke stepped outside and saw the gardener still there, and asked if there was a cleaner. There was a cleaner, and she had been in the previous day. The gardener knew her only as Violet, and she lived in Tlokweng and came once a week, always on Wednesdays. Marieke went back to the house and walked through each room, just getting the impressions that they would give her. Her thoughts were that Katse was a man of expensive taste, judging by the art on the walls, the furniture, the wine rack, and bar, built-in at one end of the living room. In his office, there were some files in the desk, and notes on a pad on the desktop. Nothing leapt out at her as unusual, so she resigned herself to the fact that there would be quite a lot of wading through documents to see if anything cropped up that might raise eyebrows. She looked through the desk drawers quickly and found a set of keys, most of which matched the set she had used to gain entry to the house. She took the spare set, presuming that at least one might be useful at his office. In the bedroom, there was a closet well stocked with clothes, expensive suits, shirts, and ties, and many pairs of shoes, far more pairs than she had. Back in the office, Marieke noticed the telephone answering machine and wondered why she had not seen it before. She pressed the play button and listened to the messages, one from a Mr Banda looking for help with a drunk driving case for his son, and one from someone who did not leave a name but wondered if Katse would meet her at the Peacock Bar and Grill on Thursday evening at six. Well, that was tonight, so Marieke would be there if she did not discover who it was before then.

Marieke went back outside, and asked Sergeant Phiri if he would canvass the neighbours to see if anyone had seen or heard anything. She then walked around the yard, across the street, and up and down the street, looking to see from which angles the house and the garage were visible. Someone either followed Katse into the garage and killed him in the car, or they accessed the garage and the car, and waited for Katse to come. Marieke thought the latter scenario more likely. The shooter hid down behind the driver's seat, then, when Katse got into the car, he was shot from behind. Marieke wondered if Katse locked his car while it was in the garage. The broken lock on the garage door might be significant, perhaps it bespoke planning, as it was broken two weeks earlier. Thabo interrupted her thoughts with some comments.

"This death is very recent," he said. "Less than two hours ago, so around five to six this morning. We found two spent cartridge cases under the passenger's seat, 9mm, and we found a 9mm semi-automatic with a suppressor under the driver's seat. Did any of the neighbours hear a gunshot?"

"We'll know soon enough," Marieke replied. "I have Phiri and Sibanda canvassing the neighbourhood as we speak. Any prints on the cartridge cases, the gun or the garage door handle?"

"Not one that I can see," Thabo bemoaned. "Our man, or woman, wore gloves, probably even when loading the gun. It looks like someone went to some trouble to plan and execute this killing. After we dig out those spent bullets from the wall there, we'll see how badly damaged they are, and whether or not we can pick up rifling marks, and match them to those on bullets we will test fire. We can certainly get a firing pin pattern from the cartridge cases, and we'll see if we can lift any prints from the cartridge cases or any parts of the gun. On the garage door handle, there are prints, but my guess is that they are those of the gardener. We'll take his prints just to eliminate him. The front car door handle has some prints, but they are most likely those of Katse. The rear door handles are both very smudged; if there are prints, they are old or are a mix of many, put there over the past few weeks. One thing more, the shots were from close enough that there would be some blood spatter back onto the shooter."

"Thank you, Thabo," Marieke said. "I think the garage has been swept out very recently, and that broom over there looks promising; you might want to check it for prints or perhaps even blood. If our villain swept out the garage after the shooting, and he or she had got some spatter on them, then maybe there will be traces on the handle. I don't think there's too much else I can do here for the moment. I'll just see if Phiri and Sibanda have learned anything; if not, I may just go to Katse's office, and interview his staff. I'll be back later to get his files to see if there are any clues there. Here are the keys we took from the car. I found another set in the house, one of which may be his office key."

Neither Phiri nor Sibanda had much to report. None of the neighbours had heard anything that sounded like a gunshot, but one neighbour had seen a strange man walking in the direction away from the house of Katse, at about six-fifteen that morning, just before the sun came up. He had been outside with his dog when the man walked past. His description was that of a white man, probably in his fifties, greyish hair, beard, glasses, between 160 and 180 cm tall, slim build, wearing a dark suit, and carrying a briefcase. The neighbour said that the man had greeted him in Setswana, and passed quickly by, then he had had to return his attention to his dog, so did not see where he went, it had not been very light, just the twilight before the sun arose, so he was not able to get a good look at the man. But it was at least something to start with. Marieke asked Phiri and Sibanda to work their way down the street in the direction that the man had gone and see if anyone else saw him. The fact that no one heard any gunshots was not surprising to Marieke, a suppressor would alter the sound enough that even if people heard it, they would be unlikely to associate it with gunfire, unless they were experts in the field.

Marieke then took a slow walk around the house, looking for anything that might be of interest. There were prints in the wet patches of the grass, but she identified those as belonging to the gardener in the flower beds. There was just nothing to be found, which itself was interesting. Whoever had done this had taken great pains to leave no clues or even be seen, perhaps with the exception of the man walking his dog. The killer had to have watched the house and the area for a while to know when it would be quiet, and when he could gain entry to the garage. The broken lock on the garage door, found two weeks earlier, to her suggested that the killer had been there for at least two weeks, and had been taking his, or her, time. That definitely pointed to planning and premeditation; this was no spur-of-the-moment killing. She walked around a bit and then found the spot that gave the best view of the house, without being too obtrusive. She cast about but found no evidence of any debris that might have been tossed from a car. Clearly, if someone had been watching the house, they had been careful to leave no overt trace. She got her car, and drove down the road, in the same direction that Phiri had gone, and stopped by him, and asked him to also enquire if anyone had seen anyone parked nearby recently, watching the house of Katse, pointing to the place she had just scouted, and suggesting that that might be a good starting point.

Marieke drove into town to the offices of Kagiso Katse. There, she was greeted by a woman she presumed was Katse's receptionist.
"Dumela Mma," she said.
"Dumela Mma," the receptionist replied. "I'm sorry, if you need to see Mr Katse, he has not yet arrived."
"I know," Marieke said. "I'm sorry to have to tell you, *Mma,* that Mr Katse is dead. I am Assistant Superintendent Englebrecht of the Botswana Police, and have just come from the residence of Mr Katse."
"Dead, but how?" the receptionist asked.
"I'm sorry, but please tell me your name," Marieke asked.
"Rachel Pule, I am Kagiso Katse's assistant, but how did Mr Katse die?" Rachel asked.
"He was murdered," Marieke said.
"Murdered, how, who by, when?" Rachel asked.
"He was killed between five and six this morning," Marieke explained. "Can you think of anyone who would wish to harm Mr Katse?"

"Many," Rachel said. "But, I think that most would be happy with money, murder seems a little extreme, even for Katse's clients."

"You are not upset by this news?" Marieke asked.

"Yes, and no," Rachel said. "I was paid well by Katse to keep the books, the appointments, and the files. I have worked for him for over ten years now, and I believe he came to appreciate my talents and contribution to the business, but I am at a point in my life where I was working up to telling Katse that I was going to leave to focus on my farm."

"Can you think of any recent cases or dealings that would elicit such an extreme measure as killing Mr Katse?" Marieke asked.

"No," Rachel said. "These past twelve months have been almost without controversy, and his dealings have all been quite legitimate, unlike some I heard of in the dim and distant past."

"Did he have any recent meetings with anyone that were contentious?" Marieke asked.

"No, nothing in the past month, there were some harsh words about two months ago with a man from Selebi Phikwe, but even that was straightened out," Rachel said.

"Who was the client from Selebi?" Marieke asked.

"A Mr Gareth Thomas, he works at the mine there," Rachel explained.

"Do you know what the issue was?" Marieke asked.

"It had to do with the defence of a drunk driving case, Mr Thomas felt that he was not adequately represented, they had words, then Mr Katse refunded all his fees, and Mr Thomas was left to just pay the fine, I think the whole affair was odd, but that was between Mr Katse, and Mr Thomas," Rachel explained.

"Do you know if Thomas is still at Selebi?" Marieke asked.

"I think so," Rachel said. "I understand that he has been here a long time, and is a permanent resident, I have a feeling that he, and Mr Katse knew each other before the drunk driving case, if he did then it would have been a business deal, which he kept quite separate from his law practice."

"Did Mr Katse have any significant debts, or people he owed money to?" Marieke asked.

"No," Rachel said. "Katse was quite wealthy, he has been careful over the years, and has a net worth in excess of 10 million Pula."

"That much?" Marieke said, surprised. "I have had many dealings with him, but until I went to his house, I had not appreciated how much he liked the finer things of life; he always wore the same suit, and seemed so down at heel."

"That was a façade," Rachel said. "He didn't want his clients to know how much he was worth; he had his work suit, and then his social suits."

"Who inherits?" Marieke asked.

"There are two cousins in Francistown; they are co-heirs, and I get a small bequest," Rachel explained.

"I have to ask," Marieke said. "Where were you between five and seven this morning?"

"I left my house at seven, and drove straight here, and opened the office at seven-thirty," Rachel replied. "We have a farm by Lentsweletau. I talked to Constable Moroka on the way, he will confirm that I was in Lentsweletau just after seven."

"Thank you," Marieke said, satisfied that Rachel was an unlikely suspect. She was sure that there were people who could verify that she had arrived at the office at seven-thirty or so, and her estimation of the time it would drive from Lentsweletau would leave little time to get to Katse's house, lie in wait, and then get back to the office by seven-thirty. "Do you have addresses for the cousins in Francistown?"

"I do, they manage a farm that Katse owns," Rachel said. "Here it is, the address and telephone number of the farm. Do you wish me to notify the cousins of Mr Katse's death?"

"We will send someone to this address with the news," Marieke said. "Who is the executor of Mr Katse's will?"

"Patel, and Patel on Queen's Road," Rachel replied.

"I know them, I will call upon them, and let them know of Mr Katse's death," Marieke said. "What will you do now?"

"Spend more time on the farm," Rachel said. "We have it to the stage now where our cattle herd is well established, and it will support us quite well without needing the income from this job. I will contact the cousins, and find out what they want to do with the legal practice, neither of them is a solicitor, so my guess is that they will say to wind the business up, and sell this building, I would do that for them, for a fee, I learned well from Katse, do nothing except for a fee."

"May I use your telephone?" Marieke asked.

"Of course," Rachel said. Marieke called her office, talked to Sergeant Maphosa, gave him the basics of the case, and asked him to call the Francistown station, get someone to go to the farm of Katse, and interview the cousins. That done, she hung up and considered what to do next.

"I would like to see Mr Katse's office," Marieke said.

"I'm sorry, *Mma*," Rachel said. "I don't have a key to his office."

"Let's see if one of these works," Marieke suggested. She took the keys from her pocket and tried a likely one, and it worked. Once inside the office, she saw a desk, two filing cabinets, two chairs for clients or guests, and a small table with a coffee maker and paper cups. The office had a window that looked out onto the street; it could be opened but was latched shut, with a lock on it. Marieke looked at the keys she had and picked the one that she presumed fit the window lock. She tested it, and it worked. "Did Mr Katse have any files that you did not have copies of?" she asked Rachel.

"Yes," Rachel replied. "I probably have ninety-five per cent of the case files, but there were some he kept in here, with no extra copies, unless he had copies at his home office."

"Do you think there were case files at his house that were only there with no copies here?" Marieke asked.

"Possibly," Rachel thought. "He also had a unit in one of those places where you can rent space, where he kept old case files. Most of my files go back seven years; anything older than that would be at the other place. I do have a key for that facility, and I would occasionally have to pull old material for cases."

"Do you have an index of those files?" Marieke asked.

"I do," Rachel confirmed. "I have a very good index of all the files I had access to, with cross-references, and everything. It took me some years to do it, but I persevered, and have a very good system now. If you needed anything I had access to, I could get it for you very quickly."

"Thank you, *Mma*," Marieke said. "We may need that in days to come as we try and work out who did this. Tell me, has Mr Katse had any dealings with a white man, probably in his fifties, greyish hair, beard, glasses, between 160 and 180 cm tall, slim build, in the recent days?"

"That rings no bells," Rachel said. "There was Thomas from Selebi, he is past middle-aged, definitely not grey, red hair, and no beard. The other recent white clients are Harris, he has a bar in town, and has been a client for about ten years; he has no hair. There is Mortimer, but he is quite plump, Williams, but he is away in Jo'burg at the moment, Smith, but he's in gaol awaiting trial, McIntosh, again unlikely, too young, Brown, probably too old, he's over seventy, there may be one or two more, I would have to dig through the records."

"If you would," Marieke asked. "I am interested in white clients, aged now possibly mid-fifties."

"I will start digging," Rachel promised. "Is there anything else I can do now?"

"I don't think so," Marieke said. "I'll lock up the office again, and may send an officer later to collect the filing cabinets. I'll talk to the prosecution service, and have them get a new defence counsel to visit Smith in the gaol, and take over his case. What is he accused of?"

"Assault and battery," Rachel said. "Not the first time, probably won't be the last time, he likes to drink, and when he drinks, he becomes very brave, and stupid. In this case, he was lucky in that the man he hit went down immediately, and didn't get in any return blows; in the past, he has come off worst in his fights."

"Oh, there was a message on Katse's answering machine at his house from a Mr Banda, looking for representation for his son," Marieke said.

"Oh, has Banda's son been arrested for drunk driving again?" Rachel asked.

"That was the import of the message," Marieke confirmed.

"I'll call Banda and let him know that he's going to need a new lawyer," Rachel said.

"There was another call from a woman," Marieke said. "She suggested that he meet her at the Peacock."

"That would be Celia Molale," Rachel said. "She's a business partner of Mr Katse. I have met her a few times and like her a lot. I cannot see her killing Katse, but I suppose it might happen."

"As far as you know, their relationship was going well?" Marieke asked.

"Yes," Rachel confirmed. "I think Katse liked her because there was no talk from her about a relationship; she was all business."

"Well, thank you for your time and help," Marieke said. "Please call me when you have finished your researches, or if anything else comes to mind, this is my telephone number."

"Thank you, *Mma*," Rachel said. "I should start calling current clients, and advise them that Mr Katse is dead, and to start looking for other representation."

"If any of them give any indication that his death is not news to them, please do let me know," Marieke said.

"I will, *Mma*," Rachel agreed.

"Goodbye, *Mma*, I am sure I will see you again soon," Marieke said.

Marieke then drove to the offices of Patel and Patel, solicitors who had a broad non-criminal practice that included estate issues, trusts, land conveyancing, and property disputes.

"*Dumela Mma*," she greeted the receptionist.

"*Dumela Mma*," the receptionist replied. "How may I help you?"

"I am Assistant Superintendent Englebrecht, and I would like to talk to whichever of the firm would deal with the estate of Mr Kagiso Katse," Marieke said.

"That would be Mr Ravindra Patel, but you said the estate of Mr Katse, does that mean he is dead?" the receptionist asked.

"I am afraid so," Marieke confirmed.

"Let me get Mr Ravindra for you," the receptionist said, then she scurried off and returned almost immediately with a man, whom Marieke knew by sight as one of the Patels.

"Assistant Superintendent, Ravindra Patel, I gather you wish to talk to us about Mr Katse?" he said.

"That is so," Marieke confirmed. "I am sorry to have to tell you that he was found dead this morning in his car, and we are investigating it as murder."

"Please come to my office, what can we tell you?" he asked.

"We have been informed that his heirs are cousins in Francistown, and that the majority of his estate would pass to them," Marieke said. "Can you think of someone who bore a grudge against Katse, badly enough to kill him?"

"Not off the top of my head," Patel said. "Katse had a chequered past, but he seemed to be able to jolly even his most ardent adversaries along, so that I cannot see anyone killing him. You are correct about the estate, and the heirs, the two cousins share it all, bar a bequest of some 20,000 Pula that goes to his receptionist. How did he die?"

"We are not releasing details yet, until we have talked to the next of kin," Marieke said.

"We will need copies of a death certificate at some point to proceed with the business of putting the estate through the probate court," Patel said.

"I will arrange for you to receive a copy from the police surgeon," Marieke promised. "Tell me, do you know of any dealings Katse has had lately with a white man, possibly in his fifties, beard, grey hair, about 160 to 180 cm tall?"

"That rings no bells with me," Patel said. "But then, we only dealt with Katse and his personal affairs, none of his cases. As far as I know, he had no white relatives, and few close white friends or business partners, most of the white men he had dealings with would likely be found in the criminal court, or magistrates court for driving under the influence or speeding, we did not deal with them, except on the odd occasion where Katse was a client, and one of his white clients also happened to be one of ours."

"Was the house of Katse still carrying a mortgage?" Marieke asked.

"No, he paid that off some years ago," Patel said.

"Did he have any other property?" she asked.

"He owns, owned, the building where he has his office," Patel replied. "He also had a storage building, one of those places where one can rent space to keep extra stuff. There are also three large industrial properties on Lobatse Road. There is also the farm near

Francistown, which is where the cousins live, they manage the farm. He is, was, a partner in several properties in town, the Peacock Bar and Grill, the Diamond Sight, the Elephant Hunter, and the Buffalo Bar. His ownership was usually around 35%, but with the Peacock, he had a 51% ownership."

"What were relations like between Katse and his partners?" Marieke asked.

"I think amicable," Patel said. "There were the usual discussions about investments and returns, but Katse was taking the long view and was not looking for quick returns. He was banking on the expansion of Gabs and the likely rise in property prices rather than returns from ongoing operations. Not that any of those properties are not returning well, the latest numbers I saw showed all of them well in the black, with no significant debt, and no off-balance sheet liabilities that could bite them in the future. If run well, the bar business is rarely unprofitable."

"I gather from the gardener that Katse entertained women at his house. Could he have annoyed one of them enough to have her, or a friend, take action against him?" Marieke asked.

"I suppose that is possible," Patel admitted. "But, he seemed to be able to end relationships without drama, so it seems unlikely to me, not impossible, but unlikely. The current one is June Matsuoka; she has a beauty salon in town that caters to the *haute monde*."

"And the previous one?" Marieke asked.

"That would have been Kolo Mutande; she went off to New York to be part of the UN mission," Patel said.

"So, an unlikely killer?" Marieke asked.

"I think unlikely," Patel agreed. "That relationship lasted two years before she moved, and as far as I know, she is currently in New York. If any of the earlier relationships went sour, I would have thought that there would have been repercussions long before now."

"If you think of anyone who may have wished Katse harm, or you think of some circumstance that may have led to violence, please call me at this number," Marieke said, proffering her business card.

"I will," Patel promised. "As your investigation proceeds, we would be interested to learn who it was who murdered Katse."

"I will tell you what I can, and I may be back to see you again," Marieke said. "Stay well, Mr Patel."

"Go well, Superintendent," he replied.

Marieke drove to her office and met Assistant Commissioner Mochage on his way in as well.

"So, Matshwana," he said. "I heard that our longtime friend Mr Katse met his maker today."

"That is so, Sir," she confirmed. "Initial indications are that he was shot from behind when he got into his car. The shooting took place early this morning, probably around dawn."

"Anything of note that you saw?" he asked.

"Well," she temporised. "The shooter left the gun behind, suggesting that he either does not care if we know who he is, or that it is a gun that we will have a difficult time tracing, perhaps it has been stolen sometime in the past. He didn't even bother to file down the serial number, so he's either confident or arrogant. Thabo is going over the garage now, but Katse still had his wallet with some 560 Pula still there; his credit cards were also still there. My surmise is that this was not robbery but either a hit for someone or some personal vendetta, nothing was taken from the house or the car, there are no clues of any kind around the house or the garage, whoever did this took great pains not to leave anything, it smacks very much of a well-planned operation. The gardener did tell me one thing, and that was that the lock on the garage door has been broken for two weeks. One might suspect that the killer had broken the lock to gain access to the garage, and then just bided his time."

"What's Katse been up to lately?" Mochage asked.

"According to his receptionist, nothing of note in the past few months, and his own solicitors, Patel and Patel, knew of nothing untoward," she explained. "I have some follow-up interviews to do with business partners he had, I gather that he was part-owner in several bars in town. I also need to talk to a Gareth Thomas from Selebi, apparently, he had words with Katse a month or so ago about an inadequate defence in a drunk driving case. Katse's receptionist told me that she thought that had been resolved amicably enough, but you never know."

"What else have you learned about our Mr Katse?" Mochage asked.

"He was a man of considerable means," she replied. "He owned several properties around town, a farm near Francistown, and his receptionist put his net worth at some 10 million Pula."

"That much?" Mochage said. "I should have become a solicitor, and not a policeman. So, what next?"

"I need to start going through his files to see if there is anything that might point to some discord or major disagreement that would lead to a murder," she said.

"Any girlfriends?" Mochage asked.

"Apparently, the current one is June Matsoka, who has a salon in town," Marieke replied.

"I know the shop, my wife goes there, she's doing well, I think," Mochage commented.

"There was another, a Celia Molale, I think she may have an appointment with him at the Peacock Bar and Grill tonight," Marieke said. "There was a message on his machine from a woman wanting to meet him at six tonight."

"You should check that out as well as Matsoka," Mochage said. "Maybe Matsoka is jealous of Molale."

"Yes, the age-old trilogy of love, lust, and lucre," Marieke said. "I will go to the Peacock this evening and see if it was Molale."

"Perhaps you should pre-empt things, and go, and see Molale, and ask her if it was she on the telephone message," he suggested. "Her shop opens at ten, so you could be there when she opens up, then if it was not her, try the Peacock, and see who's there at six. I would also check on Matsoka and see if she had reason to kill Katse. Who inherits Katse's loot?"

"There are two cousins who manage the Francistown farm; they get it all, bar a bequest of 20,000 Pula to his receptionist," Marieke replied.

"I suppose they were in Francistown at the time of the murder?" he asked.

"I'm waiting to hear from the Francistown station," she said. "Anything is possible, and if they didn't do it, did they get someone to do it for them, and get their hands on the money sooner? It's always possible that if Katse had a serious relationship that included marriage that the will would be changed, and they would be left with little or nothing. Ten million Pula is a lot, and there are plenty of people who would kill for less."

"True," he agreed. "So, possible motive, 10 million Pula, when may we hear from the Francistown station?"

"I would think fairly shortly," she said. "I instructed Sergeant Maphosa to call them while I was at Katse's office. They should have had time to visit the cousins by now. If I may use your telephone, we could find out?"

"By all means," he said. Marieke called the Francistown station and talked to an Inspector Moseki. He had been out to the farm, and his impression was that the death of Katse was news to the cousins. They had both seemed quite genuinely upset and were full of questions, none of which he could answer. He told Marieke that she might expect to be contacted by the cousins as they sought answers, and started to plan for what followed the police investigation and the probate of the will.

"So, unlikely suspects," Mochage commented.

"I agree, Sir," Marieke said. "But, I won't remove them from the list yet, it is possible that they are consummate actors, and, although they clearly could not have been in Gabs at the time of the murder, may have had someone do it for them. It may be worth looking at their finances to see if there have been any large cash withdrawals lately."

"You think they are intelligent enough to use cash, and not cheques?" Mochage asked.

"I have to assume that if they had designs upon Katse, then they would not leave a trail behind for us to follow," Marieke said.

"Very good," Mochage said. "Well, keep digging. Have you had lunch yet?"

"No, Sir," she replied. "Perhaps we could try the new place in town, the Mandarin?"

"Excellent," he said. "Chinese it is. Have you ever been to China?"

"No, Sir," she said. "The farthest east I got was to Beira once a long time ago when the Portuguese still ran the country."

"China is fascinating," he said. "It is so big, and the people, I have never seen so many people. But the Chinese need resources, and they take the long view, so the TanZam railway of the 1970s will be their entrée into the riches of copper in Zambia. We, so far, haven't sold our souls to the Chinese, but others will, like the Zims. But, apart from all that, the food is good, and even good for you."

After lunch, Marieke spent the rest of the day visiting the various establishments where Katse had some level of ownership. She had tried the shop of Celia Molale, but there was a note on the door saying that it was closed for the morning, and to come back later. By now, word had started to go around that Katse was dead, murdered, and those she visited professed surprise. As far as she could tell, Marieke saw no guile in those she saw, but genuine surprise that this had happened. They were all interested in who would inherit, and what the heir or heirs would choose to do with the part ownerships. All Marieke could do was refer them to Patel, and Patel, and suggest that they stay in contact with the solicitors at least until after the will had been probated. She found the salon of June Matsoka, and went in, and asked for her. She was directed to an office in the back, where she found June Matsoka busy with financial reports.

"*Dumela Mma*," Marieke said.

"*Dumela Mma*," June replied. "What can I do for you?"

"I am Assistant Superintendent Englebrecht of the Botswana Police, and I have some bad news," Marieke said.

"What's happened?" June asked.

"I'm afraid that your friend Kagiso Katse was murdered this morning," Marieke said.

"Murdered, by who, how, why?" June said.

"He was shot in his garage early this morning," Marieke said. "At this time, we don't know who by or why. Do you know anyone who would wish harm to Mr Katse?"

"No, no," June said. "Oh, poor Kagiso, he just asked me to marry him, why, why?" She sat down at her desk and burst into tears. Marieke waited until the first sobs were over, and she had

31

recovered some composure. Then she continued with her questions. "I'm sorry to have to ask this, but where were you between six and six-thirty this morning?"

"I was at home," June said. "In bed, I got up late, at about nine, then came here."

"Do you live alone?" Marieke asked.

"No, my sister and a cousin both live with me," June said.

"When did you last see Mr Katse?" Marieke asked.

"Two days ago, we had dinner at his house, and I spent the night. I left when he did at six thirty in the morning, and went home," June said.

"Did you often spend time with Mr Katse?" Marieke asked.

"We usually got together three or four times a week," June said.

"How long have you been seeing Mr Katse?" Marieke asked.

"About two years," June said. "What will I do now, my Kagiso gone, why?"

"That we don't know," Marieke said. "That's why we're asking all those who knew him if they have any idea who might want to harm him."

"I'm sorry," June said. "I can't help, truly I am, I want to know who killed him, but I don't know who would want to."

"Thank you for your time," Marieke said. "I may come and see you again in the future as our enquiries progress. Stay well."

"Go well, *Mma*, find out who did this, and string him up," June said.

Her last visit of the day was back to the shop of Celia Molale. Marieke entered the shop and was gratified to see that there were no customers.

"*Dumela Mma*," she said to the woman who was there.

"*Dumela Mma*," the woman replied. "How may I help you? A new dress, a new jacket?"

"Perhaps later," Marieke replied. "Are you Celia Molale?"

"I am," Celia said. "How may I help you?"

"I am Assistant Superintendent Englebrecht," Marieke said. "I am afraid I have some bad news about your friend Kagiso Katse. I am sorry to say he is dead, and we are treating his death as suspicious."

"Kagiso murdered, but how, who, when?" Celia asked, plumping down onto a chair. Marieke went to the door, changed the sign to closed, locked the door, and then went back to talk to Celia.

"We believe that Mr Katse was murdered in his garage, probably as he was on his way to his office," Marieke explained.

"But who would want to do that?" Celia asked, more of herself than of Marieke.

"That is one of the questions we have," Marieke said. "When did you last see Mr Katse?"

"A few days ago, we had a business meeting. He called me yesterday looking to discuss something, left a message on my machine, I called back, and left a message on his machine to meet me at the Peacock tonight at six," Celia said.

"Can you think of anyone who would wish him dead?" Marieke asked.

"Dead, no, destitute, yes," Celia said. "He had many dealings in the past that were not always beneficial to the other party, but death? No, I cannot think of anyone who would go as far as death. He was always there to take their cases, even if he did fare better than they did."

"I am sorry, but I have to ask this," Marieke said. "Where were you between five and seven this morning?"

"At home, in bed," Celia said.

"Can anyone confirm that?" Marieke asked.

"No," Celia said. "My first appointment of the day was at the dentist's, at eight, I go to Williams on Queen's Road. But Kagiso dead, why?"

"That is one of the things we are trying to discover," Marieke said. "Can I get someone to drive you to your house?"

"No, I'm fine, thank you," Celia said. "I have a flat above the shop that I use in the week. I'll stay here tonight. Get them for me, will you?"

"Get who?" Marieke asked.

"Whoever killed Kagiso," Celia said. "Whoever, man or woman."

"You think it may have been a woman?" Marieke asked.

"It's possible, I suppose," Celia said. "It's always possible. How was he killed?"

"We have not released any details," Marieke replied. "When we do, I will let you know more."

"Thank you," Celia said.

"How long have you known Mr Katse?" Marieke asked.

"We have a strictly business relationship that goes back about fifteen years," Celia said. "We had similar interests, he was quite wealthy, almost as wealthy as me, he was a good business partner."

"You have interests other than this shop?" Marieke asked.

"I have a farm with quite some number of cows," Celia explained. "And I also have a financial interest in several businesses in the town. That's how I met Kagiso, we both have just over a third of The Elephant Hunter and the Diamond Sight. I also have a fairly large stock portfolio. I inherited a little money from my father when I was only 25, and I decided to invest on the Jo'burg, and London exchanges, and lately on our own share exchange. I have done well over the years, I even have some appreciable holdings in De Beers, so support our local diamond industry."

"Could there have been a woman in the past who was jilted by Mr Katse or has another axe to grind?" Marieke asked.

"Possibly," Celia admitted. "His current girlfriend is June Matsoka, she has a beauty salon in town, very chic, and fashionable herself. I think Kagiso liked to be seen with her; she is very beautiful, in fact, he told me that he'd just asked her to marry him."

"Is there anything from his past that may have come back to haunt him?" Marieke asked.

"Not that I know of," Celia said. "I still can't believe that he's dead. Such a loss, he was a really funny man, and wonderful to be with."

"I'm afraid I only knew him as a solicitor representing people, some of whom I had arrested," Marieke said. "So, I never saw the lighter side of him."

"I suppose not," Celia said. "I need a drink; can I get you something?"

"Why not?" Marieke said. "I have finished for the day."

"What will you have? I have wine, spirits of all kinds, beer, what's your poison?" Celia asked.

"If you have a white wine, that would be much appreciated," Marieke said.

Celia led the way to the back of the store and up some stairs to her flat. She had quite a selection of wines and spirits. She rummaged through a wine cooler and produced a bottle of Klein Constantia Riesling. While they both sipped on their wine, Celia kept up a monologue about Katse, and Marieke learned much about him and his dealings in Gaborone. The more Celia talked, the less likely she seemed as a suspect. She had had a business relationship with Katse, nothing more. She talked about past relationships of Katse that she knew of, but none of them seemed likely as suspects, as they all had moved on to better things. It was almost eight when Marieke tore herself away from the monologue and excused herself to go home. The evening had been fascinating, and to some extent illuminating, but, for all that, she was no closer to a likely motive than she had been at the beginning of the day. She had also learned a lot about Celia. She was the daughter of a farmer from Francistown and had been educated in England, had gone to university in Oxford, and studied economics. When her father died, she had taken over the farm and had quickly discovered that she liked the proceeds from the farm, but not the work, so she had found a manager and had been happy with the results. He had not been given a completely free hand; she had kept a close eye on things, and the farm had prospered. She had used her knowledge of economics, and had invested her father's savings, and had turned that into a fortune.

The following day, Marieke stopped at the morgue on her way to work to see Thabo.

"*Dumela Mma*," he said when she arrived.

"*Dumela Rra*," she replied. "What do you have for me?"

"As we suspected, gunshots to the head, two, either would have been fatal, entry at the back of the head, and exit wounds at the front. Both bullets passed through the cerebrum, actually one through each hemisphere," Thabo said. "He was shot at close range, there is a degree of powder burning on the back of the head, which fits with a scenario of someone in the back of the car shooting him from behind. He was actually quite fit otherwise; he must have been doing some exercise on a regular basis. The main organs all look good, there is nothing untoward in the rest of the body, we're running routine checks for alcohol, and illegal substances, I expect those results in a day or two, but my intuition tells me that little will come of that, so gunshots to the head it is. We've had no luck on the gun; it's not in our registry. There were no prints on the receiver, barrel, magazine or suppressor or any of the bullets in the magazine. The gun itself is a Beretta 92S, not a model I have seen before, so perhaps easier to trace, but I can't tell you too much else about it. The ammunition is from Pretoria Metal Pressings, not surprising as they probably make most of the 9mm stock in South Africa. The headstamp marks also give us year of manufacture, and it is more recent than the gun, most of it 1990, but with two earlier from about 1988. The suppressor is well made; it would take the gunshot sound down to something barely audible outside a closed garage. We've confirmed from test firings that the spent cartridges we found in the car did in fact come from the gun, there are matches on the firing pin, and extractor marks, we were unable to get any good rifling marks from the bullets themselves, they were too damaged from impact into the wall, but I see as unlikely that the bullets that killed Katse came from a gun other than the one we found. I suppose that a good lawyer could invent a scenario where the gun we found was just fired into thin air, leaving the cartridge cases, but I doubt that anyone would believe such an improbable story."

"You are full of good news," she said. "Let me have the details on the gun, I'll see if I can get anything from the South Africans, maybe someone there has reported a gun stolen, or maybe it's a *Boertjie* gone mad, and is using his own gun."

"I doubt it," Thabo said. "But stranger things have happened. You were right about the broom; it had blood smears on it, but the blood was from Katse. So, our villain swept out the garage after he, or she, shot Katse. There were no fingerprints on the broom handle; it had been wiped completely clean."

"Well, thanks, Thabo, I'd better go and see the commissioner, stay well," she said.

"Go well," he replied.

Marieke walked over to the main police station and reported on her conversations to the commissioner.

"So, Matshwana," he said. "What have we today on our friend Katse?"

"I checked with Thabo, and it seems probable that cause of death was gunshots to the head," she reported. "Thabo is running the usual tests for toxins, but that seems unlikely. Why kill someone with some toxin, then arrange the body in the car, and shoot him through the head? The gun is a fairly standard 9mm from South Africa, as is the ammunition. I'm going to check with the South Africans to see if they will be cooperative, and tell us if it has been reported stolen. That's a long shot as they haven't been very cooperative of late, and I don't have any contacts there. The gun is not on our list of guns registered to anyone here. The ammunition was mostly of fairly recent manufacture, but with two older rounds, either the gun is not used much, or the user has stocks that have been around a while."

"Anything from the door-to-door enquiries?" he asked.

"I'll check with our people today," she said. "If the shooter kept the house under observation for a day or so to track the comings and goings of Katse, then surely someone saw him or her."

"Let me know if anything is reported," he said.

"Yes, Sir," she replied.

Marieke went to her office and found Sergeant Maphosa.

"*Dumela Rra,*" she said.

"*Dumela Mma,*" he replied.

"Have we anything on the door-to-door enquiries yet?" she asked.

"A few things," he replied. "Three people report seeing a Mercedes car parked nearby on two occasions in the past two weeks, they said that it was white with Gabs plates. Another saw a Land Rover once, blue short wheelbase, also with local plates."

"Were the cars there on the same day each week, and did anyone see if there was anyone in the cars?" she asked.

"They all said that the Mercedes and the Land Rover were there on Monday mornings, and that there might have been someone in them, but none could say for certain," he said.

"So, no way of knowing whether the driver was man or woman, black or white?" she asked.

"No, Madame," he confirmed. "The only thing in common was that they were there early, and usually gone by seven in the morning, which would usually be after Katse had left. Apparently, not many people in that place get up early, activity seems to start around seven thirty to eight in the mornings, it is only a few people who are out earlier."

"Very good, Sergeant," she said. "Widen the field a little, and ask about white Mercedes cars, and blue Land Rovers, you never know something may crop up."

"Yes, Madame," he replied.

"Oh, please check with the dental surgery of David Williams, and confirm that Celia Molale had an appointment there yesterday that she kept, and, if you can check on whether or not June Matsoka was at home between six and six thirty," she said.

"Yes, Madame," he said.

The next item on her list was to talk to Gareth Thomas. For that conversation, she would have to drive to Selebi Phikwe, which was a little over a four-hour drive, so if she left immediately, she could be there a little after lunch and be back the same evening. On the way there, she stopped and bought a sandwich for lunch, which she ate at the side of the road, just before arriving at Selebi. She was at the mine just after one, and at the gate was directed to the office of Gareth Thomas. He was just finishing a meeting and was curious about his visitor.

"*Dumela Rra*," Marieke greeted him.

"*Dumela Mma*, what can I do for you?" he replied.

"I am Assistant Superintendent Englebrecht with the Botswana Police, and would like to talk to you about Mr Kagiso Katse," Marieke said.

"Him, what's he done now, bilked another poor sap?" he asked.

"Sadly, Mr Katse will do no more bilking; he died yesterday," she explained.

"Died, and the police are investigating, so I suppose died actually means was killed?" he said. "Didn't see that coming. I suppose you heard about our disagreement. Well, for the record, I was underground yesterday from six-thirty until two. When was he killed?"

"He died early in the morning, around six," she said. "What was the disagreement about?"

"I was accused of drunk driving, and retained Katse to defend me. I thought he did a superficial job at best, and told him so. I couldn't get off the ticket, even though I still contend that the arresting officer concocted the evidence. Katse agreed to refund his fee, and I paid the 50 Pula fine that the magistrate levied. I think it was a slap on the wrist fine, because I think the magistrate also had questions about the whole affair. I got nothing on my licence out of it, so put it down to experience, stay away from sobriety checkpoints, the cops will find some way to pin something on you. Sorry about that, but you're obviously not in Traffic if you're after a murderer," Thomas said, quite bitterly.

"I'm sorry to have to ask this, but is there a way to confirm that you were here yesterday?" Marieke asked.

"No worries," he said. "There are probably 100 people who could tell you I was here, and underground, and there are the shift logs, which I suppose could be falsified, but there are enough witnesses. You want me to get one or two?"

"That won't be necessary at this time," Marieke said. "I have to ask these questions as a matter of routine."

"Of course," he said. "How was Katse murdered?"

"We have not yet released details of the case," she said. "In time, we will issue a statement, perhaps even in time to forestall the rumours."

"Good luck with that," he said. "The bush telegraph is alive and well, even here in Selebi. Katse popped, who'd have thought? I suppose there is a suspect list a mile long?"

"Surprisingly no," Marieke said. "Although there are some other people who seemed to have had similar experiences with Mr Katse as you did, most that I have talked to seem to have been mollified with cash, and even though some had been bilked, as you say, they still went back to him."

"He was a nice enough bloke," Thomas admitted. "But, he struck me as a little glib, maybe you should look way back into his past, and see who he really pissed off, or someone he defended, and lost, and they got time, and are now just out."

"We are investigating the dim and distant past of Mr Katse," Marieke said. "That will take time, so for the moment we are eliminating likely suspects."

"So, am I eliminated?" Thomas asked.

"For the moment," Marieke said. "But, we may come back to you if new information comes our way."

"I understand," Thomas said. "Just don't try, and stitch me up for this, I didn't do it."

"I'm sorry, stitch me up?" Marieke asked.

"Brit cop speak," Thomas explained. "When the Old Bill fixes the evidence so that they can charge you, and make the charges stick."

"Really?" Marieke asked.

"True enough," he said. "I'm sure you chaps have thought about fixing evidence when you know for a certainty who the guilty party is, but have nothing that will stand up in court."

"Personally, no," Marieke said. "But, sadly, there may be some truth to what you say. Before I go, I should take down your particulars. Your name is Gareth Thomas, any middle name?"

"David," he said.

"Date of birth?" she asked.

"14th of May 1932," he replied.

"And you currently reside at?" she asked.

"421 Kubelo Street," he said.

"Well, thank you for your time," she said.

"You driving back to Gabs now?" he asked.

"I am," she confirmed.

"I was going to say watch out for the speed trap that they often set up about 26 kilometres from here on the road to Serule, but they'll leave you alone, not like us common folk," he said. "Go well."

"Stay well," she replied, and left.

The speed trap was there, but they were busy writing out tickets to two other poor souls who had either not heard that this was a common place for a trap, or who had ignored the warnings, and gambled on the officers either not being there, or being busy with someone else. She did have to go through a disease control barrier, just outside Serule, but that was simply a matter of driving through a shallow pond filled with some concoction to kill off the virus of the foot and mouth disease that may have found its way onto her car. Foot and mouth might not be that important to humans, but to cattle farmers, it could be the death knell for them, so the government took precautions whenever anything showed up.

By the time Marieke got back to her house, it was quite late, she had had enough for the day, and was looking forward to a bath and a glass of wine. She pondered her conversation with Gareth Thomas and decided that he was a very unlikely shooter. He may have paid someone to do it for him, but she saw that as highly unlikely. In her view, the killing of Katse Kagiso had a deeper meaning to someone than just dissatisfaction over representation, so she would have to delve further into his past and see who might be holding a grudge, but for the moment, food and wine were more of a priority. The refrigerator was rather sparse, but there was enough to put together a quick light supper, then it was time for a soak in a bath with a glass of wine.

Possible suspects?

Before going to the office the next day, Marieke went back to the house of Katse and took another look around. She went into the garage, opened the back doors of the BMW, and sat in the back seat, behind where the driver would sit. She felt around but found nothing in or around the seat that might belong to the shooter. She could see the powder burns on the bottom of the headrest. The shooter must have put the barrel of the gun between the seat and the headrest. When he fired, the cartridge cases would have been ejected to the right, and she found very faint char marks on the upholstery of the back seat where they landed first. She surmised that the shooter must have swept them off the seat when he left. She looked at the ceiling fabric, but saw no hair, or hair treatments that might have been left, so either he was short enough not to touch the ceiling, or he was wearing some sort of cap or hat. There was nothing on the floor in the way of mud or dust, so either he was very clean or he cleaned out the floor of the car when he left. She dismissed that idea because any cleaning post-shooting would also have gathered up the cartridge cases. There was always the possibility that he wore booties over his shoes, so as not to leave anything behind. It was looking more and more as if this was a well-thought-out and executed shooting. A thought did occur to her, the man seen walking away from the scene was carrying a briefcase, perhaps it contained gloves, cap, and booties, all the items necessary to avoid leaving any evidence. But, if that were the case, why not also take the gun, why leave the gun behind. Perhaps there was a message there, perhaps the shooter wanted the investigation to lead somewhere, but where?

She went into the house and found Inspector Masisi going through the files of Katse.

"*Dumela Rra*," she said.

"*Dumela Mma*," he replied. "Are you well today?"

"I am," she confirmed. "And you?"

"I am well, but frustrated by our lack of progress," he lamented. "I can find nothing in these files that gives any hint of who might wish Katse dead."

"How far back do these files go?" she asked.

"Only about five years," he replied.

"Call Rachel Pule at the office of Katse, and ask her for older files," Marieke suggested. "Start with those five to ten years old, and see if there is anything in them, she told me that she had them catalogued, and could access them at any time."

"Yes, Madame," Masisi said. "It strikes me that this shooting is very professional; whoever did it left no clues or traces. Are we dealing with an outsider, perhaps from South Africa, here at someone's bidding?"

"That thought has occurred to me as well," Marieke admitted. "If that is so, then Katse must have really annoyed someone, and the answer surely would be in the files somewhere. We have been assuming that this was the work of someone who bore a grudge because of his position as a solicitor. What if it was a business deal that had gone bad, Katse had quite a few holdings in different businesses in town; perhaps someone wanted him out of one?"

"A possibility," Masisi agreed. "Who might know that?"

"His own solicitors, Patel, and Patel," Marieke said, "I should pay them another call. Stay well, Inspector Masisi."

"Go well, Madame," he replied.

Marieke drove to the offices of Patel and Patel, and once there, asked to speak to Ravindra Patel.

"Assistant Superintendent," he said when he came into the lobby. "Please, let's use this conference room. How may I be of service?"

"It has occurred to us that perhaps Mr Katse's killing might be a falling out among business associates. Do you know of any disputes between him and his partners?" she asked.

"As I said before, not off the top of my head," he said.

"Who were the partners in the various enterprises that Katse held parts of?" she asked.

"Well, let's see, the Diamond Sight, that would be Katse, 35%, Celia Molale at 35%, and Samson Mwendwa the other 30%," he started. "Then there's the Elephant Hunter, again Katse 35%, Celia Molale 35%, and Isaac Bwalya the other 30%, the Buffalo Bar, again Katse 35%, David Williams 35%, and Thabo Matsoka the other 30%, finally there's the Peacock Bar, and Grill, Katse 51%, Gareth Thomas 49%. Katse, Molale, Williams, and Thomas put up the money; the others were more in the line of operating partners, and were vesting their ownership over time."

"Is that the same Gareth Thomas who works at Selebi Phikwe?" she asked.

"I believe it is," he said. "Have you met him?"

"I saw him recently, yes," she confirmed. "Older, sixties, thin, red hair?"

"That's him," Patel confirmed. "Longtime resident, probably reached the end of his promotions at the mine, but probably makes more money from the bar."

"What were the details of the partnership agreements at those bars?" she asked.

"It varied," he said. "I'll get you copies, and I'll get you copies of the latest P & L's and balance sheets."

"Thank you. Offhand, do you happen to know how ownership might change in the event of the death of any partners?" she asked.

"Again, it varied," he said. "With the Elephant Hunter and the Diamond Sight, his holdings pass to Celia Molale directly. With the Buffalo Bar, his holding just passes to the estate, finally with the Peacock, the holding passes directly to Thomas, which was a reciprocal arrangement; if Thomas had died, then Katse would have received all. In the cases of the Diamond Sight, the Elephant Hunter, and the Buffalo, the managers, who were working out their share of the businesses, would automatically fully vest."

"So, in his estate, you have excluded the values of those holdings?" she asked.

"Those that pass to other owners," he confirmed. "Those that stay with the estate are included in the valuation."

"What about other enterprises?" she asked.

"Well, he has some commercial properties that are leased out. I can give you details of all of those," he said.

"Thank you, I would appreciate that," she said. "And the farm near Francistown?"

"I'll get you details on that too," he said. "If you'll excuse me, I'll have our secretary quickly copy those documents." He left the room briefly and then came back and resumed his answers about the ranch. "There's quite a bit tied up in the ranch; it must be worth 5 million Pula in and of itself."

"That much?" she asked. "How big is it?"

"Quite large," Patel said. "There is also a large herd of cattle associated with it. I think the stocking rate is about 12 hectares per livestock unit, and they have a herd of about 4,000. Some of the land is owned, and some is leased."

"Have you met Samson Mwendwa, George McIntosh or David Williams?" she asked.

"I have," Patel said.

"Describe them for me if you will," she asked.

"Mwendwa, thirties, short, glasses, tending to overweight, McIntosh, tall, almost two metres I would say, forties, red hair, clean shaven, rake thin, Williams, well-known local dentist, forties, balding, what hair is left is black, wears glasses, about one metre sixty, average build," Patel replied.

"Did you know that Mr Katse had asked June Matsoka to marry him?" she asked.

"He did tell me that he was going to, yes," Patel said.

"How does that affect the will of Mr Katse?" she asked.

"It wouldn't until after they married, and even then, it would be uncertain who could claim what unless he made a new will," Patel said.

"Thank you for your time, Mr Patel, I may be back later with more questions, if that is convenient?" she said.

"Of course, Superintendent, we're happy to help," he said.

"Well, thank you again, stay well," she said.

"Go well, *Mma*," he replied. "Let me see you out, ah, here is the package of copies that I promised."

Marieke left, kicking herself for not asking Thomas about knowing Katse before the drunk driving case. Rachel had told her that she thought that they knew each other, and she had missed the chance to dig further. She still doubted that Thomas did the shooting. If he were at the mine, as he said he was, then it would not have been possible. But that was not to say that he did not hire someone to do it for him. She needed to know if the cousins in Francistown had wind of the impending marriage, and how that might change their expectations. The loss of a ten-million Pula estate might be a good motive for killing someone. She also now needed to talk to Celia Molale again. Both Thomas and Molale might have motives to kill Katse, but so did Bwalya, Matsoka, and Mwendwa. She needed to review the financials for the two enterprises that Celia Molale now held the majority of, and the financials of the Peacock, which Thomas now held outright. That might give her a sense of whether there were motives there. She decided to talk first to Celia Molale and see what she had to say. At the shop, there was one lady being waited upon, so Marieke just bided her time until she was gone, and the shop was empty.

"*Dumela Mma,*" she said to Celia.

"*Dumela Mma,*" Celia replied. "How do things progress with your investigation?"

"It is early in the investigation," Marieke replied. "I am sorry, I must ask you some more questions."

"Of course," Celia said.

"Tell me about the business arrangement with the Diamond Sight and the Elephant Hunter," Marieke said.

"We started the businesses together," Celia replied. "Kagiso and I put in the money, and we gave the managers the chance to earn out a holding in the businesses. So, Kagiso and I stayed as the majority owners, but the operator had a stake."

"What happens now that Mr Katse is dead?" Marieke asked.

"In the event of either my death or Kagiso's, then the one's holdings would pass to the other. Also, in the event of the death of either one of us or a sale of a partner's holdings, the managing partner's share would fully vest," Celia explained.

"With Mr Katse's death, and the passing of his share of the Diamond Sight, and the Elephant Hunter to you, how much does that add to the value of your own holdings?" Marieke asked.

"What, you think I might have killed Kagiso for a measly 385,000 Pula?" Celia asked.

"I have to ask," Marieke said. "I have to explore all possibilities that might lead us to discover who killed Mr Katse."

"I suppose I understand," Celia said. "Actually, quite titillating to be a suspect, I bumped off Kagiso to get his part of the businesses. But, no, I didn't kill Kagiso or pay to have him killed. The bars run well, but the annual returns are not in the realm of what I would consider stellar. I do much better with my portfolio of stocks. I hold the ownership in the bars because it's steady cash income, and one of the few types of enterprise that are reasonably recession-proof. When things are good, people drink to celebrate, and when they're bad, they drink to forget. I know that's rather cynical, but it seems to be true."

"So, how much does each of the properties take in a year?" Marieke asked.

"Well, the Diamond does about 1,250,000 Pula a year, and the net is 20% of that, so 250,000, of which I get half, 125,000, which will now drop to 87,500 as Mwendwa becomes fully vested, the Elephant does slightly better, and takes in about 1,500,000, netting about 300,000, of which I get 150,000, which again will drop, this time to 105,000, as Bwalya becomes fully vested, but if I add back what would have been Kagiso's share, then I could get 175,000 from the Diamond Sight, and 210,000 from the Elephant Hunter, if we continue to have good years," Celia enumerated. "If I take a sell price of ten times earnings for the properties, then the total potential net worth of the two properties would be 5,500,000 Pula, of which I already would have 1,925,000, so with Katse gone, I could look at a potential sale that would net me twice that, or an annual income stream of 385,000 Pula."

"You obviously have a good sense of what the businesses are worth," Marieke said. "So, how much would Isaac Bwalya and Samson Mwendwa get from a sale or as an ongoing income?"

"Bwalya could get 900,000 Pula in a potential sale or a continued income stream of about 90,000 a year, Mwendwa would get a little less at about 750,000 in a potential sale or an income of about 75,000," Celia replied.

"So, both could be well compensated by Botswana standards," Marieke said.

"They could," Celia agreed. "But, I suppose one of them could get greedy or could have financial difficulties, not that I'm suggesting that, as far as I know, neither has any problems. At the moment, they both receive a salary as managers, but when they fully vest as partners, the salary will stop and be replaced by their share in the partnership. For both of them, it would mean quite an increase. At the moment, they get 40,000 and 35,000 Pula a year respectively, so you can see that vesting and switching to the partner income would make quite a difference. On the other hand, the partner's income is not guaranteed. If we have unusual expenditures or the businesses do poorly, then, potentially, they could actually get less, even nothing in a really poor year, partnership income only comes after all expenses have been paid, and accrued for, is our early years we were lucky to get 5,000 each, but as we have become more successful, that has grown significantly."

"How long is the vesting period?" Marieke asked.

"Five years," Celia replied. "Mwendwa has been with us three years, and Bwalya four years. If either leaves before the vesting period is complete, then they lose the opportunity; if they leave after they're fully vested, then the other partners must buy them out. So far, that has not happened. Mwendwa is the third manager we've had at the Diamond, and Bwalya is the fourth at the Elephant. The average length of service is three years, why they don't stay for the full five years, and capitalise on the ownership opportunity has always escaped me. The ones that have left have all gone to good opportunities at higher annual salaries, but it's not the same as ownership, where the potential for wealth accumulation is quite real; they don't seem to be able to grasp the mathematics."

"Tell me if Mr Katse had married, how would that have affected your partnership agreements?" Marieke asked.

"It wouldn't," Celia replied. "There were no heirs or successors clauses in our agreements; it wouldn't have mattered if he had married, it would not change the agreement."

"What about the other properties that Katse had an ownership in?" Marieke asked.

"Well, his share of the Buffalo Bar, I think, just goes to the cousins in Francistown, and the Peacock, I suppose, goes to Thomas, but Kagiso was never very forthcoming about that arrangement," Celia replied.

"Who manages the Peacock?" Marieke asked.

"George McIntosh, born here, lived here all his life," Celia replied.

"Is he related to the McIntoshes from Serowe?" Marieke asked.

"The famous, or infamous ones?" Celia laughed. "I don't know."

"How did he get on with Katse and Thomas?" Marieke asked.

"I think better with Thomas than with Kagiso, I've seen them arguing about pricing and the number of employees," Celia said. "The Peacock is a gold mine, and remember it's mostly all cash, so who knows what they actually took in, and what showed up on the books."

"Surely that would be a risky proposition," Marieke thought. "If the suppliers are checked, then the amount being delivered is known, and it would be fairly simple to estimate the probable income."

"I agree," Celia said. "I've done that a couple of times for the Diamond and the Elephant to check if the managers were being straight with us. I did discover a couple of wholesalers who suggested under-the-table sales to us. I cut them off, I've too much to lose elsewhere to be bothered by petty crimes. I know there is normally a wastage percentage, which in a well-run bar or restaurant, that's usually pretty low, so I suppose if I were the tax people, I would start there, and also look for spurious petty theft reports."

"Tell me, what kind of car do you have?" Marieke asked.

"I just bought a new Land Rover Defender County," Celia said. "It's the 110 model station wagon."

"What colour?" Marieke asked.

"Red," Celia said. "I like it, it's got the V8 engine, and five-speed gearbox, and I bought all the upgrades, and optional items I could think of."

"Well, thank you for your time," Marieke said. "I may wish to talk to you again in the future. Do you have any plans to travel outside the country?"

"Not this year," Celia said. "Perhaps next year I'll go to France, but not for the moment."

"I see, if you change your plans, please contact us before you go, stay well, Ms Molale," Marieke said.

"Please call me Celia," Celia said. "Go well, Superintendent."

At her office, Marieke sat down to write up her notes on the morning. She was interrupted by Assistant Commissioner Mochage, who always seemed to know when and where to appear.

"So, Matshwana, what have we today?" he asked.

"Perhaps suspects," she replied.

"Really, who?" he asked.

"Well, it seems that apart from the cousins in Francistown, several other people benefit directly from Katse's death, Celia Molale, Gareth Thomas, as beneficial owners of Katse's share, and Samson Mwendwa, Isaac Bwalya, and Thabo Matsoka as managers whose shares vest. They were all business partners with Katse, and according to the partnership agreements, if he dies, then in three cases his ownership reverts to the other financial partner, either Celia Molale or Gareth Thomas, and the other managing partners, Mwendwa, Bwalya, and Matsoka, fully vest. There is one thing that I need to explore, it seems that Katse just asked June Matsoka to marry him, perhaps the cousins heard about that, and decided that they didn't want to lose the estate to a new wife," she explained.

"Is the ownership in the bars worth killing for?" he asked.

"Perhaps," she admitted. "Celia Molale told me that her share in the two bars nets her about 275,000 Pula a year, which would increase to 385,000 with Katse gone. I need to review the financials to confirm that, but she seemed pretty confident in her numbers. She also suggested that if the businesses were sold outright, then the selling price might be as high as 5,500,000, of which she would get 3,850,000 Pula. Maybe that's motive enough; perhaps she wanted to sell, and Katse didn't. I also need to look at Isaac Bwalya and Samson Mwendwa; they both directly benefit from Katse's death, and could both benefit further if Celia Molale sold the businesses, but I'm wondering if the amount they would gain is enough to warrant the risk of killing Katse. What annoys me is that I omitted to explore the possible relationships with the possible suspects. I also need to dig a little into the operations of the Peacock Bar and Grill. Celia Molale hinted that they might be under-reporting revenues. She said that she had heard Katse, and the manager, a George McIntosh, arguing about pricing and staffing levels."

"Well, let me know what you find," he said. "What about the girlfriend, June Matsoka?"

"I didn't get the impression that she was acting when I told her the news about Katse. I think she was genuinely shocked and distressed. I noted that this morning, when I drove past her salon, it's closed for the day," she replied. "I would have thought that if she intended to kill Katse, then first she should have married him, then killed him to benefit as an heir or successor."

"From what I have heard from Lerato, she truly did love Katse, and would be an unlikely killer, but check on her anyway, but I agree marry him first, then kill him off," he said.

"Yes, Sir," she replied. The commissioner left, and Marieke called in Sergeant Maphosa, who had been hiding around the corner.

"He's gone," she said.

"Thank you, Madame," Maphosa said.

"Anything I should know?" she asked.

"Yes, Celia Molale did go to the dentist, Williams, on the day of Katse's murder. She had an eight o'clock appointment and was there early," he reported. "And, June Matsoka left her house at around nine thirty that morning, the gardeners across the street were there by five thirty, and saw no one leave until she did."

"Thank you," she said. "What do you know about Isaac Bwalya of the Elephant Hunter, Samson Mwendwa from the Diamond Sight, and Thabo Matsoka from the Buffalo Bar?"

"Bwalya is an immigrant from Zambia, he's been here maybe fifteen years, we've had no occasion to look at him for anything, Matsoka has had three speeding fines, but nothing else of note, Mwendwa has not crossed our paths at all, no speeding fines, no D & D, nothing," he replied.

"What about George McIntosh from the Peacock?" she asked.

"Two speeding fines, one D & D, and hints of dealing in merchandise under the table, the tax people have asked questions a couple of times, but nothing concrete ever came of it," he replied.

"And David Williams, the dentist?" he asked.

"Nothing," he said. "He's never come to our attention as the police, but I know that a few people at the station go to him, by all accounts he's a good, and thorough dentist, also known for his understanding that most people have deep anxiety when they go to the dentist, so he has the latest, music, proper anaesthetics, all that you need to relax."

"Did you know that Katse and Gareth Thomas were the owners of the Peacock?" she asked.

"No," he said. "I always thought McIntosh was the owner."

"Apparently, he's only the manager," she said. "I need to talk to Thomas again about his relationship with Katse. He was less than candid the last time I talked to him, and not very forthcoming. Do I have time to get to Selebi and back today?"

"If you left now, Madame, and used lights and siren, you could be there quickly," Maphosa suggested.

"I think I'll do that, call down, and get me a police Land Rover, would you?" she asked

"Yes, Madame," he said. "What would you like me to work on?"

"I think get warrants for the bank records of the cousins in Francistown, for Celia Molale, Isaac Bwalya, Thabo Matsoka, Samson Mwendwa, and George McIntosh," she asked. "We need to see if there have been any odd transactions recently, or if any of them had debts they needed clearing."

"Yes, Madame," he said. "Should I also get those for Gareth Thomas and June Matsoka?"

"Oh, of course, how could I forget them?" Marieke said. "Well, I'll see you tomorrow, Sergeant. Stay well."

"Go well, Madame," he said.

The Land Rover was waiting when Marieke went downstairs, and she set off for Selebi Phikwe. Sergeant Maphosa had been right, using her lights, and occasionally the siren, she was able to get there in three and a half hours, instead of the usual four and a half hours. At the office of Thomas, she saw that he was just finishing the end-of-shift briefing, and when his people had left, she entered his office.

"Superintendent," Thomas said. "I didn't expect to see you again so soon."

"Nor did I," Marieke agreed. "But, I have more questions, tell me about the business relationship with Kagiso Katse, and the Peacock Bar and Grill."

"Not much to tell," Thomas said. "Katse and I went into business about eight years ago with the Peacock. We both put up money, but in the end, Katse put in a little more than I did, so that we were sure that there was a majority Botswana ownership, in case the government got funny in the future, like the South Africans will when majority rule takes effect in a couple of years. We hired George McIntosh as the manager, and he runs the place from day to day. Katse and I have disagreed more lately on how the place should be run. I wanted to expand, and he didn't."

"You didn't think to tell me this before?" she asked.

"I didn't think it relevant," Thomas said.

"This is a murder investigation, Mr Thomas, everything is relevant. Now that Katse is dead, what happens to the Peacock?" she asked.

"Under the terms of the partnership agreement, I now have 100% of the place," he explained.

"What do you estimate that to be worth?" she asked.

"I'm not sure," he said. "Maybe a couple of hundred thousand Pula, not really sure, I'd have to check the latest P&L, and balance sheet to see. Hey, wait a minute, you're not suggesting I had Katse popped so that I could get control?"

"Did you?" she asked.

"No," he said. "We had our differences, but having a majority Botswana ownership keeps us out of the sights of the politicians."

"What kind of manager is McIntosh?" she asked.

"Pretty good," Thomas said. "He flies a little close to the wind at times, but the bar and restaurant make good money."

"In other businesses that Katse was involved in, there are managers who have an earn-out ownership stake; why wasn't that done in the case of the Peacock?" she asked.

"We offered it to McIntosh, but he wasn't interested. Said he wanted to be free of any encumbrances," Thomas explained. "Plus, it would have meant that I would have had to take a lower ownership stake to keep it majority Botswana."

"What citizenship does McIntosh have?" she asked.

"Botswana, I think," Thomas said.

"So, if both you and Katse had taken less and given an earn-out share to McIntosh, it would still have been majority Botswana," Marieke pointed out.

"I suppose," Thomas agreed. "But Katse didn't want less than 51%, and I wasn't prepared to give up more of my share, unless I reduced my investment, and we needed to full amount to open the place. It was complicated at the time."

"Is there anything else you have neglected to tell me?" she asked.

"No," he said. "I suppose I should have mentioned the Peacock, but I thought anyone who popped Katse would have been from his legal past, and not our business dealings."

"We will be looking into the finances of the Peacock Bar and Grill, and will talk at some time to George McIntosh," she said. "Is there anything you would like to tell me?"

"No," he said. "Can't think of anything."

"How much does the Peacock take in a year?" she asked.

"Last year, a little under 2,500,000 Pula," he said. "Of that, we kept about 500,000 Pula."

"So, a very successful venture?" she asked. "Your share would have been 245,000 Pula, whereas now it would be the whole 500,000."

"That sounds about right," he agreed. "But, you have to remember that it's partnership income, it could drop to nothing if McIntosh messes up, or we lose our licence or get shut down by the health department or any number of other possible scenarios."

"Do you have any travel plans?" she asked.

"Not at the moment," he said.

"I must ask you to surrender your passport until this investigation is over," she said. "Do you have it here?"

"No," he said.

"I will send an officer to your house this evening to collect it," she said. "He will issue you a receipt for it, and we will return it to you as soon as our enquiries are complete."

"You can't do that," he said.

"I can, Mr Thomas, do not try, and leave the country before tonight, and surrender your passport when the officer calls," she said.

"I'm going to file a protest with the British High Commission," he said.

"Please do," she said. "I have had dealings with them before, and have found them to be very accommodating. I will be in touch again, and I would be disappointed to find that you have been less than candid with me. Good day, Sir."

Marieke left the mine and drove to the Selebi Phikwe police station, where she spoke to the officer in charge and left instructions for two of the officers at the station to go to the house of Gareth Thomas and collect his passport. She asked the officer in charge to keep it in the station safe until such time as she authorised its release, and to send her a copy of the receipt for the passport. Thomas annoyed her, but did not really move up in the list of possible suspects. He was still a suspect, to be sure, but probably not the most likely. His bank records would be interesting to review. Any odd large cash withdrawals in the past six months would warrant further investigation. She was also annoyed with Ravindra Patel, who could have told her much more at the first interview, and with herself for not exploring all those aspects of Katse's life with Patel. Her drive home was at a more leisurely pace, but a couple of times she did get frustrated with the traffic speed and used her lights and siren to get the laggards out of the way. She arrived home well after sunset with about enough time left in the day to make dinner and reflect upon the day.

After dinner, she sat down and wrote to Melisende. She had a computer, a Macintosh SE, which she was very pleased with, and a Hayes modem, so she could send her letters as e-mails, but preferred the less speedy, but to her, more personal hand-written letters. She and Melisende did send each other messages through their computers, but it was nice to get an envelope in the mail and wonder what it contained. Marieke wrote in French, mainly to keep using the language. There were few opportunities to speak French in Botswana, except when the occasional tourist got into difficulties, and she was asked to translate, or when she ran across the members of the French legation in town, all of whom she knew. They were also a useful source of French cuisine items that she could not get in the normal grocery stores. She told Melisende about her daily activities and about the case she was now working on. That was actually a big help to her because she had to put her thoughts in order so that she could write them in French.

Sergeant Maphosa had been busy and had bank records for all those that Marieke had requested. She sat with him the next morning, and they quickly scanned through them. To her disappointment, nothing stood out as a flag that would warrant further investigation. Thomas had been remitting money back to the United Kingdom on a regular basis, but that was all quite legal. He seemed to be sending all of his earnings from the Peacock Bar and Grill and using his salary from the mine for a comfortable lifestyle in Botswana. Mwendwa looked as if he were living hand to mouth, so now he would be much better off, getting about 75,000 Pula in a good year, instead of 35,000. Bwalya was not living quite to the limit that Mwendwa was, but his bank balance was not that rosy, so he would also see quite a change in his life. But, that begged the question, was it enough to kill for. She would have to see both Mwendwa and Bwalya and talk to them.

"Sergeant, we need to pay visits to Mwendwa, Bwalya, and McIntosh. Who shall we see first?" she asked.

"I think McIntosh, Madame," Maphosa replied. "It is the closest place, and then we could go to the Elephant Hunter, and finish at the Diamond Sight."

"Very good," she agreed.

The Peacock Bar and Grill was not yet open for business, but they found the staff entrance at the back and followed two men inside.

"Who are you?" a voice said. Marieke looked and concluded that this must be McIntosh. "I am Assistant Superintendent Englebrecht of the Botswana Police, and this is Sergeant Maphosa. We would like to talk to you about Kagiso Katse."

"Better come to my office," McIntosh suggested. "What can I tell you?"

"Can you think of anyone who would wish harm to Kagiso Katse?" Marieke asked.

"Plenty who would have liked to see him less successful," McIntosh said. "But, I'm not sure about anyone wanting to kill him. I had my own issues with him. He was a bit of a penny pincher, and to make a place like this successful, you have to keep up the decor, the menus, and the staff. Can't have people waiting around without a drink in their hands, can't make money that way. Katse wanted to limit growth, I suppose growth costs money, and he wanted the most return now. Sorry, long answer to a simple question."

"In the other bars where Mr Katse had an interest, the managers got the chance to earn out a share in the business; why wasn't that done with this operation?" Marieke asked.

"My stupidity," McIntosh bemoaned. "I was offered the chance when Katse and Thomas started this place to earn out 30%, but didn't think it would be as successful as it has been, so declined the offer. Katse put up 51% of the money, and Thomas 49%, and I could have had almost a third, no money upfront, just my own commitment to work here for five years. Well, I've been here ten, so instead of my 50,000, I could have been getting 150,000 in a good year. Last year's numbers are revenues of 2,500,000 Pula, earnings of 500,000 Pula, of which Katse got 255,000, and Thomas got 245,000, if I had done the deal, then Katse would have got 178,500, and Thomas 171,500, and I would have got the remaining 150,000, how stupid can you be?"

"I heard that you and Mr Katse were seen arguing," Marieke said. "Tell me about that?"

"I wanted to add an extension out the side there, so that people waiting to be seated to eat, could sit, and be served drinks," McIntosh explained. "But that meant an expense of some 250,000 Pula, and Katse didn't want to do that, probably because it would cut into his partner's share. I also wanted to add a couple of managers, so that I could take some time off every now and then. Right now, I'm pretty much tied to the place."

"It has been suggested that you might sell the odd drink off the books," Marieke said. "Would there be any truth to that?"

"In the past," McIntosh said, obviously deciding that some degree of candour at this time would be better than not. "Not in the last seven years, in the early days I was looking for a quick return, but nearly got caught by the tax people, so we've been scrupulous since then. You can check the books if you want."

"Someone may wish to do that," Marieke said, thinking that the seven years was convenient, as past due taxes and audits only went back seven years. "But, I'm interested in who may have killed Mr Katse."

"My guess, someone from his legal practice," McIntosh said. "He used to bring in some really unsavoury-looking characters."

"How was Katse's relationship with Mr Thomas?" Marieke asked.

"They argued a lot," McIntosh said. "Gareth was like me, wanted to expand and open up a lounge over there to sell booze, but Katse wasn't buying it. I think Gareth also regretted letting Katse take 51%, because that was always something Katse could use in an argument, 'I have 51%, so I have the final say!'"

"How often would you have meetings with the partners?" Marieke asked.

"Once a month," McIntosh said. "Usually, the first Monday of the month, I would go over the numbers for the prior month, and any issues, and they would typically walk away happy."

"Now that Mr Thomas has full ownership, will you go ahead with the expansion?" Marieke asked.

"That's up to Gareth," McIntosh said. "But, my guess is, yes, I could start in a few weeks, I've already got the plans approved by the City, that pissed Katse off, said I shouldn't have done anything without his approval, but Gareth had said, go ahead, so I did, at least to clear all the permissions."

"Tell me, where were you at about six in the morning on the 27th of this month?" Marieke asked.

"Home in bed," McIntosh said.

"Can anyone corroborate that?" Marieke asked.

"I had a girl over for the night," McIntosh replied. "I suppose you'll want her name, it's Joy Matambo, you can find her at the Diamond Sight, she works there as the purchasing agent."

"Tell me about the drunk and disorderly charge," Marieke instructed.

"That was about eight years ago, stupid on my part, I'd had too much, and got into a fight with another chap, don't remember his name now, it was over a girl, he managed to take off when the cops arrived, but I was still swinging at anything, so was hauled before the beak, admonished, and fined," McIntosh explained. "Went on the wagon after that, and have been sober ever since."

"Well, thank you, Mr McIntosh," Marieke said. "We may be back at a later date for more information."

"Fine," McIntosh said. "Go well, Superintendent."

"Stay well, Mr McIntosh," she replied.

"Well, what do you think?" Marieke asked Sergeant Maphosa when they were in their Land Rover, and well away from the bar.

"He's been selling stuff off the books, and has become better at hiding it than he was before," Maphosa said. "We could probably find it, but it would take quite an effort."

"I agree," Marieke said. "But, is he a likely suspect to kill Katse?"

"I don't think so unless he got paid to do so," Maphosa said. "Madame, what is a beak? I thought it was the bill of a bird."

"It's a British slang expression for a magistrate, I don't know how it was coined, but it has been around for quite a long time. Who's next?" Marieke asked.

"Isaac Bwalya, at the Elephant Hunter," Maphosa said.

"What's your betting on Bwalya?" Marieke asked.

"Not likely," Maphosa thought. "I just don't see a motive, there's money in it surely, but is it enough?"

The Elephant Hunter opened early for the breakfast and early drinking crowd. They found Isaac Bwalya giving his instructions to the lunchtime crew, going over the menu items, and emphasising what he wanted moved.

"Mr Bwalya?" Marieke interrupted. "We are from the Botswana Police, and would like to talk to you about Mr Kagiso Katse."

"Of course," Bwalya said. "Let's use the office. What can I tell you?"

"Let's deal with the administrative first," Marieke suggested. "Where were you between six and six-thirty on Monday morning?"

"I was here," he replied. "We open early, so I normally open up, and then take a break mid-morning when it's quiet, then come back for the lunchtime people."

"Can anyone corroborate that?" Marieke asked.

"James, the barman over there, Stan the chef, Anel the waiter, any of them," Bwalya replied.

"Can you think of anyone who would wish to harm Mr Katse?" Marieke asked.

"No, he was a nice man," Bwalya said. "He was good to us here, he paid fairly, and didn't demand things."

"How does your vesting in the partnership agreement affect you?" Marieke asked.

"It is a great opportunity," he said. "But, I will need to be careful, I realise that as a partner I won't have a set salary anymore, but will get my share of the earnings, which may go up, and down. But, as the manager, that is something I can at least strongly influence if not control."

"When does the change occur?" Marieke asked.

"Apparently, thirty days after the death of Mr Katse," Bwalya said. "Mr Patel from the law firm called me, and asked me to be at their offices on Wednesday, the 27th of May, to complete the papers, then I'll be a part owner."

"How do you get on with Celia Molale?" Marieke asked.

"Fine," he said. "She is a businesswoman who understands what we do. I think that the future will be good, she is really good with the accounts, and knows how the economy works. My wife is worried that she will try and steal me away, but Miss Molale has her life, and we have ours."

"Have you seen anyone strange in the company of Mr Katse lately?" Maphosa asked.

"No, when he has been here, it has been on his own," Bwalya said.

"Thank you for your time, Mr Bwalya," Marieke said. "We may come back to you at some time with more questions."

"Fine," he said. "Go well."

"Stay well," she replied. Outside, she looked at Sergeant Maphosa, who shook his head slightly, apparently, he did not see Isaac Bwalya as a likely suspect. They drove to the Diamond Sight and found it closed. The sign on the door stated that opening time was at eleven. Around the back, they found the staff entrance, and another sign that stated that the staff were all out for a while, and would be back at ten. Well, it was only fifteen minutes to wait, so they repaired to their Land Rover and sat back to wait.

They watched as a car pulled up, and a short, tending to portly man got out. "Samson Mwendwa," Marieke said. "At least from the description that Patel gave me." They followed him to the door, and he jumped as he realised someone was behind him.

"Who are you?" he asked.

"So, sorry to alarm you," Marieke said. "I am Assistant Superintendent Englebrecht of the Botswana Police, and this Sergeant Maphosa, we would like you ask you about Mr Kagiso Katse."

"Oh, well, come in then," Mwendwa said. "I'm not sure what I can tell you. I was in Serowe when he was killed."

"You know when he was killed?" Marieke asked.

"I heard it was on Monday," Mwendwa said. "Isn't that right?"

"It was Monday, yes," Marieke confirmed. "What were you doing in Serowe?"

"My parents live there, so I was visiting for the weekend. I left there on Monday at lunchtime," Mwendwa explained. "I heard that Mr Katse was killed on Monday morning."

"If you would give Sergeant Maphosa details so that he may confirm that you were in Serowe, please," Marieke instructed. She waited until he had done so, then Maphosa left to call Serowe, while she stayed and talked to Mwendwa. "Tell me," she said. "Do you know of anyone who might wish to harm Mr Katse?"

"No," Mwendwa said. "He was a fair boss to work for, a bit conservative when it came to expanding the bar, but he probably had his reasons."

"You wanted to expand the bar?" she asked.

"We get full around eight until closing, particularly on music nights, and could sell more if we could fit more people in; it wouldn't have been that much money for the expansion, but Katse wanted another six months' results before he made the decision," Mwendwa explained.

"Now that Mr Katse is dead, and you vest as a partner, do you think that the other partner would agree to an expansion?" Marieke asked.

"I think so," Mwendwa said. "But I would need to look at things again, and see, it's my risk now as well, looking as an owner is different to looking as a manager."

"What is your relationship with Ms Molale?" Marieke asked.

"Good," Mwendwa said. "She was the financial brains, while Katse was the social one who brought the people in. He was very good at finding clients and bringing them here."

"Now that you will vest as a partner, your situation will change quite a bit. How do you feel about the extra money?" she asked.

"Well, when I came here, they explained it to me carefully, and I see Mr Patel on the 25th of May to sign the papers, but I'm a little nervous, getting a salary is good, because it's always there, getting a partner share is a bit scary, because it could be really good, or it could be nothing, I'm going to have to learn how to manage my money a lot better, right now I'm living month to month," he explained. "Patel did tell me that they would find a way to advance money to me by quarter so that I have some to live on, and then they will reconcile at the end of each quarter."

"And that concerns you?" Marieke asked.

"I don't have an overdraft, but I'm close," Mwendwa admitted. "I'm going to have to manage spending much better if I get large chunks each quarter."

"How are the finances of the bar?" Marieke asked.

"Oh, we're doing well," he said.

"But if you can manage the finances here, what is different from your own?" she asked.

"Here I've got Joy Matambo, she keeps the books, buys the supplies, pays everyone, what I do is hire, and fire, mix with the customers, and make sure the place is run well," he explained.

"And the results are good?" Marieke asked.

"They are," he said proudly. "Last year we took in 1,250,750 Pula, and netted 251,650 Pula. I'm expecting this year to be up about 10%."

"I would like to talk to Joy Matambo," Marieke said. "Is she here yet?"

"Should be," he said. "Her office is next door." He quickly left his office and was back almost immediately. "She's here," he said. "Is there anything else?"

"Not now, Mr Mwendwa, but we may be back sometime for more questions," Marieke said. "Thank you for your time, I'll just stop, and see Joy Matambo on my way out." Marieke went to the next office, introduced herself to Joy Matambo, and confirmed the alibi of George McIntosh.

Outside, she met with Sergeant Maphosa, who confirmed that Mwendwa had been in Serowe on Monday. She had been going to go back to the office, but decided that, as it was lunchtime, they would just eat there. So, they went back inside, to the surprise of Mwendwa, who, when learning that all they wanted was to get some lunch, was happy to find them a table and menus.

After lunch, their next stop was back at the police station to write up all their notes in the case file. As they entered the station, they saw the commissioner, and he came over to get a report.

"*Dumela Mma, Rra,*" he said.

"*Dumela Rra,*" Marieke replied.

"What have you for me?" he asked.

"We have just finished our interviews with the possible suspects in the Katse killing," she explained.

"And?" he asked.

"At the moment, none of them look very promising," she said. "Some have very good alibis, and none have withdrawn any odd large cash amounts that might indicate hiring someone to do it for them."

"Those with shaky or unconfirmed alibis?" he asked.

"I don't see any of them as being capable of killing Katse," she said.

"Well, keep looking," he said. "We can't have people going around, and shooting lawyers, even questionable ones like Katse. Meeting, my office at two with Masisi to go over the case."

"Yes, Sir," she replied.

At two, she reported to the office of the commissioner, who asked Inspector Masisi to first tell them if he had found anything in the files of Katse that might point to a dispute serious enough to provoke a killing. Masisi reported that, to date, he had found nothing and had asked for older files, so that he could go back a little further into history. Marieke then gave her report, which was a little more detailed than the one she had given the commissioner earlier, but with no new revelations. They had yet to uncover anyone with a strong enough motive to kill Katse. Inspector Masisi had been over the crime scene again and had found nothing new. All the evidence from the garage had been taken already, and there was nothing new. The door-to-door interviews had provided nothing new. The Mercedes car and Land Rover that had been previously reported were all that those interviews had yielded. So, all they had was the weapon, and the South Africans had not been particularly cooperative, saying that they would look into the possible theft of the 9mm pistol, in due time, whatever that meant. The one witness who described the white man leaving the area had been in and given a police sketch artist a description, but it could be any middle-aged white man. The commissioner was not thrilled with the results of the investigation to date, but admitted that they had little to go on and might never discover who had done it. The killer had covered his tracks very well, which in his mind pointed to a professional. But that suggested a serious dispute with Katse, sometime in the past, and nothing had been uncovered yet. He told Masisi to keep digging, and suggested that Marieke talk again to Celia Molale to see if she had had any intimation from Katse that he felt in danger.

Marieke called Celia and asked when it would be convenient to talk to her. Celia suggested that they meet the following morning at ten at the Bull and Bush pub. That left the afternoon to catch up on paperwork and reports. There were also other cases to check on; crime did not stop just because a murder had been committed. Marieke sorted through what she felt she should do and what could be delegated to Sergeant Maphosa. He was a slow typist, but accurate and reliable, so she gave him what she could and addressed the rest herself. At five, she called it a day and sent Sergeant Maphosa home, then drove to the house of Mbali and Jan.

"*Dumela Mma*," Jan said as he opened the door.

"*Dumela Rra*," she replied. "Are you well?"

"I am, and you?" he replied, completing the ritual. "Come in, come in."

"Marieke," Mbali said. "We haven't seen you in a few days."

"I've been busy," Marieke said.

"With the Katse shooting?" Mbali asked.

"Indeed," Marieke replied. "It's a bit of a mystery, did you know Katse?"

"He had three accounts at our bank," Mbali said. "His own personal account and two different business accounts."

"Any financial difficulties?" Marieke asked.

"Far from it," Mbali said. "He was quite well off."

"I probably should ask, but can you think of anyone who would wish to kill Katse?" Marieke asked.

"Kill, no," Mbali said. "Relieved of some of his money, plenty, he made a living representing the villains of the town, and sometimes won, much to the chagrin of some, I'm sure some of them would have been happy to recover from Katse what they had lost in the cases. But, even with those who lost against him, he managed to find a way to be charming, even though those of us who knew him quite well knew that that was a façade, and that he was really for himself."

At ten on Friday morning, Marieke went to the Bull & Bush Pub, and found it already busy, but Celia was there had had a table for them.

"*Dumela Mma*," she said as Marieke joined her.

"*Dumela Mma*," Marieke replied. "Do you have a financial interest in this place as well?"

"No," Celia said. "I just like the place. What would you like to drink?"

"I think a beer would go down well," Marieke thought.

"Which do you prefer, St. Louis or Castle?" Celia asked.

"I think Castle," Marieke said. Celia signalled a waitress who came over and took their orders. She was back quickly and brought two beers with her, plus some chips and other bar snacks.

"So, Superintendent, any progress on finding the killer of Kagiso?" Celia asked.

"Please, call me Marieke," Marieke suggested. "I'm afraid very little, we are still exploring all avenues, but whoever did this has been careful, and we have little to work with. Did Kagiso seem in any way distracted or uneasy in the past weeks?"

"Not at all," Celia said. "We had been having some discussions about the various bars, a couple of them wanted to expand, and Kagiso was chary about investing too much more cash, but even that didn't seem to bother him."

"You saw no one who could have been from his past criminal practice?" Marieke asked.

"Not that I knew," Celia said. "I would say that he was as contented as I have seen him, and there was nothing that was troubling him; he was enjoying his relationship with June Matsoka, and he had asked her to marry him, which was a departure from his previous relationships. Another beer?"

"Thank you, just one more," Marieke said. "Tell me, what was Oxford like?"

"Old," Celia said. "The place just seemed really old, just think about it, there's been education there since the early 12th Century, 11th if you accept some theories. I went to Trinity and read economics, where did you study?"

"In France, I went to university in Lyon, and studied law, and then did a Master's in law enforcement," Marieke replied. "After that, I joined the Botswana Police Force."

"Did you get the chance to visit Oxford?" Celia asked.

"Not until last year when I was working on a case," Marieke said. "It involved some Oxford academics, and murder."

"Oh, was that when the Turners were killed?" Celia asked.

"Did you know them?" Marieke asked.

"Oh yes," Celia said. "I used to spend time with both of them, I found it useful to keep me abreast of current economic trends, and thinking."

"Have you met the new economics professor at the uni here?" Marieke asked.

"Camille Frou?" Celia asked. "I've met her, but we don't get on that well; she's not as clever as David or as talented as Julia. I posed for Julia a couple of times, and I have the paintings at my house. She really was good, come, I'll show you, and make lunch at the same time."

"You're sure it's not an inconvenience?" Marieke asked.

"No, no," Celia said. "It will be good to cook for more than one. I don't entertain much at my house."

"I'll pay the bar bill here; shall I just follow you?" Marieke asked.

"That's a good idea, and in case we get separated, here's my address and telephone number," Celia said.

Marieke followed her to a house in Extension 9, one of the more fashionable and expensive parts of Gaborone, replete with diplomats and high-flying business leaders. The house was set back from the road, surrounded by a high wall, and to Marieke it was huge. She followed Celia through the gate and parked. Celia put her car away in the garage, then came and opened the front door.

"Come in, come in," she said. "It's nice to have a visitor, I get very few. I normally conduct all my business from my office in town, and try and keep business and pleasure very separate. So, what for lunch, I have lamb, beef, chicken, what's your fancy?"

"Chicken, if that's not inconvenient," Marieke said.

"Chicken it is," Celia said. "Help yourself to wine over there, and pour me a glass of the Chardonnay that you'll find in the wine chiller." Marieke did as instructed and took the chance to look around. She had been surprised by the signs of affluence at the house of Kagiso Katse, but this house had the feel of wealth. Clearly, Celia was a woman of means. There were magazines lying on a coffee table, Vogue, Marie Claire, and Harper's Bazaar, she understood, but Rally Car and Autosport threw her a little. She did not see either of the portraits that Celia had referred to, but there was a nice painting of desert elephants in the living room.

"Ah, you've seen my painting, good, isn't it?" Celia asked.

"Excellent," Marieke agreed.

"Watch," Celia. She walked over to the painting, pulled it out from the wall, and flipped it over. On the reverse side was another painting, this one a nude of her in the style of Manet's Olympia, but without the attending maid or cat. "Not everyone appreciates art," Celia said. "So, I usually keep the elephants on display, and only switch to this one when it is just me."

"Julia Turner was very talented," Marieke said. "I had the chance to see her sketchbook when we were investigating the deaths."

"That's it," Celia said. "I knew I had seen you before. I saw you at the memorial for David, and Julia at the university, you had a uniform on then. Come, and see my other Julia painting." She led the way into her bedroom, where a painting of a lion hung, which she similarly switched over, and it was another nude, this one after the style of Mengin's Sappho, but without the lyre and wrap. "I had my cleaners here today, and I don't want to offend their sensibilities, so always switch the paintings to the wildlife. Excuse me, it smells as if the chicken is catching a little." She left, leaving Marieke to ponder the painting and wonder if Celia had had a relationship with Julia Turner. She had found out during her investigation of that murder that Julia might have been married to David Turner, but her sexual proclivities lay elsewhere. Marieke went back to the kitchen, and Celia had magically produced a meal worthy of the Le Cordon Bleu cooking school.

Over lunch, Celia considered Marieke's earlier question about Katse and offered and dismissed ideas about who might have wanted him dead. In the end, she admitted that she simply could not come up with anything, and suggested that Marieke look further into his legal practice, and the people that might include. It was quite late when Marieke excused herself and said that she had better be going, as she had duty in the morning.

"Come again," Celia invited. "It's nice to have someone visit who is a kindred spirit. Go well."

"Stay well," Marieke said, wondering just what to read into the kindred spirit comment.

Another murder

Marieke arrived home late, and all she wanted now was a hot bath and bed. That wish was short-lived as she had only been in the house for a few minutes when the telephone rang.

"Hello," she said.

"Matshwana, good, you're finally home, I've been calling you for some time, we have need of your immediate services," a male voice said, that Marieke identified as that of Police Commissioner Abel Boateng, her boss's boss. Marieke was surprised that he used the name she had acquired at Tsabong. Perhaps her boss had used it, and the commissioner had picked it up.

"Yes, Sir," she said.

"Come to the house of Assistant Commissioner Mochage, there has been a shooting, and the commissioner is dead," Boateng said.

"I'm on my way, Sir," Marieke said. She hung up the telephone, sat, and looked at the wall for a few minutes, running through her head what possible scenarios there could be for shooting her boss. For the moment, at least, at a loss, she gathered up her crime scene kit and left for the house of Ian Mochage. She had been to his house often enough so knew where to go. It only took fifteen minutes to get there, and the late evening traffic was light enough.

When Marieke arrived at the Mochage house, she was horrified by the number of people milling around, including her assistant, Sergeant Maphosa. Controlling this crime scene was going to be a nightmare. She parked a little way down the street and walked to the house, motioning to Maphosa to join her. The commissioner spotted her and waved her over.

"Good, you're here," he said. "Here's what we know. Ian arrived home somewhere between six fifty and seven, and was shot as he exited his car. Lerato had been out and arrived back at six thirty, and Ian was not yet home, but he normally gets home about six forty-five, so that was not a surprise. However, when she heard the car arrive at nearly seven, and he did not come in, she checked out the front and found him dead. She called me immediately, and I came out."

"She didn't hear anything?" Marieke asked.

"Apart from the car arriving, she says not," Boateng confirmed. "Looking at the head wound, I would guess a fairly large calibre long gun, so a distance shot, not a close-range killing. Thabo has already looked at the body, and barring something odd at the PM, initial cause of death would seem to both of us to be gunshot to the head. That suggests planning, we need to find out who did this, and why."

"Yes, Sir," Marieke agreed. She took a quick look at the body and had to concur with the commissioner, it did indeed look like death was caused by the headshot. But strange things happen in life, so she would wait until Thabo Mosiwa confirmed those findings. As the body was lying down between the car and the house, it was difficult to guess from which direction the shot may have come, but Marieke guessed that it would be over the road. From any other direction, there would be too many obstacles for a clear shot. So, she left Thabo and his crew to the details of the body, and then she and Maphosa wandered over the road to see if there was anything that they could learn.

They walked up, and down the road, looking back at the house as they went, there was only one place, a piece of vacant land with some large trees on it, where the front door of the house was clearly visible, so Marieke turned on her torch, and cast around looking for anything. There were perhaps footprints, but the light was not really good enough to see clearly. She told Maphosa to get a couple of officers and have them tape off the whole area, then she broadened her search, looking for anything that seemed out of place. She did find two teenagers who were hanging around and watching the proceedings.

"*Dumela*," she said to them. "Have you been here long?"

"*Dumela Mma*," one of them replied. "Long enough to see a *muzungu* going that way."

"How long ago?" she asked.

"Maybe two, three hours," the boy replied. "He went that way, not in a hurry, just walking."

"How do you know he was he, and a *muzungu*?" she asked.

"Walked wrong for a girl," the boy said. "And, I can tell a *muzungu* from miles away, they look different."

"Can you tell me anything else about him, how old, how tall?" she asked.

"No," the boy said. "He was all in black, like one ninja warrior."

"Was he carrying anything?" she asked.

"Maybe a small bag on his back," the boy said.

"You're sure, nothing else?" she asked.

"Nothing," the boy confirmed. "What happened over there? Someone get killed?"

"Something like that," she confirmed.

"I told you there was something big," the boy said to his friend. "So, did the *muzungu* kill someone?"

"We don't know," Marieke said. "Did he drop anything?"

"Didn't see," both boys said in unison.

"You didn't think to tell anyone that you'd seen someone?" she asked.

"No one asked," one of them replied. "And, we don't normally talk to the police; we've had problems with them before."

"Why talk to me then?" she asked.

"Because you greeted us properly," the other replied. "Not the usual, *ema!*" Marieke smiled to herself at that last comment; she could just see the average policeman telling these boys to stop so that he could ask them what they were up to.

"Well, thank you for telling me," she said. "I will get my sergeant to take your statements, if you don't mind."

"Your sergeant?" the one said. "Does that mean you're a big boss?"

"Not too big," she said. "Why were you here?"

"We were moving up, and down," one said. "Then we heard the woman scream, so waited to see what would happen. Then a car came, and not long after, a police Land Rover, then more police cars, then you. You parked down there and walked to the house."

"I see," Marieke said. "You didn't hear a gunshot?"

"No, *Mma*," one said. "Was someone shot?"

"Where exactly did you see this man?" Marieke asked.

72

"Just down this road a short way," the other said. "We saw him go by, then we came here, and it was when we got here, we heard the scream."

"So, you didn't see the man with anything or among the trees?" Marieke asked.

"No," they replied in unison.

Marieke called over Maphosa and told him to take down statements from the boys. If they truly had seen someone walk away, then he was well away by now, and dressed in black, if he stayed in the shadows, finding him in the dark would be difficult. If he was the shooter, then he may have just dropped the weapon and left it, so she should concentrate on finding it. She called the constables who had been taping off the area and told them to get some help, and some lights, and do a thorough search of the area, inch by inch, on their hands and knees, if necessary. She went to her own car, got a larger, more powerful torch from the boot, and came back to join in the search. She had the team start at the road and slowly work their way towards the trees. She saw what looked like footprints, but they were either very old or had been made with something that left indistinct tracks. It reminded her of something she had read, that of wearing either feathers glued to one's feet or sheep's wool booties to make the track very indistinct. If she had to guess, then she would say that if anyone had been there, they were using something to disguise their tracks.

It took thirty minutes of diligent searching, but finally, one of the constables noticed something that caught the light and brushed aside the soil to reveal part of a rifle barrel. He called Marieke over, and she went over to supervise the unearthing of the rifle. Reasoning it unlikely that anyone would take the time to dig a hole after shooting, she wondered if the hole had not been dug ahead of time, and the rifle just dropped in with the dirt quickly kicked over it to delay discovery. She sent one of the constables over to the house to get Thabo to come and look at what they had found.

"So, what have we here?" Thabo said when he joined them. "Rifle, large calibre, suppressor, telescope, why drop it here, why not carry it away?"

"Too conspicuous," Marieke suggested. "With the suppressor, and the added telescope, it makes for quite a large, and long gun, breaking it down would take time, and still make for a quite large package, better to drop it at the scene, and walk away. That does suggest that it's a cold gun, and we may have problems identifying it, and who may have owned it."

"We'll see," Thabo said. "I'll get my people started on it right away, I'm presuming no prints extant, but if we break it down, there may be some on the receiver, and under the barrel. Who's the best gunsmith in Gabs?"

"Piet Cronje," Marieke said without hesitation.

"Well, I'm not proud, get him in for me to pull this rifle part, and tell us everything he can about it," Thabo said. "By the time you get him in, I'll have all the prints, dirt, and debris I can get. I'm looking to him for provenance of the gun itself, who bought it originally, and when."

"Sergeant Maphosa," she called to her assistant. "When you've finished with the statements there, please go to the house of Piet Cronje the gunsmith, and ask him to go with you to the morgue. I want him to tell us all he can about this rifle. Ask him nicely, tell him it's a favour for me, and we need it now."

"Yes, Madame," the sergeant said. "Where does he live?"

"Close to the Maru a Pula school, on Eland Street," she replied.

"Madame," one of the constables called. Marieke went over to where he was pointing, and saw that there were marks on a tree where something had been tied, and something had been stuck into the tree at about the same place. There were even small strands of what looked like sisal adhering to the tree. Marieke stood behind the tree, and sighted towards the house, and concluded that this was a likely place for a shooter to secure a steady to the tree to better hold a shot on anyone by the front door of the house. She played her torch around the ground in the area, but it was covered in dry leaves, and the soil beneath was firmly packed. Still, anything was better than nothing, so she told the constable to sweep up all the leaves and debris around the tree, bag it for later analysis, and make sure he had all the fibres from the tree.

"Thabo," she said. "I need to start doing a wider area search. Can I leave this area to you and your techs?"

"Of course," Thabo said. "Go, and hunt us down a shooter."

"I'll try," Marieke said. "This must be a first for us, two shootings in five days."

"I believe it is," Thabo agreed. "We're becoming like Jo'burg!"

"God forbid," Marieke said.

Marieke gathered up two of the sergeants who were standing by the police cars in the street and told them to come with her. The fact that one was the commissioner's driver did not escape her, but she had better uses for him than to stand and wait. She told one of the officers by the door who she had taken, and where she was going, and to let the commissioner know that she had borrowed his driver, and that they were following a promising lead. Then she took one of the police Land Rovers and set off in the direction that the two boys had indicated as the route taken by the white man. As they went along the street, she had the sergeants check at each house they passed to see if anyone had heard or seen anything. There was always the remote chance that someone had been outside when the white man went by, and perhaps they might remember a person dressed in black. Not everyone was thrilled to be woken up so late at night, but it was necessary. It seemed after hours of aimlessly driving up and down surrounding streets that their quarry had vanished, and there had been no sightings, other than the one of the two boys. Marieke believed that they had seen the man, and they were not just making up a story, but he had been simply unlucky when he had been spotted by them, because after that, he had gone to ground. They had also been lucky that the boys had stayed at the scene, and were prepared to talk about what they had seen. At seven the following morning, she told the sergeants to go home and rest, and she drove back to the crime scene, surrendered the Land Rover back to its normal driver, and collected her own car. Then she drove to the morgue to see what Thabo and his crew had learned.

"*Dumela Mma*," Thabo said when she got to the morgue. "You look as if you've been up roaming the streets all night."

"I have Thabo," she confirmed. "I just sent the two sergeants I borrowed home to get some sleep, I'm not sure everyone we awoke was thrilled, and delighted to be rousted out of bed in the early hours of the morning, but if there are any complaints, I'll refer them to Boateng, and he can deal with them. I'll send new people out again today to do another house-to-house, and see if we can't learn something, and I'll also have them ask about anyone seen in the last week or so watching the house of the commissioner. What about you?"

"Death caused by large large-calibre bullet to the head, one shot only, I'll have a ballistic check on the rifle we found shortly, but it's a good guess that we found the weapon," Thabo said. "Cronje's in the second office down the hall pulling the rifle apart now, along with one of my techs."

"Thanks, Thabo. Has the commissioner been by yet?" Marieke asked.

"Twice," Thabo said. "I gave him the preliminaries two hours ago, and I think he went off to see Lerato."

"Fine, I'll see him later," Marieke said. "Anything of note on the rifle?"

"Not yet," Thabo said. "We checked for prints, negative, we checked for oils, such as you would get from the body, the only oils we found are gun oil, we checked for hair, and debris, and did find some odd fibres, we're checking on those now. We found some sisal with the rifle, and it had been cut with a knife, not broken or torn, and we found strands on the tree, which suggests that the tree was used as a rest. The mark on the tree by the sisal strands was consistent with a pocket knife stuck into the tree. The serial number of the gun had been filed off, but we were able to chemically raise it, but it didn't help; it's not in our database."

"So, the likelihood is that our shooter brought the gun into Botswana somehow, and when he came to load it he used gloves?" Marieke asked.

"It certainly looks that way," Thabo agreed. "Unless we can get some line on the rifle, this is a very cold gun."

"I'll go and talk to Piet," Marieke said. "Maybe he has something."

"*Dumela Mma*," Piet said, when she went into the office he was using.

"*Dumela Rra*," she replied. "Thank you for coming in and helping us, Piet."

"*Ag* man, no worries man, here's what I have for you so far," Piet said. "Steyr Mannlicher ML79 Luxus chambered as a nine-three, manufactured 1985. Serial number filed off, but we raised the number chemically. It's not on the Botswana registers, so probably from South Africa. This chasing on the receiver was done by an *ou* in Bloem, Johannes de la Rey, it's distinctive, and typical of his work. I have his contact information here. No prints on the receiver, barrel or stock, nor on the bolt or the magazine, and none on the ammunition left in the magazine. Whoever stripped this rifle last did a good job; it's been well cleaned, cared for, and cleaned of every fingermark. It looks like he fired only one shot. The spent cartridge was still up the spout. Either he was very sure of his shot and only intended one shot, or he was disturbed and decided to forego the usual second tap. The telescope didn't come with the rifle when it was purchased, but they are common enough, and we've been able to raise the serial number of it, too. I'd suggest gun shops in South Africa to see if you can get a line on when it was bought, if it was not bought at Johannes's shop, that's a long shot because there are a lot of gun stores in South Africa, and not all keep good records of such items as telescopes, and neither they nor we require registration of scopes. It is similar vintage to the rifle, 1986 or 7, most likely late 1986. The sling is an addition, probably fitted soon after the gun was purchased. The sling is leather, and normal cowhide, nothing exotic there. The suppressor is homemade. Done in a machine shop, well done, by the way, it would have done a good job of bringing the noise down to a plop. There are traces of grease and fabric in odd places, Neo, and I have been discussing things, and we surmise that the rifle was pulled apart, wrapped up, and stuffed into something. Wild guess, it was smuggled across the border under a car or a *bakkie*. This is a good rifle for a long shot; the suppressor takes down the noise to about the same level as popping a Coke can. The scope is zeroed in for 150 yards. How far away was the target from where you found this rifle?"

"Just about that," Marieke said. "That maybe does suggest that our shooter did his homework, and picked his spot carefully, measured the distance, then went out somewhere, and zeroed in his gun."

"That sounds likely," Piet agreed.

"Thank you, Piet," Marieke said. "Was it the gun that fired the bullet that Thabo pulled from the crime scene?"

"Without doubt," Piet said. "Neo's just run a second shot from the magazine through the comparator, and it's a perfect match. What I would like to do is take it out to a range, fire off a dozen rounds, and see what kind of grouping I get, to see if this was a lucky shot or if the gun is truly zeroed in, and our shooter that good. To find out who the gun belonged to, we should call Bloem as soon as possible, and find out who he did the chasing for."

"It's a little early for gunsmiths to be at their workplace," Marieke thought. "Do you happen to have his telephone number at home?"

"I do," Piet said. "Want me to try?"

"Please do," Marieke asked. She waited while Piet dialled a number and listened for the reply. At last, someone answered the telephone, and Piet started talking to them. The entire conversation was in Afrikaans, which Marieke could follow, but Neo could not. For his benefit, Marieke kept up a simultaneous translation of the side of the conversation she could hear. When Piet finally said his goodbye and hung up the telephone, Marieke was delighted that he handed her a piece of paper with a name written on it.

"Koos van de Merwe?" Marieke said, glancing at the paper.

"That's what Johannes said, Koos van de Merwe, apparently van de Merwe bought the rifle from Johannes in 1986, and has sent it back to him regularly for different things," Piet confirmed. "Johannes said that van de Merwe had sent the rifle back for re-bluing about a year ago, and the address was in PE. He can find the address for us when he opens up his shop later today. Oh, and van de Merwe also bought the scope from Johannes."

"Let me see if the police in Port Elizabeth are cooperative," Marieke said. She called their local operator and asked for the number of the main police station in Port Elizabeth. It took less than a minute for the operator to get the number, and Marieke dialled it.

"Good morning, *goeiemôre*, SAP, how may I help you?" a voice said.

"Good morning," Marieke said. "This is Assistant Superintendent Englebrecht of the Botswana Police, and I am trying to track down a Koos van de Merwe, who I have reason to believe is a resident of Port Elizabeth."

"Hold the line, please," the voice said. There were a few clicks, and another voice came on the line. "Who did you say you were?" he asked.

"This is Assistant Superintendent Englebrecht of the Botswana Police," Marieke repeated, this time in Afrikaans. "We are trying to track the whereabouts of a Koos van de Merwe. With whom am I speaking?"

"This is Lieutenant Colonel van Dyk. May I ask what is your interest in this man van de Merwe?" the colonel asked.

"We have had a shooting of a senior police officer, and have traced the weapon used as one being owned by a Koos van de Merwe, thought to be a resident of Port Elizabeth," Marieke explained.

"*Magtig*," Marieke heard him mutter. There was silence for a while, and then he spoke again. "Well, here's the problem," the colonel said. "Last November, a Koos van de Merwe of PE was found dead near Port Alfred, his body washed up on the shoreline on the PE side of Port Alfred. The PM established that he had been murdered, cause of death, puncture wound to the liver. His boat was found beached on the East London side of Port Alfred. We are keen to interview someone going by the name of Piet Cillie, who claimed to have been in the army with van de Merwe, and who said he was looking for van de Merwe. The problem we had, was that the Piet Cillie we tracked down who had been in the army with van de Merwe had been in Bloemfontein at the time of the murder, in fact, had not been out of Bloemfontein for three years, so we've no idea who was really looking for van de Merwe. How did you trace the gun to van de Merwe?"

"A gunsmith here recognised chasing on the receiver as being the work of a renowned smith in Bloemfontein," Marieke explained. "We called the smith in Bloemfontein, and he was able to identify the purchaser from the description of the chasing. Is there a way to determine if we are talking about the same van de Merwe?"

"Did your gunsmith get the number of his Identity Card?" the colonel asked.

"I'll check," Marieke said. She turned to Piet and asked him to call Johannes back and see if he had the card number. Piet had to make another call, as Johannes had gone to his shop, but as that was only a short distance from his house, the call was picked up almost immediately. "Thank you for holding, Sir," Marieke said. "I am having someone check that information for you now. I have it, Sir, let me read it to you."

"We have a match," the colonel said. "Who got shot?"

"My boss, Assistant Commissioner Mochage," Marieke explained. "It will no doubt be in the papers today or tomorrow. Tell me, Sir, do you know if the rifle we have had been in the possession of van de Merwe?"

"He certainly had a rifle," the colonel confirmed. "His widow said that he kept the rifle, and a 9mm handgun on board his boat, they were both gone when we found the boat, and searched it. I'll check with the widow and see if she remembers anything distinctive about the rifle. Could you send me pictures of the chasing on the receiver? If you get a line on who used the gun, we would be interested in case it's the same *ou* who murdered van de Merwe."

"Of course," Marieke promised. "Do you have a Fax machine there, and a number? If so, I will send a copy of the pictures we have. I'll also send details of the gunsmith in Bloemfontein so that you can check with him yourself. Thank you for your help, may I call upon you again if the need arises?"

"*Ja*," the colonel said. "Can't have *ouks* going around shooting us cops, makes for a bad day. Here's the number of our Fax machine. When I get the pictures, I'll have someone check with *Mevrou* van de Merwe."

"Before you go, Sir," Marieke said. "We had another shooting the day before yesterday, this time with a 9mm Beretta; the shooter just dropped it at the scene when he or she left. If I gave you the serial number, would you be able to tell us if it comes from South Africa?"

"You think it could be van de Merwe's gun?" van Dyk asked.

"I don't know," Marieke said. "It just struck me when you said that van de Merwe had both a rifle and a 9mm pistol on his boat, and both went missing, that I should check."

"Fax me the details, and I'll look into it. It's not from Botswana?" van Dyk asked.

"It's not in our registry," Marieke confirmed.

"Are the shootings related?" van Dyk asked.

"At the moment, we are treating them as separate incidents," Marieke said. "We have no reason, at this time, to connect the two, but you never know, we don't often get two shootings in five days, and I don't believe in coincidences."

"Neither do I," van Dyk said. "If you get anything more, here's my direct number."

"Thank you," Marieke said. "*Tot siens.*"

"*Tot siens,*" he replied.

Marieke relayed the gist of the conversation to Neo and Piet, and then she had a thought.

"Neo, please get the 9mm Beretta and the suppressor that we found at the scene of the shooting at Katse's house."

"Yes, Madame," Neo said. He was back in about a minute with the two items.

"Piet," Marieke said. "We found this 9mm and suppressor in the back of a BMW belonging to Kagiso Katse, the solicitor. Katse had been shot twice in the head, from the back, and it looks as if the gun had just been dropped. Any thoughts?"

"Well, so someone finally popped Katse," Piet said. "I wonder who he pissed off. But, that's your problem, back to the matter at hand, this is a Beretta 92S model, which is odd because it was basically made for the Italian military and police. I don't remember all the serial number sequences, but I'm thinking this was made about 1979. It would be interesting to know how it turned up here. It fires a 9mm cartridge, and the magazine holds 15 rounds. It is a very good gun, reliable, easy to field strip, and reassemble."

"What about the suppressor?" Marieke asked.

"Now that is interesting," Piet said. "I'll need a microscope to be sure, but just a quick look at the design and the way it's made suggests that this one was made by the same person who made the one for the long gun, and on the same lathe."

"Really?" Marieke asked. If that was true, it was a really good lead as it might link the two crimes, and that might help in their search for motives, and thence possible killers.

"Same design concept, same basic mode of manufacture, same details in the baffling," Piet said. "I'd lay money that they were made by the same *ou*."

"Can you and Neo do a microscopic examination and confirm that?" Marieke asked.

"Neo, what do you think?" Piet asked.

"We can do that," Neo said. "We have the right kind of microscope next door."

"Good, I'll leave you to that then," Marieke said. "I should call the SAP *ouks* again, and ask them if the Beretta that van de Merwe had was the 92S model."

Marieke called Lieutenant Colonel van Dyk again, this time using his direct line.

"I'm sorry to bother you again so soon," she said.

"No bother," he said. "What can I do for you?"

"Our gunsmith, Piet Cronje, just took a look at the 9mm Beretta we found, and he tells us that it is the 92S model, which was used mainly by the Italian military and police. Do you know if van de

Merwe had any contacts with anyone from Italy?" Marieke explained.

"We'll check," van Dyk promised.

"One other thing," Marieke said. "Piet Conje believes that in both the case of the rifle and the handgun, the suppressors were made by the same person."

"Ah, that is interesting," van Dyk said. "We'll have to start looking around at who makes suppressors on the side. You don't think they were made in Botswana?"

"No," Marieke said. "Piet says that there are traces of grease, and fibres that suggest that the weapons and the suppressors were stripped, and then wrapped up, and secreted somewhere to move them into Botswana."

"*Magtig*," van Dyk said. "So, I may be looking for a machine shop, and a hit man, do you think your shooter is still in Botswana?"

"We've no idea," Marieke admitted. "At the moment, we're nowhere in the investigations; we're just beginning."

"Well, good luck," van Dyk said. "I'll call you if I find anything."

"*Dankie*," Marieke said. "*Tot siens.*"

"*Tot siens*," van Dyk replied.

Marieke hung up the telephone, relayed her conversation with the colonel to Piet and Neo, then she faxed all the information on the two guns and the gunsmith in Bloemfontein to the number that van Dyk had provided. She then went to report to the commissioner. He was in his office, and he had just come back from visiting with Lerato Mochage, who was still distraught at the death of her husband.

"*Dumela Mma*," he said as she hovered in his doorway. "I hope you have something for me."

"*Dumela Rra*," she replied. "Yes, and no, Sir, we have identified the weapon used for the shooting; however, we believe it was stolen in Port Alfred last November, and the owner murdered. The SAP have no idea who they are looking for in relation to that crime. The SAP also told me that a 9mm handgun also went missing at the same time."

"Whose gun was it?" the commissioner asked.

"It was identified from chasing on the receiver by a gunsmith in Bloemfontein as belonging, at least at one time, to a Koos van de Merwe of Port Elizabeth," Marieke explained. "I called the SAP in PE, and they told me that a Koos van de Merwe had been murdered last year, and they have no suspects at this time."

"So, essentially, a cold gun used to shoot Ian, is the 9mm the one that was used to kill Katse?" the commissioner asked.

"We don't yet know," Marieke replied. "The SAP is checking for us, but Piet, my gunsmith, did suggest that the two suppressors were made by the same person. The lab people are doing a microscopic examination of tool marks to confirm that."

"Now, that is interesting," the commissioner said. "That suggests that both shootings are linked, if not by the same shooter, then by the source from which he got his equipment. Can you think of anything that links Katse to Ian?"

"No, Sir," Marieke said. "I've no doubt that if we go back into history, then we'll find cases where Commissioner Mochage was on one side, and Katse the other, but why kill both now?"

"Good question," the commissioner agreed. "This is going to take some teasing out to unravel the situation. We need to do this quickly, we can't have people going around shooting at us, and at lawyers, even lawyers as disreputable as Katse."

"I agree, Sir," Marieke said.

"Did you find anything else?" the commissioner asked.

"Neo from our lab, and Piet, the gunsmith, noted odd traces of grease and fibres on parts of the rifle, and they surmise that it was somehow smuggled into the country, either in or under a car, *vanette* or *bakkie*," Marieke said.

"Anything else from the scene?" the commissioner asked.

"The rifle appears to have been held steady against a tree, one shot taken, then dropped into a pre-dug hole, and had dirt kicked over it," Marieke explained. "Piet, the gunsmith, says that the rifle is zeroed in to 150 yards, and that is about the distance from the tree to the front door. It suggests that reconnaissance was done, and our shooter probably measured the distance, then went out, and zeroed the gun to 150 yards."

"Anything else?" the commissioner asked.

"Two teenagers said that they saw a white man walking away from the scene about three hours before I got there," Marieke said. "They said that they didn't come forward earlier because their previous encounters with us have not been the best. Unfortunately, the description of the man they gave us is of little use; he, and they were both convinced that it was a he, was dressed all in black, and left walking. We followed up all possible ways away from the scene, but no one else saw anything."

"How do they know he was white?" the commissioner asked.

"They both said that he walked like a *muzungu*, they both claim that they can tell the difference, in the same way that they say that they can tell the difference between male and female," Marieke explained.

"So, in all probability, we are looking for someone white, but what white man would want to kill Ian?" the commissioner mused. "So, we know how and when, but we don't know why, and who?"

"Yes, Sir," Marieke agreed. "It does strike me, Sir, that our shooter would probably have practised somewhere, as I said before, Neo, and Piet think that the weapon was taken apart, wrapped, and possibly smuggled into the country somehow, I would want the chance to test fire before I took my shot if I was the shooter, and I would want my test firing to be close to the date of my shot, not months in advance, plus I would want somewhere to make adjustments to the zero. So, I think we should look a little farther afield, and see if anyone saw or heard shooting outside Gabs in the past week or so."

"That's probably a quarter of Botswana, but I see your point, if the gun was taken apart then reassembled, I, if I were the shooter, would also want to test fire to see that it still fired true," the commissioner agreed. "Put out the word asking for anyone seeing or hearing gunshots within a fifty-mile radius of the outskirts of Gabs in the past month."

"I was also thinking that, although the task may seem daunting, if we are dealing with a white shooter, then the pool is not that large," Marieke suggested. "We have about 21,000 white male residents, and there are probably as many white male visitors at any one time, either here on business or as visitors. We can probably start culling down the resident population, either by geography or by age, and reduce that number somewhat. It also strikes me that if our shooter is not a resident but a visitor, then he would have to enter the border somewhere and sleep somewhere. I'll have a check done on all hotels, lodges, and camps in the vicinity of Gabs, and see if any names jump out at us."

"That's a long shot," the commissioner commented. "But, yes, start with immigration, and get a list of who arrived by car since. When was the man killed in Port Alfred?"

"Last November, Sir," Marieke said. "It's probably going to be quite a long list."

"I agree," the commissioner said. "But, we have to start somewhere. If we have arrivals, get departures, and start crossing them off to see who's still here. Get some help from the university, we just need clerical help checking lists."

"Very good, Sir," Marieke said. "It strikes me that it is also possible that our man flew or drove into the country with his gun, posing as a safari client. I'll check with the airlines and the customs people to see who came in recently with a gun, and where they are now."

"I want a briefing this afternoon at five to review what we know and what we don't know," the commissioner said.

"Very good, Sir," Marieke replied.

Marieke left the commissioner's office and went to find Sergeant Maphosa. She tracked him down getting coffee.

"Sergeant, I have a mission for you," she said.

"Yes, Madame?" he replied.

"Get onto immigration, and get all arrivals, and departures from last November 1st until now, and cross-check everyone on the list to find out who is still here, also make a list of those with multiple entries, and departures," she instructed. "Don't do the work yourself, take the lists to the university, and have the Statistics students do it for you. I'm going to call the Vice-Chancellor now, and tell him what we need. We need entries by car and by plane.

Also, check with customs, and see who, if anyone, has brought in a gun by air, and where they are now."

"Will the Vice-Chancellor be willing to help?" the sergeant asked.

"He was a friend of the commissioner's; he will help," Marieke stated. "Let the university people do the cross-checking for arrivals and departures, but you check with customs and the game department for hunting licences and firearms import permits, and track down where they all are today."

Why?

The sergeant left, and Marieke made her telephone call to the Vice Chancellor's house. The Vice-Chancellor promised help and said he would have a team on standby as soon as they had the lists from immigration. Marieke then sat back and reviewed what they knew and what they did not know. Katse was killed at close range with a pistol, dropped at the scene, and they had no viable suspects. There were some that might have motive, but for the most part, they all had reasonable alibis for where they were at the time of the shooting. It was possible that a white man was involved. Mochage was killed at a distance by a single shot to the head from a rifle, dropped at the scene. They had no suspects at this time; again, there was potentially a white man involved. The one piece of evidence that suggested a link between the cases was the observation that the two suppressors used may have been made by the same person. So, what was the link between Katse and Mochage, if there even was one?

Marieke listed all the usual reasons for killing, sex, and or jealousy, greed, and money, a personal vendetta, revenge for some perceived wrong or slight, hatred, disputes over property, politics, drugs or other crimes. She then set out columns for Katse and Mochage, and started going down the list, making notes as to the likelihood or possibility of any of them applying. They needed information, and getting it was going to be delicate, it would be hard to ask if an Assistant Commissioner of police was involved with infidelity, or suspected his wife of such, and it was going to be delicate to dig into the commissioner's finances to see if there were any reason to suspect dealings in narcotics, illicit diamonds or other crime. Her musings were interrupted by a telephone call from Lieutenant Colonel van Dyk.

"*Middag*," he said.

"*Middag*", she replied, thinking that when the telephone call was over that she really should get something to eat. "How can I help?"

"We've talked to *Mevrou* van de Merwe and confirmed that the rifle you have was on his boat when he was killed. The 9mm that you have was not his; we've not been able to identify it yet," he said.

"Thank you," she said. "Does this suggest that your crime is linked to ours, or did your killer sell the rifle at some time?"

"Those are both good questions," he agreed. "We're working on the assumption that our killer disposed of the rifle by selling it, which suggests that he also sold the 9mm."

"Would it be possible to get some details of the van de Merwe killing?" she asked.

"Unusual, and probably highly irregular, but I think I can do that," he said. "What's the postal address there, and I'll send it to our marked personal? I would appreciate getting it back when we've solved these cases."

"Of course," she promised.

"I'll call if I find out anything on your other gun," he promised.

"Thank you, Sir," she said. "And, I'll let you know if we are able to identify our shooter. *Tot siens.*"

"*Tot siens*," he replied.

Marieke left the station in search of a late lunch. She was hungry, really hungry as she had not eaten in quite some time, and if she were to pursue this case, then she would need to keep up her strength, and that meant eating once in a while. She went to a place she knew, and sat down, and ordered lunch.

"Would you like company?" a voice said. Marieke looked up and saw that it was Celia Molale.

"Please," Marieke said, pointing to the empty chair opposite her.

"How are you today, Marieke?" Celia asked.

"Hungry and tired, thank you for asking, Celia," Marieke said.

"I heard that we have had another shooting," Celia said. "Are we going the way of Jo'burg?"

"I don't know," Marieke admitted. "I hope not."

"I knew Ian," Celia said. "He would come to the store at times with Lerato, did you know she used to model for me?"

"No," Marieke said. "It doesn't surprise me, I could see her as a model, what lines did she model for you?"

"Mostly dresses and skirts, but occasionally sleep attire, and lingerie," Celia said. "I employed a photographer from town, and he was most taken with her. I think he did a boudoir shoot for her as a present for Ian."

"Who is the photographer?" Marieke asked.

"Henry Curtis," Celia said.

"Is that a real name or one borrowed from King Solomon's Mines?" Marieke asked.

"I believe it was a real name, perhaps his parents were fans," Celia said.

"Did you get the impression that all was well between the two of them?" Marieke asked. "I'm sorry to have to ask, but we have to look at anything and everything as we have no idea at the moment who may have done this, and why."

"I think Ian was more invested in the relationship than Lerato," Celia said. "I think Lerato would like to have had more of her own life and career, but modelling, particularly of lingerie, is probably not the best choice if your husband is a high-ranking police officer."

"Perhaps not," Marieke agreed. "But, was that desire for free expression enough to arrange for his death, and is she a good actress?"

"I rather think not to the first, and the second," Celia said. "She chaffed a little about wanting to be her own person, but she also had a sense of loyalty."

"Why tell me?" Marieke asked.

"Because I knew that at some point you will have to consider all possibilities, and that this would surface in time, better that you should know now than have someone else dig it up," Celia explained. "I also had a long talk with Sara Turner after the death of Julia and David, and she told me that you knew how to handle matters with delicacy."

"This is delicate, but did you suspect any infidelity on either part?" Marieke asked.

"No," Celia said. "I think Ian was really devoted to her."

"Could that devotion have led to frustration, and someone else?" Marieke asked.

"I don't think so," Celia said. "But, people do odd things at times, so nothing in life surprises me anymore."

"I know that I could not afford the clothes from your shop," Marieke said. "Did you get the sense that Lerato's purchases create any financial difficulties?"

"No, Ian always paid promptly," Celia said. "I think he was a man of simple tastes for himself, but he did like to indulge Lerato, and, speaking of clothes from my store, I think I could offer you something that would not break the bank, but which you might enjoy. Come, and see me some time, and I'll let you try some things on."

"Thank you," Marieke said.

"Anything new on Kagiso's case?" Celia asked.

"I'm sorry to say, no," Marieke said. "We are at sea at the moment, so are digging through old case files trying to find something that might give us a clue."

"I've racked my brain," Celia said. "And, I've come up empty-handed. I just can't see any plausible reason to kill Kagiso. As an aside, I have to see Patel in a day or so to go over details of the partnerships that we had. I think the cousins from Francistown will be down soon as well to review his estate, and make some decisions on the properties he had here in Gabs. If I were them, I'd keep them and engage someone to manage them."

"Well, I should be getting back to the station," Marieke said. "I will treat what you have told me with discretion."

"Thank you, go well," Celia said.

"Stay well," Marieke replied.

At the five o'clock meeting, the commissioner laid out what he wanted investigated in the two cases they had. He handed out assignments to all and sundry, and Marieke got the Assistant Commissioner's finances and personal life. She would have preferred something less intrusive into the personal lives of Ian and Lerato, but murder is murder, and everything had to be considered. The commissioner had prepared the way for her and had obtained a warrant to investigate the finances of Ian and Lerato Mochage. Marieke decided that she would do that first, then she would interview Lerato. She was not looking forward to that, but she knew it had to be done. There was always the chance that Lerato had engaged the services of someone to remove her husband from her life, but Marieke hoped that she had not. The last thing the commissioner told the team was that, as the next day was Sunday, they should all take the day off, rest, clear their minds, and come in fresh on Monday morning ready to get back to work.

At about nine on Sunday morning, Marieke called Melisende. She had not talked to her in a while and was missing her.

"Marieke *ça va?*" Melisende asked.

"*Comme ci comme ça*," Marieke replied.

"Why, what's wrong?" Melisende asked.

"Two shootings in only a few days, and no suspects yet, and one of those shot was my boss," Marieke explained.

"*Mon Dieu*," Melisende exclaimed. "What is happening there?"

"That we don't understand," Marieke said. "But, what about you?"

Melisende then told her about her comings and goings, and what was new in her life. She also confirmed that she would be arriving in a few days for the holiday they had planned. That led to a long discussion about whether or not she should still come, but Marieke asked her to, even if their time together was interrupted by police work, it would still be good to see her. They talked for about an hour, until Melisende got another call, summoning her to work. Marieke prepared herself a light lunch, then got her rifle, some ammunition, and drove off to a spot she knew well outside the town to get in some target practice. She set up a cardboard box with a head drawn on it, and then paced out 150 yards and took up a firing position. There were some trees in the area, but Marieke thought that she would first try without a steady rest. Her shooting was good, but it took three shots to get exactly where she wanted on the target. Then she tried tying her rifle with some sisal to a tree and firing again. The results were much better; she managed to put the first bullet right where she wanted it. That in her mind confirmed the use of a steady rest to shoot the commissioner, and the tree with the sisal strands would have been perfect. That done, she put the rifle aside, went to her car, and got a shovel. She dug a hole long enough to take the rifle, and a suppressor if it had been mounted. Then she stuck her pocket knife into the tree, wrapped her rifle in some plastic, tied it to the tree with some sisal, took one shot, cut the string, dropped the rifle into the hole, kicked the dirt over it, and walked away. The whole process took less than a minute. Satisfied that that was the likely method used by the killer, she retrieved her rifle, stripped off the plastic, and then carefully cleaned it. As she was doing that, a police Land Rover pulled up, and two constables got out.

"*Dumela Mma*," one, who Marieke dubbed number One, said.

"*Dumela Rra*," she replied.

"What are you doing here?" number Two asked.

"Just practising," she replied.

"May we see some identification?" Two said. Marieke produced her warrant card, and the two constables stepped back in alarm.

"So sorry, Madame," One said. "We have been looking for a place where a man may have practised with a rifle. Have you been here before?"

"I have," she said. "But, this is not the place. I took a careful look before I started, and the last person here was me, about a month ago. No one has been here since."

"Thank you, Madame," Two said. "Stay well."

"Go well," she told them, and watched as they beat a fast retreat, eager to be away lest they be reported for something. Marieke packed away her things, drove back to town, and something to eat and drink.

Monday morning, Marieke made her way to the bank where Mbali worked, and where the Mochages held their accounts. She asked to speak to Mbali and was shown to her office.

"*Dumela Mma*," Mbali said.

"*Dumela Mma*," Marieke replied. "Are you well?"

"I am," Mbali replied. "What brings you to my bank this morning?"

"I have a warrant here to investigate the finances of Ian and Lerato Mochage," Marieke explained.

"Oh, I see," Mbali said. "Such a shame about Ian, who did it, and why?"

"That is what we're trying to discover," Marieke said. "If you would prefer, I could use an office here to review the statements, and only take copies of those items that may be of concern, if indeed there are any."

"We could do that," Mbali agreed. "Let's set you up over here, and I'll have the statements brought to you. How far back do you want to go?"

"Let's say five years for now," Marieke thought. "If nothing shows up there, then perhaps I'll go back further, perhaps not."

"Have you talked to Lerato yet?" Mbali asked.

"That's the next thing on my list of things to do today," Marieke said. "I know the commissioner has talked to her, but he wants a more formal interview."

A bank employee brought statements for Marieke to review, and she started to plough through them. The Mochages were quite well off, not quite as well off as Kagiso Katse, but comfortable. They had a joint account and an account each. Marieke started with the most recent accounts and went backwards in time. By the time lunchtime came, she had found three fairly large cash withdrawals, all made about six months earlier from Lerato's personal account. She took copies of those items and thought that she would check on them before going further back. Before she saw Lerato, she wanted some lunch, so asked Mbali if she was busy. Mbali said that she would be happy to take lunch with her, so they left and repaired to the newer Chinese restaurant in town.

"Tell me about Ian and Lerato Mochage," she said to Mbali after they had placed their order.

"They seemed to me happy enough," Mbali said. "They were never overdrawn, so I doubt that they had financial woes."

"I saw that they maintained separate accounts, as well as a joint account," Marieke said. "Why was that?"

"I think Lerato just liked the idea of her own money, even though much of what was in the account was a monthly deposit from Ian's account. It was also where she deposited her occasional modelling fees, which used to be quite frequent about eight to ten years ago, but which have become rare lately. The joint account was used to pay the electricity bill, mortgage, and other regular monthly items; it was topped up by transfers from Ian's account each month," Mbali explained.

"There were three fairly large cash withdrawals from Lerato's account about six months ago. Do you know what they were for?" Marieke asked.

"I asked Lerato about that, and she said that it was something she was working on," Mbali said.

"Do you know Henry Curtis, the photographer?" Marieke asked.

"Yes," Mbali said. "He's a customer, has been for some years now, why?"

"Oh, I heard his name earlier and wondered why I had never come across him," Marieke said.

"He does most of his work for fashion and glamour," Mbali said.

"Oh, that's why I've never come across him, fashion, and glamour, not exactly me," Marieke laughed. "Have you ever been to him?"

"Not me, but I know that two of the girls in the bank have been, and he did some really good work, I saw the results, and he is good," Mbali said.

"Did you know that he also does layouts called boudoir folios?" Marieke asked.

"I had heard that," Mbali said. "I've wondered about doing one for Jan, but have to say that it would be hard for me to put myself in any kind of position where the photographer could misuse the pictures."

"Do you think he would?" Marieke asked.

"I've not heard anything that would indicate that he ever has or would, but that may depend on how hard up he is?" Mbali thought.

"Can you think of anyone who would wish harm to Ian Mochage?" Marieke asked

"No," Mbali said. "But, I would have thought that you would have a list from past cases of people who had reason to be after him."

"We're looking into that," Marieke said. "Well, I should go to my next interview. Stay well."

"Go well, will we see you this weekend?" Mbali asked.

"It depends, "Marieke said. "If we are all out trying to find two killers, then perhaps not, but then again, a break is sometimes necessary to clear one's thinking, so perhaps, yes, I'll let you know."

Marieke decided to pay a call on Henry Curtis and see what kind of business he ran. She looked in the telephone book, found his address, and drove there. The studio was set back from the road a little, and there was shade under a tree. Marieke parked and went into the lobby.

"*Dumela Mma*," a woman greeted her.

"*Dumela Mma*," Marieke replied. "I was looking for Henry Curtis."

"Henry's busy with a shoot at the moment, can I help?"

"And you are?" Marieke asked.

"I am Helena Curtis, Henry's wife. I'm sorry I didn't get your name?"

"Assistant Superintendent Englebrecht of the Botswana Police," Marieke said, producing her warrant card.

"How can we help?" Helena asked.

"I am looking into the death of Assistant Commissioner Mochage, and I understand Mrs Mochage has done some work with you in the past," Marieke said. "How well did you know the Mochages?"

"We knew Lerato quite well; she used to do a lot of modelling for Celia Molale, and Henry would do the shoots," Helena explained. "Look, he's almost finished, why don't I get him."

"Thank you," Marieke said. She waited while Helena disappeared into the back and came back a minute later with a man she introduced as Henry.

"Sorry about that," he said. "Henry Curtis, I was just finishing off a roll or two on the latest men's suits. Helena tells me you want to know about Lerato and Ian Mochage?"

"I am given to understand that you did shoots for Celia Molale, and that Mrs Mochage used to model for her," Marieke said.

"That's right," Henry confirmed. "She is a great model, good posture, sense of style, looks good in almost anything."

"Does that include lingerie?" Marieke asked.

"We did do a boudoir shoot for her," Helena confirmed. "She wanted it as a present for Ian."

"When you do a boudoir shoot, what happens to the negatives, and any additional prints?" Marieke asked.

"We give them to the client," Helena said.

"You don't keep any copies?" Marieke asked.

"We used to, but then a friend of Henry's in England was arrested for blackmailing some clients; he used the shoot materials to pressure them, so we decided that it was a better business practice to surrender all the materials to the client," Helena explained.

"And those before the change in practice?" Marieke asked.

"We do have those in our files," Helena admitted. "We weren't able to contact everyone, so locked them away."

"And, those for Mrs Mochage?" Marieke asked.

"We did give her all we had," Henry confirmed.

"How did she pay for the session?" Marieke asked.

"By cheque from her own account," Helena said.

"Do you know if Commissioner Mochage was pleased with his gift from Mrs Mochage?" Marieke asked.

"She told me he was," Helena said. "She came in about a week after she had given it to him, and said that he was delighted."

"What form do the folios take?" Marieke asked.

"The final product is a series of photographs that have been edited and then bound to form a book," Helena explained.

"And you do all that here, you don't use outside bookbinders?" Marieke asked.

"No, I'm not sure I would want to trust bookbinders," Helena said. "The level of trust between us and the client has to be high, and a third party would just not serve."

"Do you know why Mrs Mochage cut back on her modelling work?" Marieke asked.

"I think she thought that she was getting too old," Helena said. "I tried to tell her a few times that age wasn't an issue, but she was less and less interested in the work. I did wonder if she had found another interest."

"Well, thank you for your time," Marieke said.

"Do you know who killed Ian?" Henry asked.

"We're pursuing a variety of leads," Marieke dissembled. "Stay well."

"Go well," Helena replied.

Marieke then drove to the house of the commissioner, admitting to herself as she did that she had been deliberately putting off this interview. She knew Lerato, not well, but well enough to call her Lerato in a social occasion, and not Mrs Mochage. Still, it had to be done, so she should get it over with. At the house, she saw a police car parked off to the side, and as she approached, an officer came to her car.

"Assistant Superintendent," he said, saluting. "The commissioner's wife is in."

"Thank you," Marieke said. She parked and knocked on the door.

"Marieke, *dumela*," Lerato said when she opened the door.

"*Dumela Mma*," Marieke replied. "May I come in?"

"Please do," Lerato said. "I have had few visitors in the last two days."

"I'm very sorry, but I have to ask you a few questions," Marieke said. "Is this a good time to do that?"

"I understand," Lerato said. "I'm over the initial shock, and am now just wondering who, and why, I suppose, being married to a policeman, there was always this chance, but I thought we were past that when Ian moved more to an administrative role. Please ask away."

"When was the last time you saw your husband before the tragic incident?" Marieke asked.

"At seven that morning," Lerato said. "He went off to work like any other day."

"And what happened that evening?" Marieke asked.

"Well, I got home at about six-thirty, and Ian wasn't home, but that wasn't unusual. I heard his car at about seven, and when he didn't come in, I went out to look, and saw him lying there," Lerato explained. "I called Abel right away, and he came around."

"When you opened the door, you didn't see anyone?" Marieke asked.

"No," Lerato confirmed. "I didn't hear anything either."

"Where had you been?" Marieke asked.

"I had been at a garage," Lerato said.

"Have you any idea who might wish harm to your husband?" Marieke asked.

"No, but I'm sure that in his past work with the police that he had made enemies," Lerato suggested.

"I'm sorry, but I have to ask this," Marieke said. "But, how were things between you?"

"Good, but not wonderful," Lerato admitted. "I used to model for Celia Molale a lot, and Ian didn't really approve. I got him a boudoir folio, and he was upset that I had done that; he was quite jealous at times. I wanted more from my life than just being the commissioner's wife, but I don't think that Ian really understood that. Does that make me a suspect?"

"Not necessarily," Marieke said. "But, tell me you made three quite large cash withdrawals from your bank about six months ago, what were they for?"

"You've been busy," Lerato commented. "I wanted the cash for a car I was buying."

"I thought you had a car?" Marieke said.

"I do, but I wanted another car that wasn't known to everyone as belonging to me," Lerato explained.

"Did you buy the car?" Marieke asked.

"I did, I registered it under another name, and keep it in a garage north of the town," Lerato said.

"Why?" Marieke asked.

"I want to enter the Safari Rally, you know what used to be the East African Safari, next year," Lerato said. "I thought that if Lucille Cardwell and Pat Moss-Carlsson could do it, why shouldn't I? I bought a Toyota Celica GT-Four, and have been modifying it."

"Who's your co-driver?" Marieke asked, not knowing what else to say. This announcement that Lerato had been thinking of entering the East African Safari had taken her completely by surprise; she never would have imagined Lerato doing something like that.

"Celia," Lerato replied. "I made her promise not to mention this to anyone, so if you've talked to her, she probably didn't mention it."

"Have you driven in a rally before?" Marieke asked, thinking that that explained the odd magazines she had seen at Celia's house.

"When I was younger, before I married Ian, I used to go into the Kalahari with an old Colt Gallant that I had, it was quite a fast car, but I had a difficult time finding a good navigator, most of them got sick. Celia is great, she researches the route well, calls the shifts at exactly the right times, and she doesn't get sick," Lerato said.

"Did your husband know about this?" Marieke asked.

"I don't think so," Lerato said. "But, he was very good at picking up little signals, and things, so he may have guessed I was up to something, he just didn't know what."

"The East African Safari requires a big support team," Marieke said. "Who was going to be your support team, and how were you going to break this news to your husband?"

"Celia is prepared to provide some sponsorship, and has already got us the racing suits, gloves, boots, and helmets, and I was thinking of talking to Mbali and Jan Lamprecht to sponsor me through MJ Motors," Lerato said. "As to telling Ian, I was working up to it. I was going to tell him before I left for Kenya, but confess to have been putting it off, not knowing what his reaction might have been."

"Does Commissioner Boateng know about this?" Marieke asked.

"No, I doubt that he'd understand," Lerato said. "He's a lot like Ian, very conservative, and not likely to view such a venture as the kind of thing women should do. It's not as if we would be the first women to do this; there's Michèle Mouton, Paola de Martini, Eija Jurvenan, and Christine Driano, to name just a few."

"I will have to include the car as part of my report to explain the cash withdrawals," Marieke said.

"I suppose it doesn't make much difference now," Lerato said. "I'm not sure if I'll go ahead with the plan now, so much changed in just that one moment."

"Did you and Commissioner Mochage have any business interests?" Marieke asked.

"We had built up a small stock portfolio," Lerato said. "But, no other interests, properties or partnerships."

"I hesitate to ask this, but I should complete the reports. Did you have any reason to suspect that your husband was interested in anyone else?" Marieke asked.

"I wondered once or twice, but there was never anything concrete, I even wondered about you for a while," Lerato said.

"Me?" Marieke said, surprised. "Why me?"

"I think because I questioned why the department would appoint a woman to such a position, and how you had got there," Lerato replied. "Then I met you, and heard about you from Mbali, and realised that that was not something you would do."

"Thank you," Marieke said. 'It's been hard to move up the promotional ladder, and I've had to contend with comments and innuendo, but I like to think that my work speaks for itself."

"Indeed, it does," Lerato agreed. "I think everyone was surprised when you solved the murders of David and Julia Turner."

"That was a challenge," Marieke admitted. "Again, I'm sorry I have to ask this, but did you have any interests outside your husband?"

"No," Lerato said. "Ian was a caring man, and if he had only been a little more sensitive to what I wanted in life, he would have been as perfect as a man can get, but I did not stray."

"Have there been any unusual telephone calls or people calling in the past few weeks?" Marieke asked.

"No calls, but I did see a car parked across the street one day, it was a Mercedes, so I thought it might have been an estate agent looking into the land across the street that is for sale," Lerato said.

"How long has that land been for sale? I didn't see any signs?" Marieke asked.

"About six months now," Lerato said. "There's no sign, but if you go to the estate agent's office, it is posted there. Now that I think of it, there was a Land Rover there one day as well, and someone doing something on the land, I thought again it was the estate agents."

"Do you remember when that was?" Marieke asked.

"I don't know, maybe two weeks ago," Lerato thought.

"Thank you for your time," Marieke said. "If you think of anything else that might help us, please call me."

"I will," Lerato promised. "Go well."

"Stay well," Marieke replied.

Marieke had missed the five o'clock meeting, so she satisfied herself by calling the commissioner when she got home and briefly reporting on what she had found during the day. She was satisfied in her own mind that Lerato was an unlikely suspect. Although the relationship between her and her husband was not as perfect as it seemed from the outside, there was no evidence of the loathing that often triggered a bid for freedom. With Katse, they were no closer; the South Africans had yet to reply to her query about the 9mm pistol dropped at the scene, and they had no viable suspects. The notion of Lerato and Celia speeding through the wilds of Kenya on the safari sounded as if it could be exciting as well as a little risky; it was something she had never tried but had often wondered about. Perhaps when this investigation was over, she would ask Lerato to take her out one day to see what it was like.

Commissioner Abel Boateng called a meeting at eight the next morning to review what they knew and did not know. He called upon Thabo first to give details on the deaths.

"Kagiso Katse," Thabo started. "Gunshots to the skull, two, either would have been fatal. Gun used, 9mm semiautomatic made by Beretta, provenance unknown at this time. No prints or other forensic evidence on the gun or ammunition. No footprints, fingerprints, hair, or fibres present at the scene. Time of death between six and six-thirty in the morning. Assistant Commissioner Ian Mochage, gunshot to the skull, single shot, fatal. Gun used Steyr Mannlicher 9-3, provenance tied back to a Koos van de Merwe of Port Elizabeth, himself murdered last November. No prints on the gun, but traces of fibres and oil, suggesting it was broken down and transported. In both cases, a suppressor was used, and our consulting gunsmith says that they were made on the same equipment, suggesting a link between the killings or killers."

"Thank you, Thabo," Abel said. "Inspector Modise, any new items on the house-to-house interviews?"

"No, Sir," Modise replied. "All we have is the one report of a white man walking near Katse's house on the morning of the shooting, and the report of another man, possibly white, walking away from the Mochage house just before Mrs Mochage discovered the commissioner. We have possible sightings of a Mercedes and a Land Rover near the Mochage house at different times."

"Thank you, Inspector," Abel said, then he went on to ask Marieke for her report. "Any new information on the backgrounds of our victims that might suggest a motive?"

"I have interviewed all the business associates of Katse that I can find, and none have, in my view, a strong enough motive for wanting him dead. I have just started with the background for the commissioner, but nothing of note yet," she reported.

"Inspector Sibanda, what about arrivals and departures?" Abel asked.

"We've got as far as February," Sibanda reported. "So far, we have 1,156 white males who entered the country since November, and have not yet left. I have the list here."

"Can anyone think of any links between Ian and Katse that might give us a clue as to our killer or killers?" Abel asked.

"Not yet," was the general reply, and then Sibanda chimed in with, "Perhaps it's a case where the commissioner arrested someone, and Katse did a poor job of defending, and they did time."

"Find out what cases Katse lost," Abel instructed. "Then find out if Ian was involved in any of them, you may have to go back a year or two, because I think Ian made his last arrest ten years ago. Very well, let's keep pursuing what we have. Inspector Sibanda, have some men start interviewing the 1,156 you have on your list."

"I'll try, Sir," Sibanda promised. "But many of them are on safaris, and may be difficult to find."

"I know," Abel said. "But, try anyway."

"Sir," Sibanda said.

"Let's meet again tomorrow at this time, and see if anything crops up. That's all for now, Assistant Superintendent, please stay for a minute," Abel instructed.

When all the others had gone, he looked to Marieke and asked her, "How was the interview with Lerato?"

"Difficult, Sir," she replied. "It seems that the relationship was not as perfect as I thought it was, but I got no sense that it went beyond some dissatisfaction, I heard nothing that suggested any infidelity on either part. I did learn that Lerato bought a rally car, without Ian's knowledge, and was planning to enter the East African Safari next year."

"What?" Abel asked. "She did what?"

"Apparently, she and Celia Molale teamed up and were going to enter the rally in a Toyota Celica GT-Four," she explained.

"Does Lerato have any rally experience?" Abel asked.

"She said that when she was younger, she had a Colt Gallant, and would take that out into the Kalahari, apparently her biggest problem was finding a co-driver, navigator, who wouldn't get sick," Marieke replied.

"Well, I never," Abel said. "And I thought I knew those two really well. I never would have imagined that she would even think of that, let alone buy a car, and enter. When was she planning to tell Ian?"

"She said that she was working towards that," Marieke said.

"Does Celia Molale confirm this?" Abel asked.

"I was going to see her today and ask," Marieke said.

"Fine, Marieke, let me know what she says," Abel said. "Well, I never, the East African Safari. Go well."

"Stay well, Sir," Marieke said.

Marieke left the office and went to the shop of Celia. It was open, and there were four customers, so Marieke waved to Celia, went out, and found herself some coffee, then went back to the shop.

The line was down to two now, so Marieke just found a chair and sat down to wait.

"So, Marieke," Celia said after the last customer left. "What brings you here today?"

"I talked to Lerato yesterday, and she told me about the East African Safari," Marieke explained.

"It's the Safari Rally now," Celia said. "Yes, she and I are, maybe were now, going to enter. She had asked me to keep it between us until such time as she had told Ian."

"Do you have any rally experience?" Marieke asked.

"Like Lerato, I had played around in the Kalahari when I was much younger. I used to drive a Beetle in those days. Then I competed in the Paris Dakar Rally in 1984," Celia said. "I wasn't nearly as fast as the winners, but I finished."

"That's an expensive proposition," Marieke said. "Who sponsored you?"

"A group of fashion magazines," Celia said. "I had brought out a line of race-wear looking clothing, so they wanted desert shots. I got OMP to make me some actual race-wear suits that looked like mine. They were very nice about it and did it all with typical Italian flair and style. I talked the magazine editors into backing a car for me, so bought a Mitsubishi Pajero, had it fitted out in Genoa by OMP, and found a co-driver, she was Italian, a very good mechanic, and fun to drive with. She went on to marry the lead mechanic on one of the teams."

"Can you see any scenario where this rally entry would cause anyone to want to shoot either Ian or Lerato?" Marieke asked.

"No, that wouldn't make any sense," Celia said. "As far as we knew, Ian didn't even know about the car, and our wish to enter, and if someone wanted to stop us, why shoot Ian, and not Lerato, or even me?"

"I would agree," Marieke said. "Well, thank you for your time, stay well."

"Go well, Marieke," Celia replied.

Marieke went in search of lunch and found some at the Bull and Bush pub. She was mulling over the things she had learned that morning when Jan Lamprecht came in with Phineas Botha from Maun.

"*Dumela Mma*," Jan said. "Are you well?"

"*Dumela Rra*, Phineas," she replied. "I am, and you?"

"Well," Jan assured her. "Phineas is in town collecting parts for some broken-down Land Rovers, so we thought we would get some lunch."

"How is your mother, Phineas?" Marieke asked.

"She is very well," Phineas said. "She's been busy with bookings for Bridget and Will, not that the season is open, they're trying to make sure the latter end of the season is booked out."

"Please, sit," Marieke said, waving to the other chairs at her table.

"So, how are the investigations?" Jan asked.

"Slow," Marieke said. "We just don't have much to go on. Did you know that your friend from long ago, Koos van de Merwe, was killed last November?"

"Koos, killed?" Jan said. "No, who by, why?"

"The SAP don't know," Marieke said. "But a rifle that belonged to him showed up here at one of our shootings."

"It did?" Jan said. "Are the two deaths related?"

"We've no idea," Marieke said. "Perhaps the killer just sold the rifle, and the buyer used it here; we don't know. Can you think of anything that connects the two?"

"Not off hand," Jan said. "The last time I had any contact with Koos, he was still in the army, after that, I don't know where he went."

"I'm hoping to get more details from the SAP," Marieke said.

"Who's Koos van de Merwe?" Phineas asked.

"An *ou* I used to know in South Africa," Jan explained. "We were in the army together, and both were here in the seventies looking for ivory. Thankfully, Marieke can't arrest me for that now, but I gave it all up when Mbali and I came here."

"How's business at the garage?" Marieke asked Phineas.

"Dad retired, and I run it now," Phineas replied. "We're busier than ever. The growth of the visitor safari business centred on Maun has meant that we're in constant demand. We've a steady business modifying Landies and Toyotas for the safari industry, and then fixing them. We also had a growing business with local car owners. I have six mechanics now, a bit different from when it was Dad and me."

"Jan," Marieke started. "Have you been asked to sponsor a rally team?"

"Oh, you heard about that," he said, grinning. "Yes, Celia Molale and Lerato Mochage came to see me about a week ago, and asked if we would be one of their sponsors."

"Will you?" Marieke asked.

"If they decide to still go, yes," Jan said. "We've got a year yet, so a lot can happen. I'd like to get a look at the car and see what kind of mods have already been done, and then take a ride with Lerato to see what kind of driver she is. Will we see you this weekend, Marieke?"

"A lot depends on the investigations," she said. "I'll see if I can. I should go and see what I can do at the office, stay well."

"Go well," Jan said.

Sergeant Maphosa was waiting for her when she returned; they had other cases they had to work on, apart from the two killings. They ranged from a car theft ring, possible diamond thefts, two assaults, and a few other minor offences. Together they reviewed the cases and the evidence they had collected, and concluded that four of them were ready to send to the prosecution service, and that they needed more evidence on the others. All this took until six that night, at which time they were both ready to go home.

"Go, Sergeant," Marieke told him. "Your family must be wondering where you are."

"Thank you, Madame," he said. "Stay well."

"Go well, we will start again in the morning," she said.

And yet another

At the eight o'clock meeting the next day, Inspector Sibanda was able to report that they had tracked down 145 of the men who had entered the country since November, and who were still in Botswana. They were all at various safari camps and lodges in the north of the country, and the camp managers all verified that they were there when the shootings occurred. That left only 1,013 to find. Marieke was surprised there were that many, but then if she added up those involved in the mining industry, the beef industry, the safari business, and just general visitors, she could imagine that number. Further business was halted when there was a telephone call from one of the inspectors who was not at the meeting. Marieke took the call and then relayed what she had been told to the rest. There had been another shooting. This time it was Jan Lamprecht. He had been found by one of his staff, dead in his office at his workshop.

Three violent deaths in only a few days were something that Botswana just did not see. She brushed away the tears and looked at the commissioner.

"You are friends with the Lamprechts?" the commissioner asked.

"I am," Marieke confirmed.

"Has Mrs Lamprecht been informed?" the commissioner asked.

"There is an officer there," she replied.

"You'd better go, and see Mrs Lamprecht, and then visit the scene, then come back, and tell me if this is just an amazing coincidence or are these shootings related?" the commissioner instructed.

"Yes, Sir," she said. As she drove to the house of Jan and Mbali, Marieke thought about the deaths, first Kagiso Katse, a well-known if not particularly prominent solicitor, a police assistant commissioner, and now a well-known businessman, who was probably a future city leader. Was there any scenario that connected these three deaths, or were any combination of two related, and the third merely happenstance. The link between the two suppressors certainly suggested that at least two were connected, but what was the connection?

At the Lamprecht house, Marieke met with the officer who was there with Mbali and her two daughters.

"Marieke, who, why?" Mbali asked, between bouts of tears.

"I don't know yet," Marieke said.

"Find him," Mbali hissed. "I'd say kill him, but the law may not like that unless they hang the bastard."

"How are you?" Marieke asked.

"I don't know," Mbali wailed. "It's such a shock. I don't know what I'm going to do."

"Would you like me to have someone come and stay with you?" Marieke asked.

"That might be a good idea," Mbali said. "Do you think we're in any danger?"

"I don't think so," Marieke temporised. "But, it's better to be safe. I'll have one of the officers here stay here until I can send an armed female officer, then I'll borrow Sergeant Constance Sephoto from Maun to come, and stay a little longer."

"Will you find the man who did this?" Nandi asked, the tears streaming down her face.

"Yes," Marieke said.

"It's Pretorius," Mbali said. "He said he would get even with them all, now he's out, he's started."

"I'll check to see if he's in the country," Marieke promised. "But is it possible that someone else wished to harm Jan?"

"I don't think so," Mbali said. "We had no enemies; there was no reason to harm Jan."

"I'm sorry to leave you, but I do need to visit the scene and see what I can learn," Marieke said.

"Of course, go and find the bastard," Mbali said. Marieke spoke to the officer who was there and told him that she would get an armed female officer to come and replace him. Before she left the house, she called the station, talked to Sergeant Maphosa, and gave him instructions to set that up.

Marieke then drove to the workshop of MJ Motors and found police cars in abundance. The parking area was paved, so no chance of getting any tyre tracks, besides which the parking area had been driven over by their own police vehicles. But, it seemed unlikely that a shooter would park outside and advertise their presence, so she took a look around for places to park that would not attract attention, and be hidden from casual view. There were a number of warehouses and buildings in the area behind which the killer could have parked, and then walked to the scene. Marieke took a walk around looking for tracks, but there were so many that without a clue as to which one she should be interested in, it would be time-consuming to follow them all. She went to MJ Motors and found the inspector in charge, Inspector Bangwata, who had the scene cordoned off and was conducting interviews while a forensic technician was collecting evidence. Just after she arrived, Thabo and Neo also arrived.

"So, Matshwana, another one, do we have a serial killer on our hands, or are these three related, or have we been hit by a peculiar crime wave?" Thabo asked.

"My money is that they are related," Marieke said. "We don't have three murders in seven days out of the blue; someone has an axe to grind. Mbali is convinced that it's Pretorius."

"Who?" Thabo asked.

"Hansie Pretorius, sent up for twenty years, just released last October," Marieke explained. "Jan told me some of the story, and Mbali filled in the bits that he left out. Jan was part of an ivory poaching group over twenty years ago; Hansie Pretorius was the leader. He was arrested by the commissioner, who was then an inspector. I'm not sure what part Katse played, but we do know that the owner of the rifle used to kill the commissioner was a Koos van de Merwe, and that he was killed under mysterious circumstances last November. Van de Merwe was another member of the group."

"Any more?" Thabo asked.

"A cousin of Pretorius, Danie Pretorius, and a South African Army colonel by the name of de Villiers, who was the buyer," Marieke replied.

"How do you know about this, de Villiers?" Thabo asked.

"Jan told me that van de Merwe recognised him when he was serving in the Caprivi, apparently they had met de Villiers in Cape Town to hand over the ivory, and get paid, and then de Villiers went to the base where van de Merwe was. De Villiers was a colonel in intelligence, so he was on an inspection visit to the Caprivi to jack up the troops," Marieke explained.

"So, what do we have here?" Thabo asked.

"Shot in the back of the head at close range," Inspector Bangwata said. "If you look over there, it looks as if that's where the bullets ended up. We have entry wounds here, and exit wounds here. Shot with a 9mm handgun, probably that SIG Sauer over there, I've got two cartridge cases here that I picked up when I came upon the scene. It looks as if the killer gained entry and was waiting, so that when Lamprecht came into the office, the killer shot him." Thabo looked around, looked at the body, and shook his head in agreement.

"I wonder where this gun came from?" Marieke mused.

"We'll check, and we'll also check the cartridge cases for firing pin marks, and we'll see if we can dig out the bullets without damaging them too much, and see if we can get rifling marks to prove whether or not this is the weapon," Thabo said. "Are you going to pursue Pretorius as your main line of enquiry?"

"I'm going to look at him, certainly," Marieke said. "But, I'm not closing off all other possibles. It is remotely possible that these three shootings are unrelated, or even if they are related, it's possible that someone else did the shooting. Inspector, was the door forced?"

"Not forced, Madame," Bangwata said. "But, see here, the scratch marks around the lock, the lock has been picked."

"MJ had no alarm system?" Marieke asked. "I thought they did?"

"They do, Madame," Bangwata confirmed. "But, again, from the very small scratch marks on some of the wires, it looks as if someone was able to bypass the alarm."

"So, we're looking for someone who has skills with alarms," Marieke said. "No one heard anything?"

"Apparently, Mr Lamprecht was the first one in, so there was no one else here. The walls of this office are fairly thick, probably to stop the noise from the shop, but would be just as effective at stopping noise from here being heard outside. Lamprecht's body was discovered by the parts manager who came in just after eight," Bangwata explained, then he went on to say, "Apparently Lamprecht's routine was to come in early, often around six or six thirty, before anyone else, then go to his office, clear up any paperwork then go out into the shop, and meet his staff as they came into work, and see if they had any issues or needs. The parts manager was in next, and went to ask him a question, and found him dead."

"No chance that it was the parts manager?" Marieke asked.

"I don't think so," Bangwata said. "He's too upset. I don't see him as that good an actor. No, he really liked Lamprecht, and his biggest worry now is who will lead MJ. We've swept the floor and found nothing. The killer was very careful; he didn't bother to file off the serial number of the gun, so either doesn't care that we may be able to trace it or is very arrogant."

"Did anyone in the neighbourhood see anything?" Marieke asked.

"We've started canvassing the neighbourhood, but so far, nothing. If we find out anything, I will report on it," Bangwata promised.

"Very well," Marieke said. "Make sure that our people also ask if anyone saw someone waiting around, and watching MJ in the past couple of weeks. This has the hallmarks of a planned job, so whoever did it must have done some reconnaissance. I'll leave you to the scene, Thabo. Inspector, when you have the interviews done, let me know if you learn anything. Take your time, we need to get this right."

"Yes, Madame," Bangwata said.

"It's interesting that this gun has no suppressor," Marieke said. "Was that bravado on his part, or did he know that the walls were thick, and he probably wouldn't need a suppressor?"

"Good point," Thabo said. "I'm sure the Inspector will be asking about people who may have been seen in the area in the past few weeks."

"Of course," Bangwata said. "Could you have one of your technicians look at the scratches on the lock, and on the alarm system, and give me a guess as to how old they may be?"

"Ah, yes, good thinking Inspector," Thabo said. "Neo, take a look, would you?"

"I should go back, and see the commissioner, and tell him what we know, and what we speculate may be going on," Marieke said. "He won't be happy. It's interesting isn't it that at each of the three shootings we've had lately, that the shooter just dropped the gun at the scene walked, or perhaps drove away. If it is one shooter, where did he get all these guns, how did they come into the country, and how many more does he have?"

Back at the police station, Marieke first confirmed with Sergeant Maphosa that he had arranged for an armed woman police constable to go to the house of Mbali Lamprecht, and to be relieved by another after eight hours. She told him that she wanted an armed constable there at all times. That done, she went to the commissioner's office and reported.

"Sir," she said, knocking at his door.

"What do you have for me Superintendent?" he asked.

"Jan Lamprecht shot in the back of the head, twice, probably between six and seven this morning, the gun dropped at the scene as in the case of Katse," she said. "The alarm had been bypassed, and the lock on the door picked. It seems likely that the killer effected entry then just waited for Jan to show up. No one heard anything or saw anything. The body was discovered by the parts manager, who went to ask a question."

"What did you say the weapon used this time was?" the commissioner asked.

"Another 9mm," Marieke replied. "I'll check with van Dyk from the SAP, and see if this is van de Merwe's 9mm".

"So, anything that connects these three deaths?" he asked.

"I have nothing concrete," Marieke said. "The only theory is one that Mbali Lamprecht advanced, and that this is the work of Hansie Pretorius who is exacting revenge for having spent twenty years in Francistown."

"How, and why?" the commissioner asked.

"Twenty-one years ago, a group that comprised Hansie Pretorius, Danie Pretorius, Koos van de Merwe, and Jan Lamprecht came to Botswana to poach ivory. The operation was discovered, and we, and the game guards moved in. We never found any ivory, but in the course of the operation, Hansie shot at our officers until he was subdued. The arresting officer was our own Ian Mochage," Marieke explained. "Pretorius was the only one who spent any time in prison, according to Ian, van de Merwe and the other Pretorius were kicked out of the country, and no one ever saw Lamprecht in the country. What the involvement of Katse was, I don't yet know. But, in those days Katse would take all manner of villains as clients, so perhaps he numbered Pretorius as one."

"So, perhaps all three related," the commissioner mused. "I can see the relationship between Pretorius, and Lamprecht, but you need to check on Katse?"

"I thought I would check the old files and gaol logs to see who visited Pretorius," Marieke said. "I'll get onto the Vice Chancellor, and ask him to have the name Pretorius looked for particularly in the immigration data, but I suspect that we won't find him on any recent entry or departure records."

"You think he's using an alias?" the commissioner asked.

"Either that, or he came across the border illegally somewhere along the Limpopo or the Molopo," Marieke replied.

"When Pretorius was here twenty years ago, how did he enter the country?" the commissioner asked.

"He came in across the border legally, but according to Mbali, one of the others used a track through the bush, and waded the Limpopo, I don't know exactly where, but believe it was somewhere near Mpepu," Marieke explained.

"What's your next step?" the commissioner asked.

"I'm going to contact the South Africans again, and see if they can track down Pretorius," Marieke said.

"And if they can, and he can account for his whereabouts in the past week?" the commissioner asked.

"Then we have a real problem," Marieke admitted.

"We will indeed," the commissioner agreed. "If I were Pretorius, and I was doing this, I'd kill one or two more at random to break any pattern or obvious relationships between the victims."

"Let's hope that if it is him, that he isn't that devious," Marieke said. "Any more shootings, and we'll have a panic in the city."

"True," the commissioner agreed. "You'd better contact the South Africans, and see if we can track down Pretorius."

Marieke went back to her office, and called the Maun police station, and asked for the services of Sergeant Sephoto. It was promised, and they said that she would leave for Gaborone that morning. Her next call was to the Port Elizabeth police station again. She asked to be put through to Lieutenant Colonel van Dyk. She was told that he was not in that day, but he had left instructions that if she called, she was to be given his home telephone number. So, she called him at home.

"*Goeiemôre,*" he said. "I didn't expect you to call back so quickly. Have you something for us?"

"I'm so sorry to bother you at home, but we have had another shooting, and have a possible link," Marieke said. "We are keen to track down a Hansie Pretorius of Zeerust, we would like to talk to him about the three shootings here."

"I thought you had only the one?" van Dyk asked. "Oh, I forgot the other one you mentioned when you called about the 9mm."

"Our assistant commissioner was the second, the first was a solicitor, and we have just had another. We suspect they may be related. Let me explain," Marieke said. She related the tale of the ivory poaching trip twenty years earlier, and the fact that the only one who had been imprisoned was Pretorius. Now the arresting officer was dead, and two of the hunting party were dead.

"*Magtig.* Who else was involved?" van Dyk asked.

"Danie Pretorius of Zeerust, and this may be delicate, but an army colonel by the name of de Villiers, apparently twenty years ago he was in Intelligence, he was recognised by van de Merwe when they met in the Caprivi," Marieke explained.

"*Magtig,*" van Dyk breathed. "I'll need to tread carefully, you're sure about de Villiers?"

"Lamprecht told me last October when Pretorius was released from prison, and kicked out of the country," Marieke confirmed.

"Let me make some enquiries," van Dyk said. "Give me a little time, and I'll call you back."

It was four hours later, while Marieke was having some coffee, and a very late lunch, and reading through the old file of the Pretorius case, when van Dyk called back.

"You were right," he said. "This is going to be delicate. De Villiers is dead, shot in December of last year. De Villiers is, was, a general, and the army are still trying to work out any motives for killing him. His driver was also shot, and there was another, apparently unrelated, death in the neighbourhood just a day before, but as you might imagine, the army is going to be difficult to deal with, they will not want to share or release any information. Danie Pretorius is also dead, died on the 3rd of March in Sin City, found the next day by the maids, heart attack apparently. Interestingly there were two other deaths related to Zeerust in February, two *ouks* that ran what used to be the Pretorius butcher's shop, apparently frozen to death, how, the Zeerust police are not sure. Their van was seen in Vryburg where they bought diesel, a witness described the *ou* who bought the diesel, and it mostly fit that of Andries Bloem, one of the *ouks* that died, but it could have been someone dressed like Bloem. The van was later found abandoned in Kimberley, with the two bodies in the cab, Bloem and Hennie Arnot. The pathologist was able to tell that they had been frozen to death, which was odd, because the cab is isolated from the refrigerated part of the van. There was speculation that the two were killed because they were known to be *moffies*. The police in Zeerust, Vryburg, and Kimberley have had no luck in tracking down anyone who may have been involved. But, it seems to me that the two must have been in the back when the van was driven from Zeerust to Kimberley, and the *ou* who bought the diesel was the killer. We haven't had any luck tracking down Hansie Pretorius yet, but I did check records at hotels, and lodges in, and around Port Alfred last November, and there is no record that he went there."

"Thank you, Colonel," Marieke said. "We have a hunt going here to try, and find Pretorius, but we have not ruled out other possible shooters or motives for the shootings. Could you get me the actual dates of the various killings, and the locations?"

"*Ja*, I'll do that," van Dyk promised.

"Thank you, Colonel, *tot siens*," Marieke said.

"*Tot siens*," van Dyk replied. "Oh, by the way, the 9mm handgun you sent me details of, was not the one taken from van de Merwe's boat. We're still checking to see if it's registered anywhere in South Africa. What was used in your latest?"

"It's another 9mm, a SIG Sauer," Marieke replied. "I'll send the details as soon as I can."

"Let me know if you find out anything more," van Dyk said.

"I'll do that," Marieke promised.

Marieke then went to see the commissioner, and related to him the news she had learned from the South Africans.

"So," the commissioner said. "Pretorius is looking more promising?"

"Possibly," Marieke agreed. "If it is him, he has done a thorough job of cleaning up after himself. The South Africans have no leads on who killed van de Merwe or de Villiers, and they have treated the death of Danie Pretorius as natural causes until now, and they have no clues yet to the killing of the two from the Pretorius Butchers."

"Go back twenty years, and go through all the old files, and see if there is anything you can find out about Pretorius, and his associates," the commissioner instructed. "I'll have Inspector Bangwata take the lead on the crime scene investigations, you should concentrate on the history of that case, and how that relates to the present."

"Very good Sir," Marieke said.

"I have called a meeting of inspectors, and superintendents, and will be assigning tasks in these cases, we'll have Bangwata look at the crime scenes, I'll get Sibanda to take over the arrivals and departures data, and the sweep of the surrounding area looking for where the shooter of Ian practised. I'll have Modise do house-to-house for all three shootings, and see if we cannot get some line on the white man seen near Katse's house, and the one that the teenagers saw near Ian's house. I'll have Masisi lead a team that looks for other connections between the three, I'll assign Pule from here, and Moroka from Maun to assist him. You stay focused on the history of Pretorius, and learn as much as you can about the South African killings. Go there if you have to; the department will cover air travel and all the other expenses. We need to find this shooter or these, if there is more than one," the commissioner instructed. "The meeting will be in one hour, so be there, I know it's late, but this is a situation where I need everyone, all leave will be cancelled for the next month, or until we resolve these cases."

The commissioner held his meeting, and went through assignments, and told them all that he wanted a daily briefing at 5:00 pm when all would share what they had learned. If they were not able to attend because they were away from town, then they needed to send a deputy who was fully briefed. The commissioner wanted no lone wolf behaviours, and no guarding information, all needed to be shared because one small item might help one of the others. His final admonition was no talking to the press, he would handle that, and he would decide what was released, and when, anyone talking to the press would suffer consequences. Then he addressed the issue that was uppermost in his mind.

"So," he said. "Are these random killings, related killings that are driven by some motive like revenge or something else personal or do we have a serial killer in our midst?"

"It's difficult to see how they are related," Inspector Bangwata said. "What do these three have in common?"

"Well, two at least are possibly linked through old criminal cases," Inspector Sibanda commented. "There have to be a number of cases where Katse was on one side, and we were on the other side."

"Marieke has suggested a link," the commissioner said. "It appears that twenty-some years ago, Hansie Pretorius was arrested by Ian Mochage, and charged with various crimes, including ivory poaching, he may have had some contact with Katse at about that time, and then he spent the next twenty years in the Francistown prison. We have also learned that another man involved in the ivory poaching, was also killed late last year in South Africa, and it was his rifle that was used to kill Ian, and another member of the gang died of an apparent heart attack in Sun City recently. The South Africans have so far treated that as a simple heart attack. Finally, the buyer of the ivory was also recently killed in Pretoria, also shot, also no witnesses, no suspects as of this time."

"I can see a revenge killing of Assistant Commissioner Mochage," Marieke said. "But, I'm debating if it's reasonable to link Katse to the other deaths. We do have a link between the Katse, and Commissioner Mochage shootings, the suppressors used in each case show the same tool marks, so were likely made on the same machine, most likely by the same person, so either the cases are linked or we have two shooters who by an amazing coincidence both bought suppressors from the same supplier."

"What does Lamprecht have to do with this?" Bangwata asked.

"We have reason to believe that he was also part of the ivory poaching," the commissioner replied.

"Lamprecht?" Sibanda asked. "That doesn't seem very likely."

"It's true," Marieke said. "He told me, and his wife confirmed it, he told me the day that we kicked Pretorius out of the country."

"But, he's such an honest man," Sibanda protested. "All his dealings that I know of have been scrupulously straightforward."

"I rather think that was the price of marriage," Marieke suggested. "I think that Mbali, his wife, laid the law down when they set up house here. No more poaching for pot or money."

"Is there anything that would rule out a serial killer?" the commissioner asked.

"The three killings only have one evidentiary thing in common," Inspector Pule said. "The victims were all shot, but even then, they were shot with different weapons, two with handguns, and one long gun, all probably stolen, so no link back to the shooter, except for the likely link with the suppressors. There were no items taken from the victims, no souvenirs, no trophies. There was nothing left at the scenes, like notes, flowers or anything else. If the American movies, and news reports are to be believed, serial killers like to let it be known that they are active, and almost have this catch me if you can bravado. These three shootings have rather the mark of one who is more professional in his or her outlook, do the job, leave, and leave no clues."

"Well, the latter is certainly true," Thabo Mosiwa said. "The only real clue that we have had, has been the long gun that we were able to track back to South Africa. The South Africans have just confirmed that the 9mm used to kill Katse did not come from van de Merwe, they are still checking to see if they can find out if it was registered anywhere in South Africa. With the Lamprecht case, we found two cartridge cases, and the bullets we dug from the wall are 9mm, and we're running our tests to confirm they came from the gun we found at the scene. The only link we have right now is the story Ian told Marieke about the ivory poaching, and later confirmed by Lamprecht."

"How was the man van de Merwe in South Africa killed?" Bangwata asked.

"A knife," Marieke replied. "He was on a fishing boat where he was killed, and his body thrown overboard. The South Africans have no suspects, and no one saw anything."

"I am going to have Assistant Commissioner Masisi look at the case assuming that the killings are the result of contract killings. He will be looking into the histories, and backgrounds of all three, and trying to find something that would link them, and that would warrant killings. To help him I am assigning Inspectors Pule, and Moroka, they will have or need access to all documents, and files that we have on Katse, Lamprecht, and Ian Mochage. I am of the mind that we are not dealing with a serial killer, so would like the rest of you to concentrate on Pretorius, and find him," the commissioner said. "I subscribe to the notion that this is revenge for spending twenty years in Francistown, but if anything else pops up in the background investigations of all three, then I will listen. We may be dealing with an opportunist as well as a contract killer, what better time to settle a personal score than when we are fully occupied with the investigation of the shooting of one of our own, an opportunist would guess that we would focus resources on that, and take advantage of the fact that we do have limited resources. I am disappointed that our reputation with teenagers caused two potential witnesses to not immediately come forward, and tell us that they had seen someone near the scene of the killing of Ian Mochage, we may have missed an opportunity there to quickly apprehend the shooter, and perhaps forestall the shooting of Lamprecht. We must do a better job of working with the people, no matter how objectionable we may find some of them. Is there anything else?"

There being no questions, the commissioner handed out copies of the photograph that had been taken of Pretorius before he was deported from Botswana the previous October, and instructed the Pretorius team to show the photograph to hoteliers, car rental agencies, shops, offices, anywhere where a man may go looking for lodging, food, and transport.

After the meeting, Marieke went back to her desk, and put together all the notes she had from her interviews on the Kats, and Mochage cases. Those she would give to Inspector Bangwata. They then pulled the history files on the old Pretorius case. She had found all Mochage's notes, and reports on the case, and she had asked for the gaol logs to see who came, and went to see Pretorius. She thought about things for a while, and decided that it would be useful to have records from outside the police, so she made a note to call Katse's office, and see if Rachel had anything.

Marieke looked at her watch, and was horrified to see it was eight thirty already. She looked out of the window, and, yes, it was pitch black. She had been so focused on the files that time had just flown by. She stacked everything neatly on the corner of her desk, and went home. She was tired, she had been constantly on the go for the last several days, so what she really wanted was a relaxing bath, something light to eat, and more than anything some sleep. Sleep was slow in coming, in her mind she kept turning over what they knew, and did not know, but eventually, fatigue won, and she fell asleep. The following day, she awoke late, or at least late for her, at seven-thirty. She made sure that she actually ate a reasonable breakfast, then called her office, and told Sergeant Maphosa that she would be there after she had called the office of

Katse, and been to see a possible source of information. Rachel answered the telephone, obviously with a now-prepared speech.

"*Dumela*," Rachel said. "I'm sorry if you have called requesting the services of Mr Katse, but we are no longer in business."

"*Dumela Mma*," Marieke said. "This is Assistant Superintendent Englebrecht again, I wonder if you could do some research for me in the old files of Mr Katse?"

"Of course, *Mma*," Rachel said. "What do you need?"

"Go back twenty years, and earlier, and find anything, and everything on a South African by the name of Hansie Pretorius who was from Zeerust," Marieke asked. "Hansie Pretorius was arrested, and convicted on a number of charges back then, and he has recently been released from prison, and deported. I want to know if there was a relationship between Mr Katse, and Pretorius."

"Hansie Pretorius," Rachel repeated. "I'll look, and call you back."

Marieke thought about the other deaths in South Africa, and they seemed straightforward enough, except that of Danie Pretorius. She wondered if he really did die of a heart attack. There were traditional medicines that she knew of that would mimic the symptoms of a heart attack, and if pathologists were not looking for the signs, it could be missed. She decided to follow up that line of enquiry while she was waiting for the various files, and reports to be dug out of archives, and made available. Marieke changed her clothes, into much older worn clothes, and left her house, and drove south to Ramotswa. She stopped at the police station there, and arranged to leave her car. She then walked to the bus rank, and found a local mini-bus that would take her to where she wanted to go. Once there, she walked the short distance to her destination, a house set back from the street. She knocked, and entered, and greeted the man there.

"*Dumela Rra.*"

"*Dumela Mma,*" he replied. Their subsequent conversation was carried on in Setswana, but it essentially went like this.

"Are you well Uncle?"

"I am well, and you daughter?"

"Well, Uncle."

"What brings you out to see an old man?"

"I am seeking information about someone who may have acquired *zwezwe*, or something similar in the past few months."

"In the past three months, there have been five people who acquired *muthi* that is either *zwezwe* or has similar uses."

"Where were these acquisitions made?"

"One in Gaborone, one in Otse, one in Lobatse, one here in Ramotswe, and one in the Pilanesberg."

"Tell me of the one in the Pilanesberg."

"It was a woman, who arrived by taxi."

"What manner of woman was she?"

"It is difficult to see that, she was not what she appeared to be."

"How did she appear?"

"As an old woman, but she was much younger, perhaps the same as you, oh ho, was it you?"

"No, Uncle it was not me."

"I know, she was younger than you, she had knowledge of *zwezwe* from an old *ngaka* who is now dead."

"Where did this *ngaka* live?"

"Goo-Kgang."

"How long is this *ngaka* dead?"

"Perhaps fifteen years."

"Is there anything else that you can tell me?"

"She was from Zeerust long ago, like you, she would be classified by the South Africans as coloured, and she has been very successful in South Africa."

"Anything on whom the *muthi* was used?"

"I see nothing else now, but perhaps another day if you come, and see an old man again."

"I would not be a good daughter if I did not look to the uncle of my mother from time to time."

"Your mother was my favourite niece, it distressed me greatly when she, and your father were killed by that landmine, I hope you stay away from such dangers."

"I will, Uncle, is there anything you need?"

"No, I will let you know if there is."

"Very well. Stay well, Uncle."

"Go well, daughter of Patience."

Marieke walked back to the bus stand where she had left the bus before, and waited. It was not long before an overladen bus appeared, and she bought passage back into town. She retrieved her car from the police station, and drove back to Gaborone, and home. She was now fairly certain that *zwezwe* had been used to kill Danie, she wondered if Danie had been buried or cremated. That was a question for van Dyk as was the identity of the coloured woman from Zeerust. Marieke changed back into her normal office attire, and drove to the police station. There, she got a quick update from Sergeant Maphosa, then she called the police station in Port Elizabeth, and asked to speak to van Dyk.

"*Middag*," he said when he came on the telephone.

"*Middag*," she replied. "I have some questions for you, if you have time?"

"Of course," he said. "What do you need?"

"Can you tell me if Danie Pretorius was buried or cremated, and can you find out the identity of a coloured woman who grew up in Zeerust but has probably moved away, and become successful?" she asked.

"You think this woman is involved?" he asked.

"I have information that someone acquired *zwezwe*, which is a native medicine that causes symptoms that mimic that of a heart attack, at about the time that Danie Pretorius died," she explained. "The *muthi* was acquired by a woman in the Pilanesburg. She had learned of its uses, and properties from an old *ngaka* who lived in Goo-Kgang, and my information is that she obtained some from a *sangoma* who lives in Mabalstad."

"You think she was involved in the death of Danie Pretorius?" van Dyk asked. "This *zwezwe*, it works?"

"The *zwezwe* works," Marieke confirmed. "Botanically it is *Strophanthus kombe*, and has been used for years in hunting, it produces effects that look to all intents, and purposes like a heart attack. Was the woman involved, I don't know?" Marieke admitted. "But it would be nice to talk to her."

"I'll see what I can do," van Dyk promised. "This is going to be difficult, Zeerust is a little out of my jurisdiction, so I'll have to rely on the local people for help."

"Thank you, *tot siens*," Marieke said.

"*Tot siens*," he replied.

Marieke was wondering what to do next when an officer arrived with files that included the old visitor logs from the gaol. Marieke pored through them until she came to entries for about the time that Hansie was there awaiting trial. Katse visited him twice in the weeks before the trial. So, there was a connection there. Also according to the notes she had just read from then Inspector Mochage, Hansie had specifically asked for Katse, stating that Katse had done work for him in the past. Now she really wanted to see what Katse's files had to say about Hansie. She decided to go to the offices of Katse, and see how Rachel was progressing. She found her amid piles of boxes, and files.

"*Dumela Mma*," Rachel said.

"*Dumela Mma*," Marieke replied. "Any luck?"

"Yes," Rachel confirmed. "It seems that Mr Katse had done quite a few small jobs for Hansie Pretorius, but the last request he declined to help because he asked for a fee in advance, and in cash, and it was not paid."

"How much?" Marieke asked.

"5,000 Rand," Rachel said. "It seems that Hansie Pretorius did not have that much on him at the time of his arrest, and his cousin Danie declined to provide the funds, so Mr Katse would not take the case. He did make one visit to the South African consulate people to tell them that Hansie was in gaol, and wanted to talk to someone."

"So, Hansie Pretorius was unlikely to be happy about that," Marieke commented.

"I wouldn't think so," Rachel agreed. "Perhaps he blamed his conviction, and sentence on Mr Katse, and decided to avenge himself."

"Perhaps," Marieke agreed. "If I could get copies of those files and notes, I would be obliged. Assistant Commissioner Masisi, and

Inspector Pule will probably be here shortly, they have been tasked to go through all Mr Katse's files, and look for possible motives for killing him."

"I will help in any way I can," Rachel said. "Give me five minutes, and I'll have these files copied." She quickly copied the files and notes and put them all in a folder for Marieke. "Is there anything else?"

"Not at the moment," Marieke said. "I presume that there is nothing in the recent files that indicates any contact between Mr Katse and Pretorius?"

"No, I would have remembered that," Rachel confirmed.

"Well, thank you for your help," Marieke said. "Stay well."

"Go well," Rachel replied.

Marieke arrived back in the office in time for the 5:00 pm meeting, and realised as she sat there waiting for everyone to turn up that she had had nothing to eat all day, apart from breakfast. That would not do; above all, she had to take care of herself, or else she would become ineffective in the investigation. She resolved to get something to eat immediately after the meeting had ended. The commissioner arrived and looked to her for a report.

"There would appear to be evidence of a link between Kagiso Katse and Hansie Pretorius," she reported. "Pretorius used Katse as his solicitor here in Botswana, but Katse declined to take a case where Pretorius had been arrested by then Inspector Mochage. The upshot of that was that Pretorius did his twenty years in Francistown and was released last October."

"Anything else?" the commissioner asked.

"My suspicion is that the cousin, Danie Pretorius, was poisoned with *zwezwe*, and death declared to be a heart attack. I am waiting for the South Africans to give me more details on that death," Marieke said.

Next up was Thabo who went through the forensics as they knew them, the details were known to most, but it did not hurt to go over them again, in case he had missed something. Katse had been shot with a 9mm handgun, left at the scene, the commissioner had been shot with the rifle, left at the scene, and Lamprecht had been shot with another 9mm, also left at the scene, they had had Piet Cronjé come in, and examine the pistol, and Thabo reported that it was a SIG Sauer P225 made in 1985, it was not on the Botswana register of guns, so probably was brought in from another country, most likely South Africa. His analysis was that Katse, and Lamprecht were both shot at close range, probably because the shooter was lying in wait, and Ian Mochage had been the long shot with the rifle. Inspector Sibanda reported that progress had been made on arrivals, and departures, and that they were already into the December data. All the arrivals so far had been accounted for with matching departures. Sibanda also reported that a villager near Sojwe had heard shots fired at a nearby pan. Sibanda was sending an officer to investigate. The door-to-door checks had so far yielded nothing, and the two possible sightings of a white man had been checked, but with no further details. They had gone back to the witness in the Katse shooting, and shown him pictures of Pretorius to see if he would recognise him. But, the man was unsure, it might have been, it might not have been. They had the same result when they showed the picture to the two teenagers, again, it might have been, it might not have been. The commissioner thanked everyone, and reminded them that he would be expecting their reports the next day.

Marieke started to drive home, then changed her mind and went to see Mbali.

"*Dumela Mma*," Nandi said as she opened the door to Marieke, under the watchful eye of Sergeant Moseki.

"*Dumela Mma*, Sergeant," Marieke replied. "Sergeant, I have arranged for your replacement. I expect Sergeant Constance Sephoto from Maun later. I will wait here until she gets here. Please go home to your family."

"Yes, Madame, thank you," she said. "There have been three visitors, one from MJ Motors, and two from the bank where Mrs Lamprecht works. I took the precaution of checking them for weapons before I let them in. I don't think they were too happy, but I do not want another death, especially while I am here."

"That's fine, Sergeant," Marieke said. "Thank you for being thorough. I appreciate the dedication, even if it offends others. If there are any complaints, I will deal with them."

"Thank you, Madame," she said. Marieke watched her leave, then closed the door and went to see Mbali.

"Marieke," Mbali said. "Thank you for coming, I suppose it's too early to ask if you've caught the man yet?"

"I'm sorry to say that it is," Marieke said. "We have over thirty officers working on the three cases, our thoughts now are that they are probably related, but we may be wrong, can you think of anyone who may have wished Jan harm?"

"No," Mbali said. "I've thought about that a lot since yesterday, and I cannot come up with any names of people who hated Jan enough to kill him. In fact, I cannot even name more than three or four who even disliked him."

"Who were they?" Marieke asked.

"Hastings Ngenda, Jan fired him about a month ago for stealing, James McBride, he tried to get out of paying for repairs done to his lorry, but Jan got the solicitors involved, and McBride was forced to pay, and Elizabeth Warden, she tried it on with him to avoid paying for tyres he had ordered for her especially. Jan rebuffed her, and she got all sour, even called me, and tried to pit me against Jan. I told your Inspector Bangwata, and I'm sure he's probably interviewed them by now," Mbali explained.

"I don't think I would want to be on the wrong side of Bangwata," Marieke commented. "He really liked the commissioner, and if he thinks the deaths are related, he won't be subtle in his questioning."

"Have you eaten anything today?" Mbali asked.

"Not really," Marieke admitted.

"I was just making something for me and the girls, there will be enough for four," Mbali promised. "If your Sergeant Sephoto stays here tomorrow, I will go to work and see about a temporary replacement while I take a week or two off. I'm going to keep the girls out of school for a week until things die down. Will we be safe here? Do you think Pretorius will come after us as well?"

"Would you feel safer at my house?" Marieke asked.

"I think so," Mbali said. "If it is Pretorius doing this, and he found the houses of Katse and Ian, he must know where we live."

"I will arrange it," Marieke said. "Let me call the station and arrange transport. We will use three different vehicles, and go first to the police station, then we'll go to my house, but the other vehicles will also leave so that anyone following will not know which one you are in." Marieke made the telephone call and was told to expect the transport within the hour. They had just finished dinner and were clearing up when they heard Land Rovers pull up outside. Marieke went to the door and saw Sergeant Constance Sephoto, two other female officers, and three male officers. Constance came in with police uniforms and suggested that Mbali, Nandi, and Khanyo change into them. When they had done that she then supervised the loading of luggage, and then sent Mbali off with two other officers, and similarly split up Khanyo, and Nandi. The rendezvous was set for the main police station, where it was possible to load and unload in the garage, and away from any observer. Marieke, in the meantime, drove home by a circuitous route to further confuse things. At the police station, Constance rearranged things, and the three Land Rovers left all bound for Marieke's house, but by different routes. When everyone finally arrived at Marieke's house, Constance was confident she had not been followed, and her own tail car confirmed that by radio.

"Feel safer now?" Marieke asked Mbali when they all arrived.

"I do," Mbali said. "I feel a little as if I am in a James Bond flic."

"It was necessary, Madame," Constance said. "I needed to create confusion and minimise the risk. I will be with you for the next week or so, or until the superintendent tells me that it is no longer necessary."

"Thank you, Constance," Marieke said. "That was well done. Let me show everyone where they can sleep. We'll have a car outside, that we'll change every two hours, so that the officers will not get bored and doze off."

"Where can we sleep?" Mbali asked.

"I have two spare bedrooms," Marieke said. "Constance, would you mind the settee?"

"I'll be fine," Constance said. "This settee looks very comfortable, and I'm sure is softer than the mattresses the superintendent and I slept on in the cells at the Kazungula station."

"How have you been, Sergeant?" Marieke asked.

"Busy *Mma*," Constance replied. "But, we have nothing that comes close to this affair."

"Probably true," Marieke agreed. "Do you remember the trip we took to the Linyanti to investigate those headless bodies?"

"I do, *Mma*," Constance said.

"Well, this current case may lead us back to the Linyanti, it seems to all hinge around a Hansie Pretorius who was poaching ivory there twenty years ago."

"Really, *Mma*?" Constance said.

"Truly," Marieke confirmed. "Look after Mbali and the girls for me."

"I will, *Mma*," Constance promised. "I have a riot gun with me, and it is loaded."

"Look out for long shots," Marieke warned. "The commissioner was taken with a single shot to the head from across the road. Don't let the officers outside in the car get complacent, I have reason to believe that Pretorius would not hesitate to just kill them if they got in his way."

"I will be careful, *Mma*," Constance promised. "I may go out tonight, and set some snares and traps to catch unwary visitors."

"Fine, then let's get you all settled," Marieke said. "Which room do you want, Mbali?"

"I think this one would be fine," Mbali said. "And the girls will be just over there?"

"They will," Marieke assured her. "You know where the bathroom is, so I'll start on some dinner, and let you know when it's ready."

Cooperation

Marieke had coffee with Constance early the next morning, and then left Mbali and her daughters sleeping and went to her office to plan her next moves. The police needed to find Pretorius, if indeed it was he doing the killing, before he got out of the country. To her, the most logical ways were to drive west towards Tsabong, and then go south across the Molopo into South Africa, or to drive east, and cross the Limpopo into South Africa. Either river would be easy to cross; the Molopo was dry for most of its western course, and the Limpopo might have more water in it, but it was easily wadable with a Land Rover or similar vehicle. There were enough people looking for Pretorius that if he was indeed in Gaborone, then someone would hear of it, so she decided to leave the searching to the others and focus on trying to find out how he might have entered the country. She saw Inspector Sibanda and asked him how the checks on arrivals and departures were going. He told her that they were almost up to date and had a number of names of visitors who were still in the country. He had a list of all those who had flown in with guns, and had tracked them to various safari hunting camps, three were still in the country, and he had arranged for local officers to visit with them, and the professional hunters to see where they had been, and if it would be possible for them to hie to Gaborone, then hie back to the safari camp, and not be missed. He also commented that there had been no Hansie Pretorius entries at all since the previous November. To Marieke, this suggested that, if they were looking for Pretorius, and he was in the country, then he was using an alias.

A thought occurred to her, how had Pretorius travelled from the border post to Zeerust, or any town for that matter. She told Sergeant Maphosa that she was going to the border post at Kopfontein. At the post, she said hello to the Botswana immigration officers and told them that she was going to walk across the border to talk to the South Africans. On the other side, she went to the office and asked to speak to the officer in charge.

"*Môre*," he said when he came to the desk. "Major Pienaar, what can I do for you?"

"*Goeiemôre*," she replied. "I am pursuing enquiries into several recent shootings, and am trying to track down the movements of people who may have information that would help us. I have been working closely with Lieutenant Colonel van Dyk of Port Elizabeth, as he has a possibly related case."

"I'm not sure how we can help," Pienaar said.

"Last October, we sent a Hansie Pretorius over the border here; he would have been on foot, if you could tell us how he travelled beyond here, it would be most helpful," she said.

"Last October, Pretorius, *ja*, I remember the case, no documents, no money," Pienaar said. "We got him a ride with a transport driver, Hennie, you remember the *ouk's* name?"

"*Ja*, Gert Theron, funny, Gert used to be a regular, but I haven't seen him in months, not since this Pretorius came through here. Pretorius said he had no documents, so we gave him a temporary identity card good for ninety days, and he was supposed to get a new one when he got to Zeerust," Hennie explained.

"Do you know what kind of lorry this Theron has?" Marieke asked.

"Nice Mercedes," Hennie said. "He told me he'd just finished paying it off, so no debts with the banks."

"That help?" Pienaar asked.

"It does," Marieke said. "Thank you. *Tot siens*."

"*Tot siens*," Pienaar said.

Marieke walked back across the border and then drove back to her office. There, she went to see the commissioner and explained where she had been and what she had learned.

"I think you should interview this Theron as soon as possible," he said. "Go to South Africa if you have to, but talk to Theron; he may be able to tell us where Pretorius went. I will instruct Sibanda and his people to look at arrivals and departures for Theron to see if he has been here lately."

"Very good, Sir," Marieke said. Back in her office, she called the police station in Port Elizabeth and asked to speak to Lieutenant Colonel van Dyk.

"*Goeiemôre*," he said. "Back again, do you have something for me?"

"Perhaps," she said. "Have you had any luck tracking down Hansie Pretorius?"

"Not a thing," van Dyk admitted. "He seems to have gone to ground somewhere, but we've no idea where, we can't find an address for him, no bank account, no mailbox, nothing."

"Perhaps we should also try and track down a Gert Theron," Marieke suggested. "He gave Pretorius a ride from Kopfontein to Zeerust when we deported Pretorius. I gather he is a transport driver and has a Mercedes lorry. Is it possible for you to get copies of the identity cards of Hansie Pretorius and Gert Theron?"

"Yes, I'll get onto that," van Dyk promised. "Any leads on who your shooter or shooters are?"

"Not yet," Marieke admitted. "It all seems well planned."

"Oh, there was one other thing," van Dyk said. "The police in Sun City want to talk to a Celia Botha, about a meeting she had arranged with Danie Pretorius, she had made room reservations for Pretorius, paid in cash in advance, then she left, and was overheard saying that she had business out of the country but would be back for their meeting. Well, on the day that Pretorius died, this Celia Botha did come for a meeting, but the local police didn't worry too much because Danie Pretorius ordered extra beer to be delivered to his room after this Celia Botha had left. They still want to talk to her, but they can't find her."

"Interesting," Marieke said. "Was there a description of Celia Botha?"

"*Ja*," he said. "Auburn hair, height 178cm, weight about 67kg, wearing a dark blue business suit, might have been coloured, might not."

"Could be anyone," Marieke commented. "Anything on the coloured from Zeerust?"

"I'm waiting for the Zeerust *ouks* to get back to me on her identity," van Dyk said. "Are you thinking that the coloured you are looking for, and this Celia Botha are the same?"

"Perhaps, would it be inconvenient if I came to see you?" Marieke said. "I would like to go over our case notes on these shootings with you, and what we have on Hansie Pretorius, and on Koos van de Merwe."

"No man, that would be fine," van Dyk said. "But, I'm not sure what you'll learn from us."

"If you can track down Theron, I would like to talk to him," Marieke said.

"Fine, just let me know when you'll be coming," van Dyk said. "Oh, I almost forgot, Danie Pretorius was cremated, so unless your *zwezwe* can survive really high temperatures, we won't be able to confirm that. I know that we can probably find mineral poisons like arsenic and antimony, but we can't manage organics, I really don't know if anyone can yet."

"That's a pity," Marieke said. "Shame he wasn't buried, then we could have exhumed the body, and checked it for *zwezwe*."

"Shame," Andries agreed. "So, see you soon."

Marieke hung up the telephone and then made another call, this time to Johannesburg.

"*Môre*, Sky Charters."

"*Môre Koos, howzit man?*" Marieke said.

"*Marieke, hou gaan dit man*," Koos Strijdom said. "Haven't seen you in a while, how's the flying?"

"I'm doing well," Marieke said. "Tell me, do you have any reason to go to Port Elizabeth in the next day or so?"

"How did you know I was going to PE?" Koos asked. "Have you got me under surveillance? You want to go to PE? How soon?"

"Soon," Marieke said.

"Does this have to do with the rash of shootings you've had in the past few days?" he asked.

"It does," she confirmed.

"Would Monday be soon enough?" he asked. "I have a charter there from Gabs to PE."

"What are you planning?" she asked. "I don't want to be party to any illicit traffic."

"No man," Koos assured her. "I was asked this morning if I would take some medical equipment to PE. It was going to be a boring ride."

"Why don't they just send it on scheduled Air Botswana and SAA flights, or send it by road?" Marieke asked.

"Because the last time they did, it didn't get there in one piece," Koos explained. "I'm flying to Gabs Sunday afternoon, and will load up the equipment, then I'm leaving at five thirty on Monday to fly to PE. Do you want to come?"

"Yes," Marieke said. "When would we get to PE?"

"We'd be there by nine," Koos said. "Maybe a few minutes after nine. I've already made arrangements for customs clearance at PE, so we'd do immigration at the same time."

"I'll be at the airport at five," Marieke promised.

"See you there," Koos said. "When do you want to come back?"

"I'm not sure," she said. "It depends on what I learn, and whether or not I can interview certain people, but probably a few days."

"Okay, well, when you are ready to come back, call me, and I'll see what I am doing, and if I can run you back, or if you'll have to fly back commercial," he said.

"Thank you, Koos, you're a saviour," she said. "Until Monday."

"Until Monday," he replied.

Marieke then called the police station in Port Elizabeth, and talked to Lieutenant Colonel van Dyk, and gave him her arrival time into Port Elizabeth. He said that he would be there when she arrived. She then went to talk to the commissioner and told him that she was going to Port Elizabeth, and why.

"Do you think this Theron can tell you anything useful?" he asked.

"I do, Sir," she replied. "And, if I can work out who this Celia Botha is that the South African police want to talk to, I suspect that she may have had a part in the death of Danie Pretorius."

"Good hunting," the commissioner said. "Keep Sergeant Maphosa informed of your doings."

"I will, Sir," she promised. She went back to her office, and put together a file of things that she felt would be useful, including the fingerprint cards, and pictures of Hansie Pretorius taken just before he was shown over the border, she also got the report from their lab on the tool marks on the suppressors, perhaps the South Africans could find where they were made, and by whom. She also dug out the old files on Hansie Pretorius, van de Merwe, and Danie Pretorius. She made copies of the relevant pages that she planned to pass on to Andries van Dyk. Then, it was time for lunch. Her eating habits had become poor of late, with sporadic meals, hurriedly grabbed while she did other things. Lunch, she decided to get at home. She was gratified to see a police vehicle discreetly parked so that they could keep the house under surveillance. She parked and walked back to them, and suggested that they take a lunch break while she was there. In the house, Constance had lunch prepared and just set another place at the table for Marieke.

"Have you found the man yet, Auntie Marieke?" Nandi asked.

"Not yet," Marieke admitted. "But, we are pursuing several lines of enquiry. I leave for South Africa early Monday morning."

"So, you think it could be Pretorius?" Mbali asked.

"He is certainly on my suspect list," Marieke said. "I'm also looking for a Gert Theron, who is a transport driver, and a Celia Botha."

"Gert Theron," Mbali said. "The name is familiar, yes I know, he used to bring parts for Jan. We got a letter from him late last year telling us that he was no longer in the business, so we had to find another haulier to bring parts from Cape Town. Who's Celia Botha?"

"I don't know, and the South Africans don't know, but she was supposed to have meetings with Danie Pretorius the day his body was found. So, the SAP want to talk to her, but they can't find her," Marieke explained. "Do you have an address for Gert Theron?"

"I'm sure we do at the garage," Mbali said. "After lunch, I'll call and get it for you from the accountant."

Marieke went back to her office armed with information about Gert Theron, that she immediately sent by Fax to Lieutenant Colonel van Dyk in Port Elizabeth. It seemed that Theron lived in

Kuilsrivier, a small town to the east of Cape Town. She found Inspector Sibanda, and he had no news yet about arrivals and departures for Theron. She then briefed Sergeant Maphosa on things and told him that he should come with her to the five o'clock briefing with the commissioner, and that for perhaps a few days the next week, he would have to take her place.

Saturday, Marieke checked with the station and told them that she would be working from home until the 5:00 pm meeting. If anything of note occurred during the day, they should, of course, let her know, but otherwise, she would prefer not to be disturbed. At about eight, her guests all surfaced, and she joined them, and Constance for breakfast.

"Have you caught the man yet, Auntie?" Nandi asked.

"Not yet," Marieke said. "We're not certain who we are chasing yet, but the whole station is working on the case, and the commissioner said that all leave was cancelled for the next month."

"Does that mean that you won't be coming to the bush with us?" Mbali asked.

"I may take you there, but I suspect that he will want me back here with the rest of the team," Marieke said. "I will be sorry to miss the time in the bush, but if we catch him quickly enough, perhaps I can still come."

"What are you going to do today?" Nandi asked.

"Washing," Marieke said. "I need some clean clothes."

"We can do that," Mbali said. "Just sort out what you need washed, and we will take care of it."

"Thank you," Marieke said. She went to her bedroom, collected all the washing that was piled up or scattered about, and dumped it into the arms of Mbali. "You're sure?" she asked.

"I'm sure," Mbali reassured her. "Go, and look at that board you have set up in the garage, and work out who it was, and how to find them!"

"I will," Marieke promised.

"When you go to South Africa on Monday, how long will you be gone?" Mbali asked.

"Probably only a day or so," Marieke thought. "I leave at five thirty on Monday morning, and may be back that night or on Tuesday. Constance will be here with you, and if there are any issues, she knows where to get help."

"Well, I hope you learn something," Mbali said. "But, I think it's more likely that they will learn from you."

"I doubt that," Marieke said. "I'm sure that they've got more experience in this kind of thing than we do."

"Maybe, but that doesn't mean that they're good at solving cases," Mbali pointed out. "So, go, and think while we wash, and iron!"

Marieke went to her garage, where she had set up an incident board, duplicating the one in her office. It had pictures on it of the three victims, and then a picture of Hansie Pretorius, their only viable suspect at the moment. She had also pasted up the names of Koos van de Merwe, Danie Pretorius, and General de Villiers, then she added the army driver, Nicolaas Smit, the carjacking victim, Adams, and the two butchers from Zeerust, and Gert Theron, also as victims, and then an empty box with a question mark in it for possible other victims that they did not know about. That one man could have successfully killed all six of the other poachers or their buyer, and the others, and not be caught was a testament to his abilities, so someone not to be underestimated. She wished she had talked more to Jan about what kind of person Hansie had been, but she did remember snippets. Hansie had not been very studious at school; he had done his military service, but without any great honours. He had organised the poaching expedition well, but had changed during the trip, which led her to wonder if he had a split personality, or something of that ilk. It was apparent that he was using an alias, perhaps more than one. To avoid detection for so long, he had to be posing as at least one other person. She broke from her musings for lunch and then spent the afternoon working in her yard, trimming and cleaning, so that the place looked a little more lived in.

She went to the office for the 5:00 pm meeting, but that brought nothing new. No new information from interviews or from the forensic people. The commissioner was frustrated by the lack of progress, but even he had to admit that they were very much in the dark and had little to go on. All the routine investigations were plodding along slowly, with immigration records being checked and cross-checked, local hotels were being questioned about guests, and anything else that anyone could think of was being looked at. But this was very much mundane police work, and it took time. Sooner or later, something might crop up that would lead to more definite progress, but for now, it was a slow process. The addition of the Theron name to the mix meant that the teams had had to go back over previous work to be sure that they had not missed it. Before, they had been looking for Pretorius and may have missed Theron. The last item that the commissioner had on his list was to let everyone know that there would be no scheduled meeting on Sunday, but that if something came up, they would all be called in for a briefing.

Sunday was a welcome day off, and Marieke suggested a day out to the Yacht Club. She suggested that they drive there and then take a boat to the club. Mbali and the girls all agreed that this was a splendid idea, so after breakfast, they all went to the club, including Constance. Mbali was a member, so they could use the facilities, so Nandi and Khanyo took Constance out in a boat for a sailing lesson. Constance looked around and approved. The reservoir was big enough that it would be a long shot from the shore, and the boat was constantly moving, so it would be a hard target, unless a shooter was really expert. Mbali spent the time talking about Jan and what their early life in Gaborone had been like. At least in Gaborone, there was not the constant threat of harassment or arrest because they were a mixed-race couple, unlike South Africa. Mbali did talk a little about the assignations she had had with Jan in the flat in Kempton Park, and how she had always been really nervous coming and going, lest someone see her and ask what she was doing there. She laughed about their first meeting in Swaziland, when Jan had won money in the casino, and had proceeded to spend a lot of it on her; they had gone through 3,000 Rand in the weekend. She told Marieke that when they first met in the bar, there was a spark that passed between them, and she knew that this was the one. It had been a weekend of passion, and she had been a little afraid that she would never hear from him again, just another *Boertjie* sampling the forbidden. So, she had been delighted when he had called her at the bank where she worked, and they had quickly arranged to meet. After that, whenever he could get a weekend off from the army, they met, sometimes in Kempton Park, and sometimes in the wilds of the Blyde River Canyon, where he knew of a camping place that was off the beaten track. It had been a happy time, but a stressful time, because of the risk, so when she had moved to Gaborone, and he had joined her, they had been able to enjoy themselves without that fear. Marieke asked her if Jan had told her much about Hansie, and all that Mbali could recall was that Jan said that Hansie was never one for the books at school, or in the army, that he had a fondness for coloured girls, but only as sex objects, he had shown no inclinations to get married, and was saving up for a trip to Britain to see castles, why castles, she had no idea, but he had said that he wanted to visit old castles. When the girls and Constance came back, Mbali changed the subject to food, and Nandi volunteered to do the cooking, which was a typical South African *braai*, lots of meat, and not much green. But, once in a while, it was fine, just not as a steady diet. When they finally got home, it was quite late, so Marieke excused herself and went off to bed; she had to be up early in the morning.

At five on Monday morning, Marieke was at the airport and found Koos in the general aviation area.

"*Môre*," Koos said as Marieke joined him.

"*Môre*," she replied. "I don't see your Cessna out there on the tarmac."

"Not flying that today," Koos said. "We have the Twin Otter over there today, needed the size for the load we have. Ever flown one?"

"No," she said.

"Nice planes," he said. "Great for STOL fields and bush strips. Not that we need the short take-off features here, the strip is much longer than anything we need. This trip will be VFR; there's no IFR vectors for Gabs to PE. I checked the weather, and it looks good for VFR, no clouds anywhere, visibility is as good as it gets. Come, let's get you aboard. I'll finish out my ground pre-flight checklist, and then you can run me through the engine start checklist."

"Whose plane is this?" she asked.

"It's mine," he said. "I picked it up recently in a bankruptcy sale. It used to belong to an exploration company, they fitted it out with the best nav equipment you could buy, and with long-range tanks, so it has much better range and endurance than a factory Twin, it's pretty new as well, built in 1987."

"Will you sell your Skymaster?" she asked.

"Maybe, do you want to buy it?" he asked.

"It depends, how much, and what shape is it in?" she countered.

"I'll get you the maintenance logs, flight logs, and the latest C Check data," he promised. "Ready?"

"Ready," she said.

Koos finished his walk around, checked the tie-downs on the load in the back, and then joined Marieke in the cockpit. He handed her a clipboard and made himself comfortable.

"Parking brake set?" she read off.

"Parking brake set," he confirmed, reaching down to check the brake.

"Throttle levers to idle?" she read next.

"Throttle levers to idle," he confirmed, tapping the throttle levers above their heads.

"Propellers to feathered?" she asked.

"Propellers to feathered," he confirmed tapping the propeller controls., and, so it went through the rest of the 25 additional items he had listed, until they got to actually start, and run the engines, each of which he ran up, and down until he was satisfied that they were functioning properly. When both engines were running nicely, he talked to the tower and got clearance to taxi out to the runway. Once out on the runway, he did a last check of the flight control surfaces and then called for clearance to take off. That given, they started off down the runway. At 90 knots, he pulled back the stick, and up they went. Koos climbed out and then made a long turn towards the east around the outskirts of the town, eventually landing up heading south. Once at cruise altitude and speed, he handed over the controls to Marieke, opened up some coffee and a packet of sandwiches.

"How long have you had this Twin Otter?" Marieke asked.

"About six months," Koos said. "I've had it in the shop for a thorough review of all systems, and a look at structural integrity, but it looks good, De Havilland does a good job, and, as I said, this one's pretty new."

"Had you flown one before you bought this?" Marieke asked.

"No, but I went to Canada about five months ago, and went through a whole training school on this type," Koos explained.

"Oh, that's why we didn't see for a while," Marieke commented. "We thought you were just avoiding us."

"No man," Koos laughed. "I was just making sure I knew what I was doing. It was winter in Canada, so it was cold. We think it gets cold in Jo'burg, but we've no idea what cold really is. I had to buy all kinds of new clothes, which I'll hopefully never have to wear again. They did send me to one place that was warmer, and was really interesting, there's a small island in the Caribbean, Saba, it's a Dutch territory, they land Twins there on a 1300 ft runway, screw up, and you're in the briny."

"That's not very long," Marieke commented.

"No," Koos agreed. "But they've been using Twins there since 1965, so they've got experience. I did it a few times with an instructor pilot; you have to be really jacked up and focused. Pretty little island, just tourists though, no real industry or anything anymore, there used to be sugar, and distilleries, now they are setting up a medical school there, odd place for a medical school, but at least the weather's good, unless you get a hurricane."

"Where does our route of flight take us?" she asked.

"We're on a heading of 181, not quite due south, but close, it'll take us between Kimberley and Bloemfontein, then farther south close to Cradock, and Somerset east, then straight on down to PE," he said. "Weather looks good, not too much traffic, so should be a good trip. So, who are you after for the shootings?"

"We have a suspect list," she said. "But, it's been hard to link the three shootings, perhaps they are not linked at all, and this is random chance."

"But, as a good cop, you don't believe in that much randomness, any more than I do," he commented. "Someone has an axe to grind."

"That is a possibility," she agreed.

"So, I heard that your friend Melisende is coming back," Koos said.

"She is," Marieke confirmed. "She should arrive soon, and if I can get time off, we'll fly up to the Linyanti to Will and Bridget's camp."

"*Ja*, they told me you had a booking, he said. "Tell me more about her."

"About who," Marieke temporised.

"Your friend Melisende," Koos said.

"Oh, she's French," Marieke said.

"I know that," Koos said. "Are you two an item?"

"What?" Marieke asked.

"Are you two an item?" Koos repeated. "It stands to reason, the only time I see you really relaxed and happy is when she comes to visit."

"And who have you shared this observation with?" Marieke asked.

"Not a soul," Koos promised. "I decided it was your business, and there was no need for anyone else to learn it from me."

"Thank you," Marieke said, relieved.

"So, are you two an item?" he asked again.

"You seem to have decided that we are," Marieke said.

"True," he agreed. "Be careful, not everyone has your best interests at heart."

"And you do?" she asked.

"I do," he confirmed. "I thought there might one day be something between us, but when I saw you two together last year, then it was obvious to me that there is only one person in your life, and she lives a long way away."

"What about you?" Marieke asked.

"Oh, I've dated a few stewardesses from the different airlines, but nothing serious," he said. "My *ouma* is the hell in because she wants to see me married with *lighties* before she dies, but she'll get over it."

"There isn't a nice *Boere meisie* out there for you?" Marieke asked.

"You rather ruined that for me," he laughed. "When I saw you in the *dambo* in your *brookies* carrying a shotgun, that did it for me."

"I'd rather you forget that incident," she said. "My boss gave me hell for it, and told me that it should have been beneath my dignity to go wading in a *dambo* in my underclothes. Anyway, the current regime in South Africa would frown upon us getting together, I'm officially classified as Coloured."

"Maybe that will change after we have elections," he said.

"You think there will be elections?" she asked.

"Sure, sure," he said. "ANC will win for sure, and Mandela will be the next president."

"How do you feel about that?" she asked.

"No man, it's fine," he said. "It's about time. I like Mandela, there's one *ou* who I could follow. I met him once, liked the *ou*. There will be those who will try and upset things, but you can't hold down the population forever. We *Boertjies* have been living in a dream world on borrowed time. Okay, that's the cement works at Slurry, so look out for the next one at Bodibe."

"How do you know it's a cement works?" she asked.

"I do know some geography," he laughed. "And mines, and quarries make good landmarks along any route, they're hard to miss. But you need to get to know them, or you could see one, and think it's another, like at Bodibe coming up, there'll be one on the right, and one on the left. After the mines and quarries, look out for roads, railways, rivers, power lines, and dams. We're going to go over two dams, one at Bloemhof and the other the Vervoerd Dam."

"I've used the mine at Orapa a few times to make sure I've my bearings right," Marieke said. "But, Botswana lacks significant landmarks."

"That's when you've got to go for geography and geology," he said. "Look for features that are easy to see from the air, but not so easy to see on the ground. You can sometimes see them like stripes across the ground. Then there's the pans, and areas like the Okavango, easy to see from the air. But finding individual strips in the Okavango can be tough. I was on a trip once with another *ou*, and he couldn't find the strip, we could hear him circling, and finally managed to talk him in, *yerra*, but his *ouks* were only green when they got on the ground! If we hadn't managed to talk him in, he was going to have to go back to Maun for more fuel."

"What about individual *kopjies* or hills?" she asked.

"If you know where they are and can recognise them, then, yes," he agreed.

Conversation went on, back and forth, until they approached the Hendrik Vervoerd Dam, then Koos warned Marieke that it could get bumpy as they flew over the mountains of the Karoo and the coastal ranges. They were fortunate in that the weather cooperated, and, apart from a few bumps, it was not too bad. Koos told Marieke that it could get really rough at times and that it was wise to carefully check the latest weather information before flying through the area. As they descended and approached Port Elizabeth. Koos let Marieke stay at the controls, giving her instructions as needed, while he talked to the air traffic controllers and then the tower at Port Elizabeth. Once on the ground, they taxied to the general aviation hardstand and went through the shutdown procedures. An immigration officer, and an obviously senior South African Police officer, came walking out to the plane.

"*Môre*," he said. "Assistant Superintendent Englebrecht?"

"*Môre*," she replied. "I am, and this is Koos Strijdom, my pilot and instructor from Gaborone."

"Lieutenant Colonel van Dyk," he said. "Welcome to Port Elizabeth. If you'll excuse us, Koos, we have business to attend to. Inspector, if you'll just take care of stamping the Superintendent's passport?" Formalities were quickly taken care of, and Marieke started to go with Lieutenant Colonel van Dyk, then she turned back, thanked Koos, and said goodbye.

"*Tot siens* Marieke," Koos said. "If you need a ride back, call me, and I'll see what I can do."

"Thank you, Koos, I'll call if I need a ride back," Marieke said. "Colonel, where do we go?"

"*Ja*, this way," he said. He handed her a folder, then led the way to his car. "We've some distance to go," he said. "We're going straight out to Port Alfred. You'll see from the items in the folder there that Gert Theron and Hansie Pretorius are one and the same."

"The border guards were clear that Gert Theron gave Hansie Pretorius a ride, so does that suggest that Pretorius took over the identity of Theron?" Marieke asked.

"It looks that way," van Dyk agreed. "I'm Andries. By the way, I gather you're Marieke. We're trying to connect Pretorius and Theron to a suspicious death near Worcester, sometime around the 23rd to 26th of October. Theron, if it is Theron, got a new identity card shortly after that, and Pretorius got one in November. We did not connect the two until we had copies of both in hand."

"Could we stop somewhere so that I can call my office and let them know this?" Marieke asked.

"I did that already," Andries said. "I talked to your Commissioner Boateng, and he said that he would alert all his officers and the border patrol to be on the lookout for the man calling himself Gert Theron. It also seems that Theron, or Pretorius posing as Theron, recently sold his place near Kuilsrivier. He took cash for the payment. He had access to a Mercedes car, I gave the licence number to your commissioner. We've been onto hotels in Port Alfred, and a Gert Theron stayed at the Halyard Hotel, which just happens to overlook the marina where Koos van de Merwe kept his boat. He checked out the day before van de Merwe went missing, but I want to talk to the hotel staff. We haven't done anything about looking for prints or other items. It seems to us that enough time has passed that if there had been anything there, it would have been long either wiped down as part of routine cleaning or smudged over with subsequent prints. The manager also told me that they repainted the room and replaced the carpets a month ago, so anything that might have been there is also gone."

"Interesting about the Mercedes," Marieke said. "One was spotted near our first crime scene, I suppose it could be the same one, or perhaps not, they are not uncommon in Gab's. What colour was it?"

"White, I believe," Andries said.

Travel time between Port Elizabeth and Port Alfred is normally about 90 minutes, but with the aid of sirens and lights, Andries did it in a little over 60 minutes. He drove straight to the Halyard Hotel. There, they met with the local police captain and the hotel manager, who had the records that indicated when Theron had stayed. Marieke asked to see the room where Theron had stayed, and they all trooped up the stairs to the room. There, the view of the marina was apparent, and Marieke asked Andries if he knew which cottage and slip was that of van de Merwe. He pointed it out, and she nodded. It would have been the perfect vantage point to keep track of people coming and going from the cottage. The question was, did Hansie know that van de Merwe had a slip there, or was it just chance that he saw him. Andries thanked the manager, and then he and Marieke left. On their way out, Marieke stopped to look at a map of the coast that was hanging on the wall in the hotel lobby.

"Where was van de Merwe found?" she asked Andries.

"He was found here," Andries replied, pointing to a place on the map. "And his boat was found here."

"What's the current drift in this area?" Marieke asked.

"It follows a line in this direction," Andries said, tracing a line with his finger on the map.

"So, if the drift pattern is that way, then it suggests that van de Merwe was killed somewhere east of here, and his body and the boat drifted back towards Port Alfred," she commented.

"I agree," Andries said. "We've been trying to work out how he worked this."

"So, was Gert Theron in the army with Koos van de Merwe?" Marieke asked as they left the hotel. "Or did he just meet him at the border post at Kopfontein?"

"We're waiting for that information from the army," Andries said. "As usual, they're chary with sharing information, seem to think it's a big state secret. We've asked the army to check their records to see if Pretorius and van de Merwe served together. I've also asked the *ouks* in the Pretoria police to check hotels to see if Gert Theron stayed there around the time that de Villiers was killed. We'll see if they're more cooperative. What's your theory?"

"I'm speculating that Pretorius gets out of prison, he's bent on revenge, so he sets about killing off all those who were involved in the ivory job that went wrong, and for which he did twenty years," she replied. "He first of all kills Theron, and assumes his identity, let me guess, Theron was not married, and no close family."

"Right, lived on his own in Kuilsrivier, known locally as a loner," Andries confirmed.

"So, Hansie takes over Gert's business, sells the lorry, and gets out of the haulier business. The proceeds from the lorry must have been enough for a while," she suggested.

"We checked, and yes, the lorry was sold, in late October, he got 125,000 Rand for it," Andries said.

"How did Hansie find van de Merwe?" Marieke asked.

"We know that a man calling himself Piet Cillie was in Bloemfontein asking about van de Merwe a few days before he was killed. I've been on to the Bloem police to see if any Gert Theron or Hansie Pretorius stayed at any hotels there," Andries said. "There was a barman in Bloem who said that he had been asked about van de Merwe, and he'd told the *ou* who asked that he thought that van de Merwe lived on the south coast, and sold cars."

"So, Hansie drives south to the first big south coast town, East London, and starts asking?" Marieke suggested.

"That seems reasonable," Andries agreed. "Let's go to the station here, and get them to call East London, and have some enquiries made." They made a quick stop at the local police station where Andries called East London, and put things in motion, to start with car dealers, and find out if anyone had come in asking about van de Merwe.

"Okay, what would you like to do next?" Andries asked Marieke.

"Can we take a drive along the coast road towards East London?" she asked.

"*Ja,*" he said. They drove out of town along the road east. When they reached a sign that indicated access to the Rufare River, she asked Andries to turn off and head towards the sea. It was the first road that led that way that was far enough away from houses to not be visible easily. They drove through wooded areas until they hit the sand hills, then Andries stopped, and they both got out.

"What do you expect to find?" Andries asked.

"I'm not sure," Marieke admitted. "But, if Pretorius killed van de Merwe, and then jumped overboard, leaving the boat the drift back to Port Alfred, he probably came ashore along the coast here. He would have had his car hidden here to get away without being seen."

"Okay, but how did he get from here to Port Alfred to go fishing with van de Merwe?" Andries asked.

"Good question," Marieke agreed. "Perhaps this will tell us," she said, pointing to some old tracks. "A car was parked here, probably overnight. My reading of the tracks is that it was a Land Cruiser or Land Rover, and something like a moped or motorbike was ridden out of here."

"You can tell that from the tracks, they're old, and not very distinct," Andries said, sceptically. "This murder took place months ago."

"No man," she said. "It's clear enough to me, a car parked there, and a motorbike ridden down there. I read the tracks as two journeys out, and one back, the trees shelter the tracks from much of the rain, and it's also sheltered from the wind here, so tracks will stay a long time, until they eventually either get ridden over or the long-term rain, and wind rubs them out. But the tracks are there all right; if you get down here, you can see them quite clearly. Probably, he did a test run of how long it would take to get to Port Alfred. Look, here's what was left of a fire, and here are some scraps of paper."

"Let me see that," Andries said. He studied the paper and then said, "*Magtig*, you may be right, this is the remnant of a receipt for a moped bought in East London last October. So, he goes to East London, probably the day before he's supposed to go fishing, buys a moped, comes back here, camps overnight, then rides the moped into town, leaves it, and goes fishing. I think East London because he wouldn't want to attract attention here, or in PE, where van de Merwe lives. After he kills van de Merwe, he swims back to shore, gets his car, and goes. The moped he sacrifices, he's not using his money, just what he got from the sale of Theron's lorry. Probably left the moped where he knew it would get stolen. We need to get the East London *ouks* to do a shop-to-shop for moped sellers. I can't tell from this paper who the seller was."

"I think you could also check those places that sell marine charts," she suggested. "If I were planning this, I would want to have charts of the area so that I could see where rocks and reefs were, and what the current drifts were like. I would have driven the boat far enough east of here to be able to jump overboard, and let the current take me back to here."

"*Ja*," Andries said. "I agree. I wonder if he, as Gert Theron, bought a new car at about the same time that he sold the Mercedes lorry? I should get the *ouks* in Cape Town to check registrations in October and November under the names of Gert Theron and Hansie Pretorius. Anything more you can see?"

"Sorry, no," she said.

"Let's get back to PE and review what we have," he suggested. "And then let's prod the *ouks* in East London, and Cape Town for results."

Back in Port Elizabeth, Andries checked with the vehicle registration people and learned that a Gert Theron had bought a used Land Cruiser in October the previous year. He got the licence number, and also the number of the Mercedes car that had belonged to Theron, and Marieke immediately called her office.

"Botswana Police," Sergeant Maphosa said when he answered the telephone.

"*Dumela*, Sergeant," Marieke said.

"*Dumela,* Madame," he replied. "What can I do?"

"Check if a Land Cruiser or a Mercedes car with South African licence plates have entered Botswana recently," she said. "I'll give you the numbers."

"Thank you, Madame," Maphosa said. "Inspector Sibanda told me that a Gert Theron has entered Botswana twice recently. The first time was the 23rd of March, he left on the 25th of March, the second time was on the 30th of March, and as far as we know is still here."

"Check on the vehicle he used to enter the country if you can," Marieke instructed.

"Yes, Madame," Maphosa said. "Is there a telephone where we can find you?"

"Use the number on my pad for the police station in Port Elizabeth," she instructed.

"Very good, Madame," Maphosa said.

"You know," Andries said when Marieke had finished her call. "This *ou* must be pretty *slim*, van de Merwe's wife tells us that her husband meets an army *china* on Friday, and on Sunday when they go fishing, and he is killed, Pretorius has a plan quickly, it looks like he's checked out a place to hide, bought transport, and who knows what else, and put his plan into action, all in the space of a day or so. He's got to have a plan to get out of Botswana, if he's still there, and probably out of South Africa."

"I agree," Marieke said. "We have circulated his picture to all the border crossings and police stations, but, like you, I suspect he has a plan, and that plan probably does not include driving through any police post."

"If I were him, I would have left a *bakkie* on the South African side of the border somewhere, I'd drive close to it on your side, and walk over," Andries thought.

"That's a distinct possibility," Marieke agreed. Further discussion was halted when the telephone rang, and Andries answered it.

"It's for you," he said, handing the telephone to Marieke.

"*Dumela,*" she said.

"*Dumela Mma*," Sergeant Maphosa said. "We have details on the vehicles that Theron used when he entered the country. He came first in the Land Cruiser that you gave me the number of, the second time it was in the Mercedes car with South African plates. When he left on the 25th, he left with a Patricia Wilson, they were in a Toyota Crown, new, that belonged to her. The border post officer remembers her because she arrived on the morning of the 25th and left the same day, with Theron. Theron said that his Land Cruiser had broken down, and he had left it for repairs. We are checking all the garages in Gaborone to see if any Land Cruiser was left for repairs. I will send by Fax the licence numbers of the cars of Theron, and the one for Mrs Wilson."

"Thank you, Sergeant," Marieke said. "Please call again after the 5:00 pm briefing, and let me know if there is anything new."

"Yes, Madame," Maphosa said.

"So, perhaps we have a clue as to the identity of Celia Botha," Marieke remarked to Andries. "Gert Theron was collected in Gabs on the 25th of March by a Patricia Wilson, she drives a Toyota Crown, the number of which should be coming through now on the Fax."

"I'll check this out," Andries said. "So, this is the Toyota Crown for Wilson, and these are the Land Cruiser and Mercedes of Theron." His thoughts were interrupted by another telephone call. He listened, and made a few notes then hung up, and looked at Marieke.

"Catching this *ou* is going to be hard," he said. "The Cape *ouks* have been out to Kuilsrivier, we knew Theron sold it recently, it seems he took 325,000 Rand cash for it as a quick sale, and the new owners have already bulldozed the buildings, and are starting to clear the land for some new houses."

"*Magtig*," she said.

"*Magtig*," he agreed. "I wonder who Patricia Wilson is?"

"Let's presume that he didn't just meet someone and recruit them as an accessory," Marieke suggested. "Given that Pretorius was away for a long time, that suggests that he knew her long ago, possibly in Zeerust, because according to Lamprecht, apart from time in the army, Pretorius did not travel much away from Zeerust, except to Lobatse to the abattoir there."

"So, I should get on to the Zeerust *ouks*, and find out if they know any Patricia Wilson," Andries thought.

"Do you have any more information on the shootings in Pretoria?" Marieke asked.

"I'm waiting," Andries said. "I did hear from a friend of mine that they now think that the three shootings on that day were all related. They found matches on the rifling marks on all the bullets. Apparently, that was just luck; one of the lab techs happened to be looking at them all at the same time and made the connection. So, now they're confused, no suspects, and they've nothing really to go on."

"What kind of gun was used?" Marieke asked.

"A 9mm," Andries said. "Not dropped at the scene. If I were the shooter, that gun would be at the bottom of a river by now." They were not to know, but the gun was in fact at the bottom of a river, several rivers in fact. After the shootings, the receiver had gone into the Vaal, the barrel into the Orange, and the magazine and suppressor into the Dwyka.

"Have you suggested to them a link to Hansie Pretorius?" Marieke asked.

"I tried, but they didn't want to hear about it, said it was too old, and that there was no evidence that de Villiers would ever be mixed up in ivory poaching or smuggling. It's going to have to go higher in the chain before anyone directs a real investigation," Andries complained.

"Tell me, back to Gert Theron for a minute, do you know if he had a machine shop at his place?" Marieke asked.

"Don't know," Andries admitted. "Why?"

"Because in our first case, the shooter used a 9mm with a suppressor, and in the second case he, or someone else, used van de Merwe's rifle, also with a suppressor, and the tool marks on the two suppressors confirm that they were made on the same lathe, and further analysis shows that they were made for the same bar stock," Marieke explained. "That reminds me, I need to check with Francistown and see if there is a machine shop at the prison that is used in the rehabilitation programs. Perhaps, Pretorius learned machining skills at our expense, and then used those skills to further his own agenda."

"I'll get onto the Cape Town *ouks*, and see if they know anything," Andries promised. They were interrupted when an officer came in and handed Andries a file. Andries looked through it quickly and then gave it to Marieke. She quickly scanned it and handed it back.

"So, our first gun belonged to General de Villiers," she said.

"*Ja*," he agreed. "An old army *china* of mine got the information quietly, as the army were playing silly buggers, and shutting off all enquiries about de Villiers. It seems de Villiers was given the Beretta 92S by an Italian Air Force officer who was here with the Aermacchi people when they were here setting up the production of the Impala."

"So, that explains why an Italian military model showed up here, it also possibly links your de Villiers case to our cases, but only through the gun, and thereby probably the shooter, it's hard to see any connection between a South African Army general, and a solicitor from Gaborone," Marieke said. "It does raise another question, I thought de Villiers was in army intelligence, why was he mixed up in an air force project?"

"Don't know," Andries said. "I'll see if I can find out, and we need to find out if de Villiers had the gun in his possession when he was killed, or if he had sold it, lost it or had it stolen before his death."

"Is there anything else we should discuss while I'm here?" Marieke asked.

"I don't think so," Andries said. "I'll give you a copy of this report, just stay mum about where it came from."

"I can do that," Marieke promised. "Would you check for me, if you can find out, who Pretorius associated with when he ran his shop in Zeerust?"

"I'll get hold of the Zeerust *ouks* and see what we can dig up," Andries promised.

"I should think about getting back to Gabs, there's nothing more I can add here. You've got it all well in hand," Marieke said.

"I don't know about that," Andries said. "Look, I don't want to be rude or prying, but how does a Marieke Englebrecht get to be in the Botswana Police?"

"My dad was an Afrikaner, and my mom was Motswana," she explained. "That didn't sit well with the *ouks* in Pretoria, so they lived in South West, and I went to *uni* in France, and then went to live in Botswana. My folks died a few years ago when their *bakkie* hit a landmine in South West."

"I'm sorry," he said. "I lost a brother in South West, landmine as well, he was in the army there. Maybe after we've had elections, the rules will get changed. My dad had an uncle who lived out near Mariental. He lived with this black *tannie*, my dad visited quite a few times, and he really liked the *tannie*. I never met her, but from his stories, I wish I had."

"They may change the laws, but it will take time to change the culture and the prejudices," Marieke said.

"*Ja*," he sighed. "Maybe in my lifetime, we'll see. Anyway, when do you want to leave? We can get you a flight this evening as far as Jo'burg?"

"I'll do that," Marieke said. "Then I'll get a flight to Gabs tomorrow."

"Okay, let's see what we can fix up," he said. He called a number, talked to someone, and then told Marieke that she was booked on an SAA flight to Johannesburg that evening.

"Who do I pay?" she asked.

"No man," he said. "My friend at SAA owes me a few favours, and he fixed you up with a jump seat ride in the cockpit. I saw that you were at the controls when you came in, and checked, and know that you have a pilot's licence. So, you'll get the jump seat ride to Jo'burg."

"Thank you," she said. "I will stay in touch after I get back to Gabs, it's possible that Pretorius may already be back in South Africa."

"*Ja*," he agreed. "I need to do some work still to piece together the van de Merwe case, and we have a lot to check out for the de Villiers murder, and the other Pretorius."

"Don't forget the others, the Pretorius Butchers *ouks*, and the others in Pretoria," Marieke reminded him.

"I won't," he said. "The challenge is going to be getting cooperation from the different jurisdictions. I may have to go over everyone's head and talk to the chief in Pretoria. I happen to know him from past cases, and he will listen to me. Anyway, let me run you to the airport and introduce you to James Butler, who'll be your pilot tonight."

At the airport, Andries introduced Marieke to James Butler and his co-pilot, Albert Nelmapius. They had both flown for the airline for over ten years, and flew the Port Elizabeth to Johannesburg route regularly. The flight was actually a continuation of a flight from Cape Town, so the time on the ground was short, and James had had to come into the terminal to meet Marieke and walk her out to the plane, a Boeing 737. Marieke had never been in the cockpit of a jet and was intrigued by what she saw. It seemed to her at first glance that there were far more gauges and switches than on any plane she had flown. But, as she looked over the panel, she recognised most things, all the gauges and instruments were what she would expect, there really were no more than on the Cessna Skymaster she had flown or on the Twin Otter, she had come down on earlier that day. James showed her how to pull down the jump seat and strap herself in, then, when he had clearance from the tower, he taxied out to take off. They took off to the east, and then circled back and around, gaining altitude as they went. The ground rose quickly from the coast to the central plateau at over 5,000 ft, so it was necessary to get up as soon as possible.

Marieke enjoyed the relatively short flight from Port Elizabeth to Johannesburg, a little over one and a half hours. She chatted to the flight crew, and they wanted to know how she knew Andries van

Dyk, and she told them that she was working on a case that related to one he was working on.

"So, you're a Botswana cop?" James asked.

"I am," Marieke confirmed.

"What rank?" Albert asked.

"Assistant Superintendent," Marieke replied.

"What's that the equivalent of here?" James asked.

"I think it would be major," Marieke said.

"I'll bet your case has something to do with that *ou* who was washed up near Port Alfred," James said. "Andries was getting nowhere with that one. Didn't I read in the paper that you'd had some shootings in Gabs just now?"

"We have had," Marieke admitted.

"I heard from some *ouks* I know in Pretoria that they'd had three there as well," Albert added. "You remember that *döes* de Villiers from the army days, he got popped."

"Who did it?" James asked.

"They don't know," Albert said. "But, I heard that they're trying to keep a lid on things, to avoid exposing what de Villiers got up to when he was in Intelligence."

"Oh, you mean, when he was smuggling arms to *ouks* in the Congo, Angola, and Mozambique?" James asked.

"*Ja*," Albert said. "There's probably a list a mile long of people who would be happy to see him gone."

"Did he ever smuggle anything else, apart from arms?" Marieke asked.

"*Ja, ja*," Albert said. "Ivory, gold, diamonds, you name it, the army did some cursory investigations, but he covered his tracks well, and they never found anything definite. I only heard about it from a mate who used to fly stuff to Angola and pick up diamonds there. He used all kinds of false names, I think Smith was one he used a lot. Imagine a *regte Boertjie* coming in, and saying he was Mr Smith, he'd been better off calling himself van de Merwe, at least that's almost as common here as Smith."

"I heard he used this Lockheed Constellation to transport cargo," James said. "I wonder what ever happened to that? So, what have you flown, Marieke?"

"I've got quite a few hours in on a Cessna 182, and about fifty hours in twins, either Piper or Cessna," she replied. "Do you know Koos Strijdom of Sky Charters?"

"*Ja*," James said. "You know him?"

"He brought me down here," Marieke explained.

"He's selling that Cessna of his," Albert said. "He picked up this Twin Otter that's cherry, man, long-range tanks, state-of-the-art nav set, got it for a steal."

"That's what we flew down in," Marieke said. "I liked the Twin Otter, it was nice to fly, but it's bigger than anything I've flown before. Koos asked me if I was interested in his Cessna. Do you think it would be a good buy?"

"*Ja*," they both said in unison. "Look, man, Koos really takes care of his equipment, and if he likes you, he won't try and jack the price too high, he'll be fair. If he doesn't like you, then look out, he'll take you to the cleaners. So, does Koos like you?" James asked.

"I think so," Marieke said. "We've had some dealings in the past."

"Wait, you're not the *meisie* who was wandering around the dambo in her *brookies* carrying a shotgun?" Albert asked.

"I would rather forget that episode," Marieke said. "I was looking for heads from two bodies we had found."

"Koos told us all about that," Albert laughed. "You're famous here, can't see any of our officers doing the same, they'd send some poor black *ou* into the *dambo*, and keep yelling at him."

"Okay, we need to focus on our approach, and landing now Marieke, so we'll be a little busy, talk to you more on the ground," James said.

In Johannesburg, Marieke thanked James and Albert for the ride, and they told her that if she needed a jump seat in the future, to call them. James gave her a card, as did Albert, so she reciprocated and handed out her cards. She said goodbye and took a taxi to the Southern Suns hotel close to the airport, where she got a room and made a reservation for the flight to Gaborone the next morning. She had missed the call from Sergeant Maphosa after the five o'clock briefing, but she was sure that he would give her all the details when she got to the office the next day.

Sergeant Maphosa was waiting when she arrived at the office the next morning.

"*Dumela Mma*," he said.

"*Dumela Rra*," she replied.

"We have news, Madame," he said. "A Gert Theron has been staying in a small hotel here in town for the past month. He left the day that Lamprecht was shot. As far as the hotel knew, he had no car, and very little luggage."

"So, as he had two cars here in Botswana, that suggests that he found somewhere to park them," she thought. "Where would you park a car?"

"There are some places where one can rent storage space, and places to park," Maphosa said. "I'll have people start looking at them right away. Was your trip to Port Elizabeth successful?"

"Instructive," she said. "Whoever is killing these people shows a talent for improvisation. We have a lot of things to follow up. Is there any more on this Patricia Wilson who came to collect Theron?"

"No, Madame," Maphosa said. "She came in with her Toyota, picked up Theron, and left the same day. The guards at the border took a quick look through her car, but they found nothing."

"If we are wrong, and Pretorius, Theron, is not our killer, do we have any other suspects?" she asked.

"Assistant Commissioner Masisi reported that he cannot as yet find anyone with strong enough reason to kill Katse or Lamprecht, for the commissioner, pick any one of about fifty people who over the years he has arrested, and testified at their trials, he also reported that their examination of files has turned up no connections between the three, except for the one you had," Maphosa said.

"I should go and report to the commissioner," she thought. "I'll be back soon, and we'll go looking for storage space."

"So, you are back," Commissioner Boateng said. "This Theron lead is most useful. I thanked Lieutenant Colonel van Dyk for the information. It is not often that we get such cooperation from the SAP."

"I have copies of the two identity cards, Sir," Marieke said. "It's the same man. He changed his appearance a little between the two photographs, but it is the same man. The South Africans are now looking again at an unexplained death near Worcester. A body was found there about a week after Pretorius was deported. They had no idea who it might be, but are now going back into old army records to get dental charts to see if they can identify the body."

"Who is Celia Botha?" he asked.

"I think she is Patricia Wilson," Marieke replied. "The South Africans are looking into her history."

"Were you able to discover anything about van de Merwe?" Boateng asked.

"Between Lieutenant Colonel van Dyk and myself, we put together a likely scenario," she replied. "He is now checking things to see if they can gather evidence that confirms our suspicions."

"What next?" Boateng asked.

"I'm looking into where Theron or Pretorius stored his vehicles. He brought two into Botswana, which suggests to me that he is going to abandon one of those he brought across the border and use the other to make good his escape. If I were him, I would use the Land Cruiser, and drive either west, and cross the Malopo or east, and cross the Limpopo," Marieke replied.

"What if he goes north?" Boateng asked.

"He could," Marieke admitted. "It means a much longer drive to a border, but perhaps he is afraid to go back to South Africa, in case they know who he is, and are looking for him. If he goes north to the Caprivi or to Zambia or Zim, he could cross their borders and disappear."

"We have the regular crossings covered," Boateng said. "But, he could just abandon the second vehicle, borrow, hire or steal a *mokoro* to take him over the Zambezi, and be in Zambia or Angola easily."

"Van Dyk suggested that he already has a plan to get out of Botswana," Marieke said.

"I think he's right," Boateng agreed. "We have to try, and think like him, and try, and imagine the best way to get out of the country. Twenty years ago, where was he poaching ivory?"

"In the Linyanti," Marieke said. "He skipped back and forth across the border into Namibia, and also did some hunting on our side of the river."

"So, he knows that part of the country quite well," Boateng thought. "If I were him, and I thought that I could drive there undetected, that's where I would go."

"I should warn Will and Bridget Martin, they run the concession now that Pretorius did much of his poaching on, and where he was arrested," Marieke commented.

"Get onto the Game Department, and have them send a couple of game guards up there," Boateng instructed. "We don't want any more deaths this month."

"Very good, Sir," Marieke said. "I'll call them now."

Marieke had just finished talking to the game department when she got a call from Andries van Dyk.

"*Môre,*" he said.

"*Môre,*" she replied. "It's a pleasure to hear from you, have you a new development?"

"Patricia Wilson," he replied. "Born Pat Russo in Zeerust, one of two daughters, the older, Estelle, went to Paris as a model. Pat Russo left Zeerust in 1973 and went to Cape Town, also to a modelling agency. She started her own travel agency and has travelled extensively. She was known to the Pretorius family and was quite a looker even as a teenager. According to one retired officer, she had a thing for Hansie Pretorius, but could not stand Danie Pretorius. Lots of *ouks* tried to get her into bed, but her old man saw them all off, at the end of a shotgun; he had quite a reputation for being protective of his daughters, maybe a little too much so, because they both left home as soon as they could. She married a Brian Wilson who had quite an estate near Stellenbosch. It seems that they fixed things up with a solicitor to get her reclassified as white, so there would be no problems with the marriage. At the same time, they changed her name from Pat to

Patricia, must have sounded more white to them. She had been classified as coloured before. Brian Wilson died in the bush war in South West, and she has had a manager run the vineyards and winery on the Stellenbosch estate. When not at her estate, she lived on her yacht, which was anchored at the Hout Bay Yacht Club. It was a pretty big boat, apparently ketch, which they tell me means two masts, 63 ft long, sleeps eight. I'll fax you details of the boat, including a couple of pictures."

"You said had, and lived," Marieke commented. "Is she dead too?"

"No," he said. "Not dead, gone. The yacht left for Rio almost three weeks ago with a ferry crew, so they're probably halfway there by now, I heard from a ship's chandler that they bought a couple of large fuel bladders to supplement the existing tanks, so they can probably cruise quite a way on the diesel engines if they have to. She sold her estate three weeks ago for 4,238,450 Rand. She took out all of that in cash and was last heard of on a flight to Paris on the 1st of May. She told one of the immigration *ouks* there, Hennie Roux, that she had a return ticket for the 20th of May, but she's gone. My guess is that she converted the cash into diamonds that she smuggled out of the country. There apparently was a suspicion that Brian Wilson had a sideline in illicit diamonds, probably to prop up the vineyard when yields were not good. She may have taken it over after his death; she would have been well placed to do so, she was in the travel business, and knew all kinds of stewardesses from the various European airlines. She probably used them as couriers. I'll bet if the Swiss ever reveal things that she's got a sizeable account there. It's interesting that her yacht was named the 'Blue Diamond', I wonder if that was her naming or if it came with that name?"

"I know someone in Paris," Marieke said. "I'll contact her and see if we cannot track down Patricia Wilson."

"Who do you know in Paris?" Andries asked.

"Someone I was at *uni* with in Lyon, she's with the Sûreté, she's one of the higher-ranking women in the French police," Marieke explained. "I'll ask her to track down Wilson. What happened to the Russo family in Zeerust?"

"Drank themselves to death," Andries said. "They received money on a regular basis from both daughters, but spent it on booze, and probably other things that are not good for you, and they both died in 1981. The PM done on the old man showed extensive liver damage from booze, and the wife was almost as bad, but what killed her was cocaine. Pat Russo knew quite a few of the shamans in the area, and was known to have contacted them, and used their services, whether for love potions or poisons, we don't know yet."

"So, Pat Russo, Patricia Wilson, Celia Botha?" Marieke asked.

"Sounds good to me," Andries agreed. "Russo didn't like Danie, and Hansie had a grudge, so they fixed things between them. We just don't know how they met again, and where, and what they've been up to. The estate manager did tell us that there had been a man staying with Mrs Wilson; this man seemed to come and go, but the manager never got the chance to talk to him. He's seen a picture of Pretorius, Theron, and he says it's possible, but he's not certain. By the way, we tracked down a shop in East London that sold a moped to this *ou*, he paid cash, and took it with him. The proprietor of the shop is fairly certain that it was Pretorius; he identified him from the picture we showed him. We've also managed to track the movements of Pretorius in East London, he went first to the Ford dealer, and talked to a Piet Botha, and asked him about Koos van de Merwe. Botha couldn't help, so he worked his way through the car dealers until he got to the Volkswagen dealer on Oxford Road. They, or at least John Roberts, the parts manager, put him onto the Toyota dealer next door. There a Jim Walters told him about van de Merwe, and the fact that he now ran the operation in PE. After that, we can speculate about the rest. My guess is that he was going to PE, stopped for the weekend in Port Alfred, and saw van de Merwe. Walters said that he called van de Merwe to tell him about the visitor he might get, but van de Merwe was confused because Pretorius had said that he was Piet Cillie, and that he had been in Australia for twenty years, but van de Merwe said that he, and Cillie were still in Katima sixteen years earlier. He also did not recognise the description that Walters gave of the man who said he was Cillie. We also found a ship's chandler who sold charts, and other equipment to a man answering to the description of Pretorius, this *ou* did recognise him from the picture we showed him. Then, we also found another store where Pretorius bought a wetsuit, two dry bags, and a boning knife. My guess is that he took the dry bags with him onto the boat, then, when van de Merwe was dead, changed into the wetsuit, put his clothes and the guns he stole into the dry bags, and swam them to shore. If he were smart, and we are beginning to see that he is, he would have dumped the dry bags and the wetsuit. We're checking with people in the area, but they could be anywhere from Cape Town to Durban."

"That was quick work," Marieke said.

"*Ja*, the East London *ouks* put almost every man onto it, and really pushed things to get answers," Andries said. "They're still digging, they say they want to find out where he bought petrol, where he ate, and where he stayed before he got to East London."

"Thanks, Andries," she said. "I'll get hold of my contact in Paris, and see if we can't find Patricia Wilson. We're still looking here, we've found the place where he sighted in a rifle, he was careless, he left some cartridge cases behind, and we were able to match firing pin and extractor marks with the weapon we found near the home of my commissioner. Now we're looking for anyone who may have seen him come or go from that place."

"Oh, I heard back from the Cape Town *ouks*, there was a machine shop at Theron's place, and they actually managed to track down the lathe, and the mill that he had in it," Andries said. "I've asked them to run some samples with the tools that they found with the machines, so that we can run a check on tool marks, and see if the suppressors were made on them."

"Thank you," Marieke said. "We've found a hotel where Pretorius has been holed up, but he left the day of our last shooting."

"*Magtig*," Andries said. "This *ou* is always one step ahead of us, he's planned this all well. I'll keep checking here. Let me know if you find Wilson."

"I will," Marieke promised. "*Tot siens.*"

Melisende was next on Marieke's list. Marieke called, and a woman answered the telephone, but it was not Melisende.

"*Bonjour,*" Marieke said, and then asked to speak to Melisende. "*S'il vous plaît, je voudrais parler avec Melisende Garnier.*"

"Et vous êtes?" the woman asked, wanting to know who Marieke was.

"Je suis Marieke Englebrecht, je suis un commissaire adjoint de police en Botswana," Marieke explained, identifying herself as a police officer.

"Attends, s'il vous plaît," the woman said, asking Marieke to wait.

"Marieke?" Melisende said when she came on the telephone. *"Ça va?"*

"Bien merci, et tu?" Marieke asked.

"Bien aussi, quoi de neuf?" Melisende asked.

"I need help finding a woman who recently went to Paris," Marieke explained.

"Of course," Melisende said. "Who is she?"

"She was born Pat Russo, then changed her name to Patricia Wilson when she married, which is the name she used when she took the Air France flight to Paris on the 1st of May. She has a sister who lives in Paris, Estelle Russo, apparently quite a famous runway model," Marieke explained. "We, and the South Africans, would like to talk to her about a rash of killings lately, they have had at least five, and we've had three, including that of my boss, that we believe are all related. She may have been working with a man who was born Hansie Pretorius but has been travelling around as Gert Theron. We think that she helped this Pretorius kill his cousin, Danie Pretorius, with a local poison called *zwezwe*. We also think that she helped Hansie Pretorius get into Botswana. We suspect that she went to Paris with a quantity of diamonds in her possession, and that she probably has additional funds somewhere in Europe, probably Switzerland. She owns a yacht that is currently being ferried to Rio, so our guess is that she may look for a crew to ferry it from Rio to France, and may be looking for a berth in France," Marieke explained.

"Sacrebleu," Melisende exclaimed. "What do you want me to do when we find her?"

"Just keep her under surveillance," Marieke said. "If she tries to leave France, then find some excuse to detain her. This woman is clever, I know I don't have to tell you about surveillance, but if she thinks she is being watched, she may try, and leave the country."

"We'll do that," Melisende promised. "Are we still going to the bush, or will this investigation upset things?"

"Honestly, I don't know," Marieke said. "But, come anyway, I long to see you again, and we will make some time for excursions."

"Bon," Melisende said. *"Alors chérie, je tu verrai bientôt."*

"À bientôt," Marieke replied.

"Sergeant Maphosa," Marieke called.

"Yes, Madame," he said when he came to her office.

"It's time for us to go looking for storage places," she said.

"Very good, Madame," he said. "I have a list here of all those places in Gaborone, all those that advertise, and some that do not."

"Which one do we go to first?" she asked.

"I think we should start in the West Industrial Estate, it has storage places and scrap yards," he suggested.

"Fine," she said. "You drive, I have some things to think about."

It took the better part of the afternoon, but they finally found the place that Hansie had rented. He had rented it for a month and had paid cash in advance, so the manager had not been to check on it as there was time to run on the rental. It was empty now, and it looked as if it had been swept out and cleaned very thoroughly. The manager of the yard recognised Hansie from the photograph that Marieke showed him. She also noted that there was a scrap yard next door, with quite a few cars that still had their licence plates. She instructed Sergeant Maphosa to get someone from the laboratory to go over the storage place carefully, and she also told him to get a couple of officers to look over all the cars, and *bakkies* in the scrap yard to see if there were any that had no licence plates, and for those to get the chassis numbers, and have the Traffic Department get the licence plate numbers from the chassis numbers. She was concerned lest Hansie had taken licence plates from an old car and used them on his, so that he had a Botswana licence plate rather than a South African plate. She had Sergeant Maphosa take her back to the office for the five o'clock briefing, but told him to get back to the location and oversee things there.

"So, what do we have that's new?" Commissioner Boateng asked.

"We've found a storage location rented by Gert Theron," Marieke said.

"Is there anything there of use to us?" Boateng asked.

"It's been cleared out and swept," Marieke said. "But I have some of Thabo's people looking for anything they can find. There is a scrap yard next door, and we're also looking into the possibility that he took plates from a scrapped car and put them on one of his cars."

"We learned that Theron also hired a Land Rover," Bangwata said. "My theory is that he used his Land Cruiser, the Mercedes, and the Land Rover to follow and find out where Katse and Assistant Commissioner Mochage lived. They both had routines that they followed, and if our man was patient, he could follow them from their offices to their houses. He would break the task up into sections, and on the first day, use one vehicle to follow them so far, then he would break off, and go back the next day to that same place with another car."

"But, what if they broke routine?" Sibanda asked.

"If he was patient enough, he would just wait another day or two, and pick them up again," Bangwata suggested. "If he used all three cars, the chances of being spotted as following would be limited. We may also have a witness who saw a car parked opposite the house of Katse two separate times, he also thinks that there may have been a Land Rover parked there one day as well."

"Fine," the commissioner said. "I think it's time to get some help from the public, Inspector Sibanda, contact the Daily News, and the Guardian, the Gazette, and Mmegi wa Digmang, and send them a copy of the picture that Pretorius used to obtain the South African ID card in the name of Gert Theron, and ask them to caption it with words to the effect that we would like to contact this man, as Gert Theron, in connection with enquiries that we are making."

"Very good, Sir," Sibanda said.

"I've just talked to Lieutenant Colonel Andries van Dyk of the SAP, and he's going to do the same thing, and he's also going to get it posted on the news on the television down there. We both agree that we will use just the Theron name now, so that perhaps Pretorius will not know that we know that he is masquerading as Theron," the commissioner said. "The SAP, or at least van Dyk, has been very cooperative on this, I suppose they don't like unsolved murders any more than we do."

After the briefing, Marieke changed into old clothes, and went back to Ramotswa, and again took a bus to her destination.

"*Dumela Mma,*" the old man said as she entered his shop.

"*Dumela Rra,*" she said.

"So, you are back," he remarked.

"I am back," she said. "Are you well, Uncle?"

"I am well enough," he said. "I feel my age at times, but I am still alive enough to appreciate a beautiful woman."

"Where is she?" Marieke asked, looking around.

"Ha!" he said. "You will have your little joke. What brings you out here to see an old man again so soon?"

"*Zwezwe,*" she said.

"You have more information?" he asked.

"I believe that the person I have been looking for was once Pat Russo of Zeerust," she explained.

"I remember the family," he said. "Piet Russo, Cecilia, the wife, and two daughters, Estelle and Pat."

"What do you know of them?" Marieke asked.

"The daughter Pat spent many hours with the *ngaka* at Goo-Kgang, but he is dead, and she went to the *ngaka* in Mabalstad," he said.

"You know she went there?" Marieke asked.

"She went there," he confirmed. "I have seen it. She took a taxi from Rustenburg. She was dressed like an old lady. It came to me after you left last time, I was going to tell you, but I do not like to be seen at your police station."

"I understand," she said. "If you remember anything else, post this letter to me, and I will come." She handed him a letter addressed to herself, with a stamp already affixed, and a small letter "z" written on the back in the bottom left corner. The envelope itself was quite empty, but if she ever received it, she would know its meaning and come as soon as she could. "Is there anything you need, Uncle?"

"I would not turn away some of this new Kentucky Fried Chicken," he said.

"I will see to it," she promised. "Stay well, Uncle."

"Go well, daughter of Patience," he replied.

Frustration

Hansie Pretorius seemed to have dropped off the map and disappeared. They had finally found the hotel where he had been staying; they knew where he had stored at least one car, but did not know which one he was driving, and what had happened to the other. Obviously, he could not drive two cars at the same time, so either he had an accomplice, or he had found another place to hide at least one car. There had been no reports of a Gert Theron leaving the country, so there was still a chance that he was still in the country. Marieke tried to put herself in his shoes and imagine what his plan might be to escape.

If he went north across the Zambezi into Zambia, he might get away. He would have to hope that the Botswanans had not requested the Zambians to hold him if he turned up, so she resolved to call Chief Superintendent Phiri of the Zambia Police and ask for his help. She had worked with him before on another murder case. The Angolans were questionable. The civil war was still going on, and if Pretorius crossed the border from Botswana into Namibia, then Angola, he would likely encounter the Savimbi supporters, how they would treat him, she was not sure. She thought it unlikely that Pretorius would deliberately get himself in the middle of a civil war, so Angola seemed to her the least desirable option. Namibia itself was fairly recently independent, and how they might treat a South African wanted for several murders was going to be a question, but her surmise was that they no more wanted murderers on the loose than Botswana did. Going to Zimbabwe seemed very unlikely; the chances that they would be at all sympathetic to a white South African wanted for murder were also slim indeed.

There was still the possibility of South Africa, but to return there suggested a plan to leave there. Marieke just could not imagine Pretorius staying any longer in South Africa than he had to. He would be hard-pressed to slip by the authorities and fly out, but going by boat was a possibility. Marieke wondered if the intention had been for Pretorius to board Patricia Wilson's yacht at some point and make good his escape. Just because the yacht had left for Rio did not mean that it was actually sailing to Rio yet; it might just be hove to offshore somewhere or cruising up and down the coast waiting for some signal to put into a remote point on the coast and collect Pretorius. The problem with this scenario was that much of the South African west coast south of the Namibia border was closed and heavily patrolled because of diamond mining operations. Picking the right spot to be picked up would be a challenge, but not impossible. The south coast was probably a better bet, but getting there would be more of a challenge; the density of towns and communities was much greater than in the northern Cape, which would be on a route to the west coast.

Marieke gave up speculating and decided to go home. If nothing else, she needed to get something to eat. When she arrived, Mbali, and her daughters were eating.

"*Dumela*," she said.

"*Dumela Mma*," Mbali replied. "Come, and eat, Constance has made the most amazing dinner."

"Thank you," Marieke said. "How are you all today?"

"Well enough," Mbali replied. "Have you any further information for us?"

"We're still pursuing all the leads we can," Marieke said. "We've found where Hansie stored at least one vehicle, we've found where he was staying, and now we've asked the papers to publish his picture to see if we can find someone who has seen him. We've published his picture with the name of Gert Theron, we believe that is an identity he is using now. We've said that we would like to talk to Theron about enquiries we are making, but we make no mention of Pretorius, it's possible that we can fool Pretorius for a while into thinking that we have not connected the Theron and Pretorius identities."

"Do you think he's still in Gabs?" Mbali asked.

"No," Marieke said. "He left the hotel where he was staying, his car from the storage place is gone, I believe he had a plan to leave Botswana, and he has put that plan into action. For me now, it is a guessing game as to which way he will go."

"Do you think it's safe for us to go home?" Mbali asked.

"I would stay here until the trip to Linyanti," Marieke suggested. "By the time you come back, I think by then that it will be safe enough to go home."

"When does your French friend arrive?" Nandi asked.

"Saturday morning," Marieke said.

"Are we still going to the bush camp?" Nandi continued.

"I see no reason why not," Marieke said. "The question will be whether or not I can come with you. The way things are going, I'll probably stay here, in which case I'll have a friend of mine fly you up there, and you can show Melisende everything there is to see in northern Botswana."

The next day, Marieke called in Sergeant Maphosa.

"*Mma*?" he asked.

"Sergeant, do you suppose it's possible that Pretorius has an accomplice here in Botswana?" she asked.

"I think it likely, Madame," he replied. "He's disappeared, and for a white man to disappear here, it would be best done with help."

"That's what I am thinking," she said. "Contact the Francistown Prison, and ask them who he shared cells with, and when they were released. If I were he, and I had been contemplating a revenge over the years, I would have taken pains to cultivate certain people so as to have help when I got out. Oh, and while I think of it, ask the Francistown people if the prison has a machine shop that they use to teach skills to the inmates as part of the rehabilitation program. If they do, find out if Pretorius took classes, and if he did, how much did he know."

"Very good, Madame," Maphosa said. "Is there anything else?"

"Not now, thank you," Marieke replied.

The telephone rang, and Marieke answered it.

"*Bonjour chérie,*" Melisende said. "*Ça va?*"

"*Bien merci, et tu?*" Marieke replied.

"*Toujours bien,*" Melisende said. "I have information for you. Patricia Wilson flew Air France, La Première, seat 3K from Johannesburg to Charles de Gaulle. She landed at de Gaulle and was met by her sister, Estelle Russo, who took her to her flat, which is close to Notre Dame. After three days in Paris, they drove south via Lyon, and Aix-en-Provence to Beaulieu-sur-Mer, a nice town on the Med. Estelle has a villa there in the hills overlooking Beaulieu. Patricia tried to get a yacht mooring in Beaulieu, but the marina is full, there is no jetty space available, so she looked for a mooring in the next bay at Villefranche-sur-Mer. She took a mooring there and said that her yacht would be there in a month. She has been looking at villas in the hills nearby, it looks as if she plans to buy one, and live there. She opened an account at a branch of Credit Agricole in Beaulieu with 120,000 Francs and told them that she expected transfers from Credit Suisse on a regular basis. Our assumption is that she has an account at another bank in Switzerland that is more secretive than Credit Suisse, and she is only using it as the conduit to move funds. She has made some flight plans to go to Amsterdam, our guess is to sell diamonds, then bank the cash. Should we let her go?"

"Can you follow her without being discovered?" Marieke asked.

"Yes," Melisende said. "I can justify the teams because there is diamond smuggling involved. I'll use several teams in Beaulieu, Paris, and Amsterdam. We've done it before with Russian agents and not been detected."

"Watch this one," Marieke cautioned. "I understand that she is very good with disguises. Can you do some illicit entry into the villa, and find out if she has multiple passports?"

"Marieke, would we do such a thing?" Melisende laughed. "We will take precautions."

"Good, are you still coming on Saturday?" Marieke asked.

"I am," Melisende assured her. "I leave here on Friday on the overnight flight to Johannesburg. One of my colleagues, Philippe Garnier, no relation of mine, is taking over my work while I am away, and I have told him the whole story, so he knows how important it is to keep Patricia Wilson under surveillance."

"I'll be at the airport when you land," Marieke promised.

"*Bon*," Melisende said. "*A bientôt chérie.*"

"*A bientôt chérie*," Marieke replied, then she sat, and worried through the details of following someone in different cities, but admitted that if anyone could manage this, it would be Melisende. When they had run exercises at the university in Lyon, it was always Melisende who was able to keep the pseudo-suspect under surveillance without being spotted, and always Melisende who had evaded the followers when the tables were turned. Marieke trusted that she had passed along her skills to those who now worked for her, so that they would not lose Wilson.

Her musings were disturbed by another telephone call, this time from Andries in Port Elizabeth.

"*Môre*," he said.

"*Môre*," she replied. "You have something?"

"I do," he confirmed. "We've just received information from the *ouks* in Kimberley about an *ou* they picked up for illicit trade in diamonds. He got some immunity from them, then sold out the whole network. Here's where it interests us, not long after the first visit of Pat Wilson to Sin City as Celia Botha, this *ou* meets with someone dressed as an SAP captain in a remote place between Petrusburg and Kimberley. He gave her a packet of diamonds, and she paid him 250,000 Rand in cash. He saw no car, but he did see the tracks of one that had gone down the road before him. The Kimberley *ouks* did some checking, and finally worked out that the uniform had been that of a female captain from Cape Town who had died in a car accident, and who had been friends with Patricia Wilson, and by friends, they suspected that there were really close, close enough that the captain would not want the information public. They are also now looking for Patricia Wilson, and I told them that our best information was that she was in Paris, and, in our view, unlikely to return. The *ouks* in Kimberley checked around the area, and believe that she stayed at the Hunter's Inn at Koffiefontein with someone else as Mr and Mrs Cronjé. We sent them pictures of Pretorius and Wilson, and they're checking with the hotel staff now. The *ou* they picked up was shown a picture of Wilson, but he said she was older, but that could easily be makeup. The *ou* said that the woman who picked up the diamonds knew what she was looking at, and that she wore gloves at all times. The Kimberley *ouks* were taken to the drop point, and checked the area out. They found where Wilson's car had been parked, and they found footprints of someone else, probably a man, who had gone to a high point overlooking the rendezvous, they guessed to cover the exchange. They did note from the footprints by the car where the diamonds were handed over that Wilson made sure that there was a clean shot at all times of the *ou* she was buying from. This is a *slim kêrel,* she seems to plan for everything. Apparently, this was the first time that this location had been used to do a drop. The *ou* said that he had used nine others in the past, and only two of them more than once."

"So, she's been in the business for a while," Marieke commented.

"It would seem so," Andries agreed. "What do you think the chances are of us getting her extradited back to South Africa?"

"Knowing the French, I have no idea," Marieke admitted. "They could just say *non, and* all the arguments in the world would not move them, but they could just as easily put her on a plane, I really don't know. It seems more likely to me that if they do extradite her, it will be to you, and not us. We still have the death penalty, but yours is in abeyance, and seems to me will be done away with soon enough. I have been thinking about what plan Pretorius may have to leave both Botswana and South Africa. We have been assuming that Pat Wilson's yacht is on its way to Rio. What if it's standing off the coast somewhere, waiting for a signal to pick up Pretorius?"

"Could be," Andries said. "But, where?"

"I was thinking that although the west coast is probably easier to get to unobserved, the shoreline itself has many diamond mines, and there are regular patrols, but the south coast has many inlets and bays where one might put in to pick someone up," Marieke said. "I know it would be a greater risk to get to the south coast, but at least the shoreline is not being mined for anything."

"I'll talk to the navy and ask them to keep a lookout for the yacht when they make their patrols. I can give the details of the yacht. If they are waiting for a signal from Pretorius they cannot be too far offshore, whatever portable radio Pretorius may have will not have much range, so they will have to stay fairly close in, I'll also keep an eye on the shipping news to see if the yacht does turn up in Rio," Andries said. "Anything more on where Pretorius may be?"

"He's gone to ground," Marieke said. "We're looking into friendships he may have made while he was in the Francistown Prison. We speculate that he may be getting help locally, which is why, although we've found evidence of where he has been, we cannot find out where he is."

"I have other news," Andries said. "The army finally provided dental records, and the body found near Worcester was definitely that of Gert Theron. They also confirmed that Pretorius and van de Merwe served together in the same regiment. Information about the Pretoria killings is scant, but the Pretoria police have found a couple of hotels where Gert Theron, or rather Pretorius, stayed. My surmise is that he did a reconnaissance trip, then another to execute his plan. I have asked them to enquire about mopeds in case he used the same strategy again. We did have one piece of luck in Port Alfred. One of the officers there knows some of the local teens, and one of them turned up with a new moped last year. He said that he found it by the side of the road outside the Halyard Hotel the day that van de Merwe was killed. Your guess looks as if it is correct. Pretorius used the moped to get into town, then just sacrificed it for his plan. The serial number on the moped matched that of the one bought in East London. We told the Port Alfred police to let the *ou* keep the moped, Pretorius is not coming back for it."

"Thank you," Marieke said. "Now we just need to find Pretorius."

"Good hunting," Andries said. "*Tot siens.*"

"*Tot siens,*" Marieke replied.

At the regular five o'clock briefing, Marieke shared what she had learned with the others and also said that they were waiting to hear from the Francistown Prison about associates of Pretorius. Inspector Bangwata said that they had found the Land Rover that Pretorius had hired. It had been wiped clean of all fingerprints and left by the railway station. The hire company had seen it and had reclaimed it after the police had gone over it. So far, they had not found either the Mercedes or the Land Cruiser. The commissioner noted that there had been no more shootings, so perhaps the job was done, and Pretorius was now executing his escape plan. Assistant Commissioner Masisi was next, and he reported that for all their diligent searches of old records, they could not find any plausible link between the three victims. The only link they did know of was the ivory poaching one. But, he commented that he had taken pains not to be swayed by that, but to dig into everything. For him, it had been an instructive but thankless task. Thabo Mosiwa then went through the crime scene information again. The killer had been very careful, and the only physical evidence they had been able to recover from the three crime scenes had been the rifle, the two spent cartridge cases, and the pistol from the Katse crime scene, the pistol, and the two spent cartridge cases from the Lamprecht crime scene, and the bullets recovered from the victims. He and his team were going to look again for fibres, footprints, hair, whatever, but he was not holding out too much hope. The door-to-door interviews had not given them anything more beyond the sighting of a white man walking near the house of Katse, about the time of his death, and the report from the two teenagers about a white man leaving the area near the Assistant Commissioner's house. Inspector Sibanda told them that two American girls had come forward in response to the newspaper item about Theron and had told them that they had met him on a train from Kimberley to Mafikeng. He had left the train at Mafikeng, and they had seen him go across to the platform where a train to Zeerust was waiting. That did not help the Botswana enquiry much, but Marieke asked Sibanda to give her all the details so that she could pass them on to Andries van Dyk.

Next on the list were the funerals of Jan Lamprecht and Ian Mochage; they had been set for the next day, and the commissioner wanted a strong police presence at both, in case Pretorius showed his face. The funeral for Kagiso Katse had not yet been set; they were waiting for the cousins from Francistown to set a date and place. There being nothing else of note, the commissioner thanked everyone for their time and diligence and sent them on their way, except for Marieke.

"So, Matshwana, where do you think he is?" the commissioner asked.

"I think he is hiding with someone he met and befriended in prison," she replied. "As I see it, he has two options: run for the border now, or wait until things quieten a little, and hope that we get preoccupied with some other case, then make for the border."

"But, if the boat is standing off the coast of South Africa, surely a run for the border is more likely?" the commissioner asked.

"Perhaps," she agreed. "Or, perhaps Wilson has betrayed Pretorius and sent the boat off to Rio, never intending to wait for him."

"If I were the boat captain, I would want to get to Rio as soon as possible, then collect my fee, and return," the commissioner said. "I would not want to be idling up and down the coast somewhere waiting for a signal. Can we ask the South Africans to find out who the ferry crew is, and whether or not they have return air tickets to Jo'burg or Cape Town?"

"I'll call Andries and ask," Marieke promised. "Sir, it seems to me that Pretorius is not sparing his expenses in these killings. We are sure that he bought a moped in South Africa, and just abandoned it after he had used it for the one task he had in mind, he has hired cars, he has stayed in hotels, he has a source of funds here, did he arrive with cash or is he moving money into the country as he needs it?"

"We need to check with the banks to see if anyone is transferring funds in from South Africa," the commissioner agreed. "It is possible that he brought enough cash, but then he would probably be looking to change Rand into Pula, that's something else we can check."

"I'll start on that tomorrow," Marieke promised.

"No, let's have Masisi do that," the commissioner said. "It will impress the banks when a senior officer comes to see them."

"Very well, Sir," Marieke said.

"Don't you have a friend arriving soon for a visit?" the commissioner asked.

"She arrives Saturday," Marieke confirmed.

"Unfortunate timing," the commissioner said. "What were your plans?"

"I was going to fly to the Linyanti with the Lamprechts and Melisende Garnier," Marieke said.

"What does Mrs Lamprecht want to do?" the commissioner asked.

"She wants to go," Marieke said. "She is of the mind that two weeks in the bush with just her daughters will be good for them."

"I'm thinking that you should take them," the commissioner said. "I want to be sure that nothing happens to any of the dependents of the victims. Lerato is at my house, and we will put her on a plane bound for London after the funeral. We've uncovered nothing that suggests that she hired someone to kill Ian, so I see no risk in letting her leave the country. Katse has no close relatives, only the cousins on the farm, and I doubt that Pretorius knows about them. That leaves the Lamprecht family. I don't want any more killings. Does the bush camp have a telephone?"

"No, Sir," she replied. "But they do have a radio, and I have used it before to talk to the Maun station."

"If you go, how long would it take you to get back here?" he asked.

"If the weather was good, and I could fly, then about two and a half hours to get there, and the same back," she thought.

"Go," he said. "I would rather have the Lamprechts well away from here. Unfortunately, I still need you here, so must ask you to return. Will your friend be all right in the bush?"

"She will be fine," Marieke said. "She is in the French police, and is quite capable, and the camp staff and trackers will know to look out for strangers in the area."

"How did you meet Madame Garnier?" he asked.

"We were at university together in Lyon," Marieke explained, deciding not to correct the commissioner about Melisende's marital status. "She was the bright one in the class, always top marks, and always with no real effort, or at least that is what it seemed to me."

"When do you leave?" he asked.

"Sunday morning," she replied. "I have chartered a plane and will be flying everyone up there myself. I just hope they all remembered what I said about baggage limits, but I suppose with one less passenger now that Jan is dead, that won't be such an issue. Terrible thing to say, I know, but it is reality."

"There is the issue of the vacancy left by Ian's death," the commissioner said.

"There is, Sir," she agreed. "But, you have many to choose from that have service and experience."

"True," he said. "I wanted to let you know that I have considered you for the post, but being purely selfish, I confess I would rather have you as you are now, solving crimes; the assistant commissioner's job is more of a desk job in administration."

"I understand, Sir," she said. "I would have thought that you would promote one of our superintendents."

"That would be the natural order of things," he said. "But, we have to look at all the possible candidates, there is nothing in the rules that says I cannot promote an assistant superintendent. But, if I did, I think I would be placing you in a difficult spot. There would be many that would resent the move, and tongues would wag."

"I understand, Sir," she said. "I would rather continue as I am for a while, before I move into the administration side of the force."

"Good," he said. "I wanted to have this conversation before I make my announcement. Take the Lamprechts north to the Linyanti, then come back, and find Pretorius."

"Very good, Sir," she said.

After she returned to her office, Marieke was struck by a thought, so she called Andries van Dyk.

"*Naand*," he said when he answered the telephone.

"*Naand*," she replied. "You're there late."

"*Ja*," he said. "I have other cases that are taking time, so need to catch up on all the paperwork. *So, wat is aan die gang?*"

"I was wondering," she began. "We know that Pretorius used the identity of Gert Theron. Have you had any reports of others who have had their documents stolen or reissued in the past month or so? He had to assume that the Theron identity would only be good for so long, perhaps he's now using another name?"

"*Ja*," Andries agreed. "I'll check on that. Any progress with you?"

"No," Marieke said. "He really has gone to ground. We're still waiting to hear from the prison about his cellmates and associates. Our theory is that he's getting help here."

"Could be, could be," Andries said. "We've stepped up patrols along the Limpopo and Molopo borders. It's always possible that he might slip over the border somewhere, but we are looking."

"I will be going north with the family of Jan Lamprecht on Sunday, but I am coming straight back to look for Pretorius," Marieke told him. "I had leave planned for two weeks, but events have rather interrupted things, so will just be flying the family north, then coming back, oh, and could you find out who Patricia Wilson hired as a ferry crew, and whether or not they have tickets booked to fly back from Rio to Cape Town or Jo'burg, that may help us establish whether or not the boat is standing off the coast, or it has really gone, and is not waiting for Pretorius."

"I can do that," he said. "I finally have some reports on the Pretoria cases. I'll fax you copies so that you can read through them all. Personally, I'd rather go there and go over the crime scenes myself. I had been thinking it would be a good idea if you came with me, you gave us a break on the van de Merwe case."

"That was luck," she said.

"Perhaps, perhaps not," he said. "But, if I get the *ouks* in Pretoria to agree, I would like you to come with me, I like the way you look at things."

"I would be happy to help," she said. "But, if we're hot on the trail of Pretorius, that will take precedence."

"Of course," Andries agreed. "If you catch him, then we'll still have to try, and build cases against him. He's been very good at leaving no trail."

"He has," Marieke agreed. "We had some response to our publishing the picture of Pretorius as Theron in the papers. Two American girls who are doing Africa on $5 a day came forward, and told us that they had met him on a train from Kimberley to Mafikeng. They said that he left the train there and went to another train that was bound for Zeerust. I'll fax you all the details. Perhaps that was part of his plan when he killed the two *ouks* from the butcher's shop. Well, I should not disturb you any longer, *tot siens*."

"Thanks for the lead on the railway sighting. I'll check it out with the SAR *ouks*, and the Zeerust police. *Tot siens*," he replied.

At home, Marieke was greeted by her guests and gave them the news that she would be flying them all up to the Linyanti that weekend.

"That's good," Mbali said. "I think it will be good for us all to get away from the town for a while. When does Melisende arrive?"

"She flies from Paris to Jo'burg on Friday night, so I am going to the airport to meet the connecting Air Botswana flight on Saturday morning," Marieke replied. "I get the plane on Saturday at lunchtime, so will do pre-flight checks then, and make sure we have enough fuel, so that on Sunday morning I can do a quick walk around, and we can go as soon as the light is good enough."

"You can't fly in the dark?" Nandi asked.

"I can," Marieke said. "I have an instrument rating, but I thought you might prefer flying in the daylight, that way you can see where we are going. At night, we can follow the main road because of the lights of the towns and villages, but you can't see much."

"Are you any closer to finding Pretorius?" Mbali asked.

"Sadly, no," Marieke said. "He seems to have gone to ground or already has left the country."

"I hope they find him soon," Mbali said. "I won't feel really safe until he's behind bars or dead."

"Will we be safe in the Linyanti, Auntie Marieke?" Nandi asked.

"I think that you will be very safe there," Marieke replied. "It's well away from the South African borders, and unless Pretorius has some other peculiar plan, I think it's safe to assume he will try, and go back there, and then, perhaps, leave the country."

"You said you will be safe there, does that mean you're not staying?" Mbali asked.

"Unfortunately, no," Marieke admitted. "My commissioner wants me back to focus on finding Pretorius, but Melisende will be with you, and she is very smart, and a crack shot. The camp guides are also experts in the bush, and will know if anyone else is around, and will let Will, and Melisende know."

"What will we see in the Linyanti?" Khanyo asked.

"Lion, elephant, buffalo, kudu, warthogs, and all kinds of other things," Marieke replied. "When I was up before we saw all kinds, and there were some visitors there who had even seen a rhino."

"Will we see a rhino?" Khanyo asked.

"I doubt it," Marieke said. "Poaching has put paid to most of the rhino in Botswana, Will, from the camp, thought that that rhino had come over from Zim."

"I can't believe it's only three days away," Nandi said. "Tomorrow, and Saturday are going to seem endless. I wish Dad were still here, and coming with us."

"We all do, dear," Mbali said. "We have the funeral tomorrow, and then it will be good to get away. Marieke, when is Ian Mochage's funeral?"

"Also, tomorrow," Marieke replied. "We have the one for Jan in the morning, and then the one for Ian Mochage in the afternoon."

"Is anyone hungry?" Constance asked. "I have dinner ready."

"Thank you, Constance," Marieke said. "Do you know if you will be staying in Gabs after Mbali, and the girls leave for the Linyanti?"

"I am, Madame," Constance replied. "I have been assigned to Inspector Bangwata until such time as the Pretorius case is resolved."

"He is a good police officer," Marieke said. "He also held Ian Mochage in very high regard, so watch that he doesn't push things too far in his zeal to find our killer."

"I will be careful, Madame," Constance said.

After dinner Marieke sat with Mbali, and then shared a companionable silence for a while, then Marieke asked Mbali if anyone had changed any large sums of Rand for Pula in the days before the killings.

"There was one," Mbali said. "A South African, he wanted to change 5,000 Rand into Pula. I remember his passport as being new, what was the name again now, James Mason *ja*, that was it, James Mason, I thought that was odd because I was sure he was a *Boertjie*, he said he was looking to buy cattle, and that the sellers wanted cash."

"Do you remember anything else about him?" Marieke asked.

"No, I'm afraid not," Mbali said. "But, the bank will have a copy of his passport details page, we do that as a precaution. If you went to the bank, they might give you a copy."

"I'll get a warrant to protect the bank," Marieke said. "But, we'll need to check on this Mason."

"I need to get some sleep before tomorrow," Mbali said. "I'll see you in the morning Marieke."

After Mbali had gone, Marieke pulled out the files she had brought from her office and started to read through the police reports of the various killings in Pretoria that were suspected to be related. First was the unhappy motorist, John Adams, the manager of a local electronics store, who had been found in the bushes near an intersection. His car, a new BMW, had been found at a traffic stop, and the police had linked the theft and the murder of Adams to the work of the same man. However, their suspect was adamant that he had merely found the BMW at an intersection with the doors open and the keys in the ignition. Further enquiry disclosed that Adams was a creature of habit and took the same route to work every day at the same time. Later the same day that Adams was discovered, there was the discovery of a burnt-out army staff car, and the remains of General de Villiers in the boot, along with those of the army driver. Both had been shot with the same gun whose ballistics were able to match as being one that was used to kill John Adams. They had not found the gun, but the rifling marks all matched perfectly.

The surmise of the Pretoria police was that someone had car-jacked Adams, and taken his BMW, shot him, and dumped his body in the bushes, then had staged an incident to stop the regular army driver who was on his way to pick up General de Villiers. The driver was then shot, and stuffed into the boot of the car, and the killer then went on to collect the general who he then also shot, and stuffed into the boot, before firing the car. That suggested that the killer had done a lot of surveillance, and planning, and knew the routes taken by both Adams, and the army drivers, and had then staged his incidents. Because the same gun had been used to kill the general, his driver, and Adams, the police had been looking for connections between the general, and Adams, and had come up empty-handed. So, they had absolutely no real suspects. The thief of the BMW had a rock-solid alibi for the time of the shooting of the general, he had been getting a speeding ticket on the road to Johannesburg at the time. The security guards at the house of the general reported that the usual army staff car arrived as it usually did, and collected the general. They had not noted the driver, but then they said they never did, merely noting, in passing, that he was wearing a uniform. They had found no witnesses to either the hijacking of the BMW or the hijacking of the army staff car. No one had seen the army staff car divert from its normal route, and it was only when the car was well, and truly burning did anyone notice that it was off the road, and burning. The fire attracted much attention but no one was noticed to be leaving the area.

Marieke read on, and found the part that stated the police had finally found two hotels where Gert Theron had stayed prior to the killings. One was a stay of almost three weeks, and ended a little over two weeks before the killings. The second stay had been for another ten days. Marieke thought that that indicated that he had done his reconnaissance, taken a break and then gone back to execute his plan. She wrote down some questions that she would ask Andries in the morning, had there been any mopeds found anywhere near the place where the general's car had been fired, had any army personnel lost a uniform at about the time of the killings. She thought of a few more questions, and jotted them down as well. These killings in Pretoria had been well planned, and executed, and the South African Police had been getting nowhere. Marieke thought that Adams was just an unfortunate who happened to have a nice car that Pretorius wanted to use to stage his incident. She surmised that an army driver might stop for a Mercedes or a BMW, but lesser brands would not have the same cachet, and would be less likely to cause the driver to stop, and offer help. The way she imagined it was that Pretorius stopped Adams, got his car, staged a breakdown where he knew the army driver would pass, then shot the driver, took his place, and drove on to collect de Villiers. He then drove de Villiers to the deserted lane where the car had been found, shot him, then fired the car then left, in her mind again on a moped, to where he had left his own car. The BMW would get stolen quickly enough, as would the moped; the police were just lucky that the finder of the BMW had been careless enough to go on a joy ride and get caught. The moped, she decided, would never be found.

The next morning, dressed in her best uniform, Marieke took Mbali, and the girls to the funeral of Jan. It was a crowded affair, with many workers from the garage, and many lorry drivers, and contractors, all of whom were customers of MJ Motors. There was also a strong police presence, both in uniform, and in civilian clothes, mingling with the crowd. After the funeral, there was a wake, held in the workshops of MJ Motors which the employees put on, and catered. Marieke excused herself after a short while, and went to her office. She called Andries in Port Elizabeth.

"*Middag*," he said when he answered the telephone. "My wife is asking me questions about this lady I keep calling in Gabs, or who keeps calling me, maybe if you come here again you should meet her, and convince her that we are merely police officers doing our jobs."

"*Middag*," Marieke replied. "Of course, I would be delighted to meet her, what's her name?"

"Anna," he replied. "So, I thought today was the day for funerals?"

"It is," Marieke confirmed. "We had one this morning, and the one for our commissioner is this afternoon. I was told yesterday that a James Mason changed a large quantity of Rand into Pula recently. The bank manager noted that she thought he was a *Boertjie*, but he had a *Rooinek* name. We're checking on all large funds transfers, because our man has been spending money, and all of it cash, so where is it coming from?"

"You want me to check out this James Mason?" Andries asked.

"If you would please," Marieke confirmed. "I am getting a warrant to get copies of the bank paperwork, which will include the information page of his passport."

"That would speed things up a lot," Andries said. "But I will start looking anyway. I have something for you. We've been checking hotels, and inns on the roads between Zeerust, and Cape Town, Bloemfontein, and Cape Town, and Bloem, and East London. It seems Pretorius stayed at a small hotel in Aliwal North for two days before he went to Port Alfred. That would make sense, it's on the road from Bloem to East London. He has also stayed in different hotels a few times in Kimberley, all around the time of the Zeerust killings. Pretorius was also seen at a hotel in Hopetown having breakfast, and the staff there noted that he met a woman there, and they seemed to know each other, but that they felt it was a chance meeting. The staff there picked out both Pretorius and Wilson from photos we showed them. Later that same day, a Mr and Mrs Wilson stayed overnight at the Royal Hotel in Beaufort West. The staff there identified both Pat Wilson and Hansie Pretorius from the pictures we have. Apparently, Wilson was well known at the Royal; she stayed there quite frequently, but usually on her own. Our guess is that that was a typical stop on her way to do business with her diamond contacts. These sightings were just after the deaths of the two *moffies* from the butchers' shop. Another thing, the Zeerust *ouks* found an abandoned building near the Pretorius Butchers shop that had been used by someone camping out. The Zeerust *ouks* got a break when one of them was talking to a friend who works for the railways, that man said that he was sure that he saw Hansie Pretorius getting off a train. That train runs from Mafikeng to Zeerust. They did the smart thing, and checked in Mafikeng, and one of the workers there picked out Pretorius from photos they showed him, and told them that he had arrived on the train from Kimberley. The railway worker also told us that he had been seen talking to two American girls who were on the train, and who went through to Botswana. That confirms what you told us. So, my surmise, he does a recce trip to Zeerust, and camps while he watches the shop, then he drives back to Kimberley, leaves his car, and takes the train back to Zeerust. He jacks the delivery van, and drives it, with the two *ouks* locked in the back, to Kimberley, dumps the van, picks up his own car, and drives back to Cape Town, meeting Wilson on the way."

"You have been busy," Marieke said.

"We've been trying to build cases, so that if we can ever get our hands on Pretorius, we have something to go to trial with," Andries explained.

"Sadly, we have not been so fortunate in our investigations," Marieke said. "We have some information, but not much. I'll send you a copy of the case files as we now have them, perhaps between us we can develop some sense of how Pretorius thinks, and what his plan is to get out of Botswana, and perhaps also out of South Africa."

"*Dankie*," Andries said. "I'll look into Mason, talk to you later. *Tot siens*,"

"*Tot siens*," Marieke replied. She went to find Assistant Commissioner Masisi to see if he had learned anything from the banks.

"*Dumela Mma*," Masisi said as she knocked on his office door.

"*Dumela Rra*," she replied.

"We have a new identity to follow," Masisi said. "We've checked all the banks in Gabs, and it seems that Gert Theron changed 3,000 Rand into Pula at one of them, and a James Mason changed Rand into Pula at the rest of them, with amounts all around 5,000 Rand. In all Mason has changed some 31,000 Rand, so he's planning something. All the bank clerks confirm his identity from photographs of Pretorius we showed them."

"Why would he take such a risk?" Marieke wondered. "To be seen at the banks, and changing large sums of money, it seems either foolish or an act of bravado."

"I agree," Masisi said. "But, perhaps there was less risk than we think. How often do the banks compare notes about who is changing large sums of money, and foreign exchange reporting data is only collected monthly, and then who knows how long it is before it is examined? I'm inclined to think that he imagined himself safe under the identity of Mason. He would not use

Pretorius, he used Theron as long as he thought he could, then to be safe he used the Mason identity. We've checked immigration records, and no James Mason has crossed the border in the past six months, so, I'm inclined to accept that he's switched identities again. I wonder how many more he has?"

"The South Africans are looking into recently issued passports, and missing identity cards to see if they can guess at other possible names he might use," Marieke said.

"We should go," Masisi said. "We don't want to be late for the funeral."

"Very good, Sir," Marieke replied. "By the way, did we get a copy of the information page from Mason's passport from any of the banks?"

"We did," Masisi said. "Here's a copy for you."

"Thank you, Sir," Marieke said. "If you don't mind, I would like to stop at my office, and ask my sergeant to Fax this to Andries van Dyk in Port Elizabeth, it will speed up their enquiries."

"Good idea," Masisi agreed.

The funeral of Assistant Commissioner Ian Mochage was attended by members of the police force, by functionaries from the university, and by the dignitaries of the town. It was a much larger affair than had been the funeral of Jan Lamprecht. Marieke looked over the throng, and thought that there was little chance of picking out Pretorius, unless she or someone else on the force got very lucky. But, she doubted that he would be there, it seemed to her more likely that he was miles away making good his escape. Following the funeral, there was a wake held at the university, and Marieke paid her condolences to Lerato, and then quietly slipped away. She wanted to check on the progress of enquiries at the Francistown Prison after the cell mates, and associates of Hansie. Sergeant Maphosa was brandishing lists when she arrived at her office, he was directing constables to various places to check on people to see if they would admit to contact with Pretorius within the last few weeks.

"*Dumela Mma*," he said when he saw her come in.

"*Dumela Rra*," she replied.

"I have information from Francistown," he said. "They report that twelve men, all recently released, were either cellmates of Pretorius or seen often in his company."

"Anyone we know?" she asked.

"Four from Gabs, I know two of them," he replied. "I've just sent people out to check on them, and the others here in town."

"What about the others?" she asked.

"Two from Maun, and one each from Serowe, Ghanzi, Bononong, Kasane, Tshabong, and Lobatse," he enumerated.

"Who from Tshabong?" she asked.

"I thought you might be interested in him," Maphosa said. "If I were looking to skip the country, out that way would be a good place to do it. The man from Tshabong is Kenneth Motsumi."

"I remember him," Marieke said. "We sent him away for five years for robbery; he stole all the takings of one of the bottle stores in town. It took me two months to track him in the Kalahari and bring him back. He knows his bush, and if Pretorius wanted help, he would be a good person to turn to. I'll call the Tshabong station and have them keep an eye on him, that is, if he's back there. Please call the other stations, and have them check on those last five."

"Very good, Madame," Maphosa said.

"Is there anything else I should know?" Marieke asked.

"No, Madame," Maphosa replied. "It is frustrating that we have made no progress."

"It is," she agreed. "I think tomorrow, we should go to Francistown and talk to the prison warden about Pretorius and his associates. We'll leave at six in the morning. I'll call the prison and tell them to expect us between ten thirty and eleven."

"Yes, Madame," Maphosa said.

"Fine, Sergeant, I'll see you here tomorrow," she said. "Get one of the new Land Rovers for us, one that has the long-range tanks, and the radio. I'll just call the commissioner, and tell him where we're going, and that we won't be back for the five o'clock meeting."

As Marieke drove home, she thought about what Andries had told her. It certainly looked as if Pretorius had been busy in South Africa. He had made trips to Bloemfontein, Pretoria, Zeerust, and the south coast. The incident with the army staff car made her wonder where had Pretorius obtained the army uniform. She presumed that he had not kept his old army uniform, which would have been probably over thirty years old, so he more likely stole one. She wondered if the South Africans had looked into that, and decided that, surely, they had done it, it was one of those things that logically would be done, or would it. She decided that before they left in the morning that she would get one of the inspectors to call Andries in Port Elizabeth, and ask him if he knew where the uniform came from. At home, she was greeted at the door by Constance, who reported that nothing untoward had happened in the day, and that no persons had been seen loitering in the area, and no cars had been seen parked anywhere near. Constance had set out tell-tales around the house, and none had been disturbed. Marieke told Constance that she would be leaving early in the morning to go to Francistown and expected to be back between six and six thirty in the evening. Mbali had been busy, and dinner was ready, so one less thing for Marieke to worry about. After dinner, Mbali told her that the girls would clear up, wash, and dry the dishes, so she was free to relax. However, relaxation did not come easily to Marieke with this case hanging over them, so she repaired to the garage and looked at her board. She added names, events, relationships and pondered the web of events that all centred around Pretorius. He had been amazingly lucky or very clever, or both. Although they were now getting reports of sightings, including those in Gaborone, they were no closer to actually finding him. Finally, she gave up and went to bed; she had an early start in the morning.

Sergeant Maphosa had the Land Rover fuelled up, and ready for the drive to Francistown. He had even managed to get some coffee for the journey. Marieke suggested that he drive for the first hour or so, and then would take over for a spell. Sergeant Maphosa liked to drive fast, so he used the lights, and siren to clear laggards from his path, not quite by the book as they were not responding to an emergency, but Marieke allowed him this indulgence.

"So, Sergeant," she said when they were on their way. "Where do you think Pretorius is?"

"I think he has gone, Madame," Maphosa replied. "If I had done this I would have left the day I shot Lamprecht."

"I'm afraid you could be right," she agreed. "What reason is there to stay? If it is Pretorius doing this, and it is related to the poaching twenty years ago, then everyone involved is now dead, so why wait?"

"If you left, which way would you go?" she asked.

"I would go west, and then cross the Malopo into South Africa, but if I know that they are also looking for me, then really west to Namibia," he thought. "I'd go north towards Ghanzi, and then head for Windhoek. If I stayed too far south, then I'd have to deal with the national park that we share with the South Africans."

"But, once in Namibia, what would you do?" she asked.

"I'd go to the coast; didn't you say that there is a boat? I'd go to Lüderitz, and then a little south, but not as far south as Elizabeth Bay, there are some nice bays there, where a boat could pull in, and pick me up, and it's away from the diamond mining," he suggested.

"So, should we notify the Namibians?" she asked.

"I did," he said. "I sent them photographs, and all the names we know he has been using, and I sent details of the two vehicles he brought into Botswana."

"Thank you," she said. "The Commissioner, and I had talked about ways he could leave the country, but we had dismissed Namibia, because we thought that he might be going back to South Africa. Now that we know there is a boat involved, then Namibia makes as much sense as South Africa. What about Angola or Mozambique?"

"Too hard to get there," he thought. "Angola he could reach easily enough, but it's a long way from the Angola-Zambia border to the coast, and that province is probably the worst for roads. Mozambique, he'd have to cross Zim, and that is not so quick. If I was him, I'd go east to the Tuli Block, slip across the border there, then go east staying just a bit north of Beitbridge, then I'd cut across the bottom of Zim, and cross the border at Pafuri into Mozambique. From Pafuri I'd go to the coast, probably Vilanculos, it's probably less policed than Maputo."

"You've thought about this?" she commented.

"I have, Madame," he said.

"The question though is, has the boat actually gone to Brazil or is it waiting for pick-up instructions, it would be good to talk to Patricia Wilson, and find out, if she would tell us, what the plan was, and even if she intended to follow it, and not just abandon Pretorius to his fate. After all, we know she's in Paris, and the chances that she'll see him again are slim," Marieke said.

"Yes, but if she agreed and then reneges, he will go after her if he can, look what he did here after twenty years?" Maphosa commented.

"True," she agreed. "Would you like me to take over for a while?"

"Thank you, Madame he said. He pulled over to the side of the road, and they switched seats, and Marieke drove them for another hour before they switched again, and then after another hour, they switched again for the last time as they were approaching Francistown. Marieke drove to the prison and parked. They were met by a warder who took them to the warden's office.

"*Dumela Mma, Rra*," he said.

"*Dumela Rra*," Marieke replied. "Thank you for seeing us."

"Of course," the warden said. "I understand that you want to talk about Hansie Pretorius?"

"We do," Marieke confirmed. "We believe he may be a suspect in the recent deaths of Kagiso Katse, and our own Assistant Commissioner Mochage."

"Well, I've been here for ten years now, so for the first ten years or so of his sentence, I'll have to rely on the reports," the warden said. "By all accounts, his first five years here were difficult for us and him. There are numerous reports of altercations with other prisoners, and he was often in disciplinary hearings, but something changed after that. He started to look after himself better; he was known to exercise regularly and got quite fit. In the past fifteen years, he has had no disciplinary actions. He did develop a circle of friends, but we never saw him as a leader of a gang, or even belonging to a gang. He kept himself apart but was friendly, if that makes any sense. The rest of the inmates left him alone, so he was not preyed upon by the gangs that we do have here. Apparently, he also started to use the library we have, and the records show that in the ensuing years, he read everything we have."

"That seems to be out of character with what I have been able to learn of his early life," Marieke commented.

"That is true," the warden said. "Our own people commented that he went from someone who had no time for books and learning to a very studious person. In latter years he also applied himself in our programs that we have for rehabilitation, studying carpentry, and machining."

"Did he indeed?" Marieke asked.

"He did, and I gather from the instructors that he was most diligent in learning the skills, we thought that perhaps when we discharged him that he would go back, and start a new life as a machinist or carpenter," the warden confirmed.

"How extensive is your library?" Marieke asked.

"It's not very large," the warden said. "But, we do have quite a wide range of books, both fiction and non-fiction. They are not very high-brow, so none are beyond the general level of education of the people we have here, but they can challenge one's thinking. I think Pretorius had read all the books at least twice, and some a third time. He also learned to speak Setswana quite fluently, and the records show that he also learned some Shona and Venda. It seemed to us almost as if he discovered who he was, and that he had an innate intelligence that had never been channelled before, and never fully realised. He did learn to play chess and was the prison champion, but I'm not sure how much that might mean outside the walls."

"Who were his associates when he was here?" Marieke asked.

"We did send of list of those that he was known to associate with, and who have recently been released, did you receive that?" the warden asked.

"We did, thank you," Marieke said. "What about releases earlier?"

"I anticipated that you might ask that, so gathered the information, we know that there were three in particular, one from

Ghanzi, one from Serowe, and one from Zimbabwe," the warden replied. "They were all released about a year before Pretorius."

"Tell me about the man from Zim," Marieke requested.

"He was in for poaching, and smuggling," the warden said. "He arrived about six years ago, and served his five years, then we released him, the file lists his home as being in Sengwe, I am not quite sure where that is in Zim."

"It's on the border with South Africa," Sergeant Maphosa said. "It's on the Zim side of the Limpopo in Venda land at the top of the Kruger National Park, not too far from Crooks' Corner."

"Ah, I see," the warden said. "I wonder if he was following in the footsteps of those who got the place its name?"

"What was this man's name?" Marieke asked.

"Kossam," the warden read. "The note here suggests that they might have known one another before their sentences."

"Well, we know that Pretorius was here in Botswana poaching ivory twenty years ago, and that he did hire some people from Zim as trackers, and skinners, so perhaps Kossam is one of them," Marieke suggested. "What happened to Kossam when he was released?"

"We took him to the Zim border, and showed him the door," the warden explained. "We do that for all foreign nationals that we have. When we release them, you, as the police, normally pick them up and take them to the closest border post for the country they came from, and see them on their way. My guess is that this Kossam will be back in Botswana before too long, he did mention to one of my staff that he had been here many times before, and liked to come here."

"I saw Pretorius just before he was taken to Kopfontein," Marieke said. "We wanted new fingerprint charts, and pictures before we deported him. Even allowing for the age, he seemed to have changed from the person who was described from the police reports at the time of his arrest, and prosecution. Is there anything in the records that might give us a clue as to this change of heart that occurred about five years into his sentence?"

"Not that we found," the warden said. "But this is a listing of those who were here at that time, I wondered whether or not he had met someone who had convinced him to change his ways. I don't think it was in the nature of a religious conversion, because my own interactions with him never indicated any strong religious fervour. Perhaps if you look through the list of people a name may strike you."

"I suppose the space that Pretorius had while he was here is now occupied by another," Marieke asked.

"It is," the warden confirmed. "Sadly, we're seeing overcrowding which doesn't help with discipline or rehabilitation. We did sweep the space that Pretorius had used while he was here, looking for contraband, or anything he may have left behind or hidden, and we found nothing."

"Is there anything else that you can tell us about Pretorius?" Marieke asked.

"I don't think so," the warden said. "But, you may wish to talk to Abel Mwanza, he was a warder here at the time Pretorius was first admitted until about five years ago. You'll usually find him at this time of day at home, this is his address, I did let him know that you might be calling on him, I also made a copy of the Pretorius file for you to take, with all the notes we made about associates, and I've included the medical records we had for him, he had a couple of fractures, and some dental work done, so there are x-rays, I've included the originals of those, which we would like back for the archives when this is all over."

"Thank you," Marieke said. "That is much appreciated. I think we've taken up too much of your time, stay well, Sir."

"Go well, Superintendent," the warden said. He called in a warder, and asked him to escort Marieke, and Sergeant Maphosa back to their car.

Marieke gave the address of Mwanza to Sergeant Maphosa, and asked him to drive them there. It only took about fifteen minutes to wend their way around the streets, and find the address. He obviously saw them arrive, because he came out of his house, and greeted them.

"*Dumela Mma, Rra,*" he said.

"*Dumela Rra,*" Marieke replied. "Are you well?"

"Well enough," he replied. "Please, come onto the porch, would you like some bush tea?"

"Thank you," Marieke said. "That would be delightful."

"I don't suppose the warden offered you tea or coffee," Abel laughed. "He just doesn't think of things like that, he's all business." When he had brought tea out and provided seats for all three, he continued, "I understand that you would like to talk about our friend Hansie Pretorius?"

"That is correct," Marieke said. "He is under suspicion at the moment, and we need to try, and understand what kind of man he is."

"I remember when he came first, from the court in Gaborone. He was an angry man, and lashed out at everyone," Abel said. "Of course, it was everyone else's fault, not his, that he had been convicted, and sentenced to twenty years, so he was still seething about that. He discovered that there were gangs in the prison that would retaliate against him, so was often in trouble and we had numerous disciplinary hearings. I think he would have eventually been seriously hurt or killed, but he seemed to realise that he needed to be less aggressive, and that helped. He was able to take care of himself if it was only two or three against him, but I think that things were going towards a severe beating. Then things took a big change, people left him alone, and he started to read, and also learn Setswana. It took me a long time to find out who it was had talked to him, and caused him to change. At first, I thought it might have been the chaplain, but Pretorius was not interested in Christianity. Then I looked at the heads of the various gangs, but it was none of them, so I was at a loss. Then I noticed one day that he was with a *sangoma* from Tshabong. He spent a lot of time with that man, and because it was known that he was a *sangoma*, people were afraid of him, and so they left Pretorius alone. The *sangoma* was only in for five years, and when he left I asked him about Pretorius, and all he told me was that he had made him see that there was a different way to look at things, and to plan for the future."

"Well, it looks as if he may have taken that advice to heart," Marieke said. "Because we have had three shootings, all possibly relating to the case that put Pretorius here, and they have all been well planned."

"And now you cannot find Pretorius?" Abel asked.

"We cannot," Marieke confirmed. "Do you know if the *sangoma* went back to Tshabong?"

"He did," Abel confirmed. "I was trying to remember his name before you came. I think it was Izak."

"A San?" Marieke asked.

"Yes, Madame, an old San, I think he was sentenced for stealing cattle," Abel said.

"I remember him," Marieke said. "It took me a month to track him in the Kalahari, I think in the end it was because he made a mistake, and came back to a water hole where I was waiting, but maybe he was just being kind to me, after chasing him around the desert for a month. He knew I was after him, and told me when, and where I had been, until he said that things got vague, and he couldn't see me. I think that's when I remembered something I had heard when I was a child, and protected myself against his viewing."

"That worked?" Abel asked.

"I'm not sure," Marieke admitted. "But it was soon after that that he came back to the water hole where I was waiting. He laughed when he saw me, and told me that it was time that I remembered the ways of my grandfathers."

"Why would he say that?" Abel asked.

"Because my great-great-grandmother was San, she was Motshaba, and lived in the north, usually near the Tsodilo Hills," Marieke explained.

"Interesting," Abel said. "Anyway, this Izak managed to do something with Pretorius, and he became a changed man."

"Maybe he worked some magic on him," Sergeant Maphosa said.

"Maybe," Abel agreed. "But, whatever he did, it made a difference. I wonder if Izak is still alive?"

"We'd better check," Marieke said. "Thank you, Abel, for the tea, and for your time, we should be thinking about getting back to Gabs."

"Go well, Madame," Abel said.

"Stay well, Abel," she replied.

Before they left for Gaborone, Marieke suggested that they get some lunch. Sergeant Maphosa suggested the Silver Spur Steak House, which he had been to before. It was busy, but they were able to get a table, and enjoy lunch. Because it was such a public place Marieke did not discuss the case at all but after lunch on the drive back to Gaborone, she asked Sergeant Maphosa if he had any thoughts.

"I do, Madame," he said. "We should find this Izak, and see if he has been helping Pretorius, and we should try, and find out who this Kossam is, if Pretorius knew him from before, and he has worked with him before, then perhaps he would turn to him for help in crossing Zim to get to Vilanculos."

"What about the machine shop skills?" she asked.

"Those would be useful in making suppressors," he agreed. "Everything seems to point more to Pretorius."

"It does, doesn't it," she said. "But, still wonder if we're not grasping at the only theory that we have, and have we missed something. I wonder what Izak said or did that make Pretorius change? I wonder if Pretorius has already gone west to Tshabong, and the border there?"

"I doubt that we will ever learn what this Izak said, and as for chasing Pretorius out to Tshabong, we should get the local station to check for us if they have seen him, or heard about a stray *muzungu* in the area," Maphosa said.

"We'll do that," Marieke said. "Perhaps you could take over the driving for a while, I need to read through this file on Pretorius, and think about what it tells me."

It was just after six when they pulled back into the police station. Marieke thanked Sergeant Maphosa for his time and his ideas, and said that she would probably see him on Monday. She drove home, and found Mbali, and her daughters busy packing, they had bags ready, and Mbali was giving them instructions on what to take, and what not to take. She understood the weight limitations of the small plane, and was going to ensure that they all came in well under those limits.

"*Dumela Mma*," she said to Marieke."

"*Dumela*," Marieke replied. "I see you have stolen a march on me, and will be ready long before I am. As I am not staying, you could take more if you needed to."

"Thank you, but no, we will be fine, it is good for us to see what we need, and what we would like," Mbali said. "I'm sorry you won't be staying, but am happy that you're still chasing after Pretorius. Are you certain it is him?"

"Fairly," Marieke replied. "We can come up with no other scenario that ties the three shootings. It's always possible that it is something else, but we can definitely link the deaths of Katse and Jan. Has Jan ever had any dealings with Katse?"

"No, we've always used our own solicitors," Mbali said. "I met Katse very soon after we both moved here, and my impression was that he was a man I would not want to do business with, so Jan, and I picked another solicitor. At the bank we've also used other solicitors, the head office would probably never approve of someone like Katse, too much gossip about him."

"Yesterday, you mentioned a James Mason," Marieke said. "Well, it seems that he changed large sums of Rand to Pula at most of the banks in town. The bank clerks in each case identified him as Pretorius from the photos we had."

"So, I met him, and didn't know?" Mbali asked.

"You almost certainly did," Marieke confirmed.

"*Hawu!*" Mbali said, slipping back into Zulu.

Flight north

Marieke watched the Air Botswana plane from Johannesburg land, and taxi up to the hardstand. She walked out onto the tarmac and waited for the passengers to deplane down the stairs. Melisende was the fourth person to come down the stairs, and Marieke waved to her.

"Marieke, *ça va?*" Melisende asked.

"*Bien, et tu?*" Marieke replied.

"All the better for seeing you," Melisende said.

"Let's get you through immigration and customs," Marieke said. They walked into the arrivals area, and Marieke led the way to the diplomatic desk. Melisende was not travelling as a diplomat, but Marieke knew the officer in charge, and he was happy to oblige.

"This would not happen in Paris," Melisende laughed.

"One of the benefits of being a small country," Marieke said. "How many bags are we looking for?"

"Two," Melisende replied. "I have a large suitcase and a smaller bag that I will use tomorrow when we fly north."

"Did you have a nice flight?" Marieke asked.

"I did," Melisende confirmed. "I spent the money, and travelled La Première, which was very comfortable, all I had to do was fend off the idiot who was next to me, in the end, the stewardess took pity on me, and moved me to another seat, where I was alone."

"I'm so happy you are here," Marieke said. "I'm just disappointed that I won't be able to spend time in the bush with you."

"I understand," Melisende said. "If my boss were shot, I doubt whether the department would give anyone even a day's leave. I did think about staying here in Gaborone, but then thought that that might hamper your investigation, as no matter how much you might try, you would still be distracted by my being here, and not fully focused on your job."

"Perhaps," Marieke reluctantly agreed. "I would like to think that I could compartmentalise things, but you are probably right, that would be difficult if not impossible."

"There are my bags," Melisende said, pointing to the carousel. She retrieved her bags, and they made their way through customs, which was a mere formality as Marieke was known to the customs officers. "How is your investigation proceeding?" Melisende asked as they walked to Marieke's car.

"Stalled, I'm afraid," Marieke replied. "Our man seems to have gone to ground, and we are having the greatest difficulty finding him. We are checking on known associates from the prison to see if he has been getting help. What news of Patricia Wilson?"

"I'll check when we get to your house," Melisende promised.

At Marieke's house, Melisende used the telephone to call Paris and took notes while the person on the other end told their story.

"So," she said after she hung up. "Patricia Wilson took an early flight to Paris, and then Amsterdam, and went to a dealer that we, and the Dutch, have long suspected as being tied to diamond smuggling. After a suitable wait, the Dutch will make their move on him. After she left the dealer, she went to Deutsche Bank and wired some 2 million Guilders to the Bank la Ferté in Switzerland. The Dutch checked, and she has been a regular customer at Deutsche, she has an account there, and frequently wires money to Switzerland, but this is the most she has sent at any one time."

"What's that in Francs?" Marieke asked.

"A little over 6 million," Melisende said.

"So, we can safely assume that she has plenty of money in Switzerland to fall back on, and after the Deutsche Bank?" Marieke asked.

"She had a late lunch, flew back to Paris, then Nice, where her sister met her," Melisende explained.

"What kind of business did she tell the Deutsche Bank people she was in to move that kind of money?" Marieke asked.

"Wine," Melisende replied. "She even took two bottles of their most recent pressing for the manager she deals with. He explained that her transactions all seemed to come after the harvest, and pressing, so he assumed they were from purchase contracts in Eastern Europe for the sale of wines, which explained the cash transactions, no banking transfers there, all cash."

"Great cover," Marieke said. "I wonder how she got the diamonds out of South Africa?"

"We found a skirt that had a weighted hem to flare out when spun, and the hem had been unpicked, and the weights removed," Melisende said. "That would be a good way to move the diamonds, wear the skirt, do some swishing twirls, make the hem flare, and everyone thinks it is meant to be that way, which in fact it is, unpick the skirt hem, pull out the weights that are there, and sew back in the diamonds."

"So, she walks right by our immigration and airport security people, and they notice nothing?" Marieke said.

"Even if they do," Melisende said. "The skirt is supposed to have a weighted hem, so one would expect to find weights along the bottom, and who is to say what shape or form the weights would be, and as the stones are all uncut, then they are roundish with no facets, and other features that would cause a second look."

"You're right," Marieke agreed. "And at Jan Smuts, she flirts with Hennie Roux, one of the immigration *ouks* that she knows, and he walks her through, against the promise of a date when she returns. She's made enough trips with her travel agency that she probably picked him out long ago and cultivated him for future use."

"You make her sound like a farmer," Melisende laughed.

"Well, how else would you describe it?" Marieke laughed. "She certainly built a legend for herself, as the spies would say. But, you didn't say how you found the skirt."

"I didn't," Melisende said. "Apparently, it took hours to get the pictures so that everything would go back as they found it, and she has been well schooled, because we found three tell-tales in the villa, and two motion-activated cameras that were hidden outside the villa."

"How did you fix those?" Marieke asked.

"Trade secret, but we did arrange for an electricity and telephone failure for the whole area within two kilometres of her house, and then went door to door saying that we were looking for the fault," Melisende laughed. "We were fortunate, we were able to detect the cameras before we looked at the villa, and then we found the other tell-tales."

"So, what does she do now?" Marieke asked.

"Buys her villa, waits for her boat to arrive, and settles down to live off the spoils she has collected over the years, without too many worries," Melisende suggested.

"Please keep an eye on her," Marieke said. "We may need to talk to her at some time to find out what she knows about these deaths."

"Philippe has that well in hand," Melisende assured her.

"Just one more thing, what language were you speaking just now? I didn't understand a word," Marieke asked.

"Breton," Melisende said. "Philippe and I both speak it, and we use it when we talk over unsecured lines; it makes monitoring difficult."

"I didn't know you spoke Breton, I don't remember you ever using it when we were at *uni*, I didn't think anyone spoke Breton anymore," Marieke commented.

"There are still some," Melisende said. "But, you are almost right, there are not too many. I was lucky, I had an aunt that I stayed with in the summer months when I was a child, she was Breton, and spoke the language in preference to French, so learned from her. Philippe grew up there, and his parents both spoke the language and made sure that he was as fluent in Breton as he was in French. When we were in Lyon together, there was never a chance to speak Breton, and when you met my parents, they didn't speak the language at all. My aunt, who did was the wife of my uncle, my father's older brother."

"Maybe we should both learn San, and that would really confuse those who might listen in," Marieke laughed.

"I thought you did speak San," Melisende said.

"I speak some San, but not fluently," Marieke said. "I only learned from those speakers we had on the farm we had while I was growing up."

"Let's go and meet the others," Marieke suggested. Constance had seen her arrive, and had nodded that all was well, and, while Melisende was using the telephone, had told her that the family was on the back *stoep*, well away from the street, and also shielded from the neighbouring yards. They went outside, and Marieke reintroduced Melisende to all. The family remembered her from her previous visit, so the only real introduction was to Constance. Melisende quickly understood that she was there to provide some measure of protection for the family. Marieke suggested that they get some lunch, then she was going to go to the airport to check over the charter plane and make sure that the fuel tanks were full.

Melisende went with Marieke to the airport and watched as she walked around the plane, a Cessna Caravan, looking for anything untoward. Finally satisfied, Marieke undid the tie-downs on the plane, borrowed one of the small tow tractors, hitched the plane to it, and then towed it out to the fuelling station for small planes. She filled the tanks and recorded how many gallons, and therefore pounds of fuel, she had taken. She needed that both for payment and for her takeoff weight calculations. Tanks full, she pushed the plane back to its place on the tarmac and put the tie-downs back, one on each wing, and one on the tail. Although no high winds were forecast, it was better to be safe. Her last action was to open the fuel filler caps and place a small seed in the space around them, something she also did with the engine nacelle cowl doors.

"That's it?" Melisende asked, noting with approval the precautions that Marieke was taking to try, and tell if someone were to try, and adulterate the fuel or tamper with the engines. "This is a bigger plane than I thought it would be; it surely can take more than just the five of us?"

"*C'est tout*," Marieke replied. "And, yes, it can. I had expected a smaller plane, but this one was available for the same price, so I was happy to take it. It does mean that I could have been more generous with the luggage allowance, but next time I may not be so lucky, and luggage will be really limited. I'm so sorry that I will not be staying with you tomorrow."

"I understand, really I do," Melisende assured her. "I will look after your friends and make sure nothing happens to them as well. Are you closer to finding this man?"

"Not yet," Marieke admitted. "One would think that we could find one middle-aged white man in this city, but it is being more difficult than we ever thought. We have concluded that he is getting help from one of his compatriots from the prison. Perhaps we're wrong, but that is our working hypothesis."

"I wish I could help," Melisende said.

"You can by making sure Mbali and the girls are safe," Marieke said. "Then I won't have to worry, and can focus on finding Pretorius."

"That I can do," Melisende assured her. Marieke looked at her in gratitude and thought, as she often did, how much she resembled Valérie Kaprisky, a famous French actress. She wondered if people ever mistook her for the actress, Melisende was older, and a little shorter than Valérie Kaprisky, but they both wore their hair the same way, and had very similar features. She remembered once asking Melisende if she was related to the famous actress, but had been assured that that was not the case. As they drove back to the house, Marieke was quiet for a while, then she said, "*Chérie, qu'est-ce qu'on va faire?*"

"*Que veux-tu dire?*" Melisende asked.

"We cannot continue as we are," Marieke said. "Letters, telephone calls, and the occasional visit will not serve. What if I were to leave here and move to Paris?"

"You would move to Paris?" Melisende asked.

"To be with you, I would move anywhere," Marieke said.

"*Oh, chérie, cela me rend si heureuse,*" Melisende said. "*Vraiment?*"

"*Vraiment,* truly," Marieke said. "I think when this is done, I will tell the people here that I am leaving. Can you arrange a visa for me to live in France?"

"Of course," Melisende said. "It will be so much fun, you are sure?"

"I am sure," Marieke said. "Each letter or telephone call I get from you tears me apart, and I stare at the wall, and wonder why I continue like this. Can your apartment in Paris accommodate two?"

"*Certainement,*" Melisende assured her. "It is as large as the one you have seen in Lyon, perhaps even a little larger, it has a nice aspect, and faces to the east, and north, so not too hot in the summer or too cold in the winter."

"Could I work in France?" Marieke asked.

"We could arrange the right kind of visa, yes," Melisende said.

"I wonder what I could do there?" Marieke said.

"We are always looking for analysts, you speak French, you know Africa, you would be of help," Melisende said.

"But, the Africa I know is only the south," Marieke said. "I know little of the old Francophone Africa where French interests must lie."

"Perhaps," Melisende said. "But, there are changes coming in South Africa, we must be prepared for those as well as seeing to former colonies. *Chérie*, when will you be able to come?"

"As soon as Pretorius is either dead or behind bars," Marieke said.

"Does that mean after a trial?" Melisende asked. "Surely that could take months?"

"Perhaps," Marieke said. "But, if I resign and leave, there will still be those who can supply evidence at any trial. I have already fully reported on all I have found, and others have reviewed what I have done and confirmed it."

"Do we tell Mbali?" Melisende asked.

"Not now, I think," Marieke said. "When you leave, then I will tell her; otherwise, you'll spend the next two weeks answering questions."

"Oh, Marieke, this is so exciting, I'm not sure I will be able to not tell people," Melisende said. "I will try, but it might slip out. Are the walls to your bedroom soundproof?"

"Not really," Marieke said. "Why?"

"Well, it might get noisy later," Melisende laughed. "If you're flying tomorrow, then no wine, but we can celebrate in other ways."

"We can," Marieke agreed. "We should try, and not be too noisy, it might shock Constance and the girls."

"Not Mbali?" Melisende asked.

"She knows," Marieke said. "Incidentally, so does the pilot you once met, Koos Strijdom, he saw us together once, and guessed, and then he has put two and two together since, and drawn his own conclusions."

"Should we be concerned?" Melisende asked.

"No, both Koos and Mbali will be discreet. Here we are at the house, let's get through the next two weeks, and then we can celebrate," Marieke suggested.

"It's a pity it's Saturday," Melisende said. "Or I could call upon our embassy, and start the process, perhaps when we come back from the bush, and before I leave for Paris, I will go and see them."

"How long will it take?" Marieke asked.

"One or two months, I would think," Melisende said. "I may be able to speed things up a little. It will help that you have a sponsor."

"Patricia Wilson got a visa to stay in France, and she had her sister to sponsor. How long did that process take?" Marieke asked.

"About six months," Melisende said. "I got her immigration file and read through it when you called about her."

"Six months?" Marieke said.

"Don't worry, *chérie*, yours will not take as long, don't forget we already have a file on you from your days at the university," Melisende said. "And, I am not without influence."

"Ah, you're back," Constance said as she opened the door. She had heard them pull up and come to see who it was. She stepped back to allow them to enter the house, then took a look around outside. Seeing nothing untoward, she followed the others into the house.

"Is the plane ready?" Mbali asked.

"It's ready," Marieke assured her. "All I need in the morning is your bags, and then we can go. Constance, will you help me put together some sandwiches for tomorrow?"

"Yes, Madame," Constance replied. "I have already made them up, and was just waiting to see if you wanted anything else. Will you come and see?"

In the kitchen, Marieke looked at the pile of sandwiches that Constance had put up and nodded her satisfaction. She told Constance that she would be back the following afternoon, late, and that they would get back onto the investigation as soon as possible after that. Satisfied that they would not starve on the flight north, Marieke then went to ask the others about their luggage for the morrow. She was shown the bags and had to admit that they had done a good job. The bags were all of the soft type, so she could easily stow them wherever they might fit, and a quick heft of each indicated that they were well under the 15 kg limit she had suggested. They remembered from the previous trip they had taken with Marieke, and had kept things to the necessities only. Marieke went to her safe and took out a pistol and a rifle. Those she gave to Melisende, along with the appropriate ammunition. Melisende took a quick look at both weapons, and then stowed the pistol in her bag, and asked Marieke if the rifle could stay as it was, or should it be broken down for the trip north.

"Better broken down, I think," Marieke said. "It will be easier to stow that way. Here's a bag that you can use."

"*Bon*," Melisende said. "I am ready now for anything."

"Nothing has changed, you're still not staying with us, Auntie?" Nandi asked.

"Sadly, no," Marieke confirmed. "We are still hunting for a killer, and we, none of us, will rest until we have him."

"Will we be safe?" Nandi asked.

"Melisende will be with you, and the guides at the camp will know if anyone is in the area," Marieke assured her.

"You will get him, won't you, Auntie?" Khanyo asked.

"We will get him," Marieke promised, but in her mind, she was not so confident. He had shown a remarkable talent for improvisation as well as planning, so the chances were that he had an escape plan already thought out and in motion. Guessing where he might go next was going to be difficult; they really needed some luck and some help from his old cellmates and acquaintances from the prison.

"So, early night tonight," Marieke suggested. "We should leave the house at five in the morning. Constance will drive us there, then I can stow the bags, run through a quick pre-flight check, and we can be on our way."

Over dinner, the girls questioned Melisende about France and Paris. She told them what she could, and suggested that in the years to come they might visit. They talked a little more about France, but what the girls really wanted to know was what was Marieke like at university.

"She was a good student," Melisende temporised.

"I may have been, but it was Melisende who was always the first in the class," Marieke interrupted.

"That was only because I had to prove to myself that I was better than all the men in the class," Melisende said. "They seemed to think that Marieke and I were not as clever as they, but we proved them wrong."

"I think the professors were afraid of Melisende," Marieke said. "They would ask a question, and she always had the answer, but would then ask them a question which they often could not answer immediately. They would have to go away at the end of the lecture and come back the next day with the answer, which Melisende had also done. There were a few occasions when her research gave us different answers from theirs, and then chaos would erupt as students asked who was right. I think by those times we all had come to accept that Melisende was right, and they were wrong."

"Sometimes," Melisende agreed. "But, Marieke was the best at putting together scenarios with little data, most would say that they needed more information, but she has this ability to extrapolate, and guess, and be right far more times than she is wrong. I remember one professor who used to try and trip her up, but it didn't work."

"How long did it take to learn French, Aunty Marieke?" Khanyo asked.

"About three months before I could converse happily, and about six months before I was really comfortable discussing philosophies," Marieke replied. "I went to Lyon about four months before the start of the academic year, and enrolled in a French class. It was an immersion class, so all I heard all day was French. For the first month or so, I would go back to the flat I had rented, and just collapse on the bed exhausted," Marieke recalled. "Then it started to get easier, and I could go to class, and come home, and not have my head feeling like it wanted to explode."

"How did you learn English, Aunty Melisende?" Nandi asked.

"English was taught at school, but I really didn't learn English until I met Marieke," Melisende explained. "We made a pact, every other day we would use exclusively French or English. Marieke had the advantage because all the classes were in French, but away from the university, we kept to our pact, and it really helped me. What languages do you speak?"

"English, Setswana, and Zulu," Nandi said. "And in school, we are taking French, but I'm not that good."

"Ah, perhaps I can help," Melisende suggested. "What if I only speak to you in French for the next two weeks?"

"I'm not sure," Nandi said. "I'm not sure my French is good enough."

"It doesn't matter," Melisende said. "It only matters that you try. Perhaps you could teach me a little Setswana or Zulu?"

"It's a deal," Nandi said.

"Well, I think we should all turn in now," Marieke said. "We've an early start in the morning."

Constance had the police Land Rover ready in the morning, with the coffee and sandwiches already loaded. She took the bags and loaded them, then watched the street as the party climbed aboard. She locked up the house and then drove off to the airport. Marieke noticed a car in front and one behind. She motioned to them to Constance, who nodded in confirmation that they were expected. At the airport, the escort cars pulled up with them, and the officers got out and took up stations where they could watch the street and the approaches to the hardstand area. Marieke first got her torch and did a sweep of the interior of the aircraft and the baggage pod underneath, but found nothing untoward. It did not take long to load the bags into the luggage area behind the seats, and then Marieke did her walk around and asked the others to get aboard. She suggested that Melisende take the co-pilot's seat and asked Mbali and the girls to take whichever of the eight seats they wanted in the back, but not all on the same side. They would have a good view of the country below as they flew, and it got light, as the windows in the Caravan were large and spaced well enough that everyone got a good view. Her last action before boarding herself was to get a ladder, and climb up to open the fuel filler caps on the wings, and note that the seeds dropped out as she did so.

The same was true for the engine nacelle cowl doors, so unless whoever might be a threat was very good at spotting tell-tales, they were likely to be safe. Once everyone was seated, she did her safety briefing, then ran through the pre-startup checklist. She waved to Constance, who pulled out the chocks and let them taxi out to the runway. It was still early, just after 5:30 in the morning, so still dark, but to the east the horizon was tinged with a thin line of colour. Marieke talked to the tower and got her take-off clearance, then she pulled out onto the runway, and off they went.

"When does it get light?" Khanyo asked.
"Sunrise is at 6:45," Marieke said. "So, we'll have a little twilight before then, but you'll get to see the sun come up over there."
"Where will we be then?" Nandi asked.
"Almost to the Orapa airport," Marieke said. "If you look out of the right window, then you should be able to see the diamond mine."

Mbali handed out coffee and sandwiches, which went down quickly. No one had eaten breakfast, so this was in effect a late breakfast. As they flew over the expanse of Botswana, they saw the occasional light from a farm or small village, and once, several cars travelling together. Marieke told them that they would be on the road from Hatsaltladi to Boatlaname. When the sun started to come up, the sky to the east was fascinating to look at. High in the sky it was still black, but as they looked lower, the sky turned dark blue, then there was a yellow tinge, and finally a red line along the horizon. Nandi was the first to see the sun as a bright red crescent showing above the horizon, and as is the case in the tropics, it was not long before it was completely up above the horizon as a red dot. As Marieke had said, off to the east, they could see the lights of the Orapa Diamond Mine, which delighted Nandi. A little farther north, they saw the sunlight glinting off water.
"What river is that?" Melisende asked.
"The Botletle," Marieke said. "It's fed by the Okavango, and empties into the pans south of Orapa."

"Does it ever dry up?" Nandi asked.

"It has," Marieke said. "It all depends on how much rain falls in Angola. Good rains there means that it flows, poor rains means we get a dry river bed. At the moment, it's doing well, with water year-round. They did some channelling near Rakops, and that changed the flow pattern a little, but it's Angola that drives things."

"How much farther?" Mbali asked.

"Not too far," Marieke promised. "Over there to the west is Maun, and coming up ahead is Khwai, then we'll begin our descent into the Selinda strip."

When they reached the Selinda strip, Marieke dropped down low over the strip and flew down it to the west, looking for anything that might be a hazard for landing. They were fortunate; there were no elephants or other large animals, just a few impala, who scampered off as the plane flew over them. Past the end of the strip, Marieke climbed out and made an hourglass turn before coming back in to land. Once safely on the ground, she taxied to the turnaround area at the eastern end of the strip and parked next to the Twin Otter that she recognised as belonging to Koos. As she was shutting down the engines, a Land Rover, filled with people, came out from under some large trees and pulled up next to them. Marieke waved, then opened the pilot's door of her aircraft and climbed out.

"Bridget," she said. "How are you?"

"Fine, thanks, Marieke, how was your flight up?"

"Not bad," Marieke said. "We saw the dawn by Orapa, and no traffic in the air. Hey Koos, you here?"

"Koos is taking our last guests out today," Bridget explained. "He flew in last night and stayed with us."

"*Howzit*, Marieke," Koos said. "You're going back now?"

"I was instructed to drop my folks off, then go back, and catch an *ou*," she replied. "Where are you off to?"

"Maun, to pick up two more, clear immigration, then Jo'burg," Koos said.

"Let's get everyone out, I should be getting back," Marieke said. She went to the back of the plane, opened the door, and pulled out the steps that were there so that Mbali and the girls could deplane.

"I need to get my *ouks* loaded too," Koos said. "Good flight back, Marieke, see you soon. See you in two weeks, Bridget." He left, and went to his aircraft, opened the door, and deployed the stairs, then came back to escort his passengers to their plane, who were milling around telling Melisende, and the others what a wonderful time they had had. Bridget said her goodbyes to them, then came over to help Marieke.

"You still after the *ou* who's been shooting people in Gabs?" Bridget asked.

"We are," Marieke confirmed. "We believe he's the same *ou* who was poaching here twenty years ago, and who Katrina helped catch. Keep an eye out, and tell your people to watch out for anyone they don't know in the area. I believe this man will kill at the drop of a hat. Bridget, this is Melisende, my friend from France, and these are Mbali, Khanyo, and Nandi."

"*Dumela, bonjour,*" Bridget said. "Let me help Marieke with your bags, there is water in the *bakkie*, please help yourselves."

"I'll be back in two weeks to collect everyone," Marieke said when they were behind the aircraft, and out of earshot. "Maybe sooner if I can catch this *ou*. Melisende has my pistol and a rifle, and she knows how to use them. Mbali is the wife of one of those shot, his name was Jan Lamprecht, and he was one of the original poaching party. The family is probably safer up here than in Gabs, so look after them please."

"Will do," Bridget said. "I'll get Jackson to put the word out with the other guides from the nearby camps to let us know if anyone shows up who they don't know."

"Bridg, this *ou* has a plan," Marieke warned. "He could have made a booking weeks ago, and be here, or expected here soon. Everything he's done so far seems to have been well planned out. Here's a picture of him, and here are some copies you could give to the other camps, and lodges, we know he's been using the name of

Gert Theron, but his actual name is Hansie Pretorius, he's also used the name of James Mason, and for all we know he has another identity or two to fall back on. If anyone sees him, watch out, and call us in quickly. If you have to, shoot him, you won't get a second chance with the usual "Stop, Police", he'll just shoot."

"We'll be careful," Bridget promised. They finished unloading the bags, and stowed them in the Land Rover then Marieke asked Bridget to come with her, and keep watch.

"What's up?" Bridget asked.

"I need to pee before I go back," Marieke said. "I need you to keep cavey for me."

"Over there is the best spot," Bridget suggested. "The bush is thick enough to screen you from the planes, I'll just check around to make sure there's nothing lurking."

They soon rejoined the others, and Bridget asked if anyone needed to go before they started out on their drive north, Mbali, and Melisende both said yes, so Bridget led them off to the thicket, and waited. Marieke made small talk with Nandi, and Khanyo until the others returned.

"All set?" Marieke asked.

"All set," Mbali said. "Is it far to the camp?"

"About an hour," Bridget replied. "Unless we see something on the way, and stop to look for a while."

"How many guests can you take at any one time?" Mbali asked.

"We usually have eight in four tents, but we only have you for the next two weeks, Marieke bought out the other tent," Bridget replied.

"Okay," Marieke said. "I'll be off, I'll wait until Koos goes then take off after him. Enjoy your stay here, Bridget, and Will are good hosts, and you'll enjoy your stay here. Keep track of what you see, and tell me all about it when I come back."

"Bye, Auntie," Khanyo said. "Stay safe."

"I will," Marieke promised. "Melisende, *à la prochaine*."

"*À la prochaine*," Melisende replied. "*Prends soin de toi*."

"I will, you take care as well," Marieke promised. "*Sans toi, je ne suis rien*."

Marieke watched with tears in her eyes as Bridget drove off with the party, then she waved to Koos as he taxied out to the strip, and then set about going through her own pre-flight checklist. Now was not the time to let emotions get in the way of proper routine, so, she steeled herself, and read off the first item on her checklist. When she had gone through the items, and started the engine, she watched as Koos took off, then she taxied down to the western end of the airstrip, and took off herself. She, and Koos exchanged a few innocuous messages on the radio, then she heard him talking to the controller at Maun. It was good to listen in on his conversations, it stopped her from feeling so lonely. She climbed out, and turned south, and retraced the route she had taken coming north. As she flew south she mulled over what she had raised with Bridget. Given the amount of planning that had gone into the three killings they had had in Gaborone, it now seemed to her very probable that Pretorius had his escape from Botswana already planned, and was just executing it. The idea of booking a safari trip, and just staying in an out-of-the-way bush camp was very alluring, but was it likely. He had to assume that at some point the police would tumble to the Theron identity switch, so he must have at least one other to fall back on. Marieke knew that he had used the James Mason identity, but were there others?

It was almost eleven when Marieke called the Gaborone tower, and got landing instructions. The flight south had been uneventful, which might not have been the best as it gave her time to brood. There were times when she resented her job, but fortunately, those times were rare, it just happened that now was one of them. But, for this particular moment, she was focused on the job at hand, which was landing. She was directed in after an Air Botswana plane, and ahead of another private plane. On the ground, she taxied over to the general aviation hardstand and parked. She watched as the other private plane followed her in, and studied the passengers who disembarked. There were four of them, all middle-aged, all white, all men, all overdressed for Botswana, they all carried briefcases, so she wondered what kind of business they were in, and who they had come to see. It was unlikely to be diamonds as the De Beers people had their own plane, and usually went straight out to Orapa. They could be connected to the beef industry, or they could be lawyers or accountants. At any rate, they were unlikely to be connected with her current case, so she just filed away the tail number of the plane, which was South African, and the faces of the four men.

"*Dumela Mma*," Constance said when Marieke arrived home. "How was the flight?"

"*Dumela Mma*," Marieke replied. "The flights north, and south were uneventful, which is good. I saw Mbali and the girls safely into the hands of Bridget, and for the next two weeks, they should be safe enough."

"I have lunch ready," Constance said. "Are you hungry?"

"I am," Marieke confirmed. "So, what did you do this morning?"

"I checked around outside, and there have been no visitors, welcome or unwelcome," Constance said. "All my tell-tales are undisturbed, and there are no new tracks, and none have been brushed out."

"That's good to know," Marieke said. "I think lunch, then a nap."

Marieke took her nap, and then went to the police station for the daily five o'clock meeting.

"*Dumela Mma*," the commissioner said when she arrived at his office.

"Sir," she replied.

"So, you have the Lamprecht family safely out of harm's way?" he asked.

"I do, Sir," she confirmed. "On Friday, I went to the Francistown prison and talked to the warden and a retired warder. It seems that Pretorius met up with a man there whom he had known before, a Kossam from Zim, who was released a year before Pretorius, this Kossam comes from near Crooks' Corner. Sergeant Maphosa has suggested a theory that Pretorius may go east to Tuli then work his way east to Mozambique, the Sergeant suggested Vilanculos as a possible pick-up place for Wilson's yacht. Perhaps Pretorius has

217

been in touch with this Kossam, and arranged to get across Zim to Pafuri, and then into Mozambique."

"Interesting," the commissioner said. "Who else did Pretorius mix with?"

"There was a San *sangoma*, Izak, who seemed to have a big impact on him, after their meeting Pretorius changed, and started reading, apparently he read every book they have, all at least twice, he learned Setswana, Shona, and some Venda, and also took classes in the carpentry and machining shops," she replied.

"He did, did he?" the commissioner said. "Well, that is interesting, so he may well have made his own suppressors."

"I will try and track down this *sangoma*," Marieke said. "I may know him, I arrested an Izak many years ago for cattle theft, and he was San, and a *sangoma*, he operated near Tshabong, where I was stationed at the time."

"Call the Tshabong station, and see if they know where this Izak may be, if he is still alive, and they can find him, fly out there, if you drive it will take you all day to get there and back, let alone how far you may have to drive to find this Izak. Talk to him, perhaps he can see Pretorius and tell us where he is and where he's going," the commissioner suggested.

"Yes, Sir," Marieke said. "I'll also call the Selebi station and see if they've heard about or seen someone that fits the description of Pretorius."

"Good," the commissioner agreed. "Let's see if there's anything else new."

There was really nothing new to report; the basic police work was still proceeding, but everyone was getting frustrated. How was it possible for a middle-aged white man to disappear in Gaborone, and where were the Land Cruiser and Mercedes that he had brought across the border. The immigration record review was almost done, and they had managed to track down 55% of those who were still in the country. That did leave quite a few yet to find and confirm their whereabouts. Further reviews of the forensic evidence had revealed nothing they did not already know. No more eyewitnesses had come forward with sightings of Pretorius/

Theron/Mason, so they were still hard-pressed to try and track his movements. It was beginning to look as if it would all hinge on some lucky event that would trigger a more focused manhunt. They were still waiting for the South Africans to let them know if Pretorius had stolen any other identities; it was entirely possible that he was staying in the best hotel in town under another assumed name. If he were, then he must have also changed his appearance somewhat, because they had taken photographs of Pretorius to all the hotels and asked if he was staying there.

Marieke went to her office and called the Tshabong police station. The duty officer who answered the telephone was a Sergeant Mokotedi, whom Marieke knew. After the usual exchange of greetings, Marieke asked him if he had heard whether Izak was still in the area. Sergeant Mokotedi told her that he was, in fact, alive, well, and flourishing in a small village about an hour's drive from Tshabong. She told him that she would be flying out the next day to talk to Izak, and asked the sergeant to have someone collect her at the airstrip at eight-thirty the next morning and drive her to where Izak was living. He promised to set things up and to let the station commander know that she was coming. Her next item was to arrange a plane, so she called the charter company she normally used and asked what might be available. They had a Cessna Stationair that could be ready in the morning, so Marieke reserved it and said that she would be out at six in the morning to do her pre-flight checks. That done, she went home for some dinner and a rest before the trip.

Constance had dinner ready, and over dinner they talked about the cases, and where they thought that Pretorius might be holed up. There was a very good chance that he was already gone, and back in South Africa, but if he was still in Botswana, they had to find him before he killed again. Marieke tried to remember all that Jan had told her about the poaching trip and who was involved. She knew about the four members from South Africa, and the buyer, she knew about the arresting officer, their own Ian

Mochage, she knew about the failed attempt to get representation from Kagiso Katse, so who was left. The files indicated that the judge was a Justice Hildyard, who had been out on a contract from England under an agreement where the United Kingdom would provide high court justices until such time as Botswana appointed their own. Hildyard would have gone back to England and would be really old now, if not dead. There was a Koos Botha from the South African legation who visited Pretorius in gaol, probably to listen to his sad story, and give him the bad news that his government could not or would not intervene. Botha was probably a junior under or assistant secretary, so not very old when he was in Gaborone. There was no way to know from the files how old he was when he was in Gaborone before, but, given that it was not a prime posting like London or Taipei, he was likely to be younger. He might still be in the South African foreign service, or might be retired, or even dead. Marieke thought that she should let Andries know that Koos Botha could be a target, or may have already been killed. The last name on her list was Dube, then Inspector Dube, now retired, and living in Gaborone. She told Constance to find him and check on him quickly; they had not heard of any other killings, but Dube was very definitely a target.

Six the following morning found Marieke signing for the aircraft she had chartered for the day. She borrowed a tug, and towed it to the fuel point, put enough to get her to Tshabong, and back, with a reserve. That done, she did the pre-flight walk-around and then climbed aboard to do the pre-flight checklist. She had flown this particular aircraft a number of times, so knew it quite well. Checks finished, she started up, and finished those checks before contacting the tower, getting her clearance to taxi out, and take off. The only traffic around was two charters taking tourists up to Maun, so would not be flying her way. Her way took her around the town, and then out towards the west, she would hold this heading for about 150 nautical miles before making a turn towards the southwest, and Tshabong. She did this to avoid flying over the South African border. The border followed the Molopo River, and was anything but a straight line, and a direct heading from Gaborone to Tshabong would have taken her briefly over South Africa, and back to Botswana. As she approached Tshabong she talked to the police station on the ground, and got the wind direction, then she flew down the strip with the wind looking for cattle, camels or other things that might cause problems landing. Finally, she made her turn and went in against the wind. As she taxied up to the hard stand, she saw Inspector Eric Matambo waiting. He had taken over from her when she had been promoted, and she had a high regard for his abilities.

"*Dumela Mma*," he said, as she exited the plane after shutdown.

"*Dumela Rra*," she said. "Are you well?"

"Well enough," he replied. "And you?"

"Physically well, but frustrated," she replied.

"So, we haven't caught this man Pretorius yet?" he asked.

"Sadly, no," she confirmed.

"How was the flight out?" he asked.

"Good," she said. "Only one hour and forty minutes, better than the five and a half hours to drive."

"Indeed," he agreed. "I understand you would like to talk to Izak, the one whom you arrested a few years ago for cattle theft?"

"I do," she said. "It seems that he spent much time with Pretorius when he was in Francistown, and I'm hoping that he will cooperate with us and tell us if he knows anything about the current whereabouts of Pretorius."

"I have a Land Rover ready," Eric said. "I have coffee for you and a small breakfast. I wasn't sure what you would get before you left this morning."

"Thank you," she said. "That is kind of you. Where is Izak living?"

"About an hour from here near Bogogobo," Eric replied.

"So, is he likely to skip across the border?" she asked.

"I doubt it," Eric said. "The South Africans know him as a cattle thief, and would chase him if they saw him on their side of the border. So, how is life in Gabs?"

"It's been interesting," she said. "I've been busy, and seem to get the odd cases. Two years ago it was the headless bodies, and this year it's the killings in Gabs."

"So sad about the commissioner," Eric said. "I knew him, as you know, and always liked him."

"What about you?" she asked. "How do you like running the station? Have you been busy?"

"I've come to appreciate how much you did for us with all the admin and paperwork," he replied. "As for busy, well, we've had the usual things, cattle theft, some brawls, and drunkenness, and the usual array of domestic, and other petty disputes, but, mainly pretty quiet, I wish I could speak Afrikaans as well as you, because I get on quite well with van de Merwe across the border, and he, and I have worked on two cross border cases trafficking in stolen cars. He's bright, good to work with, funny, but his English is not the best, and my Afrikaans is really poor, but we manage."

"I liked him," Marieke said. "I would have thought that they would have promoted him by now?"

"I think they would have, but he pissed off one of the senior officers who came to visit by calling him names when he stuck their Land Rover in the sand. The major had insisted on driving, even though Van had told him that the road was bad, and when he stuck the Land Rover, and couldn't get it out, Van let him have it, then shoved him out of the driver's seat, and got them out," Eric explained.

"I could see him doing that," Marieke laughed. "Poor Van, so he's stuck out here for a while longer."

"I don't think he minds too much," Eric said. "He likes it out here, and he doesn't get many visits from the hierarchy."

Eric finally turned off the main road, if it could be called a main road, and took a side track for about a mile until they came to a house, with a cattle kraal, and some other shanties.

"This is where Izak lives," he said. "I wonder if I should check those cattle to see if he's lifted them. Not today, I think, I'll give him the benefit of the doubt. Perhaps another day we'll do a check of all the little kraals in the area, and see what belongs to whom." He led the way to the house, and even though the door was wide open, stood in the doorway, and knocked on the doorframe.

"*Dumela Rra,*" he said.

"*Dumela Rra,*" Izak replied. "I've done nothing wrong."

"I know Izak," Eric assured him. "I've brought someone to see you."

"Inspector Englebrecht," Izak said, "I thought you had gone away?"

"I have Izak," she replied. "I have come back here to ask for your help."

"My help?" Izak asked. "What can I do? Come in, come in, tea?"

"Tea would be nice, thank you," Marieke said. They waited until Izak had made tea, and handed it around, and then she asked him about his memories of Pretorius, and if he knew where Pretorius was. He talked for about an hour in a mixture of Setswana and San, telling them of his time in Francistown, the man Pretorius, and how he had tried to direct him away from his bitterness. Marieke told him what had been going on, and he was shocked, and then sat back, and went off into a semi-trance to see if he could see Pretorius. Finally, he sat back and said that Pretorius was still in Gaborone but that seeing him was difficult as he was being protected by a *sangoma* there. Marieke asked him if he could tell her where in Gaborone, and he gave a good description of the place, something that they should be able to track down. Marieke thanked him for his help and then told him that she had to go back and see if she could catch Pretorius.

"You will catch him, *Mma*," he said. "You caught me, even if I did let you."

"You got lazy," she told him. "You should have been more alert, and then I would have missed you."

"That is true," he admitted. "But you had help, I think?"

"I did," she admitted. "But the grandfather who helped me is now dead, so I have come to you."

"I am pleased that you have," Izak said. "I am upset that Pretorius has done these things. I told him to let go of his bitterness, but all he learned was to plan and then kill. Chase him down as you chased me down."

"I will," she said. "Stay well, Izak."

"Go well, *Mma*," he replied.

Marieke and Eric left Izak pondering his failure with Pretorius and hurried back to the Land Rover. They would use the radio in the Land Rover once they were in range of the station in Tshabong, and pass on the information about the location in Gaborone. Eric drove as fast as he dared back along the road to Tshabong, and they finally got to a point where they could contact the station. Marieke relayed the information they had and asked that it be forwarded to Gaborone. Now they would have to wait to see if the information was useful or not.

"When will you come out here again, Marieke?" Eric asked.

"I don't know," she replied. "So much depends on what's happening in Gabs."

"You should try and get out here on the last Friday of any month," Eric suggested. "We have a *braai* with the people from van de Merwe's post on the last Friday of the month. We set it up in the river bed, so we can argue that we don't actually cross the border, we just pass beer and steaks back and forth."

"I like that idea," Marieke laughed. "Has anyone complained?"

"There was one new recruit on Van's side who said that he was going to report it to the higher authority, but we never heard anything," Eric said. "It helps us work together, and if either one of us needs help, the other will provide. I passed along the pictures of Pretorius, and the aliases that he has been using, Theron, and Mason, and Van had been given the same by his people."

"I've been working with a Lieutenant Colonel Andries van Dyk," Marieke explained. "He's good to work with and open-minded. He's got several murders he has to solve, and it looks like Pretorius is behind all of them. One is delicate, it involves an army general who was receiving poached ivory back in the 70s when he was in Intelligence, and the South African Army would like to hush that up. Can we stop at the station before I fly back?"

"Of course," Eric said. "We're nearly there. Would you like some lunch before you go?"

"I think I should get back as soon as I can," she thought. "If I could get a sandwich, that would be fine."

Sandwich in hand, Marieke was taken back to the airstrip where she did her pre-flight checks before saying goodbye to Eric Matambo, and setting off back for Gaborone. Her flight back to Gaborone was as uneventful as the one to Tshabong, which was good, and she landed at the stroke of twelve, giving her the whole afternoon.

At the office, she was greeted by Sergeant Maphosa.

"We missed him," he said. "If we had been two or three hours earlier, we would have had him. We did get the Mercedes and some other items, but Pretorius had left when we got there. It took us a little while to find the place. The description was good, very accurate in fact, but it took us a while to find it."

"That's a shame," she said. "Have we any idea where he's gone?"

"No," Maphosa said. "He must still have the Land Cruiser, or perhaps he traded that for another vehicle, because we didn't find it. We were so close before when we found the storage place that Theron had rented, we should have looked further, because the storage place we went to, and found the Mercedes, was less than a mile from the other, but it was rented by a Frikkie Carlitz."

"Frikkie Carlitz," Marieke repeated. "I should talk to Andries van Dyk about that name. Perhaps it's another alias, or perhaps Carlitz is a real person who's helping Pretorius. Do you know if Sergeant Sephoto found Dube?"

"I believe she's still out looking," Maphosa said. "She got his address from the records and has gone there, but that was some time ago. I would have thought that she would have been back by now."

"Did she take a car with a radio?" Marieke asked.

"Yes, Madame," Maphosa confirmed.

"Find out where she is, and if there is a problem," Marieke instructed. She then called Andries van Dyk in Port Elizabeth.

"*Middag*," he said when he answered the telephone.

"*Middag*," she replied. "How are things in PE?"

"Busy," he said. "What about you?"

"We've just missed Pretorius," she said. "We got a tip, and went looking for him, and probably missed him by an hour or two."

"So, he's still in Botswana?" Andries asked.

"I think so," Marieke confirmed. "If not, then he's just crossed the border, probably the Limpopo, it's closer than trying to cross the Molopo. I did have a couple of questions for you."

"Fire away," he said.

"When Pretorius was arrested, and in gaol here, he requested help from your legation here, and was visited by a Koos Botha. Botha apparently either could not or would not help him, so I was wondering if he's not also on the hit list?"

"Koos Botha," Andries said. "I should get onto the Foreign Affairs people, and find out if he's still with them, and if not, where did he go."

"I think it's worth checking," Marieke said. "Pretorius seems to be settling all accounts. We're checking on another here, an inspector who was the interviewing officer at the time. He may also be on the list."

"I'll check and call you back if I have anything," Andries promised. "What was the other thing?"

"Would you please check and see if the name Frikkie Carlitz means anything to you? Someone using that name rented garage space, and we found the Mercedes there," Marieke explained.

"I'll check on that," Andries promised. "I should have some possible aliases for you tomorrow, we've been running checks on ID cards, and have found some new issues with old cards that we can't explain. The interior people promised me that tonight, so if you call tomorrow, I should have that for you."

"Thank you," she said. "*Tot siens.*"

"*Tot siens,*" he replied.

Before she did anything else, Marieke wrote her report on the day's events and filed it away. She then went to see the commissioner and reported on her trip. He knew that they had just missed Pretorius, but was fairly philosophical about it.

"Sometimes, these things just happen," he said. "You did what you could, and gave us a good description of where he was. It just took us a little longer to find the place. So, where has he gone? Can your contact Izak see that?"

"I'll find out," Marieke promised. "I'll call Eric Matambo in Tshabong, and get him to go back out, and see Izak again. Izak did say that he couldn't see clearly because Pretorius was getting help here. I need to look at the list of people we were given from the prison, and see if any of them would qualify as a *sangoma*, and if not, then who do they know?"

"I understand you've sent Sergeant Sephoto out looking for Ian Dube?" the commissioner said.

"Yes, Sir," Marieke confirmed. "It struck me that Pretorius is settling all accounts, and Inspector Dube was there at the time, and features in the file."

"Let me know if you find anything," the commissioner said. "Is there anything else?" Before Marieke could reply, the telephone rang, and the commissioner answered it, then held his hand up for Marieke to stay.

"You were right to be concerned," he said. "Our people have just found the bodies of Ian Dube and his wife, who is, as I recall, Rachel, in a freezer in their house. Sergeant Sephoto is there, and Thabo is on his way. Go out there, and take a look, and report back."

"Yes, Sir," she said. She left the commissioner's office and went back to her own. Sergeant Maphosa was waiting for her and said that he had a Land Rover ready to go. He drove out to the address that they had while Marieke sat, and wondered why she had not thought about Dube earlier, and found some way to protect him. When they arrived at the house of Dube, Thabo was already there.

"So, Marieke," he said. "We have another. Is this the last?"

"There could be another," she replied. "But not here, probably in South Africa. The man I am thinking of was from their legation, and either couldn't or wouldn't help Pretorius, so I see him as a likely target. What do we have here?"

"Your Sergeant Sephoto found the bodies about thirty minutes ago," he said. "My guess is that they've been a while, exactly how long is going to take some work, as they've been sitting in a freezer. They were shot, I can tell you that, both shot from behind."

"And, no one missed them?" Marieke asked.

"Constance has all the details," Thabo said. "I'm going to focus on the forensics."

"Thank you, Thabo," Marieke said.

Marieke and Sergeant Maphosa went into the house and saw Constance talking to Inspector Bangwata.

"*Dumela Mma, Rra*," Marieke said. "This is unfortunate."

"It is, Madame," Bangwata agreed. "Sergeant Sephoto was just telling me what she found. Perhaps, Sergeant, if you would start again for the Superintendent?"

"Sir," Constance said. "Well, Madame, as you suggested, I got the address of Inspector Dube from our records, but discovered that he had moved, so I went back to the pensions office and got the new address. When I got here, there was no answer at the door. There was no mail, but perhaps he has a box at the Post Office. I asked a few neighbours if they had seen Inspector Dube, and no one has for three weeks. They all thought that the Dubes had gone away after a visit they received from a priest. They only moved here two months ago, and the neighbours did not know them well, so did not know if they attended a church or if they had family members close by. I went back to the house, and looked in through the windows, and saw nothing out of place, except the kitchen table looked like a mess, and there were ants and cockroaches all over it. I looked at the doors and windows, and noticed that the back door lock had small scratches around it, so I began to suspect something. I made entry by breaking a window in the bedroom and climbing in. I came into the kitchen and saw that the mess was blood. I traced drops of blood to this back-storage room and found the bodies in the freezer. Then I called the station, and we began our investigation."

"Thank you, Sergeant," Marieke said. "Do we know who the priest was?"

"I asked the neighbours if anyone knew the priest, but none of them did," Constance replied. "Of the neighbours I asked, four of them go to different churches, and they all said that the priest was unknown to them, and that they had not seen the Dubes at their churches."

"Sergeant Maphosa, take the information that Sergeant Sephoto collected about the churches, and start checking the other churches, and see if we can find out which one, if any Ian, and Rachel Dube attended, and or if any of them sent a priest to welcome them to the area," Marieke instructed, then she gave further instructions. "Inspector, I'll leave the crime scene to you, but I assume they were shot from behind at the kitchen table, then the bodies carried to the freezer, and dumped. Sweep the area carefully, something tells me that we won't find much, but look anyway. I'd better get back and tell the commissioner what you found."

"Well, Superintendent?" the commissioner asked when Marieke went to his office.

"Sir, Inspector Dube and his wife, Rachel, were shot from behind while they were seated at the kitchen table. The killer then carried the bodies to a storage room and put them in a freezer," Marieke explained. "The neighbours say that they have not seen them for three weeks, and a priest visited them about three weeks ago."

"Would that put this killing before or after that of Katse?" he asked,

"I suspect before, Sir," she replied. "Putting the bodies in the freezer is going to make determining exact time of death difficult."

"Damn," he said. "I don't suppose there was really much we could have done. We only went to check on Dube after we had put together a likely relationship between the killings, and that only happened after Katse, Ian Mochage, and Jan Lamprecht were killed. What was Dube's part in this?"

"My reading of the files was that he did most of the interviews here in Gabs," she explained.

"Have we forgotten anyone else?" he asked.

"The only other I can think of was a member of the South African legation at the time," she explained. "I will alert Andries in PE."

"Will you put money on the fate of the diplomat?" he asked.

"No, Sir," she said. "In my mind, if he's in South Africa, he's dead."

"Sadly, I agree with you," he said. "Now, where do we look for Pretorius?"

"As I said on Friday, Sergeant Maphosa suggested the Tuli Block as a possibility," she said. "From there, he could skip over the border into Zim, and then make his way to Mozambique."

"Yes, I remember that," he said. "I think you'd better become the tracker, and go, and find Pretorius before he does cross the border. You said he's been getting help?"

"Izak told us that he is being helped," she confirmed.

"Go carefully then, and go well armed, I don't want to lose another officer, is there anyone you want to help you?" the commissioner asked.

"The police tracker Tushay from Maun, and Sergeant Maphosa," she said. "I worked with Tushay before, and he's very good."

"Let's see, what time is it? Three-o'clock. We've missed this afternoon's flight from Maun, so fly up there yourself, collect him, and get started on the hunt as soon as you can," he instructed.

"Yes, Sir," she said. "I'll go up this afternoon, and come back tomorrow morning."

"Do that," he said. "What do you need for tomorrow?"

"One of the newer Land Rovers with the long-range tanks," she thought. "And two rifles with at least a hundred rounds of ammunition each, and a handgun with four spare magazines, plus food, and water for three for two weeks."

"Are you planning to start a war?" he laughed. "I'll have it ready for you when you get back. I'll make sure the radio in the Land Rover is working, but it won't do you much good out there."

"How disturbed is the site where we missed Pretorius?" she asked.

"Like a herd of cattle went through there," he said. "If you were hoping to pick up his or his vehicle's tracks there, I think that's a fond hope. Well, good hunting!"

"Yes, Sir," she said.

On the trail

Before Marieke left, she called the airport to find out what plane might be available for an overnight run to Maun, and back. The Stationair she had had that morning was out, but the Cessna Caravan was available. It was a little large for just two, but it was available, she told them that she would be there within the hour. Then she called Andries van Dyk in Port Elizabeth.

"*Middag,*" he said as he answered the telephone.

"*Middag,* Andries, it's Marieke, I've got something for you," she said. "We've had another two deaths, but we think they may precede the Katse shooting, which we thought was the first. A retired police officer and his wife were both killed. The officer was the interviewing officer in the Pretorius case."

"*Magtig,*" Andries said. "I found out about Koos Botha, he's still in the foreign service, but he's in Paris at the moment at our embassy there. I've something else for you, the ferry crew that Wilson hired has return tickets from Paris, eight weeks from now. I also found out a little more about the ferry crew. They're a crew of pirates, maybe not literally, but they will do anything for money. The leader is a Brit by the name of George Havelock, and his lieutenants are Bill Evans, Piet Kruger, Johannes Mulder, James Neal, and Frikkie Buys, as disreputable a group of *ouks,* as you could find, they all have military experience here, and Kruger, and Mulder served together in the Recces, so they're smart as well as being tough. This crew is interesting, they are all of about the same build, height, and weight, and at least three of them could pass as each other with only a distant casual glance, so checking who is actually who should be done carefully. Oh, and the boat was reported in Durban a while ago, and in LM a week ago, where it took on fuel, so they're not on the way to Rio, they're standing off the Mozambique coast."

"We visited the prison where Pretorius did his time," she said. "And we learned that one of the *ouks* that he used in the past as a tracker was also in for part of the time. This *ou* comes from near Crooks' Corner, so my sergeant suggested that Pretorius may be headed for Tuli, then to Pafuri then to the Mozambique coast for a pickup, he thought somewhere near Vilanculos was more likely than Maputo, less traffic, and less vigilance."

"So, he probably has a plan, and a timetable, my guess is that there's a pick-up window for the boat, and if he misses that then he's on his own," Andries suggested.

"It looks that way," Marieke agreed. "I'm getting a tracker I've worked with before, and we're going after him tomorrow, maybe we'll catch him before he crosses into Zim. If he gets to the Mozambique coast, then my guess is that they'll sail up the east coast, and through the Suez into the Med."

"That should be interesting," Andries said. "The Suez is notorious for officials looking for bribes or baksheesh, Havelock would be most unlikely to pay a bribe, he'd be more likely to hold a gun to someone's head, and force them to pilot them through, and if the Egyptians try any rough stuff, they may discover that they've bitten off more than they really want, my bet is that those *ouks* are armed to the teeth."

"I'd better go," Marieke said. "I'm going to fly up to Maun tonight, and bring my tracker back in the morning. Oh, before I go would you send me copies of the identity cards of all those in the yacht crew?"

"Of course, I'll also send you their fingerprint cards, we have one for each, either from the army or our own files," Andries said. "I'll warn the foreign service people about Pretorius. Good flight, and good hunting!"

"Thanks, *tot siens*," Marieke said. She then called the Maun police station, and talked to Inspector Moroka.

"*Dumela Rra*," she said.

"*Dumela Mma*," he replied. "How are things in Gaborone?"

"Not the best," she said. "Inspector, I know we've borrowed Sergeant Sephoto from you, may I now also borrow Tushay for the next two weeks?"

"Of course, Madame," he said. "When do you need him?"

"I was going to fly up this afternoon, and bring him back with me first thing tomorrow morning," she explained. "Is that all right with you?"

"Certainly," he said. "When do you want to leave in the morning?"

"Early, so if Tushay could be at the airport at five, I would be grateful," she said.

"Of course," Moroka said. "Are we then making progress on these killings?"

"We missed Pretorius by hours this morning," she explained. "I'm hoping that we can pick up a trail, and follow him."

"Do you need somewhere to stay tonight," Moroka asked.

"No thank you, Inspector," she said. "I'll be making arrangements with Patience Botha, she'll be picking me up at the airport this afternoon."

"I will see you tomorrow morning then," Moroka said. "Go well."

"Stay well, Inspector," she replied.

She took her briefcase, and loaded it with files, and pictures of Pretorius, in case her plans changed, and she had to go somewhere else, then she left the office, and went home to get an overnight bag, and her binoculars. She then called Patience Botha in Maun, and asked if she could stay the night, Patience was delighted to hear from her, and asked when she would be arriving in Maun. Marieke gave her an estimated time of arrival, then set out for the airport. She took a short detour, and stopped at the salon of June Matsoka.

"*Dumela Mma*," June said when Marieke went in the shop.

"*Dumela Mma*," Marieke replied. "How are you?"

"I'm returning to normal," June said. "I'm trying to stay busy, it helps."

"Are you busy now?" Marieke asked.

"No, I've an hour before my next appointment," June said. "How can I help?"

"I'm going to be going into the bush for a while," Marieke explained. "I would like my hair cut short before I go, then it's much easier to look after."

"Are you making progress then?" June asked.

"We are reasonably sure who killed Kagiso, and we're now on his trail," Marieke explained.

"Then, we should get this done quickly," June said. "You said short, how short?"

"I was thinking something like Halle Berry has, perhaps a little shorter," Marieke suggested.

"I can do that," June promised. It didn't take long before Marieke was looking at herself in the mirror, and admitting that June had done a really good job.

"Thank you," she said. "What do I owe you?"

"The news that you've caught the man who killed Kagiso," June said. "Go, go, and chase him down!"

"I will," Marieke promised, "Stay well."

"Go well," June replied.

The flight north to Maun took just one hour and forty-five minutes, and Marieke saw Patience waiting for her at the terminal building. It took only minutes to refuel the plane, ready for the morning, and tie it down. Marieke was surprised at the number of planes that were there, but perhaps it was not surprising; the tourist business was beginning to boom, and the quickest way to get to many of the bush camps and lodges was by air. She half expected to see Koos there, but perhaps he had charters elsewhere that day. The airport officials had come out to see who she was, but when they had seen her warrant card, they went back quickly to their hut to await the next arrival.

"So, Marieke," Patience said. "Are you well?"

"Well enough," Marieke replied. "And you?"

"I am doing very well, handing the garage over to Phineas was a great relief to us both, and now I can concentrate on bookings for Will, and Bridget," Patience said. "Is that all the luggage you have? Oh, there was a message for you to call a Lieutenant Colonel van Dyk in PE, he said to call him at home if you had to."

"This is it for luggage," Marieke confirmed. "When we get to the house do you mind if I use your telephone?"

"Please do," Patience said.

Marieke called the home of Andries van Dyk, and a woman answered the telephone. "*Naand*," she said.

"*Naand*," Marieke replied. "*Mag ek asseblief met Andries Van Dyk praat?*"

"Is this Superintendent Englebrecht?" the voice said. "This is Anna, his wife, it's nice to finally talk to you, let me get Andries."

"Marieke," Andries said when he picked up the telephone. "How was the flight?"

"Uneventful," she replied. "Just the type I like."

"Well, I've got some information for you," he said. "We've worked on possible identities that Pretorius may be using, and we've come up with, Piet de la Rey, Henry Porter, and Richard Anderson. I passed those on to your station in Gabs. As for associates in Zeerust, there don't seem to have been many, there was his cousin, Danie, now dead, there was van de Merwe, also dead, there was Jan Lamprecht, also dead, and there was an odd one, a Gareth Thomas who worked at the Marico Chrome mine. We checked with the Marico people, and they tell us that he left them twenty years ago, and is now working at Selebi Phikwe, apparently they used to go on hunting trips together in the northern Cape near Upington."

"*Magtig*," Marieke said.

"What's up?" Andries asked.

"Thomas was a business partner with the solicitor who was killed," she explained. "I never even thought of him as connected to Pretorius. Did you let Gaborone know about Thomas?"

"I did," he confirmed.

"Thank you for letting me know," she said. "I should call Gabs, and see if I can get some things checked." She hung up, and called the station in Gaborone to talk to Sergeant Maphosa. He was not there, but there was a message to call him at the Mochudi station. She wondered what had happened, and called Mochudi.

"*Dumela Mma*," he said, when he answered the telephone.

"*Dumela Rra*," she replied. Is there any news?"

"Have you talked to Lieutenant Colonel van Dyk?" Maphosa asked.

"I have," she confirmed.

"Well, there's more," Maphosa said. "We got a tip about Mathews Olopeng, he was one of those releases from Francistown who came from Gabs. He was a confidence trickster, and passed himself off as a *sangoma*. He was seen leaving Gabs with a white man in a Land Cruiser. We found the Land Cruiser, it was in some empty space here, we are supposing that he took back roads here. The engine was still quite hot, so we were only an hour or so behind, the Land Cruiser fits the description of the one that Pretorius, as Theron, brought across the border, it's got Botswana licence plates, but they actually belong to a scrapped Mitsubishi Colt. It looks as if he met someone, abandoned his Land Cruiser, and left with the other person. There are three sets of tracks, one we guessed was the driver of the second vehicle, which we think is a Land Rover, judging by the tracks, he's about 75 kg, and with size 44 shoes, another weighs about 80 kg with size 47 shoes, probably Pretorius, and the last weighs about 70 kg with size 42 shoes. The small man walks like a black man, not a *muzungu*, and we are certain that it is Olopeng, he walked away from the site headed towards Gabs. We tracked him for a little while, but he appears to have been given a lift by someone, so we lost him, we'll try, and pick him up when he gets back to Gabs. The others in the Land Rover turned north onto the tarred road, and we lost them too. We did find a witness who saw the white man get out of his Land Cruiser, and into the Land Rover, and saw Olopeng walk away. We're going back to the witness with photographs of Pretorius, and Olopeng to see if they can identify them."

"Thank you," she said. "Make sure that when they take the photographs they take a selection to see if the witness can really identify Pretorius, and Olopeng, and not just say yes to us, because that's what they think we want." She thought about things for a little, and then asked. "Wasn't one of the associates of Pretorius in prison who was released, from Bononong?"

"Yes, Madame," Maphosa said. "Let, me see, it was a Keabetswe Paledi, he was a poacher, and a cattle thief."

"Get onto the Bononong station, and find out if he's at home, or if he's gone walkabout," Marieke said.

"Gone walkabout, Madame?" Maphosa asked.

"Australian term, it means he's disappeared," she explained. "From Bononong to Tuli is not that far, so, perhaps he's helping Pretorius there. What about the others in Gabs?"

"Two we were able to eliminate," Maphosa said. "But, two we are still investigating, one is Mathews Olopeng, and the other is Lesitang Kgathi."

"What can you tell me about Kgathi?" she asked.

"Kgathi was a car thief," Maphosa said.

"Okay, have someone continue to check on Kgathi, and try, and find Olopeng if you can," she said. "He may have been a better *sangoma* than people gave him credit for."

Marieke thought about things for a minute then came to a decision. "How did you get to Mochudi?" she asked.

"I brought the Land Rover with the extra fuel tanks, and the supplies," he said. "I thought this might lead to something."

"You were right. Have the Mochudi people process the scene there. Get another driver, borrow one from Mochudi if you have to," she said. "And, leave now, I would like you to be at the Tuli Lodge airstrip by seven tomorrow morning. Call the air charter people, and tell them that I'm flying direct to Tuli in the morning, and that we need to make arrangements to get the plane back to them."

"You think Pretorius is running for the border?" Maphosa asked.

"With some help," she said. "We may be lucky, and catch them. We need a guide out there too, get onto the Tuli Lodge people, and tell them we need a guide, and that we're probably looking for two people who are trying to get to the Zim border, probably trying not to be seen. What kind of car does Thomas drive?"

"We're checking on that now," Maphosa said. "We're also checking with Selebi to see if he is at work."

"If you wanted to drive to Tuli, and not take the main road, how would you get there?" she asked.

"I'd take the road through Makwate, and Zanzibar," he said. "It's not as busy as the road to Selebi, it would be easy to see cars coming, and avoid them."

"Take that way yourself," she suggested. "And keep a lookout for any signs of the Land Rover that was at Mochudi. I'll see you at the Tuli Lodge airstrip tomorrow morning."

"Yes, Madame," Maphosa said. "Should I let the commissioner know where we are going?

"Yes, we'd better," she thought. "Do we have any useful contacts with the Zim police?"

"No, Madame," Maphosa said. "Nor with the Mozambique police."

"Pity," she said. "I would think that by the time any request for help goes through administrative channels Pretorius will be at sea on the Indian Ocean. Fine, Sergeant, I'll see you in the morning."

"Yes, Madame, go well," he said.

"Problems?" Patience asked after Marieke had hung up.

"Yes, and no," Marieke said. "We may have had some luck in this case of the killing, now I think it will be a matter of how fast our man makes for the border, which may depend on whether or not he thinks we're close behind. I need to be up early in the morning, I want to be in the air as soon after five as I can be."

"Won't it be difficult to find your way in the dark?" Patience asked.

"No, I'll use the Orapa mine as my first check, then I'll use the mine at Selebi as my second check, by which time it will be light, and I can then use ground landmarks to make the final leg into the Tuli strip," Marieke said. "I hadn't really thought about using the mines before, but Koos Strijdom pointed out that they're obvious from the sky, and they're typically lit up like Christmas trees, so hard to miss."

"Who are you looking for?" Patience asked.

"Hansie Pretorius," Marieke replied.

"I remember him," Patience said. "He was a notorious poacher, he is a dangerous man, he would think nothing of shooting you to get away. He used to associate with his cousin, Danie, and two others, a van de Merwe, and our friend Jan Lamprecht. They used to do business with Marais here in town."

"Marais?" Marieke asked.

"*Ja*, he had a bottle store here, and had other, less legal, dealings too, he used to go by Kobus Marais or sometimes, Piet Marais, he was eventually deported, and I heard that the South Africans locked him up for a while. I also heard that he shopped Pretorius, and his friends when Pretorius was arrested twenty years ago," Patience explained.

"I should let Andries know that he may have another potential victim," Marieke thought. She called the home number of Andries again, and he answered.

"*Naand*," she said. "I'm sorry to bother you again, but another name has surfaced that you might wish to check."

"*Naand*," Andries said. "Who should I be looking for?"

"Marais, either Kobus or Piet, it's the same person, we deported him at about the same time as we arrested Pretorius," she explained. "The story is that he shopped Pretorius, and his party to us. We also heard that you had arrested him when we kicked him out, and that he served time. So, he's likely to have a record with you."

"You are full of good news," Andries said. "I'll check on Marais, and see what I can find out."

Marieke was at the airport early the next morning, armed with a powerful torch, so that she could do her walk around pre-flight check in the dark. She saw Inspector Moroka arrive with Tushay, and waved to him.

"*Dumela Mma*," he said. "You're up early."

"*Dumela Rra*," she replied. "I think we may be onto our killer, we believe he's going to cross the border into Zim in the Tuli area. If we're lucky, and they are slow we may be able to intercept them. My sergeant should be almost at the strip, if he's not there already."

"Well, good hunting," the inspector said.

"*Dumela* Tushay," she said. "Are you ready?"

"Yes, Madame," he said. He was a little apprehensive, he had been on planes before, but was never comfortable with the idea.

"Good, then let's get aboard, Inspector if you wouldn't mind when we start our taxi, could you drive down to the windward end of the runway, and park there with your lights on," she said. They both climbed aboard the plane, and she showed Tushay how to strap himself in. She went through the pre-startup checklist, then started the engine. She waved to Inspector Moroka, and he pulled away the chocks. She waved goodbye, and taxied out onto the runway, and waited until the inspector was at the other end, then she started her take-off roll, heading towards the inspector, and his car. Once in the air, she turned to a heading of 126 degrees that ought to take her right over the Orapa mine. It did not take long before they could see the mine, and when she passed overhead she made a turn to 105 degrees that would take her over the mine at Selebi Phikwe. That leg took a little longer than the first leg, but by the time they passed over the mine it was light, and they could see everything on the ground. She then made another turn, to 100 degrees, and started her descent into the Tuli area. She found the rivers, roads, and veterinary fence line, and saw the strip ahead. She flew down the strip, and looked at the wind sock, and also noted that there was nothing on the runway, and she also saw Sergeant Maphosa waiting for her, and she saw another vehicle that was obviously from one of the game lodges. She came around again to land into the wind, and put the plane down, and taxied up to the stand area. Sergeant Maphosa greeted her, and Tushay, and then introduced Police Constable Thebe who had been his co-driver from Mochudi, and to Hastings who was the guide loaned to them by the Tuli Lodge. She had only been on the ground for a few minutes when they heard another plane approaching. It landed, and taxied up to them. It was from the charter company, and had brought guests out for the game lodge whose vehicle was there to meet the plane, and it had brought another pilot.

"*Dumela Mma*," the first pilot said to Marieke after he had seen his passengers into the hands of the lodge staff.

"*Dumela Rra*," she replied. "How was the flight up Brad?"

"Good, thanks Marieke," he replied. "I brought Charles along to take the Caravan back to Gabs. You're sure you won't be needing it?"

"Sure, thanks, Brad," she assured him. "We've got to do this on the ground now, what we could use is a helicopter."

"Sorry," Brad laughed. "Don't have one of those, who are you looking for?"

"We're looking for a Land Rover with at least two men," she said. "I didn't see any sign of it as I came in from Selebi, you didn't happen to see any traffic on your way in?"

"Nothing, man," Brad said. "Must all be still in bed. Okay, we'll be off, see you back in Gabs."

"I'll talk to you when I get back," she promised. "Go well, and you as well Charles."

"Go well, Marieke," Charles replied.

"So, Sergeant," Marieke said after the planes had left. "What do we know?"

"Madame," he said. "Thomas is on leave from Selebi at the moment, he has been off a week, and will be off another week. He does own a Land Rover, a 90 inch station wagon, colour light blue, apparently he bought it two weeks ago from a man in Gabs, it fits the description of the one seen in Mochudi."

"Thank you, Sergeant," she said. "Hastings, if you had to cross the border into Zim without being seen, where would you go?"

"When I get to the other side, will I be walking or expect a ride?" Hastings asked.

"I think expect a ride," she said. "I think he has help, and has set this up some time ago."

"Well, then Madame," Hastings said. "I would cross about here," he said, pointing to a spot on the map they had spread out on the bonnet of their Land Rover. "The crossing of the Shashi is quite wide, but it is a simple crossing between us, and Zim, and there is a road on the other side, too far north, and there's the fence line where the border pushes into Botswana in that big circle, too far south, and he's too close to the South African border, if I were him, I'd go here, there is a lodge close by, that has no guests at the moment, so they could drive to within a mile of the river, and then quickly walk over to the other side."

"Fine, Sergeant, if you'd drive please," she said. They left the airstrip, and went east essentially following the Limpopo, moving nearer, and farther depending on the terrain, and the river crossings. Eventually, Hastings tapped Maphosa on the shoulder, and told him to take the next left. As they turned off, Hastings tapped Maphosa again, and he stopped. They all got out, and looked at the vehicle tracks that were there.

"Someone went this way about thirty minutes ago," Tushay said. "These are the tracks of a short wheel base Land Rover, and dust still hangs in the air a little, and there is the smell of diesel. There are also tracks from yesterday, another *bakkie* came here, probably a Hilux or something like that."

"That could be James," Hastings said. "He's a maintenance man who works for us, I wonder what he's doing out here?"

"Let's see if we can catch up with them," Marieke said. They left, and Sergeant Maphosa pushed their Land Rover as hard as he dared along the dirt road, which was generally straight, but with quite sharp turns to avoid soft patches or other obstacles. They came to a junction, and Tushay, and Hastings both pointed to the right. Tushay pointed again, and then they all saw it, the dust plume of a vehicle, perhaps a mile or two ahead of them.

"There is the lodge just ahead," Hastings said. He pointed, and they saw the Land Rover they had been chasing. Sergeant Maphosa pulled up next to it, and Marieke got out to investigate.

"Tushay, Hastings, come with me," she said, taking her binoculars, and rifle, she also put a rifle in the hands of Tushay. "He's on foot, we'll go after him. Sergeant, Thomas is dead, shot by the look of it, and there's one other, possibly Keabetswe Paledi, start the work of the crime scene for us, and check the lodge as well, call it in, and get someone from forensics here, and tell them to bring three body bags."

"Yes, Madame," Maphosa said. He, and Constable Thebe checked on the buildings, and found them all empty, so they returned to their own Land Rover, and used the radio to contact the closest station, which was the border post at Pont Drift, and got them to relay the message about the crime to Gaborone, including the request for the forensic team. Meanwhile, Tushay, and Hastings had both got the track of the man on foot, and were trotting after him. Marieke was glad that she had kept up her runs each day, or this would have been a real effort for her. They were gaining on him, based on the chatter she heard between Tushay, and Hastings, then they came to the Shashi River.

"There he is, Madame," Tushay said, pointing across the river, where they could see their man wading through the water almost to the far bank. "Do we chase him across the river?" Marieke got her binoculars, and looked at the fleeing man. She thought about it, and reluctantly decided against it, it had to be almost 600 yards across the sand banks, and the river itself, and he had a good head start. Relations with Zimbabwe were not the rosiest, and she didn't need to create a diplomatic incident by crossing the border, hauling Pretorius, if indeed that was him and they could catch him, back into Botswana. Marieke had to presume it was Pretorius, who else would be running for the border. As she recalled when borders ran along non-navigable rivers it was usually on the median of the river. That meant that the actual location of the border was somewhat imprecise as the river channel changed over time with erosion, and water level, and at the moment the channel with water in it was very close to the Zimbabwe side of the river, so it was better to err on the side of caution, even though it allowed her man to get away. She would call the Zimbabwe Police, and tell them what had occurred, and trust to their diligence to track the man down.

"No," she replied. "I don't want to get you arrested by the Zims for illegally entering their country, particularly as one of you is armed. Let's go back, and see what Sergeant Maphosa has discovered."

"He has been picked up, Madame," Tushay said, pointing to the dust plume that had appeared just after Pretorius had cleared the far bank.

They walked back towards the lodge. Tushay pointed to some older tracks, "Two men were here about a month ago," he said. "They came from the lodge to the river, and went back."

"I wonder if it's the ones in the Land Rover?" Marieke mused. "We should check the lodge area when we get back, and see if there's any evidence of who might have been here before. When they got back to the lodge, Sergeant Maphosa came to report. "Gunshot to the head for both, Madame," he said. "It looks like Pretorius just shot them where they sat, in their seats. There are spent cartridge cases here, so that suggests a semi-automatic pistol. Thomas had his driving licence in his pocket, and a thousand Pula; there is food and water in the back, enough for a week at least. The other man is Keabetswe Paledi. Constable Thebe recognised him from previous arrests. There are some other vehicle tracks that lead that way, we were about to follow them."

"We'll do that," she said. "Tushay, and Hastings, please take a look and see what you can find. So, Pretorius gets Thomas to drive him to the border, they pick up Paledi at Bononong, and get him to guide them, then he cleans up loose ends by shooting them," she commented. "I wonder if it was Thomas, and Paledi here a month ago? When can we expect help to get these murders investigated?"

"Dr. Mosiwa is flying up now," Maphosa said. "I should go back to the Tuli airstrip to collect him."

"Fine," Marieke said. "I'll see what else we can find here."

"*Dumela Mma*," she heard a voice say. She looked up, and saw an old man walking towards her, in the company of Tushay, and Hastings.

"*Dumela Rra*," she replied. "Are you well?"

"Well, yes *Mma*," he said. "And you?"

"I am," she replied. "I am Marieke, are you James?"

"Yes, *Mma*," he said. "You have found the man you are looking for?"

"No, he ran away across the Shashi," she said. "Did you see him?"

"Yes, *Mma*," James replied. "He came here in the Land Rover, then left on foot to the river."

"Did you see him shoot the others in the Land Rover?" she asked.

"Yes, *Mma*," he said. "I was over there, and saw the people arrive, then I heard the shots, and saw the two men in the front of the Land Rover explode, then one man left, the one who went to the river."

"Did you know the man?" she asked.

"No, *Mma*," James said.

"If I showed you a picture would you be able to tell if it was him?" she asked.

"Yes, *Mma*," James said.

"Did the people in the Land Rover see you?" she asked.

"No, *Mma*," he replied. "I was fixing the water pump over there, and when I heard the *bakkie* arrive I came to see who it was. I was not told that we had guests out here this week. I saw him shoot the two men I hid until I thought it was safe to come out."

"Was this the man?" she asked, showing James a photograph of the commissioner.

"No, *Mma*," he said. Marieke then spread out about ten photographs in front of him, and asked him if he recognised anyone.

"This man, *Mma*," he said, picking out the photograph of Pretorius.

"Sure?" she asked.

"Sure, sure, *Mma*," he confirmed.

"Constable Thebe, please take the statement of James," she instructed. At least she now had a witness who identified Pretorius as being the other man in the Land Rover, and the one who fired the shots. She looked around the scene, and saw nothing of note, the footprints were apparent, but she knew which prints belonged to whom, and nothing had been dropped outside the Land Rover. Now it was a question of waiting until someone from the forensics unit arrived, then they could check out the fingerprints inside the Land Rover, and look for other clues.

Marieke was hungry, and regretted letting Sergeant Maphosa leave before taking some food, and drink from their vehicle. There was food, and drink in Thomas's vehicle, but until the forensics team had gone over things, she would leave that well alone. James came to the rescue when she heard him ask Thebe if he wanted some tea. She waited for Thebe to answer then added her request, and added one for Tushay, and Hastings. James led the way a little north of the lodge site to a small shed where the pump was located, and behind the shed was an old Toyota Hilux truck. Marieke looked back to the lodge, and noted that this area was not visible from it.

"When did you arrive here?" she asked James as he, and Hastings busied themselves with a fire, and the makings of tea.

"Yesterday, *Mma*," he said. "I slept in the back of my *bakkie* overnight, and started to work on the pump this morning. I heard the other car arrive, and went to see who it was, that's when I saw the man shoot the others, so I hid. When I saw the police Land Rover arrive I was worried that the man might shoot at you, so I waited until I thought it was safe."

"Have you seen either of those in the Land Rover before?" she asked.

"I think so," he said. "There was a man would come here to poach some years ago, a man from Bononong, I think his name was Paledi, was he one of those?"

"He was," she said. "Constable Thebe knew him, so was able to identify him."

"And the other man in the Land Rover?" James asked.

"Gareth Thomas from Selebi Phikwe," Marieke said.

"He has been here before, with Paledi," James said. "He was here a month ago, but in a different car. Not many people come here, the lodge is for guests who want to be away from others." Marieke looked at Hastings, who nodded.

"You were lucky the man didn't see you," Marieke said to James. "He seems to shoot everyone that he thinks might identify him."

Marieke sat, and drank her tea from an empty beef stew tin, James did not have mugs for all, so they used what they could. She was annoyed with herself that Pretorius had got away, and doubted that the police in Zimbabwe would make more than a cursory effort to find him. She enumerated the killings they had had, seven that she knew of, and the South Africans had eight, Pretorius had been busy. The paperwork on this case was going to be a nightmare, but had to be done in case they were ever able to get Pretorius back to Botswana. Sadly, the only case they had a witness for was the shootings of Thomas, and Paledi, for all the others all they had was a lot of circumstantial evidence. Her musings were interrupted by the sound of a vehicle approaching. Thebe took a quick look, and confirmed that it was Sergeant Maphosa back with the forensics team.

"Marieke," Thabo said when he saw her approach. "More dead bodies?"

"I'm afraid so," she confirmed. "And, to make matters worse he got away over the Shashi."

"So, who do we have here?" Thabo asked.

"Gareth Thomas, and Keabetswe Paledi," she replied.

"Hmm, both headshots from behind," Thabo said. "Lots of splatter on the windscreen, they're very dead. So, let's see if we can get anything from the back seat. I came up in the BDF Skyvan, and told them to wait, when we're done here, you can fly back with us, Commissioner Boateng wants to know all the details. Who's going to drive this Land Rover back to Gabs?"

"I think Constable Thebe," she said. "It'll need cleaning up a little so that he can see through the windscreen, so you should get all you need before we clean it out."

"Where's Thomas from?" Thabo asked, as he, and his assistant, Neo, dusted for fingerprints, and looked for other physical evidence.

"He works at the mine at Selebi," she said. "I did find out that he was in business with Katse, he had just 49% of the Peacock Bar, and Grill, and now, since the death of Katse he had 100%, now I'll have to see who his heirs, and descendants are, to see who owns it now. He used to work at the Marico mine years ago, and would go on hunting trips with our man Pretorius."

"How did you discover that titbit?" Thabo asked.

"The South Africans have done quite a bit of digging, and are trying to help as best they can, they've got eight murders to solve that they think can all be related to Pretorius," she explained.

"What about Paledi?" Thabo asked.

"A prison associate of Pretorius," she replied. "He was also known as a poacher, and cattle thief. The maintenance man here, James, knew who he was, and told us that he, and Thomas had been here about a month ago. I need to check the bank statements for Thomas, and see if he got paid for this trip."

"Well, so where's Pretorius off to now?" Thabo asked.

"My guess is Mozambique to rendezvous with a yacht," she said. "This has all been planned out most carefully."

"It certainly looks that way," Thabo agreed. "There, we've got prints, we've got other physical evidence, so we'll move the bodies, and you can wash the front out so that young Thebe can drive it back. Is there enough petrol?"

"There's enough," she said, turning on the ignition, and looking at the gauge. "And, if we do need some, we brought plenty with us in the long-range tanks that our Land Rover has."

Marieke turned over the task of cleaning out the Land Rover to Constable Thebe, he was shown by James where there was a hose pipe, and water, which he used to great effect on the messy interior. While he was doing that, they loaded the body bags into the back of the police Land Rover. Marieke asked Hastings if he wanted a ride back to the airstrip or somewhere else, he declined saying that he would ride with James. When Constable Thebe was finished, Marieke said goodbye to Hastings, and James, and joined Thabo in the police Land Rover. Sergeant Maphosa drove them back to the airstrip, then said his goodbyes as he, and Tushay left for Gaborone, followed by Thebe. Marieke climbed aboard the Skyvan while the Botswana Defence Force pilots helped Thabo, and Neo with the body bags. When all was ready, they also left for Gaborone. The flight back to Gaborone was a short hour, and twenty minutes, putting them on the ground at just before four in the afternoon. Marieke had her car at the airport, so drove herself to the police station, leaving Thabo, and Neo to supervise the transfer of the body bags to the morgue. She went directly to Abel Boateng's office, and knocked on the door.

"Come in," he said. "Ah, good, you're back, I gather we missed Pretorius by minutes?"

"Yes, Sir," she said. "A local guide suggested a most likely crossing point on the Shashi, so we went there, hoping that we might cut their tracks. But, they were just ahead of us, and Pretorius shot his driver, and guide, and then ran for the river. He's in Zim now, I need to ask them for their help."

"We'll try," he agreed. "But don't expect miracles, we're not the best of friends at the moment. Who was killed today?"

"Gareth Thomas from Selibi, and Keabetswe Paledi from Bononong," she said.

"Why kill them?" he asked.

"I can only surmise that he was cleaning up loose ends," Marieke said. "Dead, they could not identify who went over the border. But, there was a witness who saw him shoot the two, James a maintenance man for one of the lodges in Tuli. He picked out Pretorius from photographs I showed him. That may have been a mistake on the part of Pretorius. Until now, we've only been able to get circumstantial evidence against him; we can place him at certain places, et cetera, et cetera, but we had no real evidence that he killed anyone, until now."

"So, where is he going now, and how do we get him back?" Abel asked.

"Our supposition is that he's going to work his way across Zim to Pafuri then cross into Mozambique, then head for the coast for a rendezvous with Wilson's yacht, apparently it has been seen off Maputo, so I assume it's not going to Rio as we first thought," she said. "There's one name on his list yet, and he now is in Paris as part of the South African legation there."

"Who's that?" Abel asked.

"Koos Botha, he was with the SA delegation here in Gabs in the 1970s, and he was the lucky one to interview Pretorius in gaol. He either was unable or disinclined to help, so our thinking is that he's on the list, I've alerted Andries van Dyk in PE, he's the one who told me where Botha is right now. He said that he would let their foreign service people know that there might be a risk to Koos Botha," she explained.

"So, how long for a yacht to reach France?" Abel asked.

"Five to six weeks," she thought. "That is if they cruise day, and night, and if they go via Suez, longer if they go back around the Cape."

"So, there isn't much we can do for the next two weeks, we interrupted your holiday, go, take your two weeks, and come back ready to do battle, I'll reassign duties here," Abel said. "I will contact the Zim, and Mozambique authorities, and request their help in apprehending Pretorius, and I'll also advertise for anyone who may have seen him or had dealings with him, either as

Pretorius or as one of the aliases he's been using. Now that we have an eyewitness we no longer need to be coy about who we're looking for. I'll have Bangwata look into Thomas, and see what we can turn up, there may be something that we can use. I think that's it for the moment, but, before you go, write up a report on today's happenings."

"Yes, Sir," she said. "I'll have it on your desk before I leave tonight."

The report was written, and submitted before she left for the day. Then she made one more telephone call before leaving, and it was to Andries van Dyk.

"*Middag*," he said as he answered the telephone.

"*Middag*," she replied. "It's Marieke, and I have news. We missed him, he skipped over the border into Zim, I watched him go, and we think he was picked up because we saw a dust plume from a car immediately afterwards."

"So, where next?" Andries asked.

"The Mozambique border, then the east coast," she said. "He did kill two more before he skipped over the border, Thomas, and a poacher by the name of Paledi. But, there was a witness to the shootings, so we've finally got a case against Pretorius."

"That's good, you *ouks* still have the death penalty, so if you can get him back, you can take care of things once and for all. Oh, by the way, add Marais to the list of those dead. We found the remains of Marais in a freezer in his house, dead a couple of months at least. It looks as if he was shot in the back of the head, almost execution style," Andries said.

"He had quite a list," she said. "I hope that's all, and we have no more."

"*Ja*, so do I," he agreed. "I've had more paperwork with this case than I've had in years."

"I wanted to let you know that my boss told me to take my leave, so I'm going this afternoon to a bush camp in the north," she said. "I'll be back in about ten days."

"Have a good time," he said. "I'll talk to you when you get back."

"Oh, by the way, I did get those copies of the ID cards and passports you sent," she said. "They do look like a motley crew of pirates. How recent are the pictures?"

"All the passports are recent, two years or less; those are probably much more recent images than on the ID cards," he said. "Enjoy your trip."

She drove home, disappointed in not having apprehended Pretorius, but happy to be going to the bush camp. When she got home, Patience was there and wanted to hear all about the events. Marieke gave her a quick rundown, then told her that she was going to take off for the next week or so. She called the charter company she used and asked them if anyone was going up to Maun the next day. There was, and there was room on the plane, if she did the duties of the co-pilot. That suited Marieke fine, and she then asked them if they could drop her off at the Selinda airstrip. That was agreeable to them; they had a passenger pick up in Maun to drop in Kasane, but the side trip to Selinda would not be a problem, if she could be at the airport in time for a wheels up at seven the following morning. Their only request was could she wear a pilot's uniform shirt. Well, she could, she had one from a year or so ago when she had taken a trip to Oudtshoorn with Koos Strijdom, and he had given her a shirt to wear, so as not to alarm his passengers when they saw her in the co-pilot's seat. That was before she had got her pilot's licence, so she had just sat in the seat, and only kept the plane straight and level for a few minutes when Koos attended to the two passengers. Finally, she called Maun, talked to Patience Botha, and asked her to relay a message to Bridget and ask her to meet her at the airstrip the next morning at about 9:30.

Marieke was at the airport at six the following morning and saw Brad there.

"Hey, Marieke," he said. "I hear you're coming with me this morning?"

"I am," she confirmed.

"Good, you can take us up to Maun, then on to Selinda," he said, handing her some epaulettes. "Put these on your shirt, makes you the junior, and looks official. Shall we go and pre-flight the Caravan? How long since your last check ride?"

"About six months, with you, in case you forgot," she laughed.

"Oh, yes," he said. "Must have been truly memorable."

They both went out to the plane, and did the walk around, although she had just done the same thing on the same aircraft the day before, Marieke was a believer in doing things by the book. It saved headaches later. That done, she stowed her bags and climbed aboard to get ready for the pre-flight checklist, while Brad gathered up the passengers, stowed their bags, and got them seated. He then handed Marieke the manifest, "Seven pax, 1,176 lbs plus bags of 226 lbs," he said. Marieke looked at the numbers and the fuel load and decided that all looked good. There was more than enough fuel on board to take them to Maun, with the usual reserve. Brad had already said that he would get some more fuel in Maun for the trip to Selinda, Kasane, and back to Gaborone.

Marieke waited until Brad had completed the passenger safety briefing, then she started on the pre-start checklist. Together they went through all the items on the list, and then she started the engine. When it was running, they ran through the post-start checklist, then the taxi checklist. Marieke talked to the tower, and got taxi clearance, then she waved to the ground man who pulled away the chocks, and let them go on their way. They had to wait for two other light planes to go before they got their turn to take off, but the wait was short enough. When they were in the air, and at a nice level cruising altitude, they chatted for a while about things in general, and then Brad asked her about the day before.

"We missed him," she said. "We actually saw him cross the Shashi into Zim. It looked as if he got picked up there, because we saw a dust plume for a vehicle immediately after he climbed out of the river."

"So sorry to hear that," Brad commiserated. "I saw the BDF Skyvan going to Tuli, was that for you?"

"Yes," she said. "We had to bring some bodies back. It really annoyed me that we were just half an hour late, if we'd been earlier, we might have saved the two *ouks* who got killed, and got our man."

"So, if he's gone over to Zim, can you get him back?" Brad asked.

"That depends on whether or not the Zims find him, and catch him, and whether they'll hand him back," she replied.

"If I were them, I wouldn't want an *ou* who had just killed two, he might do the same again. I'd get him and hand him back," Brad thought.

"You would think so, wouldn't you," she agreed. Then she focused her attention on the plane again as they started their descent into Maun. On the ground, she shut the plane down and helped Brad with the luggage as he said goodbye to the passengers. Then he walked to the terminal to find their next batch of passengers while Marieke supervised the fuel loading. Brad came back with five people and a cart full of luggage. He handed the manifest to Marieke with the comment, "Five pax, 910 lbs, plus bags, 330 lbs." She looked at the numbers, and the fuel load, and ran some quick calculations, they would burn about 160 lbs of fuel on the way to Selinda, then another 220 lbs to Kasane, and, finally, another 725 lbs on the way back to Gaborone, that plus a reserve of 300 lbs, gave a takeoff weight of under 7,400 lbs, or well below the maximum. She thought about the passenger weight numbers and noted that this group was generally quite a bit heavier than the first group, and they had much more luggage, and cynically wondered where they came from. When Brad had the luggage loaded, he climbed aboard, and did the safety briefing, then they ran through the checklists again for the startup, and taxi out.

The flight to Selinda was quite short, just over thirty minutes, as they descended to the strip, and Marieke flew down it. She saw a herd of buffalo wandering across. She flew low to buzz them and encourage them to move a little faster, then turned around and did it again. She was about to take another run when she saw a Land Rover on the strip headed for the buffalo, who then decided that it really was time to leave. She flew around in a circle until she saw that the Land Rover was well clear of the strip, then went back downwind to begin her approach to the strip. The landing was easy enough, and she tried as hard as she could to avoid all the dung piles that the buffalo had left.

"Sorry about that," she said to Brad.

"Not a problem," he said. "I'll hose it off in Kasane."

"I hope your passengers weren't too bothered by the go-arounds," she said.

"No, I think they were thrilled," Brad said. "My guess is that at least some of them got great shots of the buffs on the strip. Is that Bridget over there?"

"I think so," Marieke said. "I'll taxi over and leave you to it."

"Thanks," he said. "Do you have a pickup planned?"

"You, or at least the company," she said. "Saturday next at ten."

"Okay," he said. "I may see you then, or it may be Charles." Marieke pulled up beside the Land Rover and waved to Bridget. She said her goodbyes to the passengers, took her bag, and joined Bridget.

"Marieke," Bridget said. "Patience told me to come out and pick up a guest. I told her that the camp was sold out, but she insisted that it would be good for business, so I assumed it was a travel writer. It's great to see you, and the rest will be thrilled that you're here. Are you here for the rest of the booking?"

"I am," Marieke said. "We reached a point in the case we're following that allowed me to take a break. So, how's the week been so far?"

"Great fun," Bridget said. "I like your friend Melisende, she's smart, and entertaining, we've heard a lot about your doings at uni in Lyon."

"Nothing really bad, I hope," Marieke said.

"No, nothing bad," Bridget reassured her. "So, did you get your man?"

"No," Marieke said. "I watched him climb out of the Shashi into Zim, and don't hold out much hope that the Zims will find him, he's got help there. I think he's on his way to Paris to finish his job."

"Perhaps Melisende can help?" Bridget suggested.

"I'll ask her," Marieke said. "So, what have you seen?"

"Just about everything," Bridget said. "Lots of ellies, lions, a couple of leopards, buffs, and I don't know how many species of antelope. Mbali and her girls have been having a great time. It's been good for them to be away, it's safe for them here, we know what's around, and there haven't been any odd visitors."

The drive to the camp took about an hour, and the others were still out on a safari drive, so Marieke just made herself comfortable and waited. Nandi was the first to see her when the party arrived at the camp.

"Auntie Marieke," she said. "Auntie Marieke, you're here!"

"I am," Marieke said. "I got some time off after all."

"Does that mean you caught Pretorius?" Mbali asked.

"No," Marieke said. "I was too late, I saw him cross the Shashi into Zim."

"Is he coming back?" Mbali asked.

"I don't think so," Marieke said. "But, how are you enjoying it here?"

"*C'est formidable*," Melisende said. "*Et, maintenant que tu es ici, c'est très merveilleux.*" Bridget then organised everyone for lunch, and they all had a chance to talk to Marieke and tell her about their adventures. After lunch, Marieke and Melisende went to their tent for some privacy.

"*Alors, chérie*," Melisende said. "What now?"

"We believe he's trying to get to Paris to kill possibly the last on his list," Marieke said. "There's a man called Koos Botha who works at the South African Embassy in Paris; he was involved twenty years ago."

"How will this Pretorius get to Paris?" Melisende asked.

"On Wilson's yacht," Marieke said. "We believe that he will rendezvous with it off Mozambique, and then sail up the east coast, and through the Suez to the Med."

"So, why don't we watch for it in the Suez and attach a tracking device?" Melisende suggested.

"We don't have the resources to do that," Marieke said.

"But, we do," Melisende said. "Can we borrow a car, and go to Maun tomorrow, and I will call Philippe, and give instructions? Plus, then we could have some time alone."

"I'd like that," Marieke said. "What would you do?"

"We'd use one of our operatives in Egypt to attach the tracking device, then we could follow the yacht wherever it goes," Melisende said.

"*Bon*," Marieke said. "*Demain, nous irons à Maun.*"

"*Bon, mais maintenant, on s'envoie en l'air?*" Melisende asked.

"*Bien sûr*," Marieke replied. "*Mais d'abord, une douche.*"

What's next for us?

Marieke and Melisende borrowed a vehicle from Will and Bridget and were on the road to Maun by six the next morning. They were in Maun by eleven and went straight to the police station.

"*Dumela Mma*," Inspector Moroka said. "I didn't expect to see you."

"*Dumela Rra*," she replied. "I have one thing to arrange, and then I'm going back to the bush. You heard that Pretorius got away?"

"I did, Madame," he said. "What do we do now?"

"That's what we're here to try, and arrange," she said. "May I use your telephone?" He handed it to her, and she called her office and talked at length to Sergeant Maphosa. Almost immediately, pages started coming through on the fax machine. She picked them up and handed them to Melisende. Then she handed the telephone to Melisende, who called her office in Paris and talked to Philippe. Moroka looked at Marieke in bewilderment at the conversation; he was not able to understand a word that was said. In an aside, Marieke explained to him that she was using Breton, a language not widely known. Melisende looked at Marieke and mouthed "pen", and then wrote down a telephone number. Finally, she hung up and said that it was arranged.

"Good," Marieke said.

"What's arranged?" Moroka asked.

"We believe that Pretorius is either on, or will be shortly, a yacht bound for France. We believe it's headed up the east coast from Maputo to pick up Pretorius, and then on north to the Suez Canal. When, or maybe if, it gets to the Suez Canal, the French have arranged to have a device attached to the boat so that we can track it," Marieke explained. "My friend Melisende Garnier here is a senior officer in the French police. We need to fax these pages to this number in Paris, and they'll be on the lookout for the boat. It should probably be at the canal in three to four weeks."

"I've also asked our people to ask for information from Dar es Salaam and Mombasa, in case the yacht stops at either port for fuel," Melisende said.

"Right, Madame," Moroka said. "Is there anything else I can get you?"

"No, thank you, Inspector," Marieke said. "We'll just pay a quick visit to Patience Botha to see if there's anything that needs taking to the camp, then we're headed back to the Linyanti this afternoon."

Patience was delighted to see Marieke and to meet Melisende, and there were a few items that needed taking to the camp. Patience called for Phineas and asked him to load the Pitse Safari Camp things into the *bakkie*, and to fill it up. Then she scurried around and made lunch.

"So, did you catch Pretorius?" she asked as they ate lunch.

"No, he got away over the Shashi," Marieke said. "I watched him on the far bank, then he disappeared."

"Well, you'll get him eventually," Patience said. "You always do."

"Perhaps not this time," Marieke said. "So, where's Kobus?"

"He's in Gabs picking up a new car for us," Patience said. "We're getting a Toyota Hilux Surf."

"Very nice," Marieke said. "Thank you for the lunch, Patience. We really should be going to get back to the camp before dark."

"Go well, Marieke, and you, Melisende," Patience said.

"Stay well," Marieke replied.

On the drive back to camp, Melisende asked about the murders.

"Well," Marieke started. "As far as we know, there have been thirteen, the first was Theron in October of last year, then there was van de Merwe in November, followed by Adams, Smit, and de Villiers in December, then there was a lull, then there was Bloem, and Arnot in February, Danie Pretorius in March, all of those in South Africa, oh, and I just earned that there was one more in South Africa, Marais, then he moved here, and the first two here were Mr, and Mrs Dube in April, then Katse also in April, followed by Mochage, Lamprecht, Paledi, and Thomas all this month."

"And you think there could be more?" Melisende asked.

"If he gets to France, then I think he'll go after Koos Botha, and who knows, perhaps he'll even try to kill the boat ferry crew, but from what the South African I've been working with tells me, that might not be so easy," Marieke replied.

"And, in all those cases, what kind of evidence do you have?" Melisende asked.

"With the exception of the last two, only odd bits of circumstantial evidence," Marieke said. "Vague descriptions of a white man seen near the scene of two of the shootings, evidence, such as hotel stays, that now shows that our man was in the area of the other killings, but no prints, hairs or fibres, nothing else. It was only the last two when the killings were actually witnessed. Put all together, it does fit, but proving it in court will be an entirely different matter."

"Well, for the next ten days you can put it aside and think of other things," Melisende said. "We're here to enjoy ourselves."

"So, what have you seen since you've been here?" Marieke asked.

"Let's see," Melisende said, marshalling her thoughts. "You dropped us on Sunday, and on the drive to the camp, we ran into a herd of buffalo, then some elephants, then Bridget showed us some kudu, and impala. On Monday, we saw lions, and a leopard, as well as waterbuck, puku, impala, hartebeest, sable antelope, roan antelope, as well as lots of small animals, and birds."

"Are you glad you came?" Marieke asked.

"I am," Melisende confirmed. "Now that you're here, it makes things perfect. What we discussed before, will you really come to Paris?"

"I will," Marieke confirmed. "The job is interesting, and I do enjoy it, but life is empty without you, so I would rather leave and be with you."

"That would be marvellous," Melisende said. "You haven't seen my new apartment yet, it's on the corner of Rue Lagrange and Quai de Montebello on the sixth floor, easy walking distance to Quai des Orfèvres. I spent all the money I got from the sale of my parents' house in Lyon, and the savings that I had, but I think it's worth it. For Paris, it is huge, it has three bedrooms, a kitchen, a bathroom, living room, and dining room. There is a lift in the building, it's a little ancient, and slow, but it does work.

"I was sorry to hear about your parents," Marieke said. "Such a shame."

"It was," Melisende agreed. "But, they did eventually catch the other driver, and prosecuted him. He was really drunk, and this was not the first accident he had had after drinking."

"How are you now?" Marieke asked.

"Well, it's been nine months now, so I've adjusted, and remember the good times with them," Melisende replied.

"You said before that I may be able to work in France?" Marieke asked.

"I'm sure we can find you a job," Melisende promised. "You're a good police officer, you speak French, you understand Africa, even though, as you said, you've not had much experience with Francophone Africa. I don't think that matters much, you are not constrained as most of us are by a European background, and way of thinking. We would have to keep you as a contractor for a while until you became a French national, but I don't see that as an issue. Because you were educated in France, and because I'm sure that you would render service of value to France, then the residence requirement would be reduced to two years instead of the usual five."

"What do I have to do first?" Marieke asked.

"Well, I have all your details, and I can get your file from the archives from when we were at Lyon, then make the application for a visa and work permit," Melisende said. "We'll do that when we go back to your house, then we'll go and see the embassy in Gaborone, and file the application."

"How long do you think?" Marieke asked.

"Less than six months, perhaps as little as three," Melisende said.

"That long?" Marieke asked.

"Perhaps," Melisende said. "You will be there before Christmas, I promise."

"I'd have to go out and buy winter clothes again," Marieke laughed. "I got rid of most of mine when I came back from Lyon. Although there were times in the desert that I wished I had kept more."

"So, has your cooking improved?" Melisende asked.

"Not really," Marieke laughed. "Perhaps I'll take some classes in Paris, and see if I can become a chef, and yours?"

"As bad as ever," Melisende admitted. "I have an arrangement with the bistro downstairs, and if I'm not inclined to cook, they put something together for me."

Conversation went back and forth for the trip back to the camp, and ranged from what they saw on the road, to shopping in Paris, and what the latest fashions were, to the winter Olympic games, held earlier that year in Albertville. When they finally got to the camp just before six that evening, the others were off on an afternoon game drive and not expected back until after the sun had gone down.

"Thank you for bringing the supplies," Bridget said. "Did you get done what you needed to?"

"We did, thanks, Bridg," Marieke replied. "We also had a good chance to catch up on gossip, and what's happening in the big wide world. So, where did the others go?"

"Do you remember that *dambo* where we found the abandoned Land Rover?" Bridget asked.

"I do," Marieke said. "Good place for leopard, as I recall."

"It is," Bridget confirmed. "And when Will came across that Land Rover, they'd just seen a rhino, sadly, he disappeared, and we never saw him again, maybe he just went back to Zim, maybe poachers got him. What can I get you to drink? I have wine, beer, spirits, and even some soft drinks."

"The other night you served a very nice Pinotage," Melisende said. "Do you have any more?"

"We do," Bridget confirmed. "Marieke?"

"I'll try some," Marieke said. Bridget brought three glasses and a bottle back and poured them each a glass.

"This is good," Marieke said. "Whose is it?"

"Kanonkop," Bridget said. "We managed to get a case from a source in South Africa, and Koos flew it up for us."

Further conversation was interrupted by the return of the others. Then Marieke and Melisende had to listen as the girls recounted the sightings of the day, both in the morning and afternoon. They had been lucky, and had seen all manner of mammals, and birds, and were racking up quite a bird list. Mbali looked more relaxed than Marieke had seen in quite a while, perhaps the knowledge that Pretorius was no longer in the country removed some of her anxiety. For the next ten days, the routine was simple: up before six, a quick breakfast, then off on a game drive or walk, lunch, siesta, then afternoon tea, and then off on an afternoon game drive. What surprised Melisende was that this never got boring or repetitive. There was always something new and different to see, and Will and his guides were excellent, with an encyclopædic knowledge of the animals, birds, trees, and plants. On their last day there, they did not go out but sat on the deck overlooking the river, and just watched what came by.

When it was time to leave, Bridget had them all up in plenty of time to make the drive to the Selinda airstrip. They had only been there a few minutes when they heard the plane approaching. They watched it land and taxi over to them, and Marieke saw that it was Brad who had come to collect them.

"*Howzit,* Marieke," he said. "Are you well and rested?"

"*Dumela* Brad," she replied. "I am, thank you, and you, have you been busy?"

"*Ja,*" he said. "Tourism is really picking up. We may have to get another plane to keep up with demand."

"Brad, this is Melisende, Mbali, Khanyo, and Nandi," Marieke said.

"Morning," he said. "Let's get you all aboard, then I'll stow your bags, and we can be off."

"Thank you, Bridget," Marieke said. "It's been a wonderful few days."

"Come again," Bridget said. "Perhaps next time you won't have a crime hanging over you."

"Let's hope so," Marieke agreed.

"Are you flying us down, or taking it easy today?" Brad asked Marieke.

"I think, taking it easy," she said.

The flight back to Gaborone was a short two hours, and Marieke was happy to see Constance at the airport waiting to pick them up. She told Marieke all the news as they drove to the house, but it was mainly all the crime scene work done at the Dube house and in Tuli. They had amassed circumstantial evidence in all the killings now, and the file was getting impressively thick. At the house, Mbali took over and said that she would prepare lunch so that the others could relax. She had been waited on hand and foot for two weeks, and now wanted to start getting back into real life, as she put it. She detailed the girls to collect all the washing that might need doing, and to attend to it.

"So, back to work, *chérie*," Melisende said as they sat on the porch and sipped some wine.

"Sadly," Marieke replied. "I'll find some time tomorrow to talk to the commissioner and let him know that I will be leaving. He may ask me to stay until there is some kind of resolution on the Pretorius case, but that could drag on for months or years if we can't find him. I won't agree to that, three months at the most."

"So, that would be August to September," Melisende thought. "That would be a good time to come to Paris, and give you time to arrange things before the winter."

After dinner, Mbali said that she and the girls would be going back to their own house the next day. Now that Pretorius was gone, probably on the high seas, the risk to them had gone, so there was no longer any need for protective custody. Marieke also told Constance that she was released from her duties of minder and could now return to her regular duties at the Maun police station. It had been an interesting experience for Constance, one that she doubted she would ever see again. That, Marieke agreed with. The chances that they would have such a string of shootings again were remote indeed. Marieke did ask Mbali what she planned to do about MJ Motors. Mbali had obviously given that much thought, and she had a plan. The parts manager was actually very good, and he, in her opinion, would make a good general manager. So, the business would continue, with her on the board as chair, and the other managers running the day-to-day affairs of the company. She, herself, would stay with the bank and continue her career with them. Life for everyone was now going to get back to a more normal pace without the chaos of the past month.

Marieke reported to work the next day, and there were meetings, and yet more meetings, putting together all the evidence in the Pretorius case. The commissioner told them that the Zimbabwe police had contacted him, and informed him that they had found an early 1980s Nissan Sunny light truck near Pafuri, and that the driver, whom they identified as Kossam Shiri, had been shot. There was no sign of anyone else. The Zimbabwe police estimated that Shiri had been dead for two days when they found him, and that had been a week ago. They said that they had informed the Mozambique police that they may have a fugitive in their territory, but it seemed to the commissioner that the Zimbabweans were merely going through the motions; he thought that they were unlikely to pursue the case with any vigour. To date, he had heard nothing from Mozambique, so had no idea if Pretorius was still there or if he had made his getaway at sea. After the meeting, Marieke asked the commissioner if she could talk to him.

"So, Matshwana, what is it that you want to talk about?" he asked.

"I have decided to move away, and will then have to resign," she said.

"I see," he said. "Where are you going?"

"To France," she said. "I went to uni there, and have friends there, and would like to try something different."

"When do you want to do this?" he asked.

"As soon as is convenient," she said. "I thought that I might make a last-ditch effort to find Pretorius, and then call it a day."

"We will miss you," he said. "You have been with the police service for twenty years, and over that time you have acquired a reputation for getting things done, and we all appreciate that."

"And I will miss Botswana, and everyone here," she said.

"Who have you told?" he asked.

"You are the first," she said.

"You will be difficult to replace," he commented.

"We have good people who will do as good a job as me," she said.

"I'm not so sure about that," he said. "You have a way of investigating that leads to results, even with the most difficult cases. Ian once told me that he saw you as a Botswana version of Napoleon Bonaparte, who featured in the Arthur Upfield novels, an excellent detective, but not a model policeman. So, how do you wish to proceed?"

"I think that's rather up to you, Sir," she said.

"Well, let me think about it for a day or so, and I will try and come up with a plan that satisfies your requirements, and mine," he said. "Could I ask you not to discuss this with the rest of the station until I have had time to consider your replacement? What were you thinking, a three-month notice period?"

"I was thinking of something shorter," she said. "But, as my visas to France are likely to take that long, I would be prepared to work out a three-month notice, if you feel I would be useful."

"I am certain you would be useful, and I'm hoping that we managed to track down Pretorius and bring him back here in that time. If we can't get him back until later, would you be prepared to come back and give evidence?" he asked.

"I could do that, Sir," she said. "But, if my presence is required for weeks or months on end, I may have to demur. I am hoping to work, and I doubt that an employer would look kindly upon a long absence."

"You have all your reports and notes on the case up to date?" he asked.

"Of course, Sir," she said.

"We had been considering you for a promotion to Ian's job," he said.

"Thank you, Sir," she said. "But, that would not change my decision."

"I didn't suppose that it would," he said. "And, promoting you over the heads of others would cause talk and speculation. Not that that would stop me, but that is moot now. So, where do you think Pretorius is at this minute?"

"Somewhere off the coast of either Tanzania or Kenya," she replied. "I think he had a plan, and stuck to it, and made his rendezvous with the boat, and is now on his way to France to finish the job. The French have agreed to have agents watch the entrance to the Suez, and, if they see the boat to attach a tracking device that they can then monitor."

"How good are those devices?" he asked.

"I think good enough," she said. "The French seem confident that if they can get one attached, they can follow the boat."

"Didn't he have an accomplice?" the commissioner asked.

"We suspect that Patricia Wilson was party to the death of his cousin Danie Pretorius," she confirmed. "Wilson is suspected of smuggling diamonds out of South Africa. She currently is in France and is under surveillance."

"Will they meet?" the commissioner asked.

"It seems likely," Marieke said. "It's her boat that we believe that he is on, why else arrange for his passage, why not just have the boat sail from Cape Town up the west coast to France, unless they planned to meet again?"

"I agree," the commissioner said. "I don't suppose the Egyptians would cooperate, and take him off the boat for us, and return him here?"

"We could ask, Sir," Marieke said. "But, I would not hold out much hope, it may depend on how bribable the local officials are."

"We'll ask anyway," the commissioner said. "Do you have the name and details of the boat?"

"I do, Sir," Marieke confirmed. "I have the boat details and copies of the passports of the crew, so if the Egyptians do a check, they should be able to pick out Pretorius."

"I'll forward them to the Embassy in Pretoria and request their help in apprehending Pretorius," the commissioner said. "Is there anything else we need to discuss?"

"No, Sir," Marieke said. "Thank you for your time, Sir."

Marieke returned to her office, pulled all her files and notes on the Pretorius case, and went through them, cataloguing them as she went. She wanted to be sure that everything she had investigated had been properly recorded, so that someone else could use the information. She thought about the various killings and reflected on how she had spent so much time on the Katse case, but less on the rest. But, perhaps that was to be expected as the other killings had followed in quick succession, and there had hardly been time to delve deeply into each before the next occurred. She also pondered the question of whether they were correct in attributing all the killings to Pretorius; it certainly made things convenient, but was it right. As far as they could tell, it all made sense that Pretorius had done all the killings, but were they being a little presumptuous and lazy. If they were, then she could not imagine where they would start to look for another or other killers. She was saved from further speculation by Sergeant Maphosa, who came to her with his reports from the killings of Thomas and Paledi for her review. She went through them and asked a few questions, the answers to which the sergeant had readily to hand, so she asked him to include those answers in the report, so that someone in the future reading them would have all the answers, and not have to go looking for the writer. At least with these last two, there had been a witness who had identified Pretorius as the shooter, so for at least two of the killings, there was little question.

She was thinking about getting some lunch when the telephone rang, and it was Andries van Dyk from Port Elizabeth.

"*Howzit*," he said. "So, how was the bush?"

"It was wonderful," she said. "I really enjoyed my time away. How are you?"

"*Ag*, fine man," he said. "We've been cleaning up loose ends. We found an army sergeant who had lost his best uniform after getting drunk with a man whom he identified as Pretorius. We found a theatrical agent in Cape Town who had rented out some outlandish clothes to a woman they identified as Wilson. We've tracked down all the merchants where Wilson converted her cash to diamonds. We've got hotels in Bloem, Pretoria, Aliwal North, and Kimberley, where Pretorius stayed, usually as Theron. I think we've got his movements fairly well tracked."

"You've been busy," she commented.

"Not me," he laughed. "I just suggested where to look, and everyone else did the work. But it is nice to have. If we ever get Pretorius back here, we can make fairly good circumstantial cases against him. Oh, we talked to the *sangoma* who sold Wilson the poison, and he finally came clean and admitted that he knew who it was who was buying it, and why. So, where is our man now?"

"My guess is somewhere off the coast of Tanzania or Kenya," she said. "We're going to ask the Egyptians if they'll detain him, and return him here, but I don't hold out much hope for that."

"What about the French?" he asked.

"They know that it's likely that the yacht will dock somewhere in France in the next few weeks, so they're on alert. They've also said that they'll try, and watch the Suez, and if the yacht transits, they'll attach a tracking device to the hull. If they can do that, they say that they'll be able to follow the movements of the boat, and know when and where it will dock," she said. "Have you warned your consular people?"

"We have," he confirmed. "I think Botha's gone into hiding, but Hansie has proven to be a *slim kêrel*, so I'm not betting on Botha, let's hope the French get him before he gets Botha."

"If we hear from the French, I will let you know," she said.

"*Dankie*," he said. "Well, I've nothing else for now, *tot siens*."

"*Tot siens*," she replied.

There being nothing else to keep her there, Marieke left the office and went home. It was strange to find only Melisende there; the house had been so busy for the past few weeks.

"*Chérie*," Melisende said, as Marieke came in. "*Ça va?*"

"*Bien*," Marieke replied. "I had my conversation with my boss today, and he has asked me not to spread it abroad until he has decided how he wants to handle things."

"*Bon*," Melisende said. "I talked to the consular staff today, and things are in motion. They want to talk to you, and I set an appointment for Wednesday at ten. Is that convenient?"

"I'm sure it will be," Marieke said. "What do I need to take?"

"Just your passport and your degree certificate from Lyon," Melisende said. "I've already given them all the background information they need. I will come with you, and then, sadly, I must return to France on Thursday and report back to my office. I will track the application and let you know how things progress."

"Thank you," Marieke said.

"What will you do with your house?" Melisende asked.

"I was thinking of selling it," Marieke said. "But, then perhaps if I kept it as an investment, I could let it out if I could find a good manager here, and tenants that are reasonable."

"What does the university do for visiting professors?" Melisende asked.

"I think they rent space for them, so perhaps that would work. I will ask Mbali when I can announce that I'm leaving," Marieke said. "Are you sure I don't need to bring the money with me to France?"

"*Absolument*," Melisende said. "I have enough for my flat, and when you get a job, we will have more than enough for living expenses, and those luxuries we would treat ourselves to. But, enough of that for now, I have made a reservation for us at a restaurant, so you have twenty minutes to bathe, and change, and we will go out, and celebrate."

Nothing was said at the police station on Tuesday, but on Wednesday morning, Abel Boateng called a meeting of his senior officers and told them that Marieke was leaving for personal reasons. He had decided to appoint Inspector Bangwata to the position that Marieke had held. He told them that Marieke would be working out a three-month notice period, so if any of them had cases or issues where they wanted her help, then they should make it known sooner rather than later. Marieke left the meeting and then went off to her next meeting with the French. She met Melisende there, and the French official, a fussy little man who kept shuffling his papers and tutting about things in general. He kept muttering about it being most irregular until Melisende asked him what was irregular. He had no answer for that, except that it seemed that he was displeased that he had been largely circumvented, as the contact that Melisende had was in a more senior position and had just told him to handle the application expeditiously. It was probably that which drew out the officialdom in him, and he was determined to show that he had the power to approve or disapprove. He was a little taken aback by Marieke's command of French, he had started to talking to her in short four or five-word sentences as one would to a child, but when she started to reply to him with elaborate discourses on French philosophy, and governmental systems, he finally looked at the file, and realised that she had gone to university in France, and must needs have a reasonable command of the language. The interview took two hours, which in the opinion of both Melisende and Marieke, was far too long; everything he asked for could have been handled in twenty to thirty minutes at most, if he had been prepared and organised. The rest of the day, they spent together talking about life in Paris and what Marieke might do when she arrived. Planning a life together was new and exciting for both of them, and it was quite late when they finally went to bed.

Marieke saw Melisende off the next morning on the Johannesburg flight, then went to the office of Mbali at the bank.

"*Dumela Mma*," Mbali said.

"*Dumela Mma*," Marieke replied.

"So, Melisende has left?" Mbali asked.

"She did," Marieke confirmed. "On the morning flight to Jo'burg."

"I'm sorry she's gone," Mbali said. "I liked her a lot. How are you?"

"I'm actually doing better than I would have thought," Marieke said. "But, that may be because I've decided to leave, and go to Paris."

"*Hawu*," Mbali said. "That is news, when?"

"I've promised to work out a three-month notice period, by which time the visas should be all organised, and I can go," Marieke said.

"Are you excited to be going?" Mbali asked.

"I am," Marieke confirmed. "But, I need advice, what do I do about my house?"

"Well, you could sell," Mbali said. "Or you could keep it, and let it out."

"But, if I did that, I would need a manager here," Marieke said.

"I could do that for you," Mbali said. "I already manage three others that belong to people who have been seconded out of the country, so one more would not be an issue."

"We would need an agreement," Marieke thought.

"It would be wise," Mbali agreed. "I have a form of agreement that I use for the others, take a copy, look it over, and let me know if you want to make any changes. It covers what I would do, what you need to do, and what the management fee structure is. What did Abel Boateng say when you told him that you were leaving?"

"He just said, I see," Marieke said. "Then he went through the usual can't do without you stuff, and then we were considering promotion for you, but I think he knew that was all to no avail. He did ask me to keep quiet for a couple of days while he considered what to do. I told him on Monday, and he only told the station yesterday. He's putting Bangwata in the assistant super's spot."

"So, can we come and visit you in Paris when you're settled?" Mbali asked.

"Of course," Marieke said. "Melisende's flat has three bedrooms and is in the heart of Paris, off the Seine, and within walking distance of Notre Dame."

"If we do come, I'll have to have a talk with Nandi and Khanyo before we come, so that they understand how things are," Mbali said. "So, what about lunch?"

"That sounds like a good idea," Marieke said. "Then I should get back to the station and see if anyone has anything for me."

For the next four weeks, Marieke busied herself getting everything set up for her move to France. She had been contacted by the French and asked to provide a couple more items, but they were minor issues, and she was able to quickly satisfy their requests. Then on the 3rd of July, she received a telephone call in the office from Melisende.

"*Bonjour chérie*," Melisende said, "*Ça va?*"

"Bien, et tu?" Marieke asked.

"Toujours biens," Melisende said. "I have news for you. Your boat has cleared Suez and is in the Med now on a course for Marseille. We have a tracking device attached, and are able to follow it."

"Thank you," Marieke said. "Do you know how many people are on board?"

"There were six who were evident on deck, and who submitted their passports to the Egyptians, but we checked carefully, and there was another who did not reveal himself. Did you ask them for help?" Melisende asked.

"The commissioner said that he was going to ask for help through the embassy in Pretoria," Marieke confirmed. "But, I always saw that as a long shot. If I were Pretorius, I would probably assume that we would contact the Egyptians, but if they don't see him, they've no reason to hold up the boat, so I'd stay hidden until they cleared Port Said, and were well into the Med, and out of Egyptian waters."

"I agree," Melisende said. "Pardon, I must go, one awaits me."

Marieke went to the commissioner's office and reported what she had just been told.

"The Egyptian Embassy in Pretoria has just called me, and they told me that Pretorius is not on the yacht," he said. "They gave me the names of six who were."

"Yet, the French insist that there are seven on the yacht," she said. "So, he must have found a way to avoid detection while the passports were being checked. I believe he hid until they cleared Port Said, and now that they are in International Waters, he is free to go up on deck again."

"I think you should go to France and await the arrival of the yacht," the commissioner said. "Perhaps also see if you can talk to this Patricia Wilson, and see what she will tell you. Now that the boat has cleared Port Said, how long before it reaches France?"

"I believe about three days, Sir," she replied. "They could also make port in Italy, and go overland."

"You are full of good news," he said, dryly. "I think their plan is France, so you should go to France, and wait until they're in

French waters, then have them boarded, and searched. How are the French on extradition?"

"To us, they may be difficult, because we still have a death penalty; if we were to promise to forego that, they might be more cooperative."

"I'll talk to the Minister," he said. "We have to be prepared for a long discussion with the French; meanwhile, we need to work on getting Pretorius into custody somewhere. If you were to leave for France tomorrow or the next day, would that give you enough time to see Wilson, and then go to wherever the tracking device suggests that the boat is heading?"

"It would, Sir," she said. "That would be more than enough time, I would probably spend much of it sitting idly by."

"Well, I think you should make your plans and go," he said. "As I recall, the Air France flight is only once a week, so if you've missed that, go via London."

Melisende was delighted when Marieke called her with the news that she was on her way to France. She promised to meet her at Charles de Gaulle and to take her to the south of France, where they could interview Patricia Wilson. She also told Marieke that they had been asked by the South Africans to help with their investigation of Wilson as a diamond smuggler, and that someone from the embassy would be joining them. Melisende said that the tracker was still working, and they had received confirmation from an agent that the boat had indeed transited the canal, matching the signals that they had been getting from the tracking device. Marieke then called the travel agent she had dealt with in the past, and got them to book her on flights to Johannesburg, then Paris. She was unable to get a seat on the once-weekly Air France flight to Paris, so was booked instead on a BA flight to London, with a connection to Paris. Marieke called Melisende back and gave her the flight information, delighted when she reaffirmed that she would be at the airport, no matter the early hour. All that remained was for Marieke to go home, pack, and then get some cash in a currency that the French would accept, francs, pounds or dollars would all do. That meant a visit to the bank, where Mbali was glad to help, and excited for her to be visiting Paris, even if it was just for work.

The flight from Johannesburg to London was cramped, and seemed to Marieke to be full of complaining tourists, complaining about the cold in Johannesburg, complaining about the lack of service at the airport, complaining about their less than expected safaris, in short, anything, and everything. The transfer at Heathrow was tedious, going from one terminal to another to catch the flight to Paris. Nothing, it seemed, was easy in London; the whole enterprise had the air of something thrown together at the last minute, perhaps as a result of the ever-expanding airport increases in traffic. It was good to finally land at Charles de Gaulle. Marieke finally got off the plane, and Melisende was there at the gate to greet her.

"*Chérie, ça va?*" she asked.

"Better now that I am finally here," Marieke said. "And you?"

"Delighted that you're here," Melisende replied. "Have you baggage to collect?"

"One suitcase," Marieke said. Melisende led the way to immigration, where she showed her badge, and the officer stamped Marieke's passport and waved them through. There was a wait for the bags to arrive, and Marieke was surprised to see hers as one of the first to arrive, cheekily mixed in with those that had priority tags on them. They left the airport through the green channel, nothing to declare, and went out to find a police car waiting for them at the kerb. She instructed her driver to take her to the Gare de Lyon in order to catch the train to Marseille. On the way to the station, she told Marieke that Wilson's yacht had passed Sardinia and was now headed north towards the French coast.

The train, at least as far as Lyon, was a TGV, Train à Grande Vitesse, and they had seats reserved. It was hard to appreciate just how fast they were going until they were running parallel to an Autoroute at one point, and they were passing cars as if they were standing still. At Lyon, the service changed to a more traditional train, but Melisende said that there were plans to improve the line south so that the whole run to Marseille could be by TGV, reducing the time from Paris to Marseille from a little over four hours to just over three hours. When they arrived in Marseille, there was an officer there to meet them, an Inspecteur Marcelle Frou. Frou had a car, and after loading their bags into the boot, he took off at a fast pace. The journey time from Marseille to Beaulieu would normally be about two and a half hours, but they were there in a little under two hours. Frou was actually from Nice and had driven over earlier in the day to meet them. They went to the police station, and there they met the representative from the South African Embassy, Johannes Cillié. The local inspector told them that they had brought Patricia Wilson to the station about fifteen minutes ago, and she was in one of the interview rooms.

Inspecteur Frou led the way, and they all crowded into the room, where Frou introduced himself.

"*Bon après-midi, je suis Inspecteur Frou et nous avons quelques questions,*" he said.

"*Comment?*" she replied.

"*Vôtre nom, s'il vous plâit?*" he asked.

"Wilson, Patricia Wilson," she replied.

"*Date de naissance?*" he asked.

"*Le quatre août mille neuf cent cinquante-sept,*" she replied, this routine she knew well from her experiences in getting her visa.

"*Où demeurez-vous?*" he asked.

"*Je reste chez ma sœur,*" she replied.

"*Et, l'adresse?*" he asked.

"*Six cent quarante et un Avenue Olivula,*" she replied.

"*Vôtre passeport, s'il vous plâit?*" he said. She handed it over, and he flicked through it quickly, then set it aside next to his file. Then he introduced Cillié as a representative of the South African government.

"Mr Cillié," Frou invited.

"I want to know all about your activities smuggling diamonds," Cillié asked. Marieke rolled her eyes at Melisende, who shook her head. This idiot was going to get nothing out of Wilson.

"What diamond smuggling?" she asked.

"You know very well," he said. "We've picked up your whole ring, and they're all singing like canaries."

"I don't know anything about any smuggling ring," she said. "You must have the wrong person, I've got no diamonds, search me if you want, search my house, I don't have any, I can't afford them."

"Maybe, but you can afford a fancy yacht, and the villa you're living in," Cillié said.

"The villa belongs to my sister, and the yacht was my husband's before he was killed in South West, did you do your time in the army or were you sitting behind some desk in Pretoria well away from the terrs?" she asked.

"What I did or didn't do in South West is not your concern," he said. "I want to know about the diamonds you smuggled out of South Africa. We know you've been smuggling diamonds, so it would be better for you if you told us all about it."

"I know nothing about any diamonds," Wilson repeated.

"*Jy kan kak praat*," Cillié interrupted. "We've got everything you've done over the past six months, where you've been, who you slept with, what you ate, the lot, so it's time to decide whether you want to cooperate or face prison in South Africa."

"Is there an extradition treaty between South Africa and France?" Wilson asked of Frou.

"No," he said.

"Well, you, Mr Cillié, can go to hell," she said. At that, Cillié threw his hands in the air and said that he was leaving, that they would get nothing from someone as uncooperative as Wilson. This surprised both Marieke and Melisende as they thought that Cillié had been briefed about the potential threat to one of the legation in Paris, and both thought that he would find a way to ask about that. Either he was sure that they had Botha protected, or did not think that the threat was real.

After he had gone, there was a period of quiet for a few minutes, then Marieke said of Inspecteur Frou, "*S'il vous plâit?*"

"*Certainement,*" Frou said.

"Tell me, Mrs Wilson, how much did you pay Thabiso Balala in Mabalstad for the *zwezwe*?" Marieke asked.

"Twenty Rand," Wilson said, without thinking. The question had been so unexpected and so direct that she had just answered.

"I see," Marieke said. "Tell me, where were you on the night of the 5th of March?"

"I don't know," Wilson said. "Probably at home."

"You weren't at the Hunter's Inn in Koffiefontein with Hansie Pretorius staying as Mr and Mrs Cronjé, oh, and did Captain Marais give you her uniform before she died, or did you take it afterwards?" Marieke asked.

"How?" Wilson started. "I want a lawyer, I'm not answering any more questions until I talk to a lawyer."

"You can get a lawyer when we say so," Marieke said. "But I think the South Africans are probably more interested right now in the activities of Hansie, how they choose to proceed with any further enquiries about diamonds may depend on how much you tell us about Hansie. When did you first meet?" Wilson looked at Marieke and the file she was consulting, and made a calculation. She was sure that in that file were details of all the transactions she had made, where she had stayed, what her various aliases were, and many other details of her life, including where she was raised, and who she knew, so she would admit what probably could be proven, and dissemble on anything else.

"I knew Hansie when I was growing up," she said.

"Then he went away to the army, and you went away to Cape Town, how did you meet again?" Marieke asked.

"I'm not sure," Wilson temporised.

"You didn't join him for breakfast at the Karoo Inn in Hopetown on the morning of the 2nd of February?" Marieke asked.

"Oh, yes, I remember now, I stopped there for breakfast, and there he was, I hadn't seen him in years, we had coffee, and chatted," Wilson said.

"It must have led to little more than chatting," Marieke suggested. "You and Hansie put up at the Royal Hotel in Beaufort West that night. So, tell us about Hansie, what did he tell you?"

"About what?" Wilson asked.

"About where he had been for the past twenty-five years, you must have been curious?" Marieke suggested.

"Oh, well, he said he'd been in the army, then he'd been in prison in Botswana for twenty years," Wilson said.

"Did he say why he had been in prison?" Marieke asked.

"Something about ivory poaching, and a shootout with the Botswana cops," Wilson replied.

"Did he say anything about what he had been doing since he was sent back to South Africa?" Marieke asked.

"He did mention a few things," Wilson replied.

"Tell us about the theatrical agency in Cape Town where you got the loud clothes for your trip to Sun City," Marieke invited.

"What theatrical agency?" Wilson asked.

"Jules Costumes," Marieke prompted.

"Oh, yes I did rent a few things from them," Wilson admitted.

"So, tell us about the trips to Sun City," Marieke invited.

"What trips to Sun City?" Wilson countered.

"Well, there was the first when you posed as Celia Botha, and called Danie Pretorius to set up an appointment to discuss, what was it, ah, yes, beef supplies to the hotel," Marieke prompted.

"That was a joke," Wilson said. "I hated Danie, I knew him growing up as well, and he once came to Cape Town when I was working as a model, and he tried to rape me. I wanted to get back at him, so I thought I'd lead him on a wild goose chase."

"If it was to be a joke where you got back at him, why pay for the room for him?" Marieke asked.

"I got the money back in the casino in less than an hour, so no loss on my part, the casino paid," Wilson replied.

"Why did you take Hansie with you?" Marieke asked.

"I thought he'd appreciated the joke, and because he'd been away for so long, that he'd be surprised at what had been built at Sun City," Wilson explained.

"Why did Hansie fly as Gert Theron?" Marieke asked.

"He told me that since he'd been out of prison, he wanted to start again, and he'd taken a new name, legally, and was trying to put all the old Hansie behind him," Wilson said.

"Tell us about the second trip to Sun City," Marieke said.

"Hansie wanted to go back there to try his luck at gambling," Wilson explained.

"And did he?" Marieke asked.

"Did he what?" Wilson countered.

"Win in the casino," Marieke said.

"Oh, no," Wilson said. "He lost a few Rand, then lost interest. I think he would have done more if he had won, but he didn't like losing."

"So, when you went to Mabalstad, why did you choose to dress as an old woman? Balala was not taken in at all?" Marieke asked.

"I was hoping that no one would see me go, certainly I fooled Hansie, but then he was never that good at seeing past the obvious," Wilson explained.

This back and forth went on for some time until Wilson finally asked, "Look, you seem to know everything about me, why are you asking?"

"We're interested," Marieke said. "I am Assistant Superintendent Englebrecht of the Botswana police, and my associates here in France have graciously agreed that we can take you with us back to Botswana to face charges of conspiracy to commit murder. When you helped Hansie, posing as Gert Theron, cross the border into Botswana, you became an accessory to the murders he committed, that we have eyewitness evidence of. I should remind you that we in Botswana still have the death penalty, and we will use it."

"Wait, wait, I'm not swinging for Hansie," Wilson protested.

"Well, a lot depends on you then," Marieke said. "Tell us what you know, and what he told you." Wilson then proceeded to unburden herself of all she knew, had heard or suspected. It all fit with what the South Africans had suspected, and with the evidence they had gathered. She told them what Hansie had told her about the killings of Theron, van de Merwe, Adams, Smit, de Villiers, Bloem, and Arnot, and finally Danie Pretorius. She told of her procurement of the Mickey Finn and the immobilising of Danie, but she put the use of the *zwezwe* squarely into the hands of Hansie. She told them, without admitting to actual knowledge, how she thought Hansie had brought the guns into Botswana, broken down, and secreted into the frame of his Land Cruiser. She also told them of the detailed plan he had put together for his escape from Botswana into Zimbabwe. She skirted around the issue of the use of her yacht, and Marieke did not press the point. They knew where the yacht was, and who was on it, and would be waiting when it approached the shore. In all, the statement took three hours to complete, and it was quite late when they finally called a halt to things and discussed how to proceed. What Marieke did not want was for Wilson to contact the yacht via radiotelephone and warn them of their impending interception. Melisende came to the rescue with an obscure clause in French law that let them detain her pending further enquiries. They might charge her, and if they did, then they would use her entry into France as the vehicle for that, citing irregularities for undeclared imported goods, meaning the diamonds. In fact, they had no actual evidence of her bringing undeclared diamonds into the country, and her subsequent visit to Amsterdam could easily be explained away as being related to the wine trade. But Wilson was not to know that, so she accepted her fate for the moment in sullen silence.

"*Alors,*" Inspecteur Frou said. "*Quoi encore?*" The whole conversation now switched back into French.
"We wait for the yacht," Melisende said. "I have already been in contact with the Gendarmerie Maritime, and they have the tracking signal and will intercept as soon as they enter French waters."
"I should send a copy of this statement to Lieutenant Colonel van Dyk of the South African Police and Commissioner Boateng," Marieke added. "Is there a fax machine I may use, Inspecteur?"
"Of course," he said. "Do you have the numbers?" Marieke gave him the numbers, and he was gone for about a minute. When he returned, he said that the faxes were being sent.
"I think if we can apprehend this Hansie Pretorius, and send him back to Botswana or South Africa, then we can make accommodation for Wilson," Melisende said. "We have nothing really to charge her with, but we'll keep an eye on her in the

future. As for Pretorius, we'd have to do it quietly, if our press learns that we are sending someone back to a country that has the death penalty, even if it is in abeyance at the moment in South Africa, there will be all kinds of protests, even for a serial murderer. This Pretorius is wanted for questioning for eight murders in South Africa, and seven in Botswana, and Marieke, didn't you tell me there was another in Zimbabwe?"

"There was," Marieke confirmed.

"So, we have a choice of South Africa, Botswana or Zimbabwe, which has the strongest case?" Melisende asked.

"We probably do," Marieke said. "We have an eyewitness to two killings in Botswana, for all the other killings we, and the South Africans, have circumstantial evidence, but nothing more concrete."

"So, in terms of an extradition hearing, Botswana can make the best case?" Melisende asked.

"I think so," Marieke confirmed.

"Is it possible that the yacht will make landfall somewhere along the coast and drop this Pretorius before they come here?" Frou asked.

"Yes," Melisende said. "We had considered that, which is why we fitted the tracking device."

"Can we intercept on the high seas?" Frou asked.

"Technically, no," Melisende said. "We will have to wait until they are within twelve nautical miles of the coastline, say about 22 km."

"Where are they now?" Frou asked.

"My last report was that they were 43 degrees north, 8 degrees east, which puts them south of Cannes, not far from our coast," Melisende replied. "We have a frigate that was returning from the Indian Ocean, and it is shadowing them, and it appears as if they've turned slightly to the northeast, and are running towards Beaulieu-sur-Mer. They are close enough, only about 40 nautical miles from here, so about six hours unless they heave to overnight, and come in in the morning. Once they enter French waters, we will board and take Pretorius into custody. We'll do a safety check, and a customs check, and we will find something."

There being little else that could be done that afternoon, Melisende suggested that they find a hotel for the night. Inspecteur Frou suggested that they travel back with him to Nice as he had a contact at the Hôtel Villa Victoria who would take care of them. It was only a thirty-minute drive into the centre of Nice, and the hotel. Frou was as good as his word, and his introduction to the front desk clerk quickly brought the manager, who proceeded to take charge of things. Melisende and Marieke were asked if they minded sharing a room, as accommodation was limited. That, they assured the manager, would not be a problem. They were given a Superior Room with a balcony and view of the garden. The hotel had no restaurant, so dinner would have to be had elsewhere. Frou suggested he take them to dinner, but Melisende told him to go and spend the time with his family; she and Marieke would manage quite well. She did ask him to pick them up at nine the next morning so that they might rehearse Patricia Wilson through her story again to see if any notable discrepancies presented themselves.

Marieke took stock of the room, high ceilings, quite spacious for a European hotel, and a nicely appointed bathroom. "*Alors, chérie,*" she said to Melisende. "*Dîner?*"

"*Oui, si tu seras le dessert,*" she replied. "I know a very nice place not far from here, perhaps a ten-minute walk." They left their bags and walked to the restaurant, which had a rooftop location overlooking the sea.

"So, now we wait until the yacht arrives?" Marieke asked.

"We wait," Melisende confirmed. "What did you think of the story that Wilson told us?"

"I'm sure that there are things that Wilson omitted," Marieke said. "But, the basic tale has the ring of truth about it. It fits many of the details we learned from the South Africans. I was surprised by their man from their embassy. I was expecting someone with a little more finesse."

"Finesse is something that I imagine is far from his mind," Melisende laughed. "So, what will you have to eat?"

They settled on dinner and the wine, and enjoyed the evening views over the sea. The restaurant was busy, but they were not chivvied along to leave, even after they had finished eating. The sun was just setting as they walked back to the hotel. Marieke had never quite got used to the late sunsets of the higher latitudes, so a 9:30 sunset to her was not the norm; it should be more like 5:30 to 6:00. But the daylight was nice, and the sunset over the sea was beautiful. When they reached the hotel, they saw Frou drive up, and he announced that the yacht had been met by the Gendarmerie Maritime and that there had been an exchange of gunfire. The yacht crew had tried to make a run for international waters, and the Gendarmerie Maritime cutter had moved to intercept. That was when the crew of the yacht tried to shoot their way out. The upshot was that four of the gendarmes sustained injuries, and three of the yacht crew were dead. The yacht was currently under tow, bound for the Gendarmerie Maritime base in Toulon. The Gendarmerie were in an ugly mood and were looking for aggressive prosecution of all involved, so the chances of Marieke getting extradition for Pretorius seemed slim.

Frou suggested that they check out of the hotel and go to Toulon to meet the boats. He had already arranged for Patricia Wilson to be moved to the main police station in Toulon, and he was sure that they could find a hotel in Toulon. The drive took a little over an hour and a half, and when they got to Toulon, they learned that the boats were still an hour out. The injured gendarmes had been helicoptered off the boat, and were already in hospital undergoing treatment, all were expected to recover, and be back on duty within six to eight weeks. It was not clear yet which of the yacht crew had been killed, so Marieke was keen to see the boat come in, and who would get off.

The waiting seemed interminable, and dawn was breaking when they saw the boats coming in. Frou drove to the wharf to meet them, and they joined the officers from the Gendamerie Maritime who were also waiting. Melisende introduced herself, Inspecteur Frou, and Marieke. When the boats had been tied up and a gangplank installed, the local commandant went aboard to consult with the captain, then came back and invited Melisende and her party aboard. They saw the body bags with the three dead, and the rest of the crew sitting on the deck, hands and feet shackled. According to the Gendarmerie Maritime officer, they had no passports; they had been dropped over the side in a weighted bag as they were boarded. Marieke got her file and pulled out the pictures of the passports she had received from van Dyk. She and the Gendarmerie Maritime officer looked at each member of the crew in turn, checking against the copies of passports that Marieke had brought with her. They had little luck trying to match the bearded faces with the passport pictures, even using the pictures that had been taken of Pretorius when he was deported from Botswana, so Marieke suggested that they separate them at the police station, and then use fingerprints to identify each, to facilitate that she handed over the copies of the fingerprint cards she had received from van Dyk. She said that separation was necessary to stop them from swapping any kind of identification mark the police would give them. The crew endured this in sullen silence, and only when Marieke and the officer moved away did they speak, and that was to each other in undertones, and in Afrikaans. Marieke did not hear anything that caused her alarm, but she decided, for the moment, to stay quiet about her knowledge of the language. A quick view of the dead bodies was a little more useful; it was possible that dead body number two was that of Pretorius, but she could not be sure. If that were the case, then her chase was at an end, but she had to be certain.

Marieke looked over the Blue Diamond and wondered what Patricia Wilson would think about all the bullet holes. Perhaps she was insured, but Marieke suspected that most insurance companies would cavil at paying out after an encounter with law enforcement. She saw the crew led away and transported to the gendarmerie station. They followed, and at the station learned that the case had been referred to Thierry Gilliéron, a *juge d'instruction*. Marieke remembered some of the powers and duties of the *juge d'instruction* but not all, and asked Melisende for a reminder. It appeared that Gilliéron had the power to do just about anything, and to order almost anything, so it would behove them to seek an interview with him, and acquaint him with the details of the cases against Pretorius, and now his confederates. The gendarmerie followed the advice of Marieke and separated the crew in the cells, and then took each in turn to get their fingerprints. As they did, they attached a wristband with a number punched into it. Marieke looked at the wristbands and approved, they were metallic, and would take cutters to be removed, and were also fitted tight enough that even an escape artist would have a really difficult time removing them. When they had all the fingerprints of the living taken and the comparisons made, the gendarmerie gave Marieke and Melisende a list of the living, the dead they would see to next.

Marieke went through the list of the living, and Pretorius was not on it. That suggested that he was one of the three dead, confirming her earlier initial identification, but, given the man's ability to survive, she wanted to be absolutely certain before reporting his death to her department and to the South Africans. So, she went to the morgue armed with all the documents she had on Pretorius from the prison, and her own police records. She talked to the pathologist and told him that the man she was looking for had had a fractured radius of the left arm, and a fractured tibia of the right leg, both about fifteen years earlier, and had had some dental work done while in prison. The pathologist had already taken fingerprints of the three men, and she gave a copy of the fingerprint chart to Pretorius to the technician, who then made the comparison and announced a match. The pathologist ordered x-rays of the limbs and of the teeth, and said that he would have those results in about an hour. Marieke left and met with Melisende, who told her that if it really was Pretorius in the morgue, then she would let the Gendarmerie Maritime handle the case, as it was potentially just a matter at sea. She suggested coffee while they waited for the X-rays to be developed.

While they drank coffee at a nearby café, Marieke asked Melisende what she intended to do about Patricia Wilson.

"Well," Melisende said. "She has broken no French laws, and we have no extradition treaty with the South Africans, so we will not be sending her there. Do you have a reason to want her detained?"

"I doubt that we have anything that could be made into any kind of case," Marieke replied. "As far as we know, all she did in Botswana was give Pretorius a ride out of the country, which a good lawyer would argue was her civic duty as he was banned from entering Botswana. So, I cannot see anything of note that would pass the scrutiny of a hearing for extradition."

"I thought that might be the case," Melisende said. "Inspecteur Frou, would you take a statement again from Patricia Wilson, and send a copy to me? Then I think, ask her if she wants to see her boat, then tell her to deal with the Gendarmerie Maritime for any information she may need for her insurance company, then after that offer her a ride back to Beaulieu, and tell her that she is free to go."

"Yes, Madame," he said. "Will you be returning to Paris now?"

"We will," she confirmed. "We just need to confirm the identity of dead man number two, and then we can go."

"Perhaps I should take you back to the morgue, and when you are done there, they will take you to the Gare de Toulon," he suggested.

"Perfect," Melisende said.

At the morgue the pathologist confirmed that the fingerprints, dental records, and fracture x-rays all matched, so he could say with confidence that they were looking at the body of Hansie Pretorius, he gave them six copies of the death certificate, and a full report on his findings, he also gave her the identities of the other two as Buys, and Kruger. Melisende thanked him for his time and efforts, and then saw the commandant of the gendarmerie station, and told him that their man was among the dead, so that they no longer had any claim on any of the arrestees, so the case was now entirely his. He was determined that the surviving crew members would serve time for having the temerity and stupidity of shooting at his officers, so he would be meeting again with the *juge d'instruction* to proceed with the case. Melisende asked him if Marieke could use a telephone to contact her department in Gaborone. She was shown to an office and given the appropriate codes for outside lines. She called her commissioner first and was mildly surprised when he answered the telephone himself. She wondered what he was doing there on a Saturday.

"*Dumela Rra,*" she said.

"*Dumela Mma,*" he replied. "You have news?"

"I do, Sir," she said. "The French made contact with the yacht, and there was an exchange of gunfire, in which Pretorius was killed. I have been to the morgue, and the pathologist confirms from fingerprints, dental records, and other medical records from the prison that it is indeed Pretorius."

"I see," the commissioner said. "I suppose that is satisfactory."

"In a way, Sir," she agreed. "But, also disappointing, we have worked so hard on this case that it is anticlimactic to have it end this way."

"It is, isn't it?" he said.

"We did get a statement from Patricia Wilson, who gave us a lot on the various killings in South Africa, which I will pass on to Andries van Dyk," she said. "But, she gave us nothing that would help us with our own cases."

"I see," he said. "Well, I will let the minister know what has happened. You will now be returning to Gabs?"

"I will, Sir," she confirmed. "I am in Toulon at the moment at the station of their maritime gendarmes, and will return to Paris this afternoon. I will book a ticket on the first flight I can get back to Gabs, either from Paris or London."

"Very good," he said. "I look forward to hearing your report when you return. Will you contact the South Africans?"

"I will, Sir," she said.

"Fine, then go well," he said.

"Stay well, Sir," she replied. She hung up the telephone and then called Andries van Dyk at home in Port Elizabeth.

"*Middag*," Andries said when he answered the telephone

"*Middag*," she replied. "Andries, it's Marieke, I have news from France."

"Good or bad?" he asked.

"It depends on how you look at it," she said. "The yacht crew tried to evade being boarded by the French cops, and there was a shootout; three were killed: Frikkie Buys, Piet Kruger, and Hansie Pretorius."

"You've confirmed that it is Pretorius?" Andries asked.

"We matched fingerprints, dental records, and other medical records," she replied. "Unless he has a stand-in who was prepared to go to great lengths, it's him."

"Anything on Wilson?" he asked.

"Your man from the embassy got nothing," she commented. "Then she asked the French police if there was an extradition treaty with South Africa, and when they told her no, she told the embassy *ou* to *gaan kak*."

"So, we got nothing from her?" Andries asked.

"I got a full statement after the embassy *ou* left, I'll send you a copy," Marieke said. "She had the tale from Pretorius about all the killings in South Africa; she skipped around her role in the poisoning of Danie Pretorius, but as you have no body there, there's not much you can do about that. She also talked about the diamond smuggling, but it pretty much confirmed what you already knew."

"What about the other *ouks* on the yacht?" Andries asked.

"They're going to be prosecuted by the French and will do time here in France, then my guess is that they'll be deported, but when I cannot guess," she explained. "Wilson may lose her yacht, I'm not sure what the French law says about that. But, in any event, it's going to cost her, because I can't see any insurance company paying out after gunplay with the maritime authorities."

"Can you get me a copy of the death certificate for Pretorius?" he asked.

"I'll fax you one to the station in PE, and then send you an actual certificate when I get back to Gabs in the next day or so," she promised.

"So, I can close all those cases?" Andries said.

"I imagine so," she agreed. "For us, it's a little disappointing that we've chased this *ou* for a while now, and now that he's dead, it leaves a lot of questions as to how, when, and where."

"For us too," he agreed. "What the hell possessed them to try and shoot it out with the French?"

"Perhaps Pretorius thought he had nothing to lose," she suggested. "The gendarmes here are going to have a difficult time with the surviving crew members; they've all switched to Afrikaans, and I've heard no English from them, and no French."

"Are you going to volunteer to interpret?" Andries asked.

"No, my boss wants me back in Gabs," she said. "If the gendarmes can't find an interpreter locally, they can always go back to your embassy."

"Well, call me when you get back to Gabs," he said.

"I'll do that," she promised. She left the office and asked if there was a fax machine she could use. The commandant directed her to the right place, and she sent off copies of the death certificate for Pretorius to both her commissioner and to Andries van Dyk.

Melisende and Marieke thanked the commandant for his help and took their leave of him. He had one of his officers drive them to the railway station, where they discovered that they would have to wait only ten minutes for the next train to Marseille. The ride to Marseille took just under an hour, and then they found a train for Lyon. On the Marseille to Lyon train, Melisende suggested lunch, and they found a place to sit and eat. The TGV line had yet to be extended south from Lyon, so there was time enough to eat in leisure.

"So, *chérie*, what now?" Melisende asked.

"I go back to Gabs, finish out my notice period, then move," Marieke said.

"You will stay the night?" Melisende asked.

"Of course," Marieke said. "If we get to Paris at seven tonight, it will be too late to get a flight to Jo'burg tonight. I'll check on availability tomorrow, either from Paris or London."

"*Bon*," Melisende said. "We need some wine to celebrate, let's see what they have." She picked out a wine, bought two mini bottles, and poured them out. "*Salut*," she said.

"*Salut*," Marieke echoed. "You know your man Frou is my vision of what Inspector Maigret would look like."

"He is?" Melisende laughed. "Well, I suppose so, Maigret is now back on the television here, and in England, so perhaps I should suggest to Frou that he offer his services as a technical consultant."

"Perhaps," Marieke said. "I'm glad this is all over."

"Are you disappointed?" Melisende asked.

"A little," Marieke admitted. "I'm relieved that it's over, but I would have liked answers to questions. I hate closing case files with so many questions unanswered. But, the good thing is, now that he is dead, there will be no trial, and they will not try and pressure me to be available to testify. That could have dragged on for months."

"That is good," Melisende agreed. "I heard that your application for a visa has been received and is being addressed. I don't expect any delays or problems, but will check again next week."

"Thank you, *chérie*," Marieke said. "It's all a little unbelievable now, it's actually going to happen, soon I will be able to look out of the window of your apartment, and see what?"

"The Seine, Notre Dame, the Palais de Justice," Melisende said. "It will depend on which window you look from. But, we must move, we are now in Lyon, and we change to the TGV here, which will put us into Paris at eighteen thirty."

The TGV from Lyon to Paris tore through the countryside at 160 miles per hour, and they arrived in Paris five minutes early, and then joined the throng looking for taxis.

"If I had thought, I would have had Philippe meet us," Melisende said. "But, it's not that far, even with some traffic, it should only take ten to fifteen minutes." The cab ride did take ten minutes, the driver seemed to be in a hurry, but that suited both Melisende and Marieke. At the apartment building, they crowded into the tiny lift and went on up to the sixth floor. Melisende unlocked the door and stood aside to let Marieke enter first.

"*Bienvenue*," she said. "I hope you like it."

"It's delightful," Marieke said.

"Please explore while I find something to drink," Melisende said.

"This bath is big enough for two," Marieke called out as she looked into the bathroom.

"That was the idea," Melisende said.

"This bed is huge," Marieke called out again. "Can anyone see in the apartment from the outside?"

"Perhaps if they're standing on the roof of Notre Dame," Melisende laughed. "But, I don't think so, I look down on most from here, and the park over there blocks the next building."

"*Bon*, may I take a quick shower?" Marieke asked.

"Of course," Melisende said. "You will see towels, and all you need by the shower, perhaps later we can relax in a bath."

"That sounds wonderful," Marieke said. "Are you pouring wine?"

"I am," Melisende confirmed.

"*Bon*," Marieke said. "I won't be long." She was not long, and shortly she was parading through the apartment as naked as a newborn, dripping very slightly. "It's been an age since I've been able to wander around without any clothes on, it feels good," she said.

"Now I understand the question about being seen," Melisende laughed. "Well, if it's good enough for you, here hold my wine while I take a shower, and rid myself of the travel dust, and my clothes!"

Eventually, they decided that dinner might be in order, and Melisende called the bistro downstairs, and had a conversation with the owner.

"Dinner will be here in ten minutes," she said. "Perhaps we should find something to wear when it comes."

Dinner was duck confit, and it was excellent. It was delivered by a waitress by the name of Camille. According to Melisende, she had worked at the bistro for the past five years, and she liked making the trek up to the sixth floor. Perhaps because Melisende was generous, perhaps it was just a good reason to get away from the hustle and bustle of the bistro for a few minutes. Whatever the reason, since Melisende moved in, whenever she ordered from downstairs, it was always Camille who delivered.

"I think Camille is intrigued by you," Marieke commented. "Have you had many people to visit?"

"Only Philippe and his wife," Melisende said.

"So, as far as Camille can see, you live alone here in this big apartment, big by Parisian standards, you get no visitors to speak of, so wonders who are you, and what you do?" Marieke expounded. "Do they know that you work for the police?"

"I don't think so," Melisende said. "But, one day when she delivered, I still had a gun on, and I think that shocked her a little."

"She probably thinks you're a Russian spy," Marieke laughed.

"I doubt it," Melisende said. "More likely a German spy, she heard me speaking Breton one day, and that puzzled her, and she thought it was some obscure German dialect. But, enough of her, what of you, are you ready for a bath with me?"

"I am," Marieke confirmed.

When they awoke the next morning, Melisende went downstairs and came back with coffee and croissants.

"So, today we check on flights?" she asked Marieke.

"I should," Marieke agreed. "May I just use your phone here?"

"Of course, here are the numbers for BA and Air France," Melisende said. Marieke called Air France first, and there was no space available, so she then called BA, and they had space on the flight to Johannesburg that evening, and could also get her on the connecting flight to Gaborone the next day. Marieke made the booking for a flight to Heathrow, then onward to Johannesburg, and finally Gaborone, and paid for the ticket. Then called her office to let them know that she would be arriving the next day. She left a message with the duty officer asking for Sergeant Maphosa to meet her off the first flight from Johannesburg the next day. That done, they had the day to kill before the flight that evening. Melisende said that as it was Sunday, she had no need to go to her office, so they could spend the day together. They split the day between a walk around the neighbourhood and more time in bed, making up for the lost years of their separation.

At two, Melisende regretfully said that they needed to get ready to go to the airport so that Marieke could catch her flight back to Gaborone. The drive to the airport was quite pleasant, only just over half an hour, quite unlike the drive on a weekday in the rush hour traffic. At the airport, Melisende went with Marieke to check in her bags, and then went with her to the gate to see her off.
"*Alors, chérie,*" she said. "Call me when you arrive in Gaborone."
"I will," Marieke promised. "I hope the visa process doesn't take too long; the waiting will seem interminable."
"It will pass," Melisende assured her. "I will see what I can do here to speed up the process, and have you here by September."
"Thank you *mignon,*" Marieke said. "I must board, *à bientôt.*"
"*À bientôt chérie,*" Melisende replied. "*Fais bon vol.*"
Marieke boarded and made her way towards the back of the plane and found her seat. The flight to London was short, then there was a wait of just under two hours for the Johannesburg flight. When she did board that flight, she was fortunate, the seats next to her were unoccupied, and gave her the opportunity to stretch out across the row of three for the flight, and get some sleep, only awakening when the crew came to serve a light breakfast just before landing. They were in a little early, so it was not even five in the morning, and still dark outside. Then there was the seemingly endless wait for the first flight to Gaborone at eight.

Sergeant Maphosa was at the Gaborone airport and helped Marieke with her luggage. He asked about her trip, and she gave him a quick résumé of what had happened. Like her, he was in two minds about the final result, relief that it was over, but disappointment that they had not been able to question Pretorius about his activities. Sergeant Maphosa was interested in who had helped Pretorius, and whether or not they had identified all his confederates. At the police station, Marieke went to report to the commissioner, who was waiting.

"So, you are back," he said.

"Yes, Sir," she replied.

"And no prisoner," he commented.

"No, Sir," she admitted. "The French took that out of our hands. I can't imagine why Pretorius, and his friends would try, and evade the French by shooting at them, perhaps he had a death wish, perhaps he really thought they could get away."

"In any event, we'll probably never find out; are the French questioning the others on the yacht?" he asked.

"They planned to, but the crew is not cooperating, so they'll have to find an Afrikaans interpreter or find some way to pressure them into speaking English. I doubt that any of them speak French, but you never know," she said. "The case is in the hands of a *juge d'instruction*, and his powers are sweeping, so he may find the pressure point that makes at least one decide to talk, and if that happens, I think they will all talk, and blame the three that are dead."

"And, you are certain that Pretorius is dead?" he asked.

"Yes, Sir," she said. "The fingerprints, dental, and medical records all match. The probability that it is not Pretorius must be one in several millions."

"Did the Wilson woman provide any useful information?" he asked.

"Not for us," she said. "She danced around her involvement here, but did give us what Pretorius had told her about the killings in South Africa. She gave nothing away on the case we suspect she was a party to, that of the killing of Danie Pretorius, but as his body has been cremated, there is nothing to be done there; the South Africans can prove nothing. She admitted to giving Hansie Pretorius a ride from Gabs back into South Africa, but a good lawyer would argue that she was doing the right thing getting him out of the country as he is banned from entering here."

"So, nothing to be done with her?" the commissioner asked.

"No, Sir, we could never get an extradition agreed to on the flimsy evidence we have on her involvement," Marieke confirmed.

"Fine, then we'll close the cases," the commissioner said. "Is there anything to be learned from the South African cases?"

"He used a few different methods in South Africa," she said. "His first killing seemed to have been a simple bludgeoning, the second a knife, three, four, and five, all in Pretoria were shootings, six was a shooting, seven, and eight were freezing, and nine was poison."

"So, he changed his *modus operandi* quite a bit," the commissioner commented.

"I think that was to suit the circumstances," she said. "His preferred method seemed to be with a gun. The South Africans also learned that their old identity cards could be forged, and I think are looking at new security measures to be embedded to make that more difficult."

"Something to think about," he said. "Are your reports completed?"

"Apart from this last in France, yes, Sir," she confirmed. "I will have that done today."

"Good," he said. "Are you still determined to leave us?"

"I am, Sir," she said.

"I'll be sorry to see you go," he said. "But, you must do what is right for you. I hope you find what you are seeking in France."

"Thank you, Sir," she said. "I will go, and write up my final report on this case, and have it to you by the end of the day."

Aftermath

Marieke went to her office, and called Melisende to let her know that she had arrived safely. Then she set about writing her final report for the Pretorius case. The report actually was quite short, there was not that much to say, Pretorius had been killed by the French authorities while trying to evade a boarding procedure at sea. She was done before lunch, so then she called Mbali to see if she was available for lunch. She was, so they agreed to meet. Marieke was first to arrive at the restaurant, and had been seated for about ten minutes before Mbali arrived.

"*Dumela Mma*," she said. "So sorry to be late, but I had an unexpected, matter to deal with."

"*Dumela Mma*," Marieke replied. "It's good to see you, are you well?"

"I am sorting out my life," Mbali said. "MJ Motors is doing well with the new manager, and the girls are slowly getting used to the idea that Jan is gone. So, tell me about Pretorius, did you get him?"

"No," Marieke said. "He tried to shoot it out with the French, and they killed him."

"Good," Mbali said. "You're sure it's him?"

"We matched fingerprints, dental, and medical records, so yes we're sure," Marieke assured her.

"And you, are you still leaving for France?" Mbali asked.

"I am," Marieke confirmed.

"I'm sorry that you're going," Mbali said. "But, happy for you that you can be with the one you love. Before I forget, I have a lessee for your house, but they want to move in by the end of the month, why don't you stay with us until you leave for France, we have plenty of room, and the girls would be delighted to have you stay with us?"

"Are you sure that wouldn't be an imposition?" Marieke asked.

"Not at all," Mbali said. "Tell me, did you want to leave the furniture, and lease the house out as furnished?"

"I think so," Marieke said. "The apartment in Paris is already furnished, all I would take are my personal things."

"Well, box them up, and move in with us, today if you like," Mbali said. "Then I'll have cleaners go through the house, and the yard."

"Are you saying I need to clean my house more?" Marieke laughed.

"No, but it's nice to be able to tell the lessees that the place has just been cleaned top to bottom," Mbali said.

"Let me see what I need to sort out at my house," Marieke said. "Perhaps by Wednesday?"

"Wednesday it is," Mbali said. "Do you need help?"

"I don't think so," Marieke said. "I will have a shipping company box up what I'm going to take to Paris, and send it off right away; that way it will probably be there when I get there."

"Do you need any help?" Mbali asked.

"I think I can manage," Marieke said. "Do you have the management agreement we talked about before?"

"I do," Mbali confirmed. "Why don't you come to the bank tomorrow, and we'll go through it?"

"Sounds good," Marieke said. "Would three in the afternoon be fine?"

"Three is fine," Mbali confirmed. "See you then, go well."

"Stay well," Marieke replied.

Marieke then went to the salon of June Matsoka, and found her there just finishing with a customer.

"*Dumela Mma,*" she said.

"*Dumela Mma,*" June replied. "Are you well?"

"I am, thank you, and you?" Marieke asked completing the ritual.

"Very well," June said.

"I have news for you," Marieke said. "Pretorius, the man who killed Kagiso Katse is dead, he was shot by the French police."

"Good," June said. "He deserved to die, you're sure it's him?"

"We are," Marieke confirmed. "How are you managing?"

"Quite well," June said. "I've been busy, which has been good, and I even have been out on a couple of dates."

"Ah," Marieke said. "Anyone I know?"

"I don't know," June said. "Edison Kwelagobe, he has a number of commercial buildings in town."

"I know who he is, but I've never met him," Marieke said. "I hope it works for you."

"So do I," June said.

"Well, I must go," Marieke said. "I just wanted you to know that Pretorius is dead, stay well."

"Go well," June said. "And, thank you."

Marieke's next stop was the shop of Celia Molale. There, she had to wait a little longer while Celia attended to the needs of two ladies who were apparently revamping their entire wardrobes. Finally, when they were gone Celia greeted Marieke, and asked her if she would like coffee. That sounded good to Marieke, so she sat, and waited until Celia came back with the coffee.

"So, you have news?" Celia asked.

"I do, Hansie Pretorius, the man who killed Kagiso Katse is dead, shot by the French police," Marieke replied.

"Good," Celia said, replying with what now seemed to Marieke as a universal sentiment. "How is June Matsoka?"

"I just saw her, she seems fine, and she is dating again," Marieke said. "Edison Kwelagobe, do you know him?"

"Edison," Celia said. "I know him, I quite like him, he has tried to buy a couple of the buildings I have, perhaps one day I will sell, but not just yet, I'm looking for the market to go up a little before I sell. So, where have you been, I haven't seen you around for a while?"

"I've been busy with this case, and I was just in France," Marieke replied.

"France," Celia said. "I like Parisian fashions, maybe a little more than those from Milan. Did you buy anything?"

"I was only there for a few days, and that was all business," Marieke said. "But, I am moving to Paris as soon as visas can be arranged."

"You're moving to Paris?" Celia said. "What will you do there?"

"I don't know yet," Marieke admitted. "But I went to uni in France, and have a number of friends there, so will find something."

"I'm envious," Celia said. "When do you go?"

"It depends on visas," Marieke said. "As soon as I get mine, then I'll go."

"Well, I hope you have fun there," Celia said. "Stay in touch, when you get settled, perhaps I'll come to Paris, and we can dine somewhere."

"I'll do that," Marieke promised. "I'm keeping my house here, and Mbali Lamprecht is going to manage it for me."

"That's a good idea," Celia said. "Never sell if you don't have to."

"I should let you get on with things here," Marieke said. "It looks like a couple of customers coming in now. Stay well, Celia."

"Go well, Marieke," Celia replied.

Marieke returned to her office and mailed a copy of the death certificate for Pretorius to Andries van Dyk, then she decided to call him.

"*Middag,*" he said when he answered his telephone.

"*Middag*" she replied. "Andries, this is Marieke. I have just sent by mail a copy of the death certificate for Pretorius to you."

"*Dankie,*" he said. "So, have you wrapped up all your cases?"

"We have," she said. "It was quite a toll in the end, seven in all, and that doesn't count those in South Africa, and the one in Zim."

"*Magtig,*" he said. "I hope we don't get another like him for a long time."

"I agree," she said. "I also wanted to let you know that I'm leaving here and moving to Paris."

"Paris?" he said. "Why Paris, it's in France?"

"I like Paris," she said. "I went to uni in Lyon, and have friends in Paris, and I was looking for a change."

"It'll be a change all right," he said. "You know that they get snow there?"

"I know," she said. "But you get snow down there in the mountains."

"*Ja,* but that's on the mountains, not down here in PE," he laughed. "When do you go?"

"As soon as I get my visa," she said.

"It's been a pleasure to work with you," he said. "I hope that if I ever have to work with the Botswana Police again, I find someone who is as professional as you."

"Thank you," she said. "If you're ever in Paris, call me, I'll send you my telephone number, bring Anna for a holiday."

"Don't tell her that you've invited us," he said. "I'd never hear the last of it until we were actually there."

"I should go," Marieke said. "My sergeant is waving papers at me to sign. *Tot siens.*"

"*Tot siens, alles van die beste,*" he said, wishing her well.

At home that evening Marieke set about sorting out her personal things that she wanted to take with her to France. She got boxes from her move-in, and repacked them with the pictures, and knick-knacks that made up her history. Finally, she addressed her wardrobe, and boxed up some clothes, and packed the rest in the suitcases, ready to take to Mbali's house. She looked over her pantry, and thought how sparse it seemed, but that was to the good now as there was not that much to pack up. The refrigerator she would empty on Wednesday when she actually moved into Mbali's house. A thought occurred to her, she had not decided what to do about her car. As taking it to France was not practical, she supposed that she should probably sell it. Perhaps Mbali, through MJ Motors would have the best contacts to offer it for sale. But that could wait until she had a departure date. Everything looked bare now, all the items that make a house a home had been packed away, and it all looked a little sterile. But, tenants would probably bring their own personal items that would make the house their home, at least for the time they lived there.

Tuesday and Wednesday, she spent clearing up issues and cases at her office, and preparing to hand everything over. The commissioner had decided not to give her any new cases, lest they not be resolved before she departed, so much of what she was given was administrative in nature, and she rediscovered why she never had aspirations for high office, where everything was administrative. She preferred fieldwork, even if sometimes it was frustrating and boring. She cleaned out her desk, gave away much, and threw away the rest. All the case files went to the archives, and her notes that were not included in any report she gave to Sergeant Maphosa, in case they might be of use in future cases. She noticed that conversation now changed, and she began to understand the term, lame duck. Everyone was nice enough, but as she was no longer part of the active team, she was not included in case briefings and discussions. But, she thought, it was to be expected; she was leaving, so they had to reorganise themselves back into a cohesive working group that did not include her. It was actually something of a relief to leave the office in the afternoon and go home.

Mbali and her daughters were most welcoming on Wednesday when Marieke took her belongings and moved in with them. They showed her to her room and left her to unpack while dinner was prepared.

"Auntie Marieke," Khanyo said, interrupting her musings over her suitcases. "Dinner's ready."

"Thank you," Marieke said. "Did you cook?"

"Not today," Khanyo said. "Maybe I'll cook on Saturday. Is it true that you shot Pretorius?"

"I didn't," Marieke said. "He was shot by the French police, actually the Gendarmerie Maritime, which is rather like the coast guard in many countries, they look after the ocean borders, and check for smugglers, and illegal fishing, and such."

"I'm glad he's dead," Khanyo said. "He must have been a nasty man."

"I think he wasn't a very nice man," Marieke agreed.

"Are you going to live with your friend Melisende when you go to Paris?" Khanyo asked.

"I am," Marieke confirmed. "She has a nice apartment on the sixth floor of a building near the River Seine, and it has three bedrooms."

"Are you going to work in France?" Khanyo asked.

"I hope to," Marieke said. "I already speak French, and have a French law degree, so expect to find a job."

"If I need to, could I come and talk to you one day?" Khanyo asked.

"Of course," Marieke said.

"It would have to be our secret," Khanyo cautioned.

"I understand," Marieke said. "Anything you tell me will be between us, and only us, rather like the confessional at the Catholic Church."

"Good," Khanyo said. "Let's go and have dinner."

Over dinner, the conversation covered all kinds of things, including their recent trip to the Linyanti area, and the return to school.

"I got information from the University of Kent the other day," Khanyo said. "I saw that the course is in Canterbury, what's it like there?"

"It's an old city," Marieke said. "I only went there once on a quick trip from Lyon. It was a settlement before the Romans invaded, and they built a fort there, and it's been growing ever since. It has a cathedral, and the Archbishop of Canterbury is based there. So, in some ways, it's where the Church of England is headquartered."

"Is it cold there?" Khanyo asked.

"It can get cold in the winter," Marieke said. "I suppose that January is probably the coldest month, you'll need winter clothes there as well as boots."

"Is it close to London airport?" Khanyo asked.

"Closer to London Gatwick than London Heathrow," Marieke replied. "But, most flights from Jo'burg go into Heathrow. Once at Heathrow I would image the best was to get to Canterbury is take the Tube to St. Pancras station, and then take a train to Canterbury."

"Time enough for all that when you get accepted," Mbali said. "Would you, and Nandi clear the table, and wash up for us, I have some things to discuss with Marieke?"

"So," Marieke said, when they were alone. "What's bothering you?"

"Pretorius," Mbali said. "I know he's dead, but I feel somewhat robbed of justice. I wanted to see him tried, and convicted, and hanged here."

"I have the same frustrations," Marieke said. "We pieced together what happened at all the shootings, and have pursued this man for a while, and then it's all snatched away from us at the last minute by stupidity on his part. Or, perhaps it wasn't stupidity, perhaps it was a deliberate gamble hoping that the French would simply lock him up for a while, and we wouldn't get our hands on him to extradite him to Botswana, and try him here."

"How do you pursue a man for weeks, then see him just gone from your grasp at the last minute?" Mbali asked.

"It happened at the Zim border," Marieke said. "We were only minutes away from arresting him, and he waded across the river into Zim and was gone. By the time we got hold of the Zim police he had vanished into thin air, but then he did have help in Zim, help that he killed when he crossed into Mozambique. So, I suppose for me this was the second disappointment, imagine what it's like for the South Africans, they finally work out who killed off eight or so people, only to find that he's out of the country, and gone, and if we hadn't made the connections for them, they never would have related the killings they had, and it would still all be a mystery for them."

"What does your commissioner say?" Mbali asked.

"I think, like us, he's in two minds, pleased that Pretorius is dead, and we don't have to go through the lengthy process of trying to extradite him, then try him, but frustrated that we didn't get the chance to ask questions, and get some answers," Marieke replied.

"So, frustration all around?" Mbali said.

"Frustration indeed," Marieke agreed. "But, for me it does mean that the commissioner won't try, and pressure me into delaying my departure while a trial is pending. But, that doesn't take away the nagging sense of failure, that I didn't bring the man to justice."

"You didn't fail," Mbali said. "If anything, you succeeded, you got him into a situation where he could not escape, he was going to be arrested by the French, and would have landed up in gaol somewhere, still I would rather it had been Francistown, and not some prison in France."

"I hadn't looked at it that way," Marieke said.

"Are you set for France?" Mbali asked. "What's Melisende's apartment like?"

"It's on the sixth floor of this building overlooking the Seine, and across from Notre Dame," Marieke said. "It's big, has three bedrooms, and living, and dining rooms, and a nice kitchen, big bathroom with a bath big enough for two, and a shower as well."

"Does Melisende cook?" Mbali asked.

"Not very well," Marieke said. "But, she's developed a good relationship with the bistro downstairs, and they are happy to provide meals, and, I have to say, their food is good."

"Do you think you'll be happy?" Mbali asked.

"Yes," Marieke said, unequivocally. "I spent a night there, and it was just so nice not to have to worry about what people might think. The French very much believe in minding your own business, and not prying into others' private affairs."

"I think that Khanyo suspects that you, and Melisende are more than just friends," Mbali said. "She was asking me the other day about gay and lesbian relationships. I tried to explain that who you love isn't always what might meet social norms, but I think she's hearing a lot at school about faggots, dykes, fairies, *moffies*, and queers, and I think she's having a difficult time relating what she hears to the person she knows."

"She may see more at uni in England," Marieke said. "So, perhaps best if she hears from you before she goes, not to judge too quickly."

"It helped when I explained to her that in South Africa, Jannie, and I would be breaking the law every time we made love," Mbali said. "I think she began to understand then, because she couldn't see anything wrong with Jannie, and I being together, after all to her we were just Mom, and Dad. She also wanted to learn more about sex itself, than she had heard at school, and then I had told her when she got her first period, so we had a long discussion, starting with the basic biology, and mechanics, then the more experimental aspects of sex between two people, and then on to the more emotional side of things. My mother had had the same talk with me, and she had been very forthright in great detail, including sexually transmitted diseases too, so when I was ready I was prepared. All I did was add to the diseases, AIDS and HIV."

"Khanyo did ask me if she could come to me sometime to talk," Marieke said. "I promised silence if she did."

"No man, that's fine," Mbali said. "I had an aunt in Jo'burg who I used to go to with things I didn't really want to discuss with my Mom. I know she kept my confidence, and it was good to have someone that I trusted completely. She was the first I told about Jannie, and she advised me to trust him, and move here, she had had a relationship in the past with a white man, and both her, and his families had found out, and had pressured both to end it, and she regretted it, it left her empty for a long time, and apparently he went off to the border war, and did something stupidly brave, and was killed, some said it was deliberate on his part because he was so broken up about the split."

"*Ag, man,*" Marieke said. "Such a shame."

"What are you two aunties gossiping about?" Nandi asked, interrupting their conversation.

"Less of the aunties," Mbali warned, laughing as she did so. "Marieke and I were talking about Pretorius, and the frustration of not seeing him tried here."

"Well, isn't it better for everyone that he's dead?" Nandi asked. "If he had come back here, we might have hanged him, or he might have been sent to prison, but that wouldn't bring Dad back, so I'm glad he's dead."

"I'm glad too," Mbali said. "And you're right, it won't bring your Dad back."

"Auntie Marieke, aren't you going to miss the bush when you go to France?" Nandi asked.

"I will," Marieke said. "But, it's a sacrifice I'm prepared to make."

"Can we visit you in Paris?" Nandi asked.

"Of course," Marieke replied. "Melisende has a big apartment with three bedrooms, so room enough. It's also right in the middle of Paris, so perfect from a tourism point of view."

"When are you leaving?" Khanyo asked.

"But, I only just arrived," Marieke laughed. "I will leave when my visa from France is approved, it's going through the bureaucracy now, with any luck by the end of the month, or perhaps a week or two after that."

"Will you come back for the holidays and stay with us?" Nandi asked.

"I will," Marieke promised.

The visa did come through by the end of the month, and Marieke went to the French Embassy to have it stamped in her passport. Then she booked a flight to Paris, spending the money to fly first class. There followed a round of goodbyes, and farewells, and bon voyage parties until the actual day arrived when she would leave. Mbali, and her daughters went with her to the airport, and there she was surprised to see the commissioner, Lerato Mochage, Celia Molale, June Matsoka, and Sergeant Maphosa, all of whom had come to see her off. She wondered what the other travellers must think, especially after she had gone around the group hugging each in turn, and when the commissioner went with her to the plane's stairway.

"Go well, Matshwana," he said, shaking her hand. "It has been an honour and a pleasure to have you in the department. I wish you well in your new life, but know that you will always be welcome back if things do not work as anticipated."

"Thank you, Sir," she said. "Stay well." She turned, and waved to the others all crowded by the fence, and boarded the aircraft before the tears came in floods. So, this was the end of that chapter in her life, it was time to start writing a new chapter, which was exciting, and yet she was also apprehensive. This was as big a change in her life as when she had returned from France, not to Namibia from whence she had left, but to Botswana, a new country in which she had had distant relatives, but no one close. Time would tell, but the anticipation of spending time with Melisende made it all worthwhile.